Witch's Daughter

Sarah A. Hoyt

Goldport Press

The Letter

It has often been said that dead men don't talk. In Avalon, this wasn't necessarily true. Dead men could talk if a reasonably talented necromancer were willing to risk the death penalty for reanimating a corpse.

But Michael had never heard of a dead man who wrote letters.

The letter lay on the breakfast table, next to the only setting on it, on a silver salve between the spoon and the porcelain creamer.

Michael Ainsling, youngest son of the late Duke of Darkwater and brother of the current titular, eyed it suspiciously, while he took his seat. His eyes widened slightly at the name of the sender, then he frowned at his own name in the space reserved for the recipient.

He hadn't slept well, and dark rings marked the pale skin beneath the dark green eyes he shared with all his male relatives.

A well grown boy at the age when one resented being called such, he had that look boys have when they've achieved adult height but not yet had time to fill in. He'd been the quiet half of fraternal twins, his sister Caroline being the garrulous and outgoing half until six months ago. Then Caroline had been sent to an academy for young ladies, where she was presumably still garrulous but far away from Michael, so that Michael had to do his own talking and endure social interaction.

It had been thought – then – that Michael's recent experiences had left him too frail to attend Cambridge. Michael frowned with distaste at the thought, as he folded and refolded his napkin. He did not understand why it had been thought better to leave him here on the deserted estate. With Caroline gone, Seraphim — now the tenth Duke of Darkwater and the prince consort of the Princess Royal — spending most of his time in London and Mama having left no one knew very well where, Michael's was the only place setting at the table designed to accommodate seventeen.

Most of the days he swallowed tea and toast and rushed off to work in his workshop. Today... He glared at the letter by his cup.

And realized that the footman who'd discreetly followed him into the dining room hovered near his chair. "You may go, Burket," he said, without taking his eyes off the letter.

"Will you need anything else, Lord Michael?" the man asked and made a broad gesture as though sweeping the breakfast spread clustered around Michael's place setting: fried kidneys and some sort of pie, and toast and butter and something else that looked suspiciously like fish cakes.

Michael didn't sigh. "No, thank you, Burket. I have everything I need."

Truly he wanted the man gone so he could look at the letter at leisure. The sender's name was Tristram Blakley, and surely there couldn't be more than one of those. The writing and the paper both looked fresh, as though someone had dashed off the note just this morning.

But Tristram Blakley had been dead for sixteen years. Michael had studied him among the great inventors of his time, the man who had created the carpetship liners that crossed the air between Britain and the Americas and took the upper classes of Avalon on pleasure cruises the world over. He remembered mama telling him, once, that she'd known Tristram in youth, that he was a lot like Michael himself, always dreaming up new magical machines, but how he'd died young and how sad it was.

"Beg your pardon, Milord," Burket said, which was when Michael realized the man had leaned over to pour him tea, and had almost poured it on Michael's lap as Michael lifted his head.

"Thank you," Michael said. "But you don't have to pour my tea."

Only now the man was buttering Michael's toast and setting it on a plate, and smiling enticingly at Michael while nodding at the toast as though, for all the world, Michael were a toddler in need of being tempted to his food. "I know, milord, but you haven't been eating, and what are we to tell his grace, should he ask? And he does ask, you know?"

Michael picked up the toast, with what he knew was ill-grace, and took a bite, while still frowning at the letter. He could well believe that Seraphim worried about his eating and his health and everything else. And that was nothing to what Gabriel, his older half-brother, once Seraphim's valet and now the king of fairyland would do. Those two had always mistook themselves for parents of Michael and Caroline. Michael was sure someone in the household was in Gabriel's pay, too, and sent him regular reports.

When you have two older brothers who are far more powerful than you, and determined to protect, cosset and annoy you within an inch of your life, sometimes all you can do is play along. But Michael wished they'd let him read his letter in peace.

He took another bite, gulped down the tea, which was still hot and made his tongue sting, and then took another bite of toast, doing his best to simulate appetite he didn't feel.

He had spent a restless and turmoil filled night, dreaming of fairyland and his recent captivity in it, and it was all he could do not to allow a long shudder to go through him at the confused and patchy memory of that dream. That was the problem, too. In dream and memory fairyland was never anything clear and solid, anything you could rebel against and resent. It was a foggy, threatening recollection, in which places and people changed shape and essence, and in which pain and worse happened to you without warning.

"That is better, Milord," Burket said, in the sort of kind, patronizing tone that made Michael wish they hadn't forbidden duels and that it weren't frowned upon to duel one's social inferiors.

"Would you fancy a kidney? Perhaps a fish cake?" At Michael's head-shake, Burket stepped back, but didn't leave, as Michael expected. Instead, he cleared his throat and looked towards the entrance door to the room, set next to the window that looked out over the gardens.

There was movement, and then two women and a man came in, all of them smiling widely, but all of them looking just the slightest bit embarrassed, as though they were doing something they shouldn't be doing. The women were Mrs. Hooper, the housekeeper, starched and stiff in her black dress with its immaculate white collar, Mrs. Aiken, the cook, and the man was Dyer, the Butler.

What on Earth could be the matter?

Before Michael could even think to ask, Mrs. Hooper advanced, curtseyed, advanced again, curtseyed again, then beamed at him, again, as if he were an infant in the nursery, and spoke, "Lord Michael, since today is your seventeenth birthday, we thought it only fair..." She stopped and sniffled, as though she were fighting strong emotion, though Michael had no idea what that could possibly be. "That is, last summer, Milord, we thought you lost, and we wish you to believe we all hold you in the greatest affection, and therefore..." She blushed, which gave Michael all he could not to let his jaw drop in astonishment. Mrs. Hooper had never seemed fully human, much less capable of embarrassment. "Therefore we got you this gift, from everyone on the estate, to commemorate your seventeenth birthday Milord."

She dropped a parcel wrapped in silver paper, and neatly tied with a silk ribbon upon the table, just north of the letter from the dead man, then beat a hasty retreat.

Michael's turn to blush, and to fumble with the paper. And then he had the devil's own time concealing the expression of astonishment on his face, and overlaying it with gratification. "Oh, thank you," he said, staring at the tiny gold box with the miniature scene of Zeus in judgment worked painted upon the porcelain lid. A snuff box? Why in heaven's name did they think he'd take snuff? Even Seraphim didn't.

But he also understood, immediately, how expensive such a thing was, and how much of a sacrifice it had been to the servants to contribute to it. That colored his voice and his expression, as he stood and said, "I am not good at flowery speeches, but—" He lifted the box and looked it over, "I am most gratified at your kind thought. Thank you. I thank you most heartily."

The four of them curtseyed of bowed according to their different sexes, looking gratified, and left.

Which is when Michael opened the letter from the dead man.

Escaping The Tower

THE PROBLEM WITH A wicked stepmother, Miss Albinia Blakley thought, as she stood in front of the mirror, wearing William's clothes, and tucking her abundance of red hair into a hat rakishly set on her red curls, was when the wicked stepmother was in fact your real mama.

It was all very well, after all, for Miss Albinia's brothers—who always called her Al—because Mama was just the woman who had married Papa when William, the youngest, was three, and was in fact no blood relation to them. So they had nothing to be either sorry or worried for. It wasn't their mama who mistreated them so.

Oh, it had been terrible for them, from what they'd said, to find that their kind and absentminded father had married a forbidding and interfering woman who was a powerful witch, to boot.

But at least all of them, even William, remembered Papa. Albinia didn't. She didn't remember anyone but Mama, the sole authority and arbiter in her fifteen years of life. Albinia locked the door to her room as she thought this, and sighed, because now she was on limited time.

Mama didn't like her to lock her door, ever, and there was no point at all imagining that Mama didn't spell that lock, so that she knew the moment Al locked it. Mama spelled everything and kept track of everything Al did, which is what made this so devilishly difficult.

But spell or not, Albinia had to lock the door, to at least delay Mama and give her a chance to escape.

Because the thing was, Mama or no Mama, Al must leave and go find the boys.

She didn't know if the boys had felt this way when Papa left shortly after marrying Mama. She didn't know, because they never spoke to her of that time, before Al was born.

What she knew was that Papa had disappeared shortly after marrying Mama, and had never returned. Presumed dead, everyone said.

And now the boys had disappeared. Al didn't know where, but she knew two things. One, that Mama had made them leave against their will. And two, that wherever they were, they needed Al. And at any rate, Al needed them. She had been raised by them since she was in leading strings, and their presence had made life at Wulffen Downs less than torture. Even if Mama was her real mama, Al was not going to stick around and have the full benefit of Mama's full attention for the duration.

Whatever the duration was. It had been miserable enough since William had left.

She scrunched under the bed to find the old sheets she had torn and tied together. They had to be old and discarded, because that was the only way to make sure they were no longer bespelled. The spells wore out and weren't renewed when the sheets were ready for the rag bag. It had taken her six months to find some and to braid them into a passable rope, in the few minutes a day Mama left her alone.

Tying the sheet rope to the foot of the bed and throwing it out the window was the work of a moment. Al's mind ticked through where Mama would be now.

Even if she were close by—say, in her room, as she would be at this time—she had to come up the North staircase, down the hallway and up to the door. Right now, she would be on the top step.

Al got the magical kit, likewise assembled painstakingly over a year, from discarded bits and ends, so that she could be sure no one had bespelled or could track any part of it. The hard part of it had been buying the herbs, because she'd had to spend her allowance on them, in a shop at the other end of Wulffen Downs, so that Mama wouldn't hear about her purchases. And she'd had to wrap them so they looked like candy.

It had earned her a sermon from Mama about spending her money on tooth-rotting sweets. But she had got the herbs necessary for enchantments. She tied the pouch to a cord under her jacket, and then slipped the few silver coins left of her allowance into a pouch in her sleeve.

She could now hear Mama's step in the hallway outside. Mama was clearing her throat, preparing to call her name.

Albinia pushed the window fully open, knelt on the parapet, and held on to the rope with both hands. She had remembered to put knots on the rope, and she set her feet on the first one, carefully; otherwise, it would be like when she tried coming down from the cliff when she'd been bird-watching with Edmund, and had got her hands burned, with the speed of sliding down the rope.

She clambered down the rope as, from above, came the sound of knocks and Mama calling, "Open up. Open up immediately, young lady."

She felt the little puff of magic as Mama opened the door with a spell, and she moved faster down the rope, because she had to be on the ground and running by the time Mama got to the window.

She had to go to her brothers. Samuel wouldn't be able to look after them. He thought he could, but the others resented his attempts at invoking authority he didn't have. And Geoffrey needed someone to help him make himself understood when he started stuttering and Edmund would turn his clothes, his room and everything into an aviary, and Aaron would lose everything, including specimens of marsh plants, Jeremy and Joshua would argue about everything and end up with ruined canvases and paints from throwing them at each other, and William was likely to disappear into his music, and Samuel would just go all extremely disappointed at all this, which helped nothing.

Albinia looked down to see how far the ground was. She had measured the tower where her room was situated. She'd calculated the height to the window five different ways.

But as her stomach sank to her feet, she realized none of that mattered now. Because she was not suspended from her own home manor's window, but from a window open on a façade of glass. In fact, it looked like she was hanging from a giant glass rectangle. Except that as she looked forward, she could see these were windows and that oddly dressed people inside the building were pointing at her and a woman was covering her mouth, but looked like she was screaming something.

Gone was the tower of the manor house on the cliff, overlooking the ocean and the familiar marshes. Mama. Mama and Mama's magic!

She could feel as though an abrasion upon her magic, as if something in this strange place were trying to get through her magical shields.

Beneath her, there were flashes of moving things that she couldn't understand and the sound of klaxons, superimposed on a low roar as of a million voices.

She had no idea where she was, dangling here, between Earth and sky, on her fragile ladder of sheets.

All she knew was that the ladder ended far short of the ground. More than the height of Al's tower.

Far above, Mama leaned out the open window, and Mama's voice called, "Albinia Blakley, you little idiot. Hang on. I shall pull you in."

But if Al let Mama pull her in, she'd never ever get away again. Al let go of the rope.

She let go before she could think. She let go knowing only that she couldn't stand to go back in and explain herself to Mama. She let go knowing that she must get to her brothers, somehow, but not knowing how, except that she must get away from Mama and Mama's magic, first.

She tumbled downwards, head over heels, wondering how it felt to hit the ground so far below. All her carefully constructed protective and helpful charms in candy wrapping rained down onto that distant pavement. They wouldn't save her.

Would it hurt? Would she even feel it? She hoped she didn't land on some innocent and kill them, even as air escaped her lungs and she couldn't find the voice to scream.

Rescuing the Dead

MICHAEL FROWNED AT THE letter. It was undoubtedly addressed to him, by a man who couldn't possibly have known of his existence, unless he had read the announcement of Michael's birth in some society newspaper once upon a time.

Swallowing tea and toast as fast as he could, Michael put the snuff box in his pocket and retreated to his workshop.

Properly speaking, he had two workshops: one in the house, a room that had taken his father a substantial portion of the family fortune to build for his ingenious and precocious son, and the other deep in the garden, where Michael assembled and tested those experiments that might explode or otherwise cause damage to the family.

The workshop in the depths of the garden, he'd all but abandoned. Even if a changeling had been left in the inside workshop, it was from the outside workshop that he'd been abducted with a cunning spell from the—now fortunately deposed and dead—king of Fairyland. And though Michael was quite sure the present king of Fairyland, his brother Gabriel, had no intention of kidnapping him, he felt alone and vulnerable in that building. It had been violated once, and so it could be violated again.

The inner workshop would be harder to breach. For one, when it had been claimed from its previous use as a ballroom, it had been lined in leather between two layers of copper, the whole bespelled, forming an impassable barrier to both organic- and inorganic-affecting spells from outside.

In the ballroom, a sort of platform had been built, and up on it, Michael had his sky-observing apparatus, designed to help him calculate the form of spell to use.

The rest of the workshop held machines of Michael's own invention, many of which now seemed impractical and childish to him. Take, for instance, his careful replica of the world of Avalon, in brass, rotating in proportional time around a miniature sun. It had been fun to build, but what practical use was it?

Since Seraphim had visited the Madhouse, the strange parallel world without magic where the Princess Royal had been raised, and brought back ideas for useful machines like shavers and mixers and clothes and dishwashers, Michael had been working hard on magical replicas for such wonders.

The clothes washer was a success, except that the housekeeper had banned its use, saying it was an abomination and would run laundresses off their jobs by the score. However, Seraphim had arranged to have it tested in the royal palace and it was well on the way to becoming accepted in other, less hidebound households than the Darkwaters' country estate. Seraphim said it would make Michael a fortune.

The automated barber, though... Michael frowned at his creation standing by the workbench near the far wall of the room. It was not a little portable thing, as Seraphim had described, because Michael had believed by making it large and capable of giving haircuts as well as shaves, it would be more popular. Particularly if it could also dress the hair of young ladies.

But all the thing had done, in actual fact, was chase Michael through the house, trying to cut...not his hair. The bits of his jacket it had got had been enough. Michael was not sure what had gone wrong with the animating spell, because when a cylindrical, man-high thing is wheeling after you brandishing knives, razors and scissors in its many arms, the only possible thing to do was to run as fast as possible.

Which he'd done, until Dyer had shot the mechanical barber through the head with a fowling piece. Michael stared at the multiple holes perforating the creature, right through the space where its directing magic had been. Well, never mind that. This was not a good time to attempt to reproduce that...experiment.

Michael perched on a high stool near the model of Avalon and tore into the letter, breaking the seal which showed—he'd swear to it—a lamb devouring a wolf, with the words *Scientia et Astu* beneath.

The letter started formally enough. "Dear Lord Michael Ainsling: You'll forgive my addressing this letter to you, though we've never been formally introduced, or, indeed, introduced at all."

And it proceeded strangely. "You might have heard of me, and have some idea that I am dead, but do not let that concern you, as rumors of my demise have been greatly exaggerated."

Michael chewed the corner of his lip, perceiving that the person who'd written this letter, in strong angular handwriting, was what Mama would have called an original. And by original, she normally meant that they needed help finding their way across a street, and were none too certain where they might have placed their head that day. She had been known to describe Michael himself in such a way.

"Whether you think me dead or alive, I suppose it will be a matter of some concern to you how you come to be receiving a letter from me, and also possibly some curiosity as to what you can do to help me, or hinder me, or indeed do anything in my case.

"I'll tell you the truth. I do not know. I have cast and recast these runes, and all I can tell is that there is only one person in the world capable of understanding my work—and you must understand what keeps me prisoner here is my own work turned against me—and disabling it, so I might perhaps be set free.

"I have never had the pleasure of meeting you, and the last thing I'd expect would be that the Ainslings would throw any kind of magical genius in the normal way. Pardon me for saying so, but your father was one of the accredited adventurers of my time, in more ways than one, meaning he was rather more adept at using other men's magic all too often in order to use their wives likewise. And although your Mama was one of the beauties of her day, and indeed a diamond of the first water, I never found that she had an inquisitive and mathematical turn of mind. But then, of course, sometimes every breed throws a sport, and my runes assure me that you are that. A magical genius, I mean, not a sport, though I suppose that, also."

By this time, Michael's head was whirling and he felt he should have had rather more than one cup of tea to fortify himself to deal with this very strange missive. Or perhaps he should have had brandy, except that none of the servants would let him have it, or at least not without telling Seraphim. And maybe Gabriel. And all he needed was for his older brothers to decide he had turned into an alcoholic.

"However, before I can request that you rescue me—though I do, of course, request that—I must ask you to find my sons. The rest of them, as one has found me. You see, the woman I married, in what I'm sure now seems to me like a fit of madness, has applied some sort of spell to them, so I can no longer track them nor communicate with them.

"I'm afraid she means to do away with them and use the lands of my ancestors to form a dowry for her whelp. And while I have nothing against the mite, who was not born by the time I got confined to this place, and whom my sons inform me is a pretty good sort in the way young females sometimes are, and not at all like her mother, I do not wish for my legacy to pass wholly into her hands and those of whichever rogue Augusta chooses to marry her to.

"I presume you have a rowboat of some sort on your property, as I vaguely remember there was a lake there, in which much boating was done in the summer. I remember the lady your mother looking very fine in a lace dress upon a boat, in fact. At any rate, if you apply the formula I enclose onto a rowboat, it should bring you where you need to be to start unravelling this knot.

"Since the full extent of the knot laid by the one I must call my lady wife is not known or understood even by me, I must trust in the formula and in the kindness of a total stranger to do what must be done. And my scrying assures me you're the only stranger who can do so.

"In full hope, if not trust, of your doing what is needful, I subscribe myself your most grateful and devoted servant, Tristram Blakley."

Having laid the letter down on his workbench, Michael stared at it, fully wondering whether the person who'd written was the—presumed dead—author of magical carpet travel on a grand scale, or simply a madman possessed of illusions of being such a parsonage.

It was not till he turned the page and looked through the formula, written in a hand that gave the impression of impatience with writing itself, that Michael blinked, whistled under his breath, and realized that this was indeed the work of Tristram Blakley.

No one else, barring an equal genius, could have come up with such a strange mix of magical formulae, turning a simple rowboat into a vehicle of both magical transport *and* divination.

And Michael knew, as he knew his own name, that he would have to try it out. It was like climbing the tallest tree or exploring the most dangerous part of the woods. He'd like to believe he was doing it for the sake of the unknown Mr. Blakley, who seemed to be in a terrible position, but in his heart of hearts, he knew he was doing it for the thrill of it and to prove that he could.

Enough of nights hemmed in with nightmares of Fairyland, and of moping about the otherwise deserted estate. Michael wanted to be doing—no matter how strange the doing. He must answer the call to adventure.

The Kindness of Strangers

Miss Albinia Blakley didn't scream. Or at least she tried, but as she turned over, her hair falling out and her cap tumbling lost to the street below, it seemed to her that the air robbed both her ability to breathe and her ability to make a sound. From above, she heard her mother's scream, but not what her mother said. From below, other screams joined, together with some sort of strange musical instrument that sounded like a crazed goose. Or, rather, many geese honking.

She caught glimpses of the street below, the glint of something like metal boxes but in many colors. She tried to use her magic to slow the fall, but of course it didn't work, when she couldn't even think clearly.

And then from somewhere, she heard a male voice. It said a jumble of words. Or at least the words sounded like a jumble in her ears, though of course, right then anything would.

Her fall halted. Not suddenly, but first slowing down, like a leaf falling gently from a tree onto the welcoming ground.

Only she didn't fall on the ground. Or get a chance to straighten up. Instead, she fell face-first onto something hard and wooden. As she recovered breath, she realized that the something she'd fallen on was moving, gliding rapidly through the air. Or perhaps not gliding, because... She blinked as she picked herself up to sitting on the floor of a small rowboat and looked at the boy who was rowing it. He was tall and dark, scowling, and plying the oars with a will. They were charging through the air, weaving and twisting, while Mama screamed above, ever more distantly, and below, the screams had changed from a horrified to a strangely excited tone as the honking stopped.

"What?" Albinia heard herself squeak as she picked herself up. "How? Who—"

"Not now," the boy said, between panting breaths. "We must get out of here before the location affects the spell. In the madhouse, no magic persists for long."

Like that, they seemed to push through...something, and there was the brief cold of what Albinia had learned to call the In-Betweener. She'd never experienced it, of course, not being allowed to perform spells that dangerous—or, really, to escape Mama's orbit that easily—but she'd read about it in her instruction books. It was supposed to be the time you slipped between one world and the next, and you were nowhere. There were horrible warnings against getting stuck in the In-Betweener, unable to breathe, forever. Albinia had always wondered how anyone knew you could get stuck there, or if you died or if you just stayed suspended forever. Since there was no time in the In-Betweener, could you die there?

When she'd tried to ask such questions of Mama, Mama had told her that young ladies of refinement didn't ask stupid questions. But she'd never explained to Albinia why the questions were stupid, or, indeed, what refinement had to do with it.

Now going through, for however brief a moment she was, she realized what had originated the talk of dying in the In-Betweener. Even if no one could know if it had ever happened. Only that someone hadn't arrived at the place where they'd meant to go. The seconds—minutes?—In-Betweener felt like she'd been dragged headfirst through hell. No. Not hell. Hell would have been something, even if the something was pretty unpleasant. This was just...nothing. Humans couldn't live in nothing.

She'd had no more than a moment to think this—or perhaps think was too clear a word. She'd in fact only had a moment to feel it, like one groping in the dark for an unfamiliar shape—and then they were out, into cool clear air, with bright sun and a smattering of snowflakes dancing in it.

And the boat was falling.

The young man whose boat it was—unless, of course, he'd stolen it—rowed more frantically, and the fall slowed down and changed into a glide.

"We're in London," Albinia said delightedly, recognizing things only seen in woodcuts, the Thames and the Bridge, the tower of London, as they turned and glided in the air above the city.

The boy only gave her a dirty look. But maybe he couldn't speak. He was red in the face and rowing fast enough that if they were on water, they'd be achieving quite a speed. Maybe. Because he was rowing faster with one hand than the other, and seemed to be controlling the boat to make them fall slowly in circles.

They weren't the only traffic in the air. There were magic carpets, as she expected, some of them pretty scruffy and small, probably pieces of bigger gliders cut and sold at a knock-off price. Those seemed to be barely above the trees, and piloted by untidy boys carrying packages. She'd never thought of that, but she supposed it made sense, to deliver purchases to ladies—and gentlemen—not willing to carry them.

There were only a couple of floating carriages, both with crests on their doors, and both, fortunately, well above them, so that there was no fear of being hit by them. She'd heard of those, or rather, read of those, in romantic novels of the kind Mama most strenuously disapproved of. They were expensive, both to build and to bespell, which meant that only the wealthiest who could command the best magicians had them. A lot of them were connected to the royal family.

The only other air traffic, too far away for her to see clearly, was what appeared to be a sort of airborne building. It would be one of those carpet-liners, the vast magic carpet supporting a first-class hotel. Such plied the routes between Europe and other continents, and Albinia had often dreamed of going on a round-the-world tour on one of them. Papa had invented the spells for those, so they could be done by normal magicians with an economy of power.

She was looking longingly towards it, thinking it was unfair she'd never be on one of those when her papa had invented them, when the boat dipped and swayed abruptly. They careened downwards at speed, towards a sort of little wilderness in the middle of busy London streets.

She screamed and held to the side of the boat. The boy was almost not rowing. Was he mad? He didn't even look at her when she screamed, his eyes fixed downward.

They fell past the small rug messengers, past the trees. Albinia kept trying to keep her eyes open, while they closed in sheer terror, and she forced them open again.

She must have closed them momentarily, because the first she knew about the small lake was when they splashed with force into the water. Water splashed on her face. Ducks screamed. She opened her eyes to see a flurry of feathers and ducks.

The boy was bent forward, his hands clasping his arms, his breath coming in ragged gasps.

She was dripping water, trying to wipe at her face, her hair sodden and soaked on her head, when the boy recovered enough breath to look up and fulminate her with as hateful and dark a glare as he'd given her before. "I—" he said. "I think you must be the most cowardly boy in the whole world. Why did you scream like that?"

Answers flitted through Albinia's head, including that she had screamed because she'd been scared, that she didn't think she was cowardly at all, and finally, that she wasn't a boy.

But the truth was that there was a reason she'd put on Geoffrey's long outgrown suit. It wouldn't do for a young woman, much less what Mama called—heaven only knew why—a "gently reared female" to be traipsing around by herself and under her own recognizance. Men—if Albinia understood correctly from the novels she'd consumed—were forever wanting to do something called "stealing the virtue" of women. She had absolutely no idea what that meant. No book she consulted explained it—just like not really explaining if you could die in the In-Betweener —but she assumed that it meant they could take your magic or steal your magic, because after all, when a magical object stopped working, it was said to have lost "its virtue."

But that had never been very clear, because a lot of the protagonists in the novels didn't have any magical power.

All the same, and just in case, she made sure there were protective spells over her so he couldn't steal any of her magic—however that was done—and decided to not tell him she was a girl. Instead, she said, her voice scathing and her diction precise, "Well, and you're quite the rudest boy I've ever met."

To her surprise, he laughed aloud at that, the anger disappearing. "I suppose you can't help it," he said. "You're just a scrub, aren't you? How old are you, twelve? I see your parents never even had your hair cut."

She started to protest, then grunted something that could be taken either way.

"And what's your name?" he asked. "I presume you're Master Blakley..."

How did this rude boy know her name? "I'm Al," she said. "Call me Al."

He opened his mouth. Closed it. "I'm Michael," he said.

He took up the oars again and started rowing more gently towards the edge of the lake. You'd think there would be people gathering and pointing at them by now, even if it was a cold day. Albinia wondered why there weren't, and if the boy realized this was wrong. Then she realized he hadn't given her a last name and looked at him curiously. Right. Well, then she wouldn't ask. You could tell from his clothes and the way he talked he was a gentleman. But why wouldn't he give her his name?

"Where are we going?" she asked instead.

He looked embarrassed. "I thought you might want to get dried and changed before I explain."

Clear as mud, wasn't he?

She wouldn't give him the satisfaction of getting upset, though. "Very well," she said. Could it be any worse than being caught by Mama?

It wasn't till they'd stowed the boat, and he'd done something that obscured it so it had become invisible, then led her across a busy street and galloped up the steps of an elegant townhouse, that she wondered if he was kidnapping her for nefarious purposes, like those things she had read about. Again she ,made sure the shield was fastened over her magic. She wondered if he had enough magic to feel her spell work, as he looked over at her out of the corner of his eyes, the green in them flashing in the light in a way that made her think he was amused.

He knocked at the door to the townhouse and stood back, waiting, his posture denoting impatience. She wanted more than anything to ask him who they were calling on. But she didn't fully realize how much trouble she was in until the house was opened by a liveried footman, whose face seemed permanently arranged in an expression of something like disdain. Which changed almost immediately. The man's eyes widened, his mouth dropped open, and he said, "Lord Michael!"

She was well brought up. Well, in some things. One of the things Mother had made sure she consumed was the manuals of peerage and etiquette. All of them.

If this young man was being addressed with Lord and his first name, that meant only one thing: not only was he of a noble family, but one of the noblest.

After all, only the sons of dukes merited that courtesy title.

Michael forged ahead with a look over his shoulder, calling her, “Come!”

And they were into the house, the footman barely jumping out of the way.

“Is Seraphim in?” Michael asked.

And then she realized the name was unusual enough...she had to be at the home of the Prince Consort. There was no other possibility.

She couldn’t swoon. It just wasn’t done in boy’s clothes. But she wished she could.

Embarrassment

MICHAEL FORGED AHEAD, DRAGGING Al into his room at the townhouse, and casually tossing over his shoulder at the butler, "Hodges, can you get someone to bring up water and clothes for us to change? Will Seraphim be in at dinner?" He turned to Al by way of explanation. "We probably should dress for dinner. I don't know if my brother will eat in our house or at the palace. I'm not sure how they manage, but—"

"Lord Michael!" The butler sounded shocked to his core, and Michael stared at him in complete confusion. It was his experience that he sometimes couldn't even remotely guess at what other people were thinking. This seemed to be one of those situations, as he had no idea what the look of deep reproach in the old retainer's face was all about.

Hodges cleared his throat. "You cannot possibly mean to wash and change in the same room with your guest."

Michael paused, suddenly alarmed. It wasn't so much that he could guess what the butler was thinking—he couldn't—but the man looked as if there would be some high impropriety in changing clothes in the same room with a friend. Michael couldn't really guess why, since in the past he had brought home playfriends and changed for dinner in his room, if they weren't staying overnight.

However, that had been some years ago. Without being able to fully comprehend it, Michael had a strong feeling that some threshold had been crossed since he'd started having to shave. Once a week, maybe, but all the same.

To this was added the memory that his half-brother Gabriel was known to prefer the company of males to that of females. At least, Michael had heard that without fully understanding it, and it seemed to him it meant he fell in love with gentlemen, not ladies.

Michael didn't fall in love with anyone. The whole thing seemed to him a passel of trouble. Look at Seraphim, having his life upended ever since he fell in love with a woman whose social consequence was greater than Seraphim's own. And as for Caroline and her romance—well. Her fiancé wasn't even human, in some ways.

In Michael's world, which he intended to keep as rational as possible as long as possible, romance was not only an infernal nuisance, but an irrational one. And he would have none of it.

And certainly he'd never, under any circumstances, have anything to do with a scrubby schoolboy who fell out of windows in other worlds. At any rate, Michael—for all he didn't care at all—had started to realize that some women—particularly very beautiful and intelligent ones, like that Miss Monkton who had given a talk on magical electricity, which he had attended last summer—had...effects on him. His palms sweated, his throat grew tight, he couldn't think of anything to say, and altogether, a lot of effects took place which Michael had never expected and didn't like in the least. So he knew for an absolute fact that when it came to avoiding romance, it was romance with women that he was avoiding.

Which meant that he should be offended by Hodges's implication. He tried to sound severe when he said, "Oh, no one cares for that. We should have some clothes that fit Al. Maybe from when I was younger? I don't think he'll be staying the night. He's only here till dinner, I think. Just have some clothes and warm water brought up. Er...not a bath. We'll just wash our hands and faces and change?"

"Sir!"

"No, Hodges, I must insist."

"And I, sir, must insist that no such thing will happen under His Grace's roof. If you please, follow me." And Hodges led them into the small parlor.

Michael blinked. Either his brother's butler had gone completely insane, or there was something of a magical nature going on that messed with people's heads.

It wasn't just the refusal to let them wash and change in the same room. No. It went well beyond that. It was that they were being shown into the parlor.

Michael paced like a caged tiger by the windows, while Al sat, subdued, on a chair, his hands in his lap, as if he were still in the nursery. Good heavens, *was* the boy still in the nursery? Was that why Hodges was acting so strangely?

But next a maid came in, bringing tea and cakes, which was a crowning insanity.

Surely Al was too young for liquor. Michael was too young for liquor, besides not liking the stuff. But lemonade and cake would be a more appropriate snack for a schoolboy, would it not?

"I have no idea—" he began, but Al was already pouring tea for both of them and helping himself to cakes. There was a vertical wrinkle between his eyebrows, as though he were trying to decipher a very difficult puzzle.

There was noise in the hall, noise unheard of in this elegant house: an argument and raised voices, between a man and a woman. And Mrs. Hodges came in. She was the housekeeper at the townhouse, a very respectable woman, who wore somber colors and whom Michael had never before seen disturbed.

He'd always assumed that she could plan a party for three hundred or nursery tea without getting flustered. But now she looked flustered. Or she looked flustered until three steps in. And then she looked like she was trying very hard not to laugh.

She curtseyed to Michael, but spoke to Al. "Well, my dear," she said, a hint of a smile on her lips. "He has no idea, does he?"

Al shook his head.

"So I take it your acquaintance is recent?"

"Yes, ma'am," Al said, his voice sounding a little shy and strangled.

"I see. And here is Hodges," she looked over her shoulder at her husband, "saying that Lord Michael is getting ready to set up a Corinth. You must forgive them. They are fools. They never actually grow up: they just stop having spots."

Michael would have been offended, if he had the slightest idea what she was talking about. Except, of course, that it included him and Hodges. Hodges, whose eyes he met, looked as dumbfounded as Michael himself.

"Go, Lord Michael," the housekeeper said, sounding exactly as commanding and maternal as she had when Michael had been ten years younger. "To your room. Have a proper bath and change."

"But Al—"

"I'll take care of your friend, sir. Do not fear. We'll bring... We'll bring you both here when you're done. Word has been sent to your brother, but whether he will be in for dinner or not, we do not know. There is some crisis involving Fairyland, and it is that important. But never fear, we'll take care of the two of you."

Michael was so confused that he not only let himself be herded to his room, but he let his brother's superior valet choose his attire after bath, so that when he dressed, he realized he was wearing the most formal of dinner attires, complete with breeches.

He thought to protest, because while his brother might be married to the heir to the throne, he was still very much at home, and if anyone else were at dinner, it would be family and...

And he forgot it all when he entered the drawing room.

There was a young lady there who had a passing resemblance to Miss Monkton. At least she had the same red hair, a mass of it, loose down her back, and very large green eyes with a startled expression in them.

Oh, she also had freckles, masses of them, but Michael had never understood why people would mind freckles. He found them charming. She wore a very beautiful dark green gown, with... Well, he was sure it was very nice lace, though he had no words to even think on it, much less describe it.

"Miss— Madam—" He stumbled.

Suddenly, the features rearranged themselves, and he realized she was... "Al!" he said.

She curtseyed. The damned chit curtseyed, very proper and all to him, as though he were some kind of important person and she a stranger! As though she hadn't fallen from a window onto his magical rowboat. As if—

"Albinia Blakley, Milord. At your service."

Michael realized, with a start, this must be the whelp that Tristram Blakley had spoken of. A bastard child?

He opened his mouth to answer, though he was not sure with what.

That was when the window exploded.

Shadow

BEFORE ALBINIA HAD REALIZED what was happening, Michael had jumped on her, and was holding her down, while a curious sound like hail rattled all around, combined with a sound of howling wind. And she tried to protest, but he wasn't letting her up.

Things that Mrs. Hodges had told her flitted through her mind in sudden panic. When she'd told Mrs. Hodges that she'd rather not let Michael know she was a girl because, she thought, men could steal a woman's virtue, Mrs. Hodges had told her not to let him touch her, or force her into any position, and that she'd be all right. Though it was also a good idea not to be alone with him behind closed doors.

The latter accorded so much with things Mama had said, that Al could only imagine it meant that when alone with a girl or in a position of command over her, a man could then steal her magic and do with it as he wished.

Panicked, unable to see, because part of Michael's—or should that be Lord Michael's?—cravat had come undone and flopped in front of her face, Albinia made futile attempts to get up.

The worst part is she knew they were futile even as she tried. First, because the big lump of Lord must outweigh her by double, and second, because as the youngest sister of six boys, she knew that it was almost impossible to overpower them, even the ones who were about her size. Which was why she'd learned early on to use her magic—

The thought was useful. She didn't need to maim him, or even seriously hurt him. She'd learned early on that sharp and concentrated force applied to a vulnerable area would get the young man distracted enough for her to then fight free.

Of course, if he's already stolen my virtue—

But she'd try. The other thing she learned, growing up, is that you always tried.

With everything in her, she closed her eyes and concentrated on the back of his neck. She'd had a view of it as they came into the house, and remembered it clearly: the pink skin beneath his hair. And then under her breath she muttered the easiest incantations for effect. If she still could do it, and had it right, it would feel like a giant mosquito sting on the back of his neck.

She aimed for effect and let it fly.

"Ouch!" came from above, and for just a moment, she felt his reaction, a slight movement, as probably his hand went to the back of his neck.

She took the opportunity to lever herself on one elbow, dig the other into what she hoped was his midriff, as she shoved with her whole body to get him off her, and then, before he could get hold again, before she even blinked, to leap away from him and—

That was when she slowed down enough, even as Lord Michael shouted, "Hey, I was trying—" to realize that the window that had been behind them: a vast affair composed of many little squares of glass encased in a framework of lead had broken inward, with force.

There were little pieces of glass all over the floor. She assumed that was the sound like hail that she had heard. She realized he'd been trying to protect her, probably guessing—accurately—that the impact of the glass would be less on the sturdier fabric of his suit. Even so, she realized that the back of his neck wasn't exactly as her mental image had been. There were now myriad tiny cuts, as though he'd been excoriated by the glass, which, now that she thought about it, he had been. As he turned around, anger in his eyes, she said, "I'm sorry. I know you were trying to protect me, but I couldn't see— I had to see—"

He looked confused, but only for a moment.

The gale force winds, which must have blown the window in, hadn't abated at all, and now, through the window, came something dark and formless, something immense and man-shaped but which looked like it was made wholly out of smoke.

Al didn't even mind that Lord Michael stepped in front of her. She could feel him, vaguely, because she sensed that he was working with forces bigger than she could command, assembling something magical. But it was complicated, and difficult, and the figure coming through the window swatted it aside with a giant hand made of shadow and smoke before it was fully assembled.

And then...

She would never be clear precisely what happened next, but she saw the thing grab Lord Michael, like a kitten by the scruff of the neck.

Albinia didn't think. If she'd thought, she'd have hidden, or perhaps tried to run. But her body reacted before her mind could. She grabbed for Lord Michael, around his midriff.

And suddenly, she was suspended midair, holding onto the young man's warm body, while—inexplicably—they both flew suspended over London, much higher than even the boat had flown.

Beneath them, very far, were the roofs and streets of London, people as small as flies walking the streets, and carriages not much bigger than that trundling along. If they fell, they would be dead.

Albinia was not stupid, or at least no more stupid than anyone else. At least, from reading novels and listening to Mama's stories of Mama's own youth, Al thought she might be rather cleverer than the common run of people.

But right now, all her belief in her excellent intellect amounted to nothing. What a dangerous and yet ridiculous situation to be in.

Now she recognized what the monster was, of course—any half-trained witch would do so, and she was a little more than half-trained—he was a Gather. Gathers were creatures created entirely by a spell, and formed of the nearest, most abundant material. She should possibly be happy that the creature had been made of the pervasive coalsmoke that permeated the city and not, say, from the equally pervasive stone used to make the buildings. Or perhaps from people, she thought, as that, too, was abundant in London. She shivered. She was not absolutely sure if Gathers would assemble out of people, should they be directed, say, to form in the middle of a crowd. She was sure, however, no people would survive such an experience.

Her arms aching, getting increasingly cold this high, where the wind blew with an extraordinary chill beneath her elaborate skirts, she returned to her impossible predicament. The problem was that, while she knew very well how to form a Gather, and therefore was absolutely capable of unforming it, to dissolve this one meant to fall headfirst into London. And die. There was no way in that short space she would have time to say a spell to break her fall. But her arms hurt where she held onto Lord Michael, and she was cold, and she was sure wherever the Gather was taking them, it could be no good place.

Just as she thought that, she heard Lord Michael shouting, "Miss Blakley!" As he spoke, he reached out his arms, and held her in turn. "You should not have held onto me. My family would have given you hospitality. There is—"

It occurred to Albinia, and what a time to think of it, that not only had she been very forward and rude in holding onto a man she barely knew, but that he might very well think she was trying to trick him into marriage. She had some idea that Mama and her friends had tried such tricks when young, and even though she didn't know much of society, she knew they were morally wrong.

"I couldn't let you be taken alone. The creature is probably evil. And you saved me before," she shouted back. Her voice was not very loud, and he looked back at her, and she could see he was trying to make an attempt to understand. Just as she thought this, she saw his lip twitch in amusement and didn't know why.

"I thank you," he said, his voice very formal. But she could tell he was upset.

The Tower

MICHAEL HAD NEVER UNDERSTOOD why people fell in love. It seemed an extraordinary thing to happen, to experience a feeling that suddenly upended all your thinking and all your plans for the future. A very uncomfortable thing, too, since he couldn't imagine marriage would be very peaceable or easy, forever having to consider another person in your plans. Bad enough that one had siblings whom one had to consider and plan for. And indulge in their senseless fears.

And of course he was not falling in love with Al— Miss Blakley. For one, he barely knew her. And for another, he wasn't quite sure what falling in love was like. When Caroline had come back from her adventures in Fairyland, it had all been about how Akakios gave her flutters in her stomach and made her mouth dry. Michael had thought that it might be successfully treated with a purgative and some bleeding, but when he'd told Caroline that, she'd punched him.

However, now, being carried by a smoke Gather over the city of London—and what a spectacle it must be. He could almost hear the shouts from the people below—he realized that while he still did not have any intention of falling in love, he could almost understand why people did.

Not only was Al quite beautiful—well, maybe not conventionally beautiful, but he found her very pleasing to the eye—but also, she was the bravest girl he'd met since his sister Caroline. Ridiculous, of course. What she thought she could do to save him from someone who had sent this large a Gather was quite beyond him. And she must know, from the spelled boat, that he was quite a competent magician himself.

But of course she had not thought of that. She had simply charged in to protect him. Which was beyond stupid, yet very endearing. He held on tighter to her, her warmth welcome, and did a minor spell so he could speak and be heard without having to shout. "I have no idea where it is taking us."

"Nor I," Al said. "Though I can't believe something that broke into your brother's house can have good intentions towards us."

"No," Michael agreed. "And it is quite stupid, too. Because whoever summoned it must know that the moment the Gather took us, my brother would be called and there would be quite—"

At that moment, he stopped. Not because he wanted to, but because everything must stop in the In-Betweener.

He did not even know you could take any Gather through the In-Betweener, and he held his breath—not that it made any difference, since you couldn't breathe in the sheer nothing of the place, and hoped that the creature, such as it was, had enough purpose to be able to drag them through and to wherever it had come from.

This, of course, resolved the problem of how the smoke Gather had dared to break into the house of the Prince Consort, let alone how he intended to get away with it.

You could track people through the In-Betweener. Unless where they landed was time dislocated or indeed a parallel universe, he would be found. Sooner, rather than later.

But the finding would take time. And Michael had learned, long ago, that there was only one reason for someone to take him and delay pursuit, for they must know they could not evade it. That reason was undoubtedly murder.

Oh, sure, there were times when kidnappers wanted money, but the son of a duke and brother of the future Prince Consort from a family with extraordinarily high magic, would be too dangerous a prey for kidnappers for ransom. If all they wanted was money, there must be far less dangerous people they could kidnap. And with more to give.

And also, kidnappers would need to be reasonably sure they could extract money before the victim was found. No such thing here. Not when the guard of the Princess Royal would descend on the kidnappers at very heart-stopping speed.

So the only reason they could have for kidnapping Michael in this fashion was because they wished to kill him, and then perhaps disappear into the multi-verse before they could be traced.

The idea was obscene, and he felt his stomach clench in a ball of ice. He'd brought Albinia, an innocent, into this perilous situation.

Just as he thought that, they came out of the In-Betweener, and the Gather strode in seven-league steps through the fog over the tops of a seemingly endless green forest. In the far distance, he could see a stone tower, but in the fog he couldn't even tell if it was a functional tower or just ruins.

Why would anyone want to kill him? People might have vendettas against his brothers, both very important people, or even against his father, though his father was vanished and officially dead. But why kill him?

The Gather was moving lower.

"Do you think we could survive the fall?" Al asked, showing she was at the same point in her thoughts.

He shook his head. And then the reason they might want to kill him came to mind with a startling clarity.

He had never paid much attention to Seraphim's job as the Royal Witchfinder. The position entailed going to other worlds and rescuing people from where magic might be forbidden. But Seraphim said one had to be careful. Loathing magic, per se, was not a bad thing, if most people in the world were without magic. Because magic practitioners, given their immense advantage, could do very bad things indeed. One of which was gather power through virgin sacrifice. And those sacrifices seemed to work better with a person of high birth.

The Gather was now at a point where they could jump and perhaps even survive the experience.

Feeling cold all through, with a cold that had nothing to do with what appeared to be a pleasant, cool morning in this universe, he frantically assembled the spell that would disassemble the Gather. As he clamped it on the creature, he had a feeling it would fail, which meant the magic creating the creature was immense.

"Hold," Al said, before he could pull the final twist that would cause the Gather to— Well, probably not to do much, given his insufficient power. "I will help."

On top of his, she threw her magic, which he was surprised to find was quite powerful.

And then she pulled the piece holding the creature together.

It sounded exactly like a balloon out of which air had been let: a long prolonged whine of air escaping. And then it came apart, suddenly, in a noxious smell of coalsmoke.

And they were falling.

Michael tumbled to the branches of a tree, managing to shift position just enough to land solidly on his behind. It rattled his brains, nonetheless, which must explain why the first thing he did, as soon as his head cleared, was to look around and yell, "Al, where are you?"

Strangers In the Night

AL WASN'T SURE WHERE she was, but to her, Michael's voice—

No, *Lord* Michael's. She had to remember she was consorting with the highest levels of nobility in the land. Mostly, she had to remember because she wasn't sure what the rules were and she despised situations where she had no idea what was expected of her. It was the type of situation in which she did something that made Mother scream at her, or worse, put watchers on her.

Lord Michael's voice seemed to come from an entire world altogether. For a moment, she wondered if she'd got stuck in the In-Betweener and his voice was coming at her from one of the real worlds.

Was that what happened when people got lost in the In-Betweener?

Then she realized she was most uncomfortable. There was something poking her in the back, and something else covering her eyes. She could feel rough leaves on her forehead. And of course, this was not the sort of thing that should happen in the In-Betweener, where nothing existed but yourself. She drew a deep breath, and it came in scented with pine. Moving her arms, and hands, she felt fairly sure she was laying on a pine branch. A pine branch that was wider than her body, and—

"Al?" Somehow, a Lord's voice shouldn't sound that tremulous, should it? They were trained from infancy to know exactly what to do, right?

"I think I'm on a tree," she managed. She cleared her throat. "Or *in* a tree, really. It's just really dark."

"Oh," he said, and she could tell his voice was somewhere beneath her. She thought he chuckled, though he tried to make it sound like he'd just cleared his throat.

Al sat up and felt for the branch she was lying on, and then towards the trunk. "I'm not sure I can get down, without seeing the branches. I...haven't a great deal of experience climbing trees," she said, and her own voice trembled, which made her feel like a fool. But there weren't that many trees around Wulffen Downs Manor. Cliffs, and scrubby bushes, yes. But no trees.

"Um," he said, which wasn't exactly informative. Or the sort of speech one expected from a high nobleman.

And then there was a long, long silence.

"Mich— Er... *Lord* Michael?" she asked.

And then there was light. It was a ball of it, climbing, climbing. By its light, Albinia saw that she was up a very tall and ancient pine tree. "I think," she said, "the branches are close enough for me to climb down."

He didn't answer. She could see him far below, a small figure, his face a pale oval looking up at her.

Right. She was going to have to climb down, and the distance seemed as high as the tower where her room was in her father's house. But this time, she didn't have a rope ladder made of old sheets.

For a moment, she considered asking if someone who had the kind of power where he could conjure a big light out of nowhere with so little effort, and keep it shining and stable, couldn't somehow float her down. But then she took a deep breath. No. She'd be damned if she'd ask for his help and catch herself at his mercy. She didn't even know him very well.

So, fighting an inner certainty that she was about to lose her footing and crash down, she slowly slung herself off the branch, searching with her feet for the branch below her. She found it, solid, under her foot, let go of the top branch, and sat on that one, before she managed to swing herself from it, holding onto it with her hands, while her feet looked for the next branch.

There was a dangerous moment, after several hundreds of branches—okay, probably dozens, but it felt like hundreds—when she couldn't quite reach the branch below with her feet, and then she heard Lord Michael's voice. "Pardon me, I'm going to touch your ah, limbs," and then his hands clasped around her ankles.

She screamed, but his hand guided her foot to the branch, while her hands groped around for a hold, and then found the trunk, and looking down, she realized her feet were at head level with Lord Michael. He let go of her ankles, as though he'd been burned.

Well, it was shocking to be touched like that, but she didn't think her legs were actually on fire. She managed another branch down, and then she jumped, falling on what felt like springy moss.

And Lord Michael was reaching out with a hand, as though offering her balance.

He let go of the energy that kept the light going. She could feel him withdrawing his magic and she said, in a shaky voice, "I thank you. I know that must have taken a lot of power." In fact, she was starting to wonder if he needed her virtue at all. Though there had been something strange when she'd added her power to his. Suddenly, her own had seemed much larger than she was used to. Almost unmanageable.

"It's not the power," he said, and his voice sounded tight. "I'm afraid someone will find us by the light. We can't be sure everyone in this forest is friendly."

Just like that, out of the dark forest, they heard the sound of a howling wolf.

The howling wolf had a sort of magical property of its own. Albinia had heard wolves before, of course. She'd been born and raised in a remote domain, except for that very brief—and odd—visit to London when she was six. And the domain was called and near the village of Wulffen Downs. There were wolves there. Samuel had said his ancestors had been Royal Wolf Hunters. But this wolf sounded like a thing composed of magic, night, darkness and fear. It was like the wolves one heard of in fairy tales, who got into cottages and devoured entire families.

There was a feeling of hunger and frustrated rage to its voice, a sense that there lived within it something more than a mortal, common wolf. And Albinia found this created a telekinesis of sorts that propelled her against Lord Michael's all-too-human and comforting warmth.

She expected a shocked sound from him. She understood from Mama that only quite abandoned females flung themselves headlong at men. Not that she didn't sympathize, if the poor things had been abandoned and had no other means of comfort, but she also didn't understand what flinging oneself at a gentleman would do. Unless, of course, the gentleman's arms were broken and he couldn't fend such an attack off?

Like most of what Mama said, it seemed a complete mystery. On the other hand, now she had actually flung herself at a young man, and she fully expected some sort of reproof. What she got instead was Michae— Lord Michael's arm going around her middle. It seemed to her it trembled a little, but she was sure that couldn't be true. Not of someone with so much magic. It must be her shaking, communicating itself to him.

She was of two minds on whether to ask him to make the light shine again or not. She couldn't remember the lore servants and woodsmen had told her in childhood and didn't know if light scared wolves or attracted them.

But just at that moment, as though some malevolent intelligence controlled it, a waxing moon, pale and bloated like something drowned, peeked from behind clouds and cast its cold light onto the scene.

What it revealed was both more and less scary than Albinia expected. The forest showed again in its dark glory, bringing to mind all the stories of children abandoned in forests to die. The trees were tall enough they seemed to disappear into a sky where a few scraps of violet or grey cloud floated, looking much like curdles in spoiled milk.

The wolf was not visible, though it sounded again and closer, that sound that was hunger and anger and terror, all lashed together.

Lord Michael's arm tightened around her. "There is nothing to be afraid of," he said, even as his voice cracked a little with poorly hidden fear. "Wolves are afraid of light, see."

And with that, he made a gesture, and she could feel the magic going from him, and quite suddenly—above them—a light appeared, the same light that had guided her down from the tree, but larger, brighter and very, very comforting.

"Oh," she said, stepping away from him, just as he seemed to leap away from her, as though shocked he'd been grasping her so tight. "I'd been wondering if light attracted or repelled wolves."

He frowned a little, and seemed to be trying to remove twigs and leaves from his clothes. Looking down at herself, she, too, seemed to be impersonating a tree, and she forebore to think of what her hair must look like. She was sure it was a mess all around her head, and filled with twigs and branches. She must look quite demented.

"I actually don't know," Lord Michael said hesitantly. "Whether light attracts or repels wolves. I don't think anyone ever told me." And then, as though embarrassed by his lack of knowledge, "You see, the domain at Darkwater, where I was raised, is...quite large, and we have...ah, gamekeepers and groundskeepers to keep the wild animals at bay. Besides..." He looked uncomfortable. "Besides, I was never the sort of child who goes for rambles in the woods or has adventures. That would be my brothers, at least from what I heard. My... I have a workshop, see, and I like to invent magical things."

She didn't see at all. If she'd been allowed to roam, instead of being locked in the tower all the time, she'd have roamed. She'd have known every inch of the domain, including the woods and the beach. And she'd probably know all about wolves, including whether or not they liked light. But she knew, from dealing with her brothers, that it didn't do to laugh at a boy or say he was silly. They were quite ridiculously fragile in their pride.

At any rate, right then the wolf howled again, quite close. Lord Michael ceased his brushing of his clothes, and Al stepped closer to him, though not quite touching, and this time she forebore from flinging herself at him.

"It appears," Lord Michael said, his voice gone unsteady again, "this one doesn't fear light."

"No," Albinia said, and looked into the darkness, trying to see the creature.

It was odd, because though she could hear it, she couldn't see it at all. Perhaps it was just a figment of her imagination? Or perhaps an insubstantial creature, like the smoke Gather, and not real in any sense?

But just as she thought this, her eyes adjusted, and like in the moment when you blink your eyes in the dark and realize what you thought was a monster is really only the curtain blowing in the wind, she saw it.

It was only that it was so large and so dark, she'd thought he was a dark spot in the trees. He—and from the feel of the creature, there was no doubt it was a he—was a vast beast, his shoulder towering above her head, his eyes glimmering yellow and feral.

As she looked, he opened his mouth to howl again, and long, sharp fangs, as long as her fingers, glimmered in the light.

Lord Michael was pushing her behind him. "It's not a natural wolf," he said.

"I know," she said, because she did. No natural wolves grew to that size.

And just as she was thinking what to do, the creature advanced on them, a low growl coming from its throat.

She forgot everything she was thinking. Her mind blanked, and she couldn't move if she—

She felt the magic work, and didn't even know if it was flowing from her or Lord Michael. It seemed much larger than her magic had been until yesterday, only yesterday—

She didn't know which of them threw the fireball, which went flying to strike the animal on the nose. It screamed.

In that second, Lord Michael screamed, also. "Run!" And grabbing for her hand, he pulled.

They ran headlong into the dark forest, while the light of magic above them extinguished itself.

Comfort

IT WAS DARK AND Albinia was tired.

They'd run madly through the forest, leaves and twigs poking up through her indoor slippers and catching at her gown.

And then she stumbled, and Lord Michael put out a hand to stop her falling. For a moment, they stayed like that in the dark. She realized she couldn't hear the sound of pursuit. There was no way that a wolf that large could be chasing them without making any sound.

"I don't hear it," Lord Michael said with a kind of gulp, as if he were trying to get air in, as though he too were breathless after their run.

Albinia shook her head, then realized he couldn't see her, and said, "I don't, either. I don't think it...it is following us."

For a while, they stood. She could hear him breathe, but all she could think of was how much her legs hurt.

"We...should find a place to...spend the night, until the light comes up."

She had a moment of fear, wondering whether the light *would* come up. Her heart thumping, she wondered if they were in some unnatural land, where the light would never come, day never break.

"I believe it's just night time," Lord Michael said, his voice hesitant. "I can't...be absolutely sure, but it doesn't feel like a place of night." He sounded very tired, too, and not just physically. "Perhaps..." he said, "we can make a bed of leaves or—"

A shriek like a child screaming cut him off. His hand, which had let go of her arm, came back again, and held her wrist. Albinia wondered if it was meant to reassure her, or if he was seeking reassurance.

The cry sounded again.

Memories of early childhood when they'd visited Albinia's paternal grandmother came to Albinia, and she said in relief, "It's a swan." Grandmother had fed dozens of the creatures, and no matter how dreadful they sounded, they were *not* soul-stealing monsters.

The cry echoed again, and then Albinia felt a beak against her leg. It wasn't hitting her hard or viciously, but more as though calling her attention. And then she heard the sound again and Lord Michael said, "Ow."

She felt him move power, and the light came on again, a witchlight, the size of a candle flame and soft in glow. Albinia knew how to do it, of course, but she also had been taught not to use it unless in absolute necessity, because it used a high level of power and would make you very tired. By rights, Lord Michael should not be able to bring the light up, as tired as he sounded before he did.

But the light was enough to see a very large swan. It seemed completely unsurprised by the sudden light, and in fact—though it was impossible for a swan to do such a thing—Albinia had the impression it was smiling.

It flew near the ground, ahead of them, a short flight, then stopped and waited.

"I think it wants us to follow it?" Lord Michael said. Albinia forebore to say, "Obviously."

"I sense no evil from it."

Albinia also didn't, but all she did was nod, and the two of them followed the swan. After a while, through the trees ahead, they saw a sort of glow.

"If it's a spun sugar cottage, remember how the story ends," she said, mock-sternly, mostly to distract herself from her own fear.

"This is not Fairyland," Lord Michael said. "I'd know if it were." His voice sounded very odd.

The swan led them nearer the light. As they got close, they realized it was the tower they'd seen from a distance. Only it wasn't a tower as such. Or, rather, it was, but the tower was attached to a small cottage built onto the front of it, as though the cottage had grown a three-story-tall carbuncle. The light shone through a window on the bottom floor while the tower proper was dark, though she could now see it had glass in its windows, so presumably it was useable.

The swan opened the door. Albinia was sure of it, though she couldn't see how.

It went in, and they followed it. But when they got in, the swan was nowhere to be seen.

Instead, they were in a tidy room, with a fire burning. There were eight comfortable-looking armchairs disposed around, and bookshelves on the wall.

Albinia hesitated. "You are sure this is not Fairyland?" she asked Lord Michael.

"Absolutely," he said. "I was kidnapped into it, you see." He said it very simply, like he might say that he'd spent some time at a country estate. "A year ago. And I had to be rescued. I know Fairyland."

She felt the dread in his voice and didn't want to dwell on it. She'd heard things about Fairyland... "This is good, because I am very hungry," Albinia said brightly. "And this looks like the kind of place that will have a kitchen."

And then she heard light steps downstairs. A door opened next to the fireplace and a familiar voice said, "Al, I'm so sorry. I had to go put clothes on, or it would be quite shocking to receive you."

Standing in the doorway, impeccably dressed in a brown suit with white shirt and neatly tied cravat, was a young man ten years older than her. She knew this precisely because they shared a birthday.

"Geoffrey!" she said, and ran into her brother's arms.

Happy Families

When it came to having strange relatives, Michael Ainsling felt he couldn't throw stones. Or, rather, he could, but it would be akin to standing atop a tower made entirely of glass and throwing stones at your neighbors' windows. Sooner or later, it was your tower that would come crashing down.

After all, his brother was the Royal Witchfinder and had continued his avocation for years, while the king himself had forbidden it by decree. Seraphim, in fact, had broken royal edict to go to other worlds where magic was forbidden and punishable with death, and rescue magic users and shifters from the jaws of death. In this, he'd been aided by his valet, whom they all knew to be his father's by-blow. What they didn't know was that Gabriel was also half-elf and in the royal line of Fairyland...of which he'd eventually become king. In fact, he already had. And Seraphim, despite his transgressions against royal decree, had become the Prince Consort of the Princess Helena, who would eventually inherit the throne.

His father, who wasn't dead, had faked his death and gone adventuring among the many worlds, with his mother. His twin sister, Caroline, had gone to Fairyland herself—he'd never understood why, and no one had ever explained—and fallen in love with a centaur named Akakios, who had, for reasons also never made clear, been banned from Fairyland forever, thereby.

During the adventures leading to that outcome, Michael had been kidnapped into Fairyland. He wasn't sure what had happened to him there.

He had memories. They were all unpleasant ones. But he couldn't pin them down. The details, the certainty of what happened to him, tended to twist and turn in his mind when he tried to think of them, leaving him confused and more scared than the son of such illustrious parentage should be. He couldn't dodge the feeling that while in Fairyland, he had become something less than fully human. Sometimes he wondered if his family suspected the same and if that was why he'd been left alone at their country home while everyone else pursued their destinies.

But at least, he thought, none of his siblings had ever turned into a goose. He thought. At least, he hoped not. Certainly not where he could see or hear of it.

He ran his hand over his face, feeling as though he'd been sandblasted since he'd first read the dead man's letter over breakfast. He'd come to the conclusion the dead man was Al's father. But did that make her the whelp he'd talked about? Or was it instead one of his sons he referred to?

He watched, past wonder, as Geoffrey, a tall lanky youth who should have finished his schooling and been presented at court to start his adult life, were this any kind of sane world, hugged Albinia, then gently nudged her aside. Albinia was crying and wiping her eyes on her sleeve. Since neither Albinia nor—Michael was sure—himself were noticeably clean after their adventures, this meant she was adding grey streaks to her face, to replace the dirt the tears were washing off.

He felt as if he'd fallen headlong in some kind of dream—at least it wasn't the screaming nightmares he experienced after his return from Fairyland—and waking up was long delayed.

Geoffrey advanced on him, full tilt, and extended a hand. "Lord Michael," he said. "My father talks much of you. He considers you the only genius to equal his to come along...well, ever. Or since Da Vinci's magical inventions, whichever you prefer."

"Your father talks..." Michael said. He remembered heated discussions about the evil of necromancy around the dining room table and one thing he was absolutely sure of: without necromancy, dead men didn't talk.

"Oh. You imagine him dead," Geoffrey said. He did not look a thing like Albinia, not having even the vaguest shred of red-headed bone structure. His hair was dark, very straight, unruly, and looked like he'd cut it himself, in irregular swathes, by the method of chopping off whatever protruded onto his field of vision. His eyes were also dark, and he had the jagged nose that Michael knew best from certain statues of antiquity. At the moment, he looked amused, his lips twisting in a smile that made Michael want to scream. It was the sort of smile his older brothers knew better than to engage in, though they were much older and really royalty, or perhaps in Seraphim's case, close to it. It was the smile of an upperclassman laughing at the follies of a new student, or of a young man laughing at a toddler.

Michael refused to answer, because a succession of nannies, tutors and, yes, his older brothers, had beat into his skull that politeness was the requirement life placed on the gently born, no matter what the temptation. Instead, he raised an eyebrow inquiringly.

The trick—which had taken him weeks to acquire, in front of the mirror, having seen their butler reduce an under-footman to incoherence by that expression—worked. Geoffrey seemed discomfited, which an outright rude response wouldn't have managed.

"Oh. Well. Perhaps it is not surprising. But he's not. He was put under a spell, you see, and whisked...well...here."

Albinia made a sound of shock, as if the air had been punched out of her stomach. As Geoffrey turned to her, she said, "It was Mama, was it not?"

Geoffrey seemed to have forgotten his sister, so he looked surprised, then sighed. "Well, yes, Al. Who else? Who could have thus gotten under his guard?"

"And you?" Albinia said. She clenched her fists at her side, and for the first time looked like she didn't trust this man, whether he was her brother or not.

"Myself? What do you mean? I did nothing to Father!"

She made a huff of impatience. Michael felt as if he were familiar with it, having experienced it a few times during their adventures. He was also fairly sure that Albinia didn't know she made that sound.

"Stupid," she said, with remarkable forthrightness. "Of course I didn't mean that. I meant, did Mother also spirit you away? Here? Wherever here is?"

Geoffrey pursed his lips. It was an odd expression, as though he were considering what to answer. Which made Michael think meanly of his mind. After all, if he knew he was going to meet them, and clearly he did so, and if he knew Albinia's curious nature, shouldn't he have a slew of answers ready, whether they were the full truth or not?

Yet, Geoffrey demurred and said, "Well, not precisely, but I think we can safely say it was at her command and instigation. At any rate..." He sighed. "The thing is, our father was turned into a werewolf and sent back in time...or perhaps to a world that doesn't show to anyone's scans, being a pocket universe. And our attempts at freeing him have only locked him tighter.

"And our father worries, which is why he decided to recruit you, Lord Michael, into helping us. We wanted to do it earlier, but Father said we had to wait until you'd reached the age of reason and could decide whether to help or not."

Various things fell into place in Michael's mind, starting with the fact that the letter, and possibly the fetch, as well, had been sent by that old wizard who had set the modern age in motion. And that he'd—or probably she'd—hit Albinia's father on the nose with light and force. Well, that was an introduction.

But then his reason intruded, as it had the habit of doing. "What do you mean I could decide? You as good as kidnapped me and brought me here."

Now it was Geoffrey who looked pained, as though his head hurt. He rubbed with—Michael noted—exceedingly well-manicured fingers at a spot above his nose. "I'm not sure of that, Milord," he said. "As nothing is as we planned. We did not, for instance, plan to have Al come with you, and I'm at a loss for how you even met."

Albinia and he spoke at once. She said, "He saved my life," while Michael, his memory on that moment when she'd grabbed onto the smog-fetch and came with him, said, "She tried to protect me."

Then Michael cleared his throat. "That is a discussion for another day," he said. "Are you saying that if I don't wish to help you, I can just return to my family's estate and my normal life?"

The smile was still sardonic, but Geoffrey looked bitter. "Father says without a doubt. Is that what you wish?"

"Geoffrey," Al interrupted. "You shouldn't be the one doing this. Where are our brothers?"

"Well," Geoffrey said. "That is part of the trouble. It's...complex." He then turned to Michael. "So, Milord, you'll turn tail and run and leave us mired in our own difficulties? I guess it's your prerogative."

Michael tightened his jaw so hard, it hurt. He knew what he must look like, having watched both his brothers do it. He knew he'd thrust his chin forward, and that his eyes reflected his anger at this Turkish treatment. He took a deep breath, and when he spoke, his voice was so precise, so cultured, no one could accuse him of incivility, but he knew he was being grossly uncivil all the same. "You have a curious means of applying for a boon." He dusted an imaginary speck of dirt from his sleeve, which in fact was so tattered and soot-covered that it would be impossible to tell dirt from fabric, and spoke in tones that did their best to ape Seraphim's. "Let's suppose you behave like a normal human being seeking a troublesome favor from another and tell me what this is about, all of it."

He looked over at Al, who hesitated. For a moment, he wondered if she'd be offended at him, and for some reason, the idea bothered him, though he could not say why.

But Al squared her chin, and stepped over to stand next to him. "Yes, Geoff, suppose you tell us. Everything, please. Half truths are no way to go about requesting someone leave everything to help you. It pains me to agree with her, but you know what Mama always said about your manners and temper!"

Geoff opened his mouth, then snapped it closed. He flushed a dark red, which proved that Al's hit had gone home. "Very well," he said. "If that's what you wish. But it is a great waste of time."

Complex

ALBINIA WAS MORTIFIED.

She'd read novels—to be truthful, mostly because Mama had forbidden her from reading novels. In those works, it seemed that whenever a young lady brought home a suitor of higher status or magical rank or fortune, the young lady's family would conspire to unwittingly embarrass her mortally.

Albinia had read with great amusement a hundred such scenes of the character being mortified by the behavior of her relatives.

Fine, so Lord Michael wasn't her suitor, but still! He was the son and brother of a duke, and here was Geoffrey behaving as though he'd been reared in a stable...or worse.

She scratched at her nose, as he promised to explain everything and how everything was so complex. It wasn't so much that her nose itched, as that she felt something was very wrong, but couldn't quite figure out what. Other than the fact that her brother apparently could change shapes and become a swan, and that Papa might be the werewolf whose nose they'd burned. She was trying very hard not to think of the implications of this, since Papa had never met her. If she understood the timing correctly, he had left—disappeared—around the time Mama was approaching her confinement with Albinia. How terrible to first meet one's father with such an unfilial action as burning his nose.

Scratching at her nose was what Albinia did when she was confused and trying to gain time. Usually, trying to gain time to think of something not quite a lie to tell Mama in order to stop her asking inconvenient questions.

Geoffrey made a big show of being offended by Lord Michael asking perfectly reasonable questions, then crossed his arms on his chest and said, "Very well. We're under a geas, you see, when no two of us can be human at the same time. So I was trying to say my piece, because I don't know—" Suddenly, his voice shook, which to Al was the scariest thing of all, because she thought Geoff was going to break down and start crying. "I don't know if the others might have need of changing at any time."

More to ward off his possible tears—she knew from when they all lived together how much any of the boys hated crying—than because she was incensed, she said, "What do you mean by that, Geoff? Surely you could leave each other notes and plan your human—"

To her horror, this made things worse. Geoff's lips trembled, and his eyes shone, and he said, "W-w-we d-d-d-did f-f-f-—"

And Al realized what had been bothering her. Geoff hadn't stammered at all through the previous speech, but now it was back, in full bloom. Out of the corner of her eye, she saw Lord Michael's horrified expression and wasn't sure why, but she reverted to what always worked. "Geoff! Deep breaths, and speak slowly."

This brought a wan smile to Geoffrey's face. He said "D-d— Darn it, Al. I rarely stammer anymore, because I have had years of solitude to p-p-practice, but..." He took two deep breaths. "Forgive me, Lord Michael." Then to Al, "You see, at first we did just as you said. We had a big board in this house, and w-we used to have a schedule. And we also left notes and letters to each other. That's how Father told us that L-Lord Michael should be able to free us from this geas, and also how he told us to wait until he came of age. B-b-b—" Geoff took a deep breath. "We couldn't wait, you see. You have no idea how terrible it is to spend years and years really alone. Though I can see the others when in swan form."

"Swan, not goose," Lord Michael muttered under his breath in a tone of enlightenment, but Al chose to ignore that ornithological observation. She didn't suppose that sons of dukes spent much time in the poultry house.

Geoff looked at Lord Michael and the wan smile became more pronounced, even if still wan, "Right. Swans. My stepmother got the idea from some old tale or other. But seeing each other as swans doesn't help much, as there's a limited degree of what you can communicate by body language. And Papa— Well, it is best at any rate for any of us not to meet Papa when he's a wolf, since he becomes quite a ferocious beast." He paused for a moment. "To be fair, even as a human, he used to be ferocious if we interrupted him while he was working, though at least as a human, devouring people was not in his range of ideas."

"I imagine not," lord Michael said drily, and stepped back till he sat on one of the chairs.

"But as I said, we grew impatient. And we had some idea of how to break the spell. Or at least—" He paused. "Papa thought it involved taking the path out the back door and meeting the challenges. He just thought the challenges required g-g-g-genius. And he said none of us had it to that degree... So the others—"

Albinia knew her brothers too well not to know what was coming next. "They took the path?"

"One by one," Geoff said. "Till only I was left."

She opened her mouth, closed it. There was a cold feeling of dread in her middle. "And none came back?"

Geoff shook his head. Now he sat on one of the chairs, as well, and his hands were visibly trembling. "Till only I am left." He looked at Michael. "And if you won't help us, I'll have t-t-t-to go myself. Only if none of the others could do it— And Papa doesn't know. I didn't dare leave him a note telling him what happened. And, oh, Al, it's been hell."

And Al fell into the role she'd had all through childhood, when she—incongruously—tried to look after all the boys. "There, there, Geoff, it will be well," she said. But she didn't dare ask Lord Michael to help. They'd already put him to so much trouble.

She looked to the side, where he—under the grime and dust of their adventure—looked very solemn.

Well. Never mind. If he wouldn't, she'd have to do it. Even if she wasn't a genius. Not even as much of a genius as the boys.

The Wolf Returns

MICHAEL FELT AS THOUGH his head were reeling.

To an extent he—the part of him that was charitable, at least—understood the frustration of the young man and how he wished they would simply do what he told them to.

To another extent—

To another extent, the truth was that he'd been shanghaied into an adventure he'd not signed up for, and the idea that he should now risk his life on some ill-defined magical road for the sake of people so wholly unconnected with him made him feel both tired and put upon.

But he didn't know how to express his problem without sounding rude, or as though he didn't care for Al, who had, in fact, saved his life twice over. Or had almost probably saved his life. While embroiling him in the most horrendous adventure, of course, but all of it—he was sure—unmeant.

As she told the young man how he was being rude, sounding like she'd lost all patience, he put out a hand. "No, I understand," he said. "It is just that I did not mean to be embroiled in any of this. I did not choose it." He looked towards Geoff. "And it sounds to me as though your brothers, with far better knowledge of the situation, just got lost, so I can't understand what I can be expected to do." He realized he sounded whiny, something he was prone to, at least to his own ears. Chalk it up to being the much youngest in a brood of—de facto, if not in law—three boys, whose two older brothers were far more powerful in their own ways. He didn't have to like it to recognize it. Mostly, he guessed he sounded tired, which he was.

Al must have picked up on the implication. She gave him the sort of look women were likely to give men when they overexert. Michael had seen it from his twin, Caroline, who was bound to think she was much older than him—not a bare fifteen minutes—and therefore entitled to looking after him like a second mother. But most of all, he saw it from housekeepers and nurses, and even maids, who all tended to think—he thought it was distributed as household rules to new hires—that he worked too much at his machines, and didn't eat enough or take enough healthy exercise.

Al gave him that look, then looked back at her brother. "Before we can decide what to do or how, we must have a bath, and clothes, and food, too. You must understand we've been precipitated from adventure to disaster for what I would judge to be a whole day, and we're not going to set off on any magical road without resting and eating." She paused. "At least I am not. Lord Michael is free to make his own decision."

Geoff looked angry, or maybe puzzled. Without knowing the young man better, Michael could not determine exactly what the frown that crossed his face meant. Geoff opened his mouth as if to speak, but what came out of his mouth was *blert*. It was exactly the same sound as you'd expect at the beginning of a trumpet fanfare.

Then, before Michael's shocked eyes, the man hiccupped, hiccupped again, made a sound that amounted to *blert!* but which was not made by any vocal organs, but rather as if his entire body had imploded inward. And trumpeted again. Only the creature trumpeting now was a swan—had to be a swan, geese didn't make that sound—standing in a welter of male human clothes. He put out his neck and trumpeted again, indignantly.

At the same time, there was the sound of footsteps approaching the tower door, and presently the door swung inward.

Michael had once seen a portrait of Tristram Blakley. It was one of the very early portraits, where magic had first allowed the affixing of an image to paper, but it tended to fade and lose sharpness over a very short time. It had been copied, many times over, in pencil and woodcut, and appeared in every schoolbook, under the heading of "Tristram Blakley, the father of modern magic."

It showed, sketchily, a thin man with a patrician nose and heavy eyebrows, and a mass of unruly, fanning-out dark hair. This man looked like that.

Only— There were changes.

Add several decades, make the hair white, and emphasize the nose. Also give the nose a wound at the very tip that looked like someone had hit it with a red-hot poker. Or a fireball. And you'd have the same Tristram Blakley. And he looked angry.

Michael suppressed a sigh and told himself that hiding behind Albinia would be a despicable act of cowardice.

The man looked upset, very upset. And his glare favored Michael, Albinia and the goo— Swan in turn.

To Michael's relief, he was wrapped in a tattered, disreputable-looking grey cloak. Seeing a legendary magician in the altogether was no part nor parcel of Michael's ambition, frankly.

He said, "Good evening" but in a tone that might mean, "The better to eat you with."

The swan trumpeted indignantly and Blakley answered, in a mordant tone, "No doubt, Geoff, but I thought I was more suited to explaining what must be done and why."

The swan made a half-muttered "trumpet" sound that managed to convey sullen acquiescence.

Albinia—as far as Michael could see out of the corner of his eye, without turning—at first looked surprised, shocked, then dejected, and had now hunched into herself and become unreadable.

Tristram Blakley's eyes, just as intelligent and piercing as in his portrait, turned back to the pair of them, lingering on Albinia. "I presume," he said, "you got some version of our intent, but have not yet understood the whole."

Michael cleared his throat, but before he could speak, Tristram hiccuped, and Michael fell back on his left foot, ready to leap in front of Al and protect her, should this person turn into the wolf again.

Instead, Tristram covered his mouth. "Pardon me," he said. "Voles. Worst part of this business, I swear. Very erratic diet. And now, what do you wish to know?"

Albinia stepped forward then, managing to project a dignity much older than her years, and said, "No, Papa. Before we wish to know anything at all, we must have baths, food, clean clothing and probably a bed. Because you are violating every law of hospitality or simple humanity and this will not stand."

Tristram opened his mouth, closed it and swallowed. Something like both shock and fear crossed his features. Michael expected him to say something unkind, but all he said was, “Oh, very well!” in the tone of a great concession.

Problem And Path

MICHAEL HAD NEVER THOUGHT of swans as particularly sarcastic. Which probably just went to show the limited understanding he had of poultry. Because, though he could not understand what Geoff Blakley said in swan *blerts*, as he led Michael up the stairs and—by use of his beak—opened a closet door to reveal much male clothing of varying sizes, Michael was sure there were sarcastic comments along the lines of, "Help yourself, why don't you?"

The same in the bathroom, whose ingenious construction fascinated Michael. He found piped-in hot water, whose temperature you could regulate with a turn of a dial, and Michael was sure the swan-trumpeting about that meant, "The old geezer had a lot of time alone here and pleased himself by making the place comfortable."

But it was only as Michael, carrying a change of clothing, stood by the bathtub and stared at the swan, and before leaving the swan made a particularly trenchant trumpeting that Michael thought meant, "Right, I'll leave. It's not like I want to see you naked, bucko," that he was absolutely sure that swan had a sarcastic turn of phrase.

After Geoff left the bathroom, Michael washed. The warm water on demand, and as much as he wanted, without having to worry about putting the servants out by making them carry endless buckets, was an amazing convenience. Particularly as the first tub-full was gritty with glass particles from Michael's hair.

He wondered if Seraphim had got home, and what he'd found after the Gather had broken his window and stolen his brother. He knew that Tristram Blakley had said that he was in a place impossible to find, but between Michael's brothers, surely they would find him.

Then he sighed, because that was probably true, but it also meant that once more Michael would be rescued, and once more reveal himself the helpless younger brother who had to be saved from peril. Yet again.

He wondered what had possessed Tristram to send the Gather to get him. Surely, he knew it would bring retribution from two very powerful men.

On the other hand, considering the magician's position, isolated and with his sons gone missing, one by one, perhaps he was desperate enough not to care?

When he finally felt clean and dried himself on a towel also magically kept warm, and dressed in the really good quality but grey and rather bland clothes, Michael wondered how the clothes had got here. Had they been magicked in? He doubted that. He had some idea of what it took to get magic objects past the In-Betweener if you couldn't get out. He could just about believe a Gather, but anything else, particularly the parts to make the elaborate water piping or the material for these clothes...no.

He had to talk to Tristram Blakley. He must be a transmuter of no common skill.

It was only when fully dressed that it occurred to him he'd taken an untoward amount of time, and that surely he was being ungallant. He should have let Albinia wash first.

He hurried out the bathroom and almost collided with Albinia, looking much as she had in the drawing room of the Darkwater townhome: her hair properly dressed, and wearing a dark green dress.

He stopped, once more afflicted with not knowing what to say or how to say it. So instead of speaking, he cleared his throat, twice, finally managing to say in a voice not quite his own, "Oh, I see you already bathed. I didn't know there was another bath."

She smiled a little. It was amazing how being washed and in fresh clothes made her look so grown up, like she knew more than a mere girl, like she was some ancient and powerful entity. "They have three other baths, here. Remember: for some time, there were eight people living here. It is more than a simple cottage with a tower."

"So I perceive," Michael said, and could kick himself for how stupid and supercilious he sounded. To make things worse, a divine smell of fresh-cooked food wafted in to surround them, and his stomach growled most embarrassingly.

And almost immediately, Tristram's voice echoed up the stairs. "Dinner time, Milord and Miss."

And like that, on cue, the swan appeared, making a sound that could only be interpreted as, "Come on, you ninnies."

Albinia gave Michael an embarrassed smile and blushed under her freckles, which made him feel slightly better, as they followed the swan, who moved at a pace just a little too fast for comfort.

He took them down the stairs, but instead of staying in the deceptively simple entrance room, they veered down a corridor, and into an ornate dining room, where Tristram sat at the head of the table, and three chairs slid back to allow them to sit. Well, Geoff simply jumped up on the chair, in front of a plate piled high with meat and chopped greens.

"When I first got confined here," Tristram said, conversationally, "there was only the front room, but I amused myself by adding the tower to the house. For about ten years, there was nothing else I could do, really. So I had my fun. And then once the boys joined me... Well, I did what I could to make this a civilized habitation for the Blakley family."

He looked at Al. "I see you made something feminine out of the provided clothes. Not a mean feat, Madam."

It was quite a compliment from Tristram Blakley, and yet Michael found himself wondering at that "Madam." Like calling her "whelp" in the letter, it was a very strange way for a father to refer to his daughter. Or to speak to her. He supposed there was no love lost between Blakley and Albinia's mother, but really. Then again, it seemed to him, Blakley must be a very strange man.

As they sat, plates circulated, unseen, as though being presented by accomplished servers. There were cauliflower patties, and lobster, and some kind of roast fowl which made Michael look askance towards Geoff, wondering if he'd take offense. Not that there was any logical reason he should. It wasn't as though he were naturally a fowl, after all. Just under an enchantment.

"It is a very ingenious setup you have here, sir," Michael said, trying to break the ice. "The kitchens, like the bath, I presume, run by magic. I would at some time like to discuss what spells you used and how. But—" He took a deep breath. "I'd like to know how you got the smog Gather past the In-Betweener—"

"What?" Tristram had been eating steadily, with manners but with what was obviously a great appetite. Michael supposed the transformation to and from wolf took a lot of energy. It normally did. Even when not voluntary, it was a great magic. But at Michael's mention of the Gather, he stopped abruptly and let out that startled, "What?"

He set his knife and fork down. "Young man, the Gather was no magic of mine. I'd not kidnap someone, much as I need rescue, and I know your family is not one to trifle with." He paused. "I merely sensed it, and controlled it to come here, instead of taking you back to my lady wife."

"But the In-Betweener..."

"It's the nature of this...prison of mine," he said. "Not as difficult as you'd think to pull things here. It's not a full-fledged universe, you know? Just a pocket one, existing within a few square miles. That's how I built it."

"You built it? Sir, I don't understand."

"Oh, I don't mean I created the world to be imprisoned in. I'm not so daft as to accidentally bespell myself. I created this world..." Tristram Blakley glowered briefly at his son and daughter. "I created this world, the few square miles of it, as a way to get away from domestic strife. Not my wife only, mind you. The boys were always excited over something..."

The swan made an irritated sound at that point. Tristram smiled. "True," he said, as though the words had been completely clear and human. "You do have a point about there being quite a lot of you." He sighed. "At any rate, I created this place so I would not be found, and I did not pay attention to how my lady wife used my own magic against myself, by making it so that I *could* not be found. And when the boys came after me, they, too, were trapped in here. At which point, I realized it would take more than my magic to escape it."

The swan squawked, and Tristram sighed again. "Well, I know. I shouldn't have let you boys know about the magic way. I never thought you would be so foolish as to try to follow me when I told you that your magic wasn't sufficient."

Al made a sound, and as Tristram looked in her direction, said, "Well, begging your pardon, Papa, but that was a great piece of nonsense. All my brothers are right 'uns. If you told them there was some means to save themselves, how could you think they wouldn't try, even if they might not have quite enough magic? They would think that, with a little more effort and a little more cunning—"

Tristram, Michael noticed, looked a little shocked at being called Papa, or perhaps at being addressed so forthrightly. He folded and refolded his napkin and said, "Well, I didn't expect them to be that foolish. It's magic, yes, but also cunning, and I told them they'd just be irretrievably lost. We just know they're all alive, because of the transformations that come over us without warning."

The swan made a noise, and Tristram smiled. "No, not now. I'm holding my transformation. Yes, I'm aware I'm the one who is dangerous, even with a surfeit of voles. I felt one of them try to change, but held it down. Hopefully, he's not in too much trouble." He turned to Michael. "Unless I'm wrong, you're the only person who can get us out of this. I can't walk the road myself, because one shift to wolf at the wrong time could be disastrous. And I don't know what the challenges are out there, or if I'd be near people or other beings when I change. I hesitated to ask you both because your family tends to be so...conventional, and because of the... Well, I don't imagine either of your older brothers will be happy at this."

"I was just thinking what Seraphim and Gabriel might do, when they discover I was pulled from Seraphim's house by a Gather."

"Not much they can do here. Well. I suppose one of them might be able to get in here. Probably your human brother, as I've made my own place fairly proof against Fairyland. No insult meant to your elf brother, whom I'm sure is excellent, but that place—"

"No, no. Trust me. I had some experience of it." And quickly, to disguise the shudder that shook him, "But then you have kept up with what's going on in the real world while you've been here? How?"

Tristram made a gesture. "The usual. Scrying on a crystal ball. But it won't show me what is going on with my sons, and I'm concerned."

Michael nodded. "And you think I can do it?" Part of him was screaming that he was stupid for even considering it. After all, what did he owe Tristram Blakley? He barely knew the man. And he knew enough of magical paths—roads designed to have a spell worked or unworked through walking them—to know it would be hazardous.

And in this case, it was a road where his brothers couldn't help him.

Only the leap of excitement in his heart, the sudden feeling like he would very much like to do this, made him realize what truly enticed him. Indeed, if he could walk this road and win out, without either of his all-too-powerful brothers being able to help him—or stop him—wouldn't that be proof, once and for all, that he was a man grown, and that no one need watch over him or keep him in cotton as though he were fragile?

Most of all, wouldn't that be proof for himself?

"Of course, I'd also walk the road with you," Al said. It was not a tone of voice that brooked dissent.

Michael knew the offer should irritate him. It should make him think that she would diminish his achievement. But mostly, it made him feel it wouldn't be so lonely. And besides, weren't they about even on saving each other?

He realized he'd been looking into Al's eyes perhaps a little too long, as they widened in surprised response to his stare. He spoke quickly into what seemed like too long a silence. "I...wouldn't object to that at all."

Tristram looked from one to the other of them with his eyebrows drawn together, and Michael felt his cheeks heat with embarrassment.

"Well," the older magician said. "Now that that's resolved, let's finish dinner. You can sleep here tonight, though I enjoin you to lock your room doors from the inside, as I'll have to give in to the change sooner than later. But then you can start bright and fresh tomorrow morning."

Brothers!

AL WAS RELIEVED THAT the bedrooms they were escorted to were reasonably clean. After all, you never knew when what Mama called "mere males" set up housing together. Not that she liked agreeing with Mama, of course, but she had had opportunity—before the boys disappeared—to realize they simply didn't see dust or think of laundry as something that needed to be done. And living here without servants, they were bound to forget household chores, even if they had magic to do them.

But other than smelling a little musty, the room she was escorted to under the eaves of the house was perfectly clean. Someone, or perhaps Papa's spell, had cleaned and repaired the beautiful dress she'd been given at Darkwater House, and it was hanging in front of the wardrobe.

That gave her a momentary pang, since she appreciated the thought, felt that this was the most beautiful dress she'd ever owned, *and* was more than a little doubtful that she should undertake the voyage through the magical road, whatever that was, in a dress. Wouldn't boy's clothes be more practical? After all, even in getting here, she and Michael seemed to have made a practice of being dropped from heights suddenly, and often upside down.

But she supposed one couldn't tell one's brother and father that one had decided to eschew petticoats.

So immersed was she in her thoughts that she—momentarily—forgot to lock the door, a lapse remedied when she heard a bloodcurdling howl coming from downstairs.

She'd no more turned the heavy key in the sturdy lock than she heard a heavy clomping of oversized paws—definitely a four-pawed gait—up the stairs, and then the howl was in the hallway outside her door. The walls and ceiling seemed to shake with it.

Al backed till her back was against the opposite wall, while she hoped that Michael had been more diligent about locking his door than she had.

The howl was followed by heavy snuffling under the door. And then heavy paws scrabbling at the woodwork. Al gave the sturdy-seeming door the weather eye. She stood ready to send another fireball at the wolf's nose. And spied by the side of her eye a cane leaning against the wall. She'd use that, too, if she had to, even if it seemed rather heartless to attack one's Papa. But really, if he were in wolf form, he should expect it, shouldn't he?

Presently, the scrabbling stopped, and she heard the snuffling further away, from what she thought was Michael's door. Then scrabbling at that. She listened, tense. If the door went down, then she would rush out and...do what she could. Between the two of them, perhaps they could keep Michael from being devoured.

She had a distant suspicion that Mama would be very upset at her for letting a duke's son be devoured. Particularly devoured by Papa. No matter if Mama had caused Papa to become a werewolf—she didn't know if that was true, but it sounded within Mama's possible repertoire of tricks—she would disapprove of his eating the quality. It would quite cut up her plans to climb the social ladder.

When Al found herself laughing at that thought, she realized that she might be hysterical. Fortunately, for her peace of mind, an authoritative voice, sounding much like Papa's, spoke in some arcane language. The wolf whined.

At length, she heard it descend the stairs, and relaxed muscles she wasn't aware of clenching. She poured water into the basin on the dresser and washed her face and hands and most of her upper body. Then she took the quite new toothbrush and a tube of patent tooth powder that Papa must have either magicked here, or copied from memory, and brushed her teeth.

She had just bathed before dinner, of course, but the habits that had been ingrained into her as what one did at bedtime were not to be gainsaid, even if she knew that rationally her face and hands, arms and neck didn't need extensive cleaning.

The wardrobe contained, on the left, a neat stack of clean nightshirts. From the size, she guessed William's, as they were much too long for her, but not overly wide. She solved the length problem by tying a knot near her ankles, pulling up a good deal of the fabric, and making the nightshirt almost a sack.

That was when the knock came at the door, and she tensed. Papa had said not to open the door to anyone. Could it be there was some magical trap? She heard the wolf howl outside the house, but really, what did she know of this place or how things worked here?

There were new knocks at the door and Geoff's voice, impatient, "Al, for heaven's sake, let me in. We need to talk."

Al frowned so intently, her eyes crossed. "Papa said—"

"Well, yes, but you know P-p-papa."

In fact, she did not. However, rather than argue, she made use of that stock of magical abilities no girl who grew up with Mama could have survived without. First, she sent out a magical probe, through the door, and found no spells active anywhere around.

Then, with the expense of a little magic, she called up a true sight of the other side, to be regaled with Geoff's face in deep and frowning concentration, glaring at the door.

And then—

"Ow," Geoff said. And glared at the door. "Did you magic-probe me, you b-b-b-brat?" There was almost approval and a chuckle in his voice.

Al turned the key and opened the door, and Geoff came in, locking the door after himself. "You never know when he might decide to double down. He warded this floor against himself, and will drive himself out again, with recorded spells, but it doesn't mean he can't come up and do much destruction before the spell activates."

"Then it was Papa's voice!"

"Well, yes." Geoff looked embarrassed. "He tries to keep himself under control, you know."

"I would expect nothing less of a Blakley," Al said, and noted that for reasons inexplicable, Geoff looked embarrassed.

He was fully dressed, too. Well, she supposed that made some sense. Why should he have changed, if he intended to speak to her? Sure, when they'd been much younger, he'd come to Al's room in his nightshirt to read to her, and tell her stories till she slept. But they'd been such...babies then.

She tried to ignore the pang of nostalgia, and noted that Geoff was wearing a very proper outfit, as though dressed to go out.

And that he looked mortally embarrassed. He stood by the door, with his back to it. "Al, why are you running about the countryside in company with a nobleman?"

"Well, you see, I fell into his boat," she said. And realizing that explained nothing, she told of her adventures.

Geoff frowned. "Papa wanted him to come, but I don't think you were involved in that request at all." He paused. His frown grew thunderous. "Al, are you— Are you i—i-involved with him? Was there some reason for him to be there when you fell?"

"No," Al said, and had to prevent herself from saying n-n-no. Really, Geoff was much better than he had been, and she'd long since outgrown that trick of imitating his way of speaking, but his disapproval and suspicions made her nervous. "And you need not be scared, because I have taken every possible precaution to avoid his taking my virtue."

Geoff's eyes went wide, his cheeks went bright red, and for a while, he imitated a goldfish with remarkable success. Finally, looking a little wild, as if he feared an answer, he asked, *"Precautions?"*

"No more than sensible," Al said, frostily. Did he think she was a baby when it came to magic? Hadn't probing him shown she wasn't? "I made sure that my magic is protected, and that he can't touch it when I activate a spell."

Geoff went into goldfish mode again, then cleared his throat and seemed to be having some difficulty speaking. "Al," he said at last, in a strangled sort of voice. "What do you think stealing your virtue means?"

"I— I presume it means taking my magic. It happens all the time in novels, and though I don't understand the process precisely, it always seems to mean that the ah—gentleman—" They were, in fact, usually scoundrels in novels. "Ends up in control of the lady's magic. Geoff, if you're going to open and close your mouth like that, I'm going to cast a spell on you and make you into a goldfish."

He blinked and laughed nervously. "I suppose it would make a change from being a swan, unless they happened at the same time, in which case, it would be...ah...interesting." He sighed. "Al, that's not what it means." And then, blushing to his hair roots, he told her what it meant. Or at least what he thought it meant.

"Geoff, you're either making up odious lies, or you were grossly misinformed."

"Al, I assure you!" He was red enough that he seemed to glow and rival the candle by her bedside.

"Well! You misunderstood something, and I'm sure I thought better of your understanding, but for your information, Lord Michael hasn't even tried to kiss me or...or touch me in any way, much less that. And let me assure you, if he tried that, I would—"

"Yes?"

"Probably set his hair on fire with a fireball. Not that Lord Michael would try any of that. He's not... He's not absurd. Other than a tendency to get up on his high horse, which I suppose he drank with his nursemaid's milk, he's quite a good sort, sound as a roast."

For some reason, this wholly failed to reassure Geoff. At least, he didn't say anything, but she could see from his eyes that he was still worried. "Very well," he said at last. "But I would feel better if you took two things with you tomorrow morning, and I don't know if I'll see you in my human form again, since Papa doubtlessly will want to guide you to the path and give you your instructions." From an inner pocket of his jacket, he removed a wrapped-up bundle of fabric. "Should Lord Michael attempt to...to lay hands on you, snap this string, and the spell will take care of it. No, don't argue, Al. I'm older than you and I know better." He also removed a whistle. "And this is should you find yourself in trouble. If you blow it, I'll know you're in trouble, and where you are." It was a small silver whistle on a chain, which he put over her head. He then looked at her in embarrassment. "I wish to heaven you wouldn't go with Ainsling, Al. And that's the truth. You're too good a sister to lose."

And on that, she forgot his boorish behavior and crazed ideas of how men and women related to each other and fell into his arms, hugging him, then kissing his cheek.

This embarrassed him worst of all. He patted her shoulder. "Well, well. You're a good girl. I'll go now, and get back to my room before Papa comes back. Mind, lock after me."

She obeyed him, but sat on her bed for a while, thinking, "Brothers!" in some exasperation.

Truth be told, she had missed them greatly.

****

Across the hall, Michael was confronted with his own brother problems. He had tensed during the snuffling, ready to go to Al's rescue, should it become needed. Then he heard Geoff blundering around the hallways.

He didn't think very highly of Geoffrey Blakley's intelligence. If all Tristram's sons were like him, no wonder that Tristram Blakley had sent in for someone wholly unrelated to him. Honestly, the man seemed to have no sense in matrimonial affairs. For him to have produced dumb sons, his first wife must have been a paper skull, and Albinia's Mama sounded like a dangerous termagant, much too free with witchcraft and maybe evil, too.

He'd tired of trying to hear what was going on across the hall after Albinia had opened the door—he assumed she'd done some checking, since, as he knew, she was no ninnyhammer—and let her brother in. He heard voices talking, but couldn't discern the words, and after a while, he realized that it was grossly indelicate of him to eavesdrop. Only, of course, in this strange situation, it seemed like self-defense.

Grudgingly, he'd changed into a nightshirt. The suit he'd arrived in, perfectly repaired and cleaned—he really would like to know the spells Blakley used—hung in front of the wardrobe, and though the idea of walking magical paths in evening wear was strange, it was also oddly reassuring, since doing it in borrowed clothes was just as strange.

He'd thought he'd stay awake, but no more had he lain his head down than he was asleep.

Asleep and dreaming.

Seraphim was in his study, at Darkwater, which was unlikely, since he'd been in the capital. But in Michael's dream, he was in his study at Darkwater, and pacing.

This wasn't the only thing that struck Michael as funny. There was to Seraphim a wild and rumpled look, as though he'd ridden night and day, and put his clothes on every which way.

"Michael," he yelled. "Where in bloody hell are you?"

It was the first time Michael heard Seraphim swear, too. Much less at himself.

"In a pocket universe, where Tristram Blakley is prisoner."

"Tristram who?"

Michael explained, and found himself, in dream, between words and images, telling the tale of his adventures.

Though in his dream, Seraphim was in his study, while Michael was in bed in the Blakley house, it seemed to him that Seraphim tried to come through the dream, to come through into Michael's room. Michael felt himself flinching on the bed, ready for the eruption of his angry brother into the room. But Seraphim seemed to fight an invisible barrier, and made a sound of frustration. "Michael, you are not to walk this magical path. You are not to expose yourself to the dangers of a challenge path in a made-up world for the sake of a stranger. I forbid it."

"Well, it is too bad you forbid it," Michael said. Really, Seraphim's behavior was beyond the pale. Michael's older brother he might be, but he was not his father. "I've given my word and you would not wish me foresworn."

And before Seraphim could answer—if he could answer, considering that his face was purple enough to look like he was dying—the dream shifted.

Now he was in a throne room. It was an odd throne room, built of what seemed to be blown glass, a material too frail to support those tall arches, and those vast ceilings. Stranger still were the courtiers assembled on the edges of the room, because Michael couldn't see them.

It wasn't that they were invisible. It was that he couldn't turn his head to look. He had an impression of sparkle and silks, of feathers and fluttering wings. And he had an idea the wings, butterfly-like though they were, were attached to humans. Well. To something close to humans.

But he could see the man on the throne. And he knew him very well.

"Gabriel!" he said, in exasperation.

Like Seraphim, Gabriel had curly dark hair and eyes as green as Michael's. Like Seraphim, Gabriel was Michael's brother. Well, half-brother. Michael had been given to understand that due to his father's proclivities, there were a lot of half-brothers. But Gabriel had been raised with them. And even if, officially, he was Seraphim's valet, he had always been one of the family.

Becoming king of Fairyland, through inheritance on his mother's side, hadn't changed Gabriel at all. Or at least that was Michael's first thought. Gabriel wore his hair long and tied back, and though his clothes were now silk and velvet, they were still as dark as they'd been when he was a servant at Darkwater.

But then he realized there was something else, something different. And it wasn't just the gold crown resting negligently on Gabriel's dark hair, as he sat on the throne. There was something else, not visible but perceptible, a majesty and a power of magic that overspread the room and which radiated from Gabriel.

And worse, the power and the magic both communicated that here was a man—well, an elf—both anxious and angry.

"Michael, I heard your interview with Seraphim. I am adding my injunction to his. You will not do this thing. You will not risk yourself on a challenge path. There are reasons I cannot tell you why this is a very bad idea."

Michael straightened his back, vaguely aware that he'd knocked his head on the headboard, but without waking. "And to you, Your Majesty," he said, deliberately cold, "I say the same I said to Seraphim. I will not be forsworn."

"You insolent puppy. You made Seraphim miss the birth of his son, and you—"

That was when Michael realized this was a true dream and that his brothers had somehow gotten hold of his sleeping mind. And that Seraphim had indeed ridden to Darkwater, presumably to check on the beginning of the boat-spell.

He made a very rude remark about what both Seraphim and Gabriel could do with their worry, and then he snapped his magic shut, and forced himself to wake up.

He woke up shaking and sweating on his bed, took a deep breath, and wove magic protections over his bed before going back to sleep.

He would not, could not walk the path without a good night's sleep.

His last conscious thought before falling into deep sleep was, "Brothers!"

Hurried Out

Michael woke up with a swan trumpeting outside the door. The worst part of it was that in the space between sleep and waking, he could understand the swan completely, and what those sounds meant was, "Get up, you lazy bastard. Everyone else is up and at them."

Of course, everyone else in this case was Al, Geoff-the-swan, and of course, Tristram Blakley, hopefully in wholly human form. Maybe. With luck.

Michael managed to sit up and peel his eyelids back just in time to see the curtains open, as though pulled by an invisible servitor, and a tray with a teapot and teacup slip through the door—somehow—and deposit itself on the bedside.

Right.

Michael fumbled himself off the bed, and found a banyan held out for him, as though there were indeed an invisible valet in the room.

He was frowning at it when a voice boomed through the room, "If you can get yourself bathed and presentable, Lord Michael, it is time you were on your way. If you are indeed going to keep your word to me and follow the path."

The voice was inevitably that of Tristram Blakley, but Michael had seen enough of floating trays and invisible servitors to suspect a distance spell, and cleared his throat and asked, "Do you mean it is safe for me to leave the room?"

"Yes, indeed," Blakey answered, in a tone that implied this was indeed a two-way conversation. "I am...very much myself, and will stay that way until you are well on your path."

The wording confused Michael, and while inclined to, perhaps, take offense at the man assuming he'd not keep his word, he felt as though he should forgive him, since Blakley was obviously anxious to have his sons restored to him and to be released from this pocket universe.

Between Blakley's awkwardness when talking of his daughter and his near rudeness this morning, Michael reflected, the man must have troubles with social interaction. Perhaps that explained his problems with his second wife. Michael remembered Mother telling him that men of his stamp, who cared more for mathematics and machines than for people, would always be easy prey for a forward woman. Which formed part of Michael's decision never to marry, of course.

He couldn't find his suit, which he'd worn from home, until he literally stumbled over a valise, and came to find, inside it; his carefully repaired suit and also three other suits, of a practical grey kind all folded up and ready for the road.

He frowned at them, wondering which one to take out and wear, but as he straightened, a suit slapped him in the face, as though propelled by an impatient valet. Michael picked it up, as it was ready to drop from his nerveless hands, and found that it was a perfectly serviceable pair of breeches, a coat, and a shirt distinguished only for being very fine linen. As he shook it, a pair of underwear fell to the ground. He picked it up and sighed. It was all clean, and it was obvious he was meant to wear it. He wasn't sure if he should be grateful to Blakley for the clothes, or resent being given clothes to wear. It was bad enough to be treated as a child by his older brothers, but to receive the same treatment from this man who was demanding Michael's help was beyond the mark of pleasing.

But he grabbed the suit, and made his way across the hall to the bathing room, banyan flying behind him like a child demanding his attention. He ignored it.

The tub filled with warm water, and he bathed, feeling slightly guilty for the expenditure of magic on his behalf for a warm bath, but unwilling to forego the comfort when he knew that he would be enduring hardships of various kinds in this endeavor.

He dressed in the clothes assigned, glad that he wasn't at least supposed to wear something scratchy or inadequate, and was surprised to find a set of sturdy boots next to the attire, and in his size, too.

With a sigh, and not even bothering to question it, he put them on. After all, he hadn't even seen his civilized slippers in the room, and they were wholly inadequate to a forest path.

Of course, this was a magic forest path. Various cautionary tales told him by his nanny came to mind, and he shivered, as a bad feeling like a hangover from his time in Fairyland overtook him. It wasn't exactly a memory, not even a memory of his nightmares, more of a feeling that he should know what awaited him, and that he should be more terrified than he was.

At the top of the narrow stairs, he stood, and had a moment of doubt. After all, his siblings were right, in his dream—if it had been a dream, and not a true seeing—he had no business doing this for a man he didn't know; a man that, truth be told, he didn't even like. Or at least didn't understand.

But at the same time, there was Al. And Al was worried about her brothers. And though he didn't know her very well, he had a feeling he'd come to like her, and that she was, as Blakley had said in his letter, "A pretty good sort."

He really couldn't let Al down.

But as he got to the breakfast room, Al wasn't there. Instead, there was a fantastical breakfast on the table, composed of all the options he was routinely given at home, from fish cakes to fried kidneys.

And there was Tristram Blakley, standing, as though guarding the food. He smiled at Michael. It looked forced, and he said, with an echo of false cheeriness, "Ah, my boy. Have some food, my boy."

The display was enough to make Michael forego breakfast. But as with a hot bath, he had a strong feeling it might be his last chance at such a luxury in a long time, so he ate buttered toast, and some ham, and drank his tea.

But Blakley standing by, as though Michael was late for a journey, didn't help anything. Nor did the unseemly haste with which he grabbed Michael's arm, as Michael rose from the table.

Michael clutched at his suitcase. "Al..."

"Oh, surely you don't want her along, my boy. You know what girls are. She will be all worried about her hairstyle, or perhaps a stain on her gown. That is the last thing you want to do, take a girl along on your journey."

Michael opened his mouth, to tell the older magician that he was sure Al would be an asset, then realized that for whatever reason the man said he was keeping Al behind, it was, in fact, probably to protect her. After all, Al was his daughter, and he had a duty to protect her. In that, at least, he was a natural father.

At the door, Blakley awkwardly shook Michael's hand. "I think you'll find you travel faster without her. Just...er...remember to stay on the path, no matter what the enticement to leave it. And do bring me back my sons, or at least find a way to rupture this gilded bubble I'm kept prisoner in. We must find what that woman, my lady wife, is intending and what she is planning. I suspect she wants the domains for the girl. But why?"

He blinked confused eyes at Michael, then stepped back and slammed the door.

Michael could swear that distantly, he heard a swan's indignant *blert*, but it was from the side of the house.

In front of him lay a garden path, and he wondered if the magical path started here or out of the garden gate into the forest. It could be either. He sighed. Well, he'd stay on the path from here on out, anyway.

It was going to be a cold and lonely journey, and unworthily, even knowing it meant more danger to her, he wished that Al had come.

From the side of the house came another indignant *blert!* and a sound like breaking glass.

And then, in what he'd swear was Al's voice, the most unladylike sound of, "Oh, blast it!"

Not Without Me

Albinia woke up with someone or something knocking on her door. Which would have been fine, except that the knock sounded odd and as if it came from very low on the door.

And it was followed by an eloquent series of, *Blert, blert, blert!*

She couldn't precisely understand what he was saying, but she knew it was Geoff, and that he was in a mood.

So she opened the door, and looked at her brother, arms crossed as he waddled in. But instead of saying or doing something to explain to her what he wanted, he turned around and used his webbed foot to close the door.

Then he turned to her and *blert blert blert* with such intensity that she backed away from him in a hurry, which in turn seemed to upset him. He gave a particularly vexed *blert*, then hurried to a corner where there stood a writing stand with ink and paper.

Taking a quill, he fussed around a while, then *blert*ed in a tone that indicated he was proud of himself.

Al didn't say anything about the blots, the crosses and the letters so strangely formed that they might be completely wrong. Or not. After all, she supposed, writing with a pen in your beak was different from doing it with hands.

Instead, she read, *My father is sending Lard Michael out on the parth right now. He believes it would be a mistake to allo wrong for you to go. But I don't think Michael Ainsning Ailing will survive without you.*

Al had to read it twice to make full sense of it, and then she turned to her brother. "He's going to do what? But he can't send Michael out without me. He doesn't know anything about our family or about...about Mama. Nor what Mama is likely to do to interfere with him, if she can just get her hooks into this bubble. And surely she can, since she locked Papa in it."

Geoff's emphatic *blert*s of agreement were gratifying, but they truly didn't help the situation. Which was why Al, with a sense of growing panic, rushed to the wardrobe, and put on the dress she'd worn the day before at the Darkwater townhouse, and shuffled her feet into the very proper slippers the housekeeper had given her.

Geoff helped as he could, but truth be told, he couldn't do much when he had no use of two hands and two opposable thumbs. And thinking about it, he wasn't much use when he had hands and opposable thumbs. None of her brothers were when it came to clothing. Geoff used to curse her dresses for a bloody nuisance, even as he tried to help her magically repair them when she tore the flounces climbing cliffs. And she always had to take them out of his hands to finish fixing them.

Fully dressed, Al dove for the door, and found her path blocked by a swan with extended wings.

"Oh, Geoff, don't be daft. I have to go! How else do I get to—"

But Geoff was indignant and Al stopped. All that *blert*ing was going to attract Papa's attention and Papa— She stopped trying to fight her way past Geoff. "Wait, you mean I shouldn't get out that way? Because Papa won't let me out?"

The swan nodded enthusiastically.

"I see, but then how do you plan for me to get down and to the path?"

Geoff half-flew across the room and tapped his beak against the window.

"We're on the second floor?"

Geoff did what in human form would have been waggling his eyebrows, a capacity that Al detested, because she could not do it, then dove for the bed and started pulling at a sheet.

"Oh, no," Al said, while, with a sinking feeling, she remembered her climb down from the tower. But Geoff looked puzzled at her, and of course Mama wasn't here to try to spell the window or her way out of it. So she might be able to do it.

Except, as she pulled the sheets from Geoff's beak and tied them together, she thought they were on the side of the house, not the front where the path was. And if she understood this properly, she and Michael—well, Michael, but she'd be boiled in oil if she let him do it alone—were supposed to walk the path and not leave it.

Rushing to the window, she threw it open, and indeed, they were on the side of the house. Estimating by eye—her far-seeing magic was not the sort that could be deployed at the whim of the moment—she came back to the bed and tied the coverlet and the bedspread to the end of the sheets.

When she was young, she had gone climbing the cliff-side with Edmund and Jeremy. Edmund liked bird watching. And Jeremy liked getting away from Aaron, his twin, and loved sitting atop the cliffs by the sea, particularly if there was a storm coming. Why he'd taken her with him so often was anybody's guess, but he did, and on that particular day, he'd taken her with him, and tried a new path to a favorite spot.

When they couldn't climb any further on one cliff, due to encountering a very smooth expanse ahead, Jeremy had taught Al to swing to the side by hitting the cliff with her feet and increasing her swing out, before throwing all her weight to one side.

It hadn't felt quite safe, truth be told. And it would be worse here. The window of her room was, fortunately, near the corner of the house, but she'd still need to swing well away from the house, and then somehow throw herself around the corner and to the other end, where—

Where she might or might not be able to reach the path. From her memory, the front of the house was much narrower, maybe ten feet across, and the front door and the path were centered, but heaven only knew if she could swing that far. Also, she didn't know if the garden path counted as part of the path when walked with intent, or if it was merely a garden path and the magic started past the gate. But she wouldn't risk it. Things changed when you were determined to walk a magical path, after all.

She took a deep breath, and tied the end of the sheets to the leg of the bed—while swatting away Geoff's enthusiastic attempts to help with his beak—then threw the other end of the sheet down from the window.

Climbing down in what amounted to a tea dress was very difficult, and it wasn't helped by Geoff's enthusiastic *blert*ing and wing-beating from above.

She ignored him, and concentrated on hitting the side of the house beneath the window with both her feet to swing out as far as she could. It took her a good three or four kicks to get distance, and a window downstairs opened, and Papa yelled upward, "Here, what are you doing, you infernal hoyden?"

Which was too bad, since she barely knew Papa and had been hoping to keep him ignorant of her failings longer.

But right then she must—she thought as she pulled very far from the house indeed—swing around the corner...

It worked, or almost worked. Except Papa sent a fireball at the sheet between the window and Albinia, which was very unsporting of him.

As the sheet parted, burned by the flame, Albinia's careful swing turned into a sort of sideways fall. She kicked at the front of the house, trying to get a hold that would keep her from falling far short of the path. There was a sound of shattering glass, and she yelled, "Oh, blast it."

In the path below, Lord Michael ran back towards the house and towards her. And she...flung herself at him. The one thing Mama had always said was inappropriate.

She would have fallen short of the path, but he somehow grabbed her by the shoulders and pulled, even as she was falling. He might have used magic.

At the end of it, she fell on top of Lord Michael with shattering force. For a moment, her brain rattled, she couldn't breathe and she certainly couldn't think.

As thought returned, she heard Lord Michael groan. She hastened to get up, though she felt achy, as though she'd been beaten. But the poor man was beneath her, and had taken her fall with full force. What if she'd killed him?

"Mich— I mean, Milord, are you well? Did I injure you?" He didn't look broken, just undignifiedly sprawled and barely raising his head. "Dear me, if I've kill—"

He laughed. He raised his head fully, and then pulled himself to sitting. "No. No. No harm done, though I expect I'll have beautiful bruises in a day or two." He struggled up to standing and gave her a smile, and a courtly bow. "I presume, Miss Blakley, you wish to join me in walking the path?"

She nodded.

"I'm delighted. Though if I may? I wish you'd learn to fall from windows, not on top of me."

She knew he was teasing, but had no idea how to respond, so she cuffed him on the shoulder as she would have done her brothers.

To her surprise, he laughed and blushed. Then he bent his arm and offered it to her. “Shall we, Miss Blakley? I believe we have a path to walk.”

The Path Winds

ALBINIA FELT BRUISED AND sore, but other than that, this was almost a normal morning walk, down a lovely path, winding amid roses with a lovely young man by her side.

She noted that Papa had set benches on the side, and in front of them a sundial surrounded by roses. It struck her that it seemed a very strange thing for Papa to have built since Papa had never cared either for roses or sundials.

She was so intrigued by the scenery, she stopped staring at it. She didn't realize she'd started walking towards the sundial, till Lord Michael grabbed her around the waist and pulled her back. "Al," he said. His voice sounded slightly hoarse. "I mean, Miss Blakley. Do not walk off the path."

She blinked. And like that, the roses and the benches and the sundial disappeared, leaving the sort of straggly grass and weeds that she expected around Papa.

"I presume you saw something out there?" Lord Michael asked.

"Yes, roses and benches and a sundial, and it seemed so... It didn't seem like something Papa would do, and this is his constructed reality. So...I—"

"You were about to walk off the path." Lord Michael took a deep breath. Then he squared his shoulders. "Well, this solves the question of where the path starts, does it not? We are on the path."

Albinia nodded, and put her hand on his arm again, and concentrated on looking only at the path. She found herself angry that she almost had lost herself and left the path when it wasn't even anything needing her attention, or even something that fooled her. She'd not been fooled. She'd almost walked off the path because she *hadn't* been fooled.

Just as she clenched her fists in anger, Lord Michael said, in a reassuring voice, "You weren't even sure you were on the path yet, and the trick of making you doubt something you're seeing is very subtle. So perhaps you'd have walked off the path, but in fact this is why I'm very glad you joined me on the path, Miss Blakley, because right now I pulled you back on the path but next time, perhaps you'll be the one who saves me."

Albinia giggled. She couldn't help it. Despite her tenseness, and her anger at herself, she giggled.

"Do I amuse you, Miss Blakley?" Lord Michael asked. There was something to his voice that was both scared but also teasing. But beneath it, she could sense his uncertainty, as though he weren't sure that she wasn't thinking less of him.

"Not you, Milord, but how good you are at reassuring me that though I was the one who almost lost the path, I'm not likely to do it again. It is charmingly different from what my brothers would have done, Milord. Being the youngest, I'd be more likely to hear from all of my brothers how addlepated I was, or how funny it was that I'd almost strayed from the path, and how only a babe unborn would be simple enough to do that."

This brought a chuckle from Lord Michael. She both heard it and felt his body shake with his laughter, which was a strange sensation and one she'd never thought to experience. She thought of Geoffrey's warning and felt her cheeks warm.

"I, too," Lord Michael said, "am by far the youngest in my family. I am further cursed with having two very accomplished and very powerful brothers. Had it been me making a similar mistake, they'd save me, very kindly, and they'd never let me go on without being tied to them." He paused. "I beg your pardon. That sounds dangerously close to bitterness. Possibly because it is."

She wondered what that meant. Surely, he hadn't been on a magical path before. If he had, he'd have told her, would he not? She didn't know how to ask, and paused as he opened the gate. She passed through it, and noted that he never was more than arm's reach away from her as he followed. Which was fine. On this side of it, she reached for his arm again, glad of its solidity.

Which was just as well, because as soon as they closed the gate behind them, the gate disappeared. Turning back, Albinia realized that the gate, the fence, the little path, and the house beyond it had all disappeared. She despised herself for the whimper that escaped between her lips.

But again, Lord Michael did not laugh at her, or tell her she was a hapless ninny for not realizing this would happen. Instead, his other hand came and laid for the briefest of spaces on hers. "It is very disconcerting, for sure," he said. "Please do not leave the path. I don't think I'd be equal to making it alone on this very strange path."

She bit the corner of her lip. The problem with all of this was that Geoffrey's warnings were looming larger and larger in her mind. It wasn't that she thought Lord Michael would, as Geoffrey had so politely phrased it, impose on her. It was that if he said things like this more often, and made it sound like she was saving him from a dread fate—somehow more dread than walking this path to save her brothers and father—she might very well impose *on him*.

After all, she thought, as they walked into the tree-shaded portion of the path, how much worse could it be than literally throwing herself at him? In fact, if she did much worse, she'd probably break him. This time she managed not to giggle, which was good, because she had done no more than suppress the impulse when she heard the cry.

It was high, disconsolate, and lost: the sound of a baby abandoned in the dark of night, who has no hope of ever being loved or comforted again.

The Baby

Michael hadn't been looking at the sides of the path. When he caught glimpses of it, he found it disturbing, an amorphous shifting mass, with flashes of light in the midst of dark swirls.

It reminded him of nothing so much as Fairyland, and it made him feel as if danger hemmed him in on all sides.

The sound of a baby crying made him turn, suddenly, to see the dark swirls and flashes were gone. On the left side of the path, reality had settled into a green, manicured lawn, as perfect as the one back home, which was tended by gardeners with sharp scythes and a passion for order. Amid the green, perfect grass, little bunches of blue flowers grew, also perfectly arranged as though by an aesthetically inclined landscaper. Around the glade were trees, beautiful and green, though the shape of their leaves evaded his eye, almost like the leaves were really a hazy illusion.

In the middle of it all there was a bundle, wrapped in a blue blanket, and moving just a little while it emitted a desolate cry.

Without even looking, Michael put his arm out, just in time to prevent Albinia Blakley from stepping off the path. "Miss Blakley, for Heaven's sake," he said. Then shifted to hold her in a way that Seraphim would say was compromising if he saw it, with both his arms around her waist. The little shrew ripped up at him, too, trying to escape.

"Let me go. The baby—"

He tightened his hold. "I'm not going to do any such thing," he said. "You know as well as I do that likely there is no baby, but only an illusion!

If you step away from the path, your magic will be aggregated to whatever out there is keeping your father and brother captive. You yourself will be gone, likely forever."

For a moment, she continued struggling and it seemed to him as though she hadn't heard him. He added, "I will not let you go, Albinia Blakley. I'm not willing to let you be destroyed." His voice echoed earnest and urgent, filled with his own disquieting memories of Fairyland, and his terrible fear of what could become of this brave and beautiful girl, out there, in the shifting landscape of magical energy.

Her body went limp. She gave a sigh. Then her hands went up to cover her ears. "I cannot stand the cry," she said, her voice small and urgent. "I'm sure there is something out there, really, a small creature that needs our help." She shook her head, and took her hands down. "I can still hear him even through my hands. And I can feel him. He's lost and afraid."

He didn't tell her to be her age. Oh, he could have. But he didn't. There was something to her distress that cut at his heart, and he remembered her talking about how she needed to save her brothers. This was a girl who had grown up looking after everyone else. She would of course want to look after this creature, magic construct or not.

He eyed the blanket. "There is nothing we can do for him. He's well off the path. We can't reach him. Even if he's real!"

She remained limp in the circle of his arms, dejected, like all willpower had gone out of her. "We can't just abandon him."

And through Michael's head there went the words, "What if your family had just abandoned you in Fairyland?" He felt like a kick in the gut at the thought. If this was a baby, a real human baby, kidnapped into Fairyland, he'd have to be a kind of monster to let him live and grow up here. And it wasn't like Fairyland was above stealing human babies just to set a trap for them. He cleared his throat. "Miss Blakley, if I promise to do my best to retrieve the poor thing, do you promise not to step off the path?"

She nodded, but as he pulled his arms from around her, she grabbed at his sleeve. "Do not step off the path yourself."

He shook his head. "No. I will not do so." And with that, he turned away, and looked around. The amorphous reality on either side of the path was pretending to be a very pretty woodland. Which meant there were branches of trees overhanging the path, both ahead and behind them.

It would be difficult, but... He put down the valise he'd been carrying from the beginning, and strode purposefully towards the nearest overhanging branch. Holding onto it with both arms, he pulled it sideways, so it would break. It resisted the pull. He felt Miss Blakley's arms around his waist, pulling at him.

Between the two of them, the branch bent and strained, till with a mighty crack, it broke from the tree. As they fell, Michael threw himself sideways to keep them on the path.

And the branch in his hands writhed. He opened his eyes, momentarily closed by the shock of falling, and realized he was holding not a branch but a cobra.

The sane thing would have been to let go, but all he could think was that if he let go, he'd be left with nothing to reach the baby.

The head at the end of the snake, cruel and merciless, turned towards him, fangs revealed by the open mouth. Was that dripping venom?

From his side, where Albinia had fallen flat beside him on the path, he heard a stream of syllables. He felt the power in them, and the back of his mind said it must be some kind of magical language he'd never learned.

Suddenly, the snake—still a snake—went rigid in his hands, its eyes glazed. Its shape was roughly that of a shepherd's crook, but while it retained the shape and look of a snake, it slowly turned into a branch again. Just a snake-shaped one.

"Thank you," he said on a thread of breath.

"No," she said. "Thank you. I see what you mean about the things off the path not being as they seem. You probably saved me, before..."

He nodded. Getting up, he oriented himself, then knelt on the side of the path, and extended the branch towards the crying bundle.

Of course, it fell just short of it. But he remembered a spell that Seraphim had taught him, when he was barely out of leading strings, and they were fishing out on the river at home. He muttered it. It didn't make the branch grow as such, it just stretched it, so it became thinner.

From beside him, Albinia Blakley scoffed. "It would have been very useful," she said. "To know that to lengthen sheets."

"It makes them thinner, too," he said. "So they might have torn." But he was bending all his concentration to maneuvering the now ridiculously long and unwieldy branch to get the baby. He hooked the curved end around the bundle, and pulled it closer, closer.

The crying redoubled in force, and the bundle shook as its inhabitant struggled to emerge.

But obviously the baby was too young to break free.

It took careful maneuvering, step by step, to pull the bundle next to the path. As soon as he was reachable, Miss Blakley reached for it with both hands, and lifted the child. The crying stopped on a surprised coo.

And Michael felt the branch wreathe and threw it from him. A snake hissed and wound away from them into the undergrowth.

He turned around to see Miss Blakley looking in shock at the bundle in her arms. She'd pulled back the blue cloth. Looking at it, he first thought it was a baby eagle. Then he saw the little paw waving in the air.

"It's a baby gryphon!" he said in some shock. "We should return it."

But Miss Blakley gave him a look of withering disdain. "Don't be stupid. It's a living thing in distress. Of course we're not returning him to that evil place." She looked towards the clearing, which now looked like a bracken swamp with green things floating. "We're going to keep him and find his mother." She hesitated for a second. "I shall call him Bug."

Bug

MICHAEL WISHED TO BE in charity with the small gryphon they'd picked up. He truly did. But the little beasty kept crying with an oddly human infant-like voice. And all Al did was rock it and make weird sounds like "tshshsh." And, "Now, now."

And now she'd started singing to the creature as they walked.

It wasn't that she sang badly. It was that no one should actually sing *row row your boat* back-to-back for an hour to something with a beak and four paws, who didn't stop crying, anyway.

After an hour, Albinia stopped in the middle of the path. "I think he's hungry."

"Miss Blakley," Michael said, controlling his voice. "I don't know what you think I can do about it." Then he realized his voice sounded unnaturally angry, and that the anger was not directed at Albinia so much as his suffering for the last hour.

And, after all, he realized, the fact Bug—what a ridiculous name—was crying was not Albinia Blakley's fault. She had rescued Bug, yes, but that surely had been the right thing to do. What horrible things might befall the poor creature if let all alone, he could imagine very well. In fact, no one knew better than him.

He wondered if it was because of the former king of Fairyland—a cruel and evil elf—or the inherent nature of the place. It seemed to him that whatever made up Fairyland, there was a very strong element of predation and enjoying the hurt of others. Particularly helpless others.

Sighing, he turned around. Al stood there, holding Bug, who had somehow worked free of his wrapping, so that his head poked out. His eyes were huge, blue and full of tears. He opened his beak forlornly. And Albinia...well, she looked almost as forlorn, staring at him as though he'd slapped her. What a beast he was.

"I beg your pardon. I should not have spoken as though it were your fault. I didn't realize his crying had been grating on my nerves for the whole time since we picked him up. And I realize that's not your fault, either. You... You sing very well. It's very...pleasant. It's just I—"

"You lost your patience," Albinia said, looking very determined. Mostly looking very determined not to look offended, Michael thought. "It is not your fault. Or mine. But we do have to do something for this creature before he cries us both to insanity."

She sighed, and Bug cried, blinking huge forlorn eyes at Michael.

"I think he's hungry," she said. "Perhaps if we can find him a berry bush or something."

Michael shook his head. "Oh, no. I don't think that's a good idea at all."

"Gryphons don't eat berries?'

"No, no," Michael hastened to clarify. "I don't have the slightest idea what gryphons eat." He tried to think back through any stories he might have heard, but his mind was a blank. There was an unpleasant one of gryphons eating a whole horse or something. He hoped that was not what the beastie ate, because he was not about to feed him parts of himself or Albinia. "But we shouldn't feed him anything that grows in Fairyland. Because if we do, he might never be able to leave it."

Albinia looked up at him, eyes wide. "But isn't he a creature of Fairyland?"

"Not necessarily. A lot of these creatures... There are other worlds in which they live. And we can't risk his becoming a prisoner in Fairyland or this path forever."

Albinia bit her lip. She seemed to be contemplating something very difficult. It was the face that Caroline made when she tried to do her maths, which were never her strong point.

He reached out and touched her hand. He said, realizing they were both talking really loudly to be heard over the crying gryphon, "I beg your pardon, but what is distressing you?"

"We have to eat something on this path, too, Michael Ainsling! I mean Lord Michael, I mean! We've been walking for hours, and I'm already... I'm already starving." And then she dropped on her behind, gracelessly, still holding the crying gryphon, and looked up at him, her eyes filled with tears and as pathetic as Bug's.

"Oh, not you, too," Michael said, but he was smiling through his exasperation. He felt he should make it all good for both this brave girl who had chosen to put herself through this with him, and the poor little creature they'd rescued. He started to put down the bag that Tristram Blakley had given him, when it occurred to him he had no idea what was in the bag.

He opened it and for a moment stared at the inside, not sure what it contained. It was... Strangely murky, as though the bag held a small, very dense fog.

"What?" he said.

"A bag of plenty!" Albinia said. "You're carrying a bag of plenty."

Feeling very stupid, he said, "I beg your pardon? Your father gave me the bag, and I have no idea what it means."

"Oh. I thought everyone knew about bags of plenty. Mama always sent us with one when we went on a trip. They're..." She leaned over and reached in the bag, and out of it she pulled a sandwich. She started taking it to her mouth, but before she could, Bug gave a strange screech, and reached out his paw, which somehow was able to hold the sandwich like a small hand.

He took a bite of it and chewed, seeming perfectly contented.

Albinia laughed and reached in again, and got another sandwich.

Michael sat beside them on the path. "How...does it work?"

"You put your hand in and think of what you want," Albinia said.

He did and withdrew a meat pie. It tasted exactly like the meat pies the cook in their townhouse made.

"How can it work? Where does it get the things?"

"Out of possibility. They are... They are made from potential. It's like pulling something out of the In-Betweener, I think." She frowned. "I don't fully understand the theory. The ones Mama had, Papa had made. So I suppose he knows the theory. And you probably could understand it. You should definitely ask him. When we return."

Her certainty that they would return warmed him up.

Moments later, they were sitting on the path, eating a very nice picnic lunch—which Bug possibly enjoyed more than either of them. He kept nodding his head side to side and making happy noises—and drinking tea, which had come out of the bag on a little tray, complete with teakettle and teacups.

"What do we do with all this when we're done?" he asked.

"Oh, you put it back in the bag. It returns to its potential."

Michael was trying to understand how that worked when someone cleared his throat behind him, and he looked back over his shoulder.

There was a man on the path behind him. He looked like an older Seraphim. Or Raphael. But not quite. He was...more chiseled, less handsome than his sons. But he was someone Michael remembered well, even though he'd not seen him in years.

He stood up. "Papa!"

Family and Faery

ALBINIA SAW THE MAN standing behind Michael. Had he approached gradually? Or did he just materialize? It shouldn't matter either way, of course, except the only way someone from outside the world could appear on a magical path was if they, too, were dislocated. In which case, they could not simply appear in the middle of the path.

Perhaps he had walked up and neither she nor Lord Michael had noticed it. They'd both been starving.

But she felt a cold prickle in the back of her neck, as the man told Lord Michael, "I cannot believe you'd undertake this, son. You are too young to attempt a magical path."

Michael looked abashed, but shook his head. "I'm not too young, Father, and Tristram Blakley called on me, because he needed someone who understood the mathematics of magic."

His father made a sound like "Pah," and said, "I cannot believe that someone who is just sixteen would say that. You might know mathematics, Michael, but how much magic can you know? Do you remember what happened with the automated barber?"

"The— How did you know about the automated barber?" Michael asked, and there was a tone of suspicion in his voice now. "You... You'd gone, adventuring between the worlds, or something, by the time that incident happened!"

The older man waved his hand. "Oh, your brother told me."

"Seraphim?" Michael asked, and now his voice was sharp—suspicious. "Or Gabriel?"

"I don't rightly remember, but one of them. He said that the barber almost decapitated you. That is not the sort of thing that should happen to someone who has the knowledge to untangle a magical path."

Albinia wished she were about twenty years older and had three times as much magical knowledge. She wasn't absolutely sure what they were dealing with. And maybe it really was Lord Michael's papa, though she couldn't fully understand why his brother was the duke if his papa was still living. But if it was his papa, he was in the grip of something strange. Albinia was sure of it. Her hair had stood on the back of her neck for minutes now.

But what did one do about a shadow semblance in a magical path?

The only thing she could remember was what to do for a changeling. So she reached into the bag of plenty, and wished for eggshells and a cup of water.

She set the eggshells up on their rounded ends, and started measuring water into them.

She worked as though this were her entire concern, even though she could hear the talk of Michael and whoever this was go on. She wasn't paying attention to the words, but she could tell it wasn't going well. For one, Michael's voice kept rising. He was denying the person's authority, and refusing to give any information.

She started pouring water from filled eggshell to empty eggshell, holding them high, and working as if the water were precious.

Suddenly, the voices stopped. There was a silence, and then the voice that was not Michael's said, "You, girl, what are you doing?"

Without looking up, Albinia said, "Oh, I'm making elf beer."

And held her breath, and waited to see if the trap worked.

She felt as though her heart were beating in her throat. The silence lengthened.

Michael cleared his throat, and she hoped against hope he wasn't about to intervene, but of course he had to. He said, "Er... Miss Blakley."

She looked up, shooting him one single, intent speaking look, and hoping against hope he would read her mind in her eyes.

Then she went back to measuring and pouring water from eggshell to eggshell, as though it were the most important thing in the world.

"But that—" the man said. Then stopped.

"No, no, go on Papa," Michael said, heavily emphasizing the last word. "What were you about to say?"

Without Breadcrumbs

MICHAEL HAD BECOME VERY sure that whatever this creature was, it was not in fact his papa. Though he'd not had much contact with his father, the missing—and believed in Avalon to be dead—duke, because as the much younger son all his problems got mediated by everyone else, including his two powerful brothers, his twin sister, and his mama, he knew Papa knew his date of birth.

Papa would never have referred to Michael as being sixteen when Michael was in fact seventeen.

From everything he'd gathered about Papa, mostly from the stories Seraphim and Gabriel told, whatever else Papa was—and he had some slight impression that Papa had been a loose fish, not quite the thing as far as behavior—Papa understood the parenting of young men. He would not call a young man too young for the same reason he wouldn't call an elderly man decrepit. Because he did not need to flatter himself by demeaning other men.

He looked at the creature, whatever it might be, standing in front of him. It seemed to have lost its thread when Al had done her strange pantomime with eggshells. When Michael challenged him, it was quite undone.

Michael had an idea things were about to get dangerous, but he couldn't quite understand how, since they'd been told that as long as they stayed on the path, they would be safe. And they were assuredly on the path.

But while they'd been promised safety for themselves, they had not been promised they would stay together.

Just as he thought of this, there was a sound like leaves in the wind. "Go back," it said. "Go back if you know what's good for you."

He had time, just barely, to bend and reach out both hands, as a sound like wind blowing through a flute filled his ears and his mind. One hand grabbed a human hand, and the other a paw. He heard Bug cry, like a baby who cannot be consoled.

And then, suddenly, while the voice screamed, "Go back," he was enveloped in a whirlwind, and twirling with it in a gray fog that made everything invisible.

He heard Al mutter something under her breath, and it had the tone of a spell.

The whirlwind dropped them.

"We are on the path," he said as he opened his eyes, which felt gritty. His skin felt tender, too, as though he'd been scoured with sand.

Bug had fallen beside him in a seating position, having somehow lost his blanket, and was whimpering disconsolately, his blue eyes unbelievably huge and forlorn. And Albinia was spilled most ungracefully on the ground, one hand still touching his and the other—bless the girl—holding firmly onto the handle of the bag of plenty.

"I am glad you brought the bag," Michael said.

"Yes, but—" Albinia pulled herself up to standing, brushed at her clothing, pulled her hair back, and looked very upset. "Where are we, exactly?"

"On the path," Michael said. "So they cannot hurt us."

"Good, good, great," Albinia said, but her tone of voice and expression did not match the words. "Oh, Bug, leave off, do," she told the whimpering baby gryphon. Reaching into the bag of plenty, she brought out a slice of bread with cheese and...tomatoes? And handed it to Bug, who made hungry sounds. Then she handed him a cup with a lid, the kind you give to very small children. "Drink some milk. And don't eat the bread too fast. You will choke and have hiccups."

She looked at Michael, who was staring at her bug-eyed. "It's not magic," she said. "Some of Mama's friends had small children, and I always ended up being in charge of them when those friends visited."

"I...I presume their friends weren't gryphons," Michael said in a thready voice, but immediately reoriented to the important matter. "But I don't understand what's distressing you. Other than Bug crying, I mean."

"Oh," Albinia said. "I'm distressed because I meant to banish the...semblance of your Papa. But he didn't seem to operate by the laws of changelings. He didn't scream and explode or vanish. He did something instead, and I think it's what he came to do."

Michael only blinked at her, because he couldn't imagine what she meant. "You're very acute. I cannot follow your reasoning," he said.

She sighed, and suddenly, with an impression of great despondency, fell down to sitting beside Bug. Michael noted she was still clasping the bag and thought that was wise. Then he wondered if he should hold Albinia's hand, but before he could say so, something made him realize how it sounded, and he held his tongue. Which was just as well, because Albinia said, "Look around, Lord Michael. Which way did we come? And where are we going?"

Michael looked. The problem—and he'd been aware of this before—was that the scenery on the sides of the path tended to change and flow at seeming random, sometimes showing beautiful scenes, sometimes desolate pathways, but mostly showing something that would entice them off the path, of course. Because of that, perhaps, both of them had started ignoring the scenery—which, again, would change, anyway, even while they stood still. Right then, the right side displayed misty mountains in the distance, and up close, the sort of lakes that were only normally seen in the paintings of fanciful artists.

To the right, there was a shoreline that reminded him of when he and Mama and Caroline had gone to the seaside at Ramsgate. Michael and Caroline had been very small, maybe all of ten years of age, and they'd run and played in the water.

He stood up and looked up the path one way. He remembered the path as perfectly straight as they walked, but what he could see meandered up hillsides and seemed to curve. Well, he thought, that would surely be the way ahead. He looked the other way, expecting to see, beyond the straight path, something familiar, but there was nothing.

He sat down, as despondently as Albinia. "Which way should we go?"

"That," Albinia said. "Is what I think the creature wanted to accomplish. They can't hurt us, but they can make us walk backward and never get to the end of the path or unwind Papa's magical trap."

Michael wanted to say something consoling, but he couldn't. Because she was right. "We should have dropped bread crumbs from the bag of plenty as we walked," he said.

"Yes," she said. "We should. But then birds would have eaten them. Or something like."

For a moment, he thought she was going to cry, but then she started laughing. "I believe you've never read a single fairy tale, Lord Michael. And perhaps that is fortuitous. Perhaps you can find a way to get out of this situation that the path won't anticipate."

The Machinery of Discovery

MICHAEL SAT ON THE path, quite oblivious to the feel of the hard ground beneath him.

It was quite the strangest way he'd ever worked, but also fascinating, because every time he reached in the bag of plenty, he found absolutely what he needed, even if he hadn't quite taken time to consider his next step.

"I wish I'd thought of a bag of plenty for my tools and needed parts long ago," he muttered.

"I don't see who would have enchanted it," Albinia challenged. Michael looked over to see her sitting in the shade, with Bug beside her. "Surely you understand that Papa, whatever else he is, is an exceptional enchanter. I suspect most other such bags are used for food, or drinks, or something else quite particular, not all-purpose."

Michael, working rapidly with his hands, and squinting, because he didn't want what he created to be larger than a watch, chuckled. "Madam," he said. "I would like to inform you that one of my older brothers is the king of Fairyland. When it comes to enchanting, he's something special in that...er...realm."

He looked up in time to see her twist her lips in a *moue* of doubt or perhaps pain at his pun. This made him want to chuckle more. It had long since become obvious to him that Miss Blakley would defend and honor her family above all, even the royal family, of this world or others if it came to it. He smiled at her, instead of arguing, and tipped his head. "I will grant you that Gabriel might not wish to give me such a boon. If it was his true appearance in my dream, he is exasperated with my insistence on going on the path."

"Do you think it is a true appearance?" she asked, smoothing her skirts.

Michael nodded once, then shrugged. "Sometimes," he said. "It's hard to tell what's a true dream and what is merely the memory of being hectored by Seraphim and Grabriel my entire life. It is difficult being the youngest."

Bug climbed into Albinia's lap with a smug expression, curling up on her skirts. Michael noted that her hand petted the gryphon unthinkingly. It was one of the things that he liked about her, her tendency to look after all creatures that needed her. Himself included.

He sighed. "I suppose it is also hard being the oldest. Seraphim has always felt responsible for the entire family and its members, more so than Papa. And it must be even harder for Gabriel, since until very recently, though he is our illegitimate brother—and perhaps more our brother than he should be, since his Mama is an elf who took the semblance of our mama when they were both young—he was only Seraphim's valet. So he had to look after us, without seeming to, and he often managed to scold me, while seeming to only make suggestions." He paused and tilted his head a little, as Albinia petted the gryphon. A part of Michael felt a deep peace, and wished he could stay here with her forever on this path, in the sunshine, building machines while she sat close by and watched and listened to him. Forget the world. Forget defeating the path or unwinding the magic that had created this pocket universe.

He wished he could stay here, in peace, just himself and Albinia with her flame-red hair, and a little gryphon who acted just like a sweet and cute toddler.

To distract himself, he said, "I always liked Gabriel. Well, I always liked Seraphim, too. To be fair, they are kind older brothers, positively ideal save for their tendency to lecture me much too much."

"I wonder if my brothers view me that way. I mean as someone who should be lectured. They don't normally do it, or not so I perceive," she said. "I mean, I am much the younger, because William is my next oldest brother and he's three years older than I. Samuel, the oldest, is almost fifteen years older than I and...I didn't realize, but he must be thirty-one now. He disappeared so many years ago.

"But the thing is— The thing is that the boys are not very good at looking after themselves. And so I find myself having to do things like remind them to eat and not let them get lost in their thoughts. They all take after Papa, you see?" She blushed. "Oh, now you'll be thinking me what Mama calls a bumptious managing female. Truly, I'm not. It's just... Though I had no memory of Papa, I always thought he'd be the kind that was better at magic than at life. You see, that's what my brothers are. And though I didn't know Papa's first wife, of course, and she is said to have been a brilliant scientific magician, as brilliant as Papa, she must have been more competent at the real world. Had to be, or they'd never have raised seven boys past childhood. She and he would have disappeared into their laboratories, and left the children to starve or be kidnapped."

"Ah. Yes, my Mama is the practical one, though my Papa is... Well, he was the king's Witchfinder, who would go and find people who had magic, in worlds where that was forbidden. Papa, I understand, is much addicted to adventure and...and finding new things and—" He paused and blushed. "And people. Obviously. I mean," he waved his hand. "Gabriel exists, after all, so— But Mama reconciled with Papa in...interesting circumstances, and though he's presumed dead, they're adventuring somewhere." He shrugged.

"Do you wish to adventure, too?" she asked. There was a careful prodding in the words, and for a moment, Michael wondered if she, too—despite being a beauty and also much too young to consider any relationship—felt that she would much like to spend the rest of her life with himself and Bug, in peace and quiet. He realized he probably only thought that because he'd like her to.

He answered honestly, "Oh, no. I have... Seraphim has given me to understand that the proceeds from my inventions have been laid by, and that I'll have enough money to buy a small property in four or five years. I'd like a little property, large enough for walking paths, and for the workshop to be far enough from the house that no explosion or burning debris will reach the main house. I, too, tend to disappear... How did you put it? Up a magical spout. Only mine is magic mechanics. And when I go up the spout, I sometimes forget to eat or drink, or bathe. My sister, Caroline—my twin—is likely to come and drag me out after a couple of days and force me to eat and drink, and shove me in the general direction of a filled tub."

"An ideal sister, then. Is she—I mean, do you mean to set up house with her, then, when you come of age?" Was that a primming of her lips? Al was trying very hard to keep a smile on, he guessed, and she was almost succeeding, but he could see for some reason she didn't like the idea of his setting up house with his sister. And he wasn't so addled that he didn't think this might connect to him, and her growing liking for him.

He could have toyed with her. He could. He could also pretend to himself he didn't understand the direction of her thoughts. But the truth was that in the end, Michael was a practical young man. He'd thought, for a long time, that he'd never marry or have a family.

Not that he had anything against marrying, such as it was, but because he thought it would be very complicated providing himself with a wife, or children. He'd probably have to go to London for the season, and dance with a lot of young women, and try to make conversation with them.

He'd assumed he'd be single forever. Most of all, when one took into account that he tended to become mute in the presence of young women, particularly if they had red hair. And one could not forget that most of the young women he'd talked to—Caroline's friends!—only wanted to talk about *on dits*, gossip, and who was doing what to whom in society, or else ruffles and lace, or else again—and the most trying—Michael's own multifold perfections, which were the stupidest things ever, like the way his hair curled, or his eyes, or even his clothing or the way he sat a horse.

But Albinia— Well, she talked of real things. Sure, family, but also magic. And he didn't miss the way her eyes were following what he did in assembling the path tracker, or the fact that, slightly narrowed, they were almost certainly keeping track of the magic used in the endeavor. Albinia was real. He didn't think if he talked to her about thaumaturgic mathematics, she'd smile and say, "Oh, you are so brilliant, Lord Michael." And he didn't think she knew how to simper. And, what's more, she had climbed a rope out a window to join him on this path.

He realized silence had lengthened, and he was looking at her in the rudest way, while her eyes had narrowed just a little, perhaps thinking that he was evaluating her.

"No," he said. "No such thing. Caroline is, as it happens, engaged to a centaur named Akakios, who has abandoned Fairyland. They're both attending schools. Boarding schools. So it's—" He almost said he was very lonely. But what an addlepated thing that would be to say. It wasn't as if he were old enough to make his addresses to anyone. And while he'd like Albinia to know he cared, perhaps know enough to hold until he was old enough to do so, he was not about to ask such a question, or even prompt some thought here in a magical realm. For all he knew, the magic would take anything he said or did, and use it to attack him. "That is, this means that for the last year or so, there hasn't been anyone to remind me to eat and bathe."

"And does that mean your servants all stand upwind from you, Lord Michael?" she asked with a smirk.

"Not noticeably," he said. "That is, I made an automatic bather." He was about to explain the problem with that when the last piece fit in place in his construction, and he said, triumphantly, "Oh, here we go. It is now finished."

Path Finder

AL LOOKED WITH SOME misgivings at the tool in Lord Michael's hand. It didn't inspire confidence, though that perhaps was saying too little.

It looked exactly like a garden trowel, of the type one would use to weed the flowerbeds, only it would be very ineffective at that, too. Because instead of a solid blade, it had a mass of gears and what looked like glowing marbles of various colors, all of it linked together by a bright gold wire, which also went around the rim to give it shape.

She stood up and almost said she didn't think it would be very good for gardening. And she wasn't sure that would be a joke, either. On the other hand, well... Lord Michael was a mathematical and magical genius, which was why Papa had most brazenly involved him in their family problems. So instead, she smiled and said, "Would you tell me how it works?"

"If I did what I think I did," Lord Michael said, "it will fulfill two functions. One is to show us the path, the other is to show us if a person, creature or...or object, or even food is hostile or good or neutral to us." He showed her a notch on the handle, then covered it with his thumb. A white pencil of light emerged from the pointy tip of the object. "If used like this," he said. "It should tell us which way is forward in the path." He pointed it behind himself, and the light pencil turned bright red. He pointed it the other way and the pencil turned blue. "See, the blue side—that way—is the way to walk." He smiled.

"And as for good or evil?"

"Well, not that. Some good people or forces might be hostile to our purpose," Michael said. "Good or evil, that is harder to test. But opposition to our purpose, that should be easy in a magical path. See this other notch?" He pointed at the notch about a thumb's width down. "If you cover it," he demonstrated, "and point it at someone or something—" He demonstrated again by pointing it at Bug. A bright yellow light, somehow soft in nature, came out and played over the gryphon, causing him to blink awake. "Bug is neutral to our walking the path. That is good to know, since I've felt for very long that he might very well be an obstacle put in our path by forces unknown."

Both Albinia and Bug squawked at that, and she was slightly amused, because she knew that what Lord Michael said made sense. Looking after a small creature of any kind was not conducive to moving fast or well. Besides, she thought, Bug was a magical creature. But to disguise the fact that she sounded exactly like Bug in her indignation, she said, "How can you say that about such a pretty creature who is so very fond of bread and cheese?"

Lord Michael smiled, in turn, as though catching her humor. He pointed the tool at her, and she found herself surrounded in a blue glow. "Ah. See, you are friendly to our progression."

"I should hope so," she said. "I am already longing for a bath, and I've never walked such a long time, sustainedly, in my life. And I don't know what it will be like to sleep on the path, either."

He smiled and reached in the bag for a hook, which he used to suspend the tool from his belt loop. "So, let's hope we don't have to stay here overnight."

"Yes, let us," she said. As he offered her his arm to help her walk, she said, "But no. Would you be so unkind and make me carry Bug all the way? Or would you have him walk his own way, when he might, in all innocence, walk off the path, as children would?"

Lord Michael tilted his head sideways, which he seemed to do when in deep thought, and said, "How do you propose we carry him, then? Perhaps a proprietary sling? Or a pram?"

"I don't propose we carry him at all, Milord. I propose we each take one of his hands and walk him." She looked at him challengingly. "That will also allow him to work off some energy, and perhaps sleep better, if we do have to spend the night on the path." She paused. "Do keep the idea of the pram in mind, though. It might become necessary."

They each took one of Bug's paws, which in grasping felt more like a child's hand, though covered in fuzz and with a pointy nubbin of claw at the end of each finger, which Albinia understood to mean that he was sheathing his claws.

They walked in the direction the blue light had shown a while.

After a few steps, Bug didn't slow them down at all, having picked up a trick of lifting his feet and flapping his wings, and doing a long jump by leveraging his hold on their hands. After a longer while, a little happy shout joined the wing-aided jumps.

Looking down, Albinia saw that Bug looked very happy indeed. She looked at Lord Michael, who also looked strangely contented.

"So, Milord," she said, her voice only half-teasing. "Do all your inventions work that well, first time out?"

He grinned. "Oh no. This one is very easy. You see, it is in the nature of a magical path to start at a point of low magic, and increase steadily as you walk it, so all I had to do was measure the power of magic at any point in the path, and whether it increased or decreased as we walked."

"Shouldn't it be the other way around?" she asked. "Starting at a point of very high power, and then winding down?"

"No. Think about it a moment and you'll understand. That wouldn't work at all. The challenges rise as you walk the path— Oh, no. What did I say?"

She realized he was responding to the way that her face had frozen in horror. "Your... Your false Papa was an easy challenge?"

"Undoubtedly," Lord Michael said. "You see, if it weren't, both of us would not have immediately realized he was a construct. Yes, yes, I failed to realize what he had come to do, but that is on me, not on the cleverness of the construct."

"And Bug was easy?"

"Bug, I think, was a trap more than a challenge. Whoever set him there was hoping you would abandon the path and render yourself lost. And fall into their power."

"I see. So the challenges will grow?"

"Yes, I believe so. You see, the charge will increase till the end, when your charge, in succeeding at various challenges will increase, too, until you can defeat it and leave. And hopefully…" He paused. "No. And needfully explode this universe and let your family go free."

"I worry about that," Albinia said. "We should have seen another of my brothers by now."

"I worry, too," he admitted. "But I'll admit I don't know very well how this works when others walked the path before you. Perhaps they are caught in their own sub-paths."

"Or perhaps they left the path and are lost." She didn't like the sound of panic in her voice.

"Well…let us not think of that," Lord Michael said. "But the thing with indicating if people are for or against our reaching the end of the path, you see, I'm using the path's own energy. The path itself was designed so that… Well, it's not sentient, of course, but it is something like. Its design is such that it doesn't wish us to reach the end, but to trap us forever, so it reacts to anyone we encounter in response to whether they help us or hinder us."

"But," Albinia said. "Wouldn't that mean that the path would show blue for those that would prevent us getting to the end?"

"Oh, no. I codded the lights myself, and wanted them to coordinate with the ones on the other notch. So, helpful for us is blue."

"I see," she said. "And so other of your inventions didn't go so well?"

He smiled, and his lip curled. "Since you were privy to the rowing boat disaster—"

"Which nonetheless saved my life. Also, I don't think that's your invention so much as Papa's designed to kidnap you."

"Possibly. But you should know I've done much worse."

He entertained her with good-natured descriptions of inventions that exploded and inventions that caught fire, and the barber-groomer that chased him all around seeking to cut…not his hair until a retainer blasted it.

She giggled and laughed, and appreciated his willingness to sound the fool in order to entertain her and almost didn't feel the distance they'd walked until, topping a rise, they came across the most dispiriting view yet.

Choices

MICHAEL STOPPED, STARING, AND drew in breath sharply. There, at the bottom of the hill, the path forked, one sub-path heading each direction.

"It's a trap," Albinia said, and he desperately wanted to believe her. They walked slower towards the place where the path became two paths, headed one right and one left. Bug must have sensed their mood, because he stopped doing his little swooping jumps and, instead, trudged along, dragging his clawed feet. He was making a little odd sound, not like crying, but not very far off it. Like a child whimpering in fear.

Michael stopped at the end where the path bifurcated, and Albinia stopped beside him, taking Bug up in her arms. Bug's little tail was swooping in circles, as though he were a disturbed cat, Michael noted.

"I'm not sure it's a trap," he said. "Except insofar as it is, of course...a...a dashed inconvenience, pardon my frank speech."

"We could just follow one of the paths," she said. And then with great animation, "What if one of them is quite the wrong path?"

Michael took the path finder off his belt loop and checked one path, then the other. Both glowed blue.

"We could both take a branch, then. Since they're both right?"

Michael didn't know what to say, or how to explain. He'd been feeling this for a while. Magical paths were a thing that differed for each person, depending on who they were. They were as personal as anything else about an individual. The challenges presented were different. Albinia was different from him, admittedly. Perhaps his own path would be easier, but probably not. He didn't know about hers. However, he could imagine there were challenges they could be presented together. Except the path didn't believe so.

Albinia's breath came loud and fast. He thought he could feel her panic. Well, he felt his own panic, as well, to be sure. And he didn't want to walk a path without her. He'd just been thinking...

"Pardon me," he said, and put his arm around her, turning them both towards the right hand path. He used the path finder. It glowed evil red. He turned them in the opposite direction. Evil red again.

"I'm sorry, Al— Miss Blakley. I don't think we can walk together."

He reached into the bag of plenty. "Once something is invented, it can be duplicated." He handed the duplicate pathfinder to her, and she almost dropped it, since it was obvious her fingers were nerveless.

"But—" she said.

"Here," he said. And pulling the bag of plenty from his own shoulder, he draped it on Albinia. He felt his eyes fill with tears, and he really didn't want to cry. If there was one thing he was sure of, it was that he should not cry right now. Not because of any rules of conduct, but because he didn't want Albinia to know that he hated the idea of walking alone, and was sure that they'd each perish without the other. It was not the thing at all to implant doubt in her mind right then.

For the first time since they'd been spirited away from his family's town-home, he wished she weren't in the adventure along with him. What a wretched thing to do to such a wonderful young lady. He should have insisted she return to the tower and stay safe-ish there. Because even living with a werewolf was better than being caught forever in a path of Fairyland.

He cleared his throat and squeezed Bug's hand a little harder, as if to keep him from running away. This, of course, prompted Bug to struggle, which was not at all what Michael wanted. "I...will keep Bug and look after him, I promise."

And then Albinia turned waspish. He saw her purse her lips, and knew she was going to be cutting, though he couldn't quite understand about what. He'd been trying to make it as easy on her as possible. "To be sure," she said, in a sarcastic tone, eyes flashing at him. "And how do you intend to look after Bug, pray tell? What do you intend to feed him? If you're not going to take the bag of plenty, are you going to feed him on wishes and air?"

"Perhaps the path will be short," Michael said, aware he sounded like a zany.

"Oh, yes, of course. Your path will be short and straightforward, so you'll have no need of anything, and can burden yourself with every kind of problem. You must be all about in your head, or think I am."

"No, no. It's just..." He heard his voice sound as though he were crying, and this wouldn't do at all. He wasn't crying. Why did his voice waver suddenly? "Miss Blakley, I'm simply trying to make it more likely that you'll come out of this, even if— Even if—"

"Even if you don't?" she asked. And she must have tightened her hold on Bug, too, because now the little gryphon was fighting to pull away from both their hands. "Why do you think the path will unwind if only one of us comes out? My brothers haven't managed to unwind it, and they're lost somewhere on the paths. Perhaps no one comes out unless everyone does."

"But then—"

"But then we'll have to find them, for sure. Or not. But you can't know. We started the path together, and it might well be a double, joint path."

He wanted to yell back that this was not possible, and that she should take what advantages she could and get out of here, before she was stuck in this pocket universe with himself forever.

"But—" he said.

Albinia reached into the bag, and pulled out a shoulder bag. "It doesn't work to pull a bag of plenty from inside another. Something about equations."

"It is protected against it," Michael said. "I heard it could dissolve the universe."

"Very well," Albinia said. She set the satchel on the ground, and, removing the bag of plenty, handed it to Michael. "Would you be so kind as to pull out a pram for Bug? Preferably with a belt so I can belt him in place, and prevent him going gallivanting off the path." She looked down. "No, Bug. Be calm. We'll look after you."

Michael pulled out a sitting pram, folded, and then unfolded it and manhandled Bug into it, closing the belt around his middle. "I spelled it. You'll be able to remove it," he said. "But he won't."

He tried to hand the bag back to Albinia. Albinia shook her head, and put the large satchel on her shoulders. "No, we have sandwiches and drinks for myself and Bug for three days, which I believe is the normal time of this endeavor. If we go hungry a little while after, it will be well. No. Don't worry, the satchel has a spell to make it light. I'll be well."

"But," Michael said. "You should take the bag of plenty. What if you should need something? Or...or what if Bug should?"

Albinia shook her head. Her features still looked pinched, but she didn't look angry. Michael knew a wild impulse to promise her that he would court her if both came out of this free. But it was the stupidest thing. Why would she even want that? Yes, he'd interpreted her questions as leading, but what if she was merely making conversation? What if, growing up with her brothers, the last thing she would want to do was spend her life with a mathematically inclined magician? "No, Milord. You might very well need the bag of plenty for your wondrous inventions." She lifted the path finder a little, as though to demonstrate her point.

He wanted to argue, but she was right. He wanted to invent things to make it easier for her, but how could he do that without knowing her challenges? And he realized that was the nature of the path. To isolate you and make you face things on your own.

He had a wild impulse and reached into the bag. He pulled out something that Seraphim talked about. Two of them. Except that, of course, they weren't the things that Seraphim had talked about but magical things that worked the same, because Seraphim had talked about a magic called "electricity" and something called a "network." He brought out two dark glass rectangles. "Here, Miss Blakley, take one of these. Even if I can't come to your rescue, you can update me on how... How you are doing. They're communication devices. If you say my name into one, it will tell me." He wasn't sure at all that was how it worked, or at least how the Madhouse devices worked, but he had an idea it should be. And since that was what he requested of the bag, and it wasn't an invention so much as a piece of activated glass, it should work. "At least, I hope it does."

She laughed a little. "And if it chases me, attempting to cut off pieces?"

"Don't be silly. It doesn't have a scissors arm," he said, smiling a little. "And, well, we can try them when we walk a little off. If it won't work at all, you can toss it to the side of the path."

She nodded.

"Thank you for... For everything," he said. "I'm very glad you joined me on the path and only very sorry we have to part."

She looked up at him. Her red hair was wild, and there was a strangely intense but indescribable expression on her face. "Thank you for catching me when I fell from high buildings. Twice. I don't know how to... How to express my gratitude. I'm afraid— Well, if we shouldn't meet—"

"No such thing. We will meet again at the end of the path."

She nodded once, lips tight, and he thought she didn't believe it. Not even a little bit.

They parted abruptly. Each tested their path. His left, hers right. When the pathfinder glowed blue, they started walking.

He had gone maybe a hundred steps when the glass square in his hand glowed. "Lord Michael?" Albinia's voice came from it.

"Yes?" he asked, with some trepidation. Had she got in trouble? He turned around and saw her standing on her path, looking at him.

"It appears to work," she said.

"Indeed," he said.

She waved and turned to walk, pushing Bug's pram.

He turned and walked his own path with a lighter heart.

Bug Out!

THE PATH BECAME BEAUTIFUL. Or rather, the land on either side did, making Al wonder what could have caused it. Either side of the path, vast fields of flowers extended out of view, filling the path with a heady perfume like roses in full bloom.

The sun shone above in a perfectly cloudless sky, and Al found herself singing a little song she'd heard the village children sing.

And Bug in his carriage joined in, humming the tune, and waving his front paws around. For the first time, she noticed that though he had an eagle's head, the eagle's head had little adorable tufted ears like a lynx's.

She reached over and petted his ears and he turned his head this way and that, offering now one ear and now the other to her petting.

The path wound, but looked perfectly clear. She'd just push this carriage...

Suddenly, the ground went out from under her. She felt herself—still clutching the carriage, and with the bag of plenty draped around her middle—falling into darkness.

Down and down, it went. Down and down and down, into a dark tunnel in the Earth without her knowing how deep the hole, or if it was a physical hole. Or even what was around it.

She landed hard on something, and must have been knocked out because she woke up to a tuneless, high-pitched humming and what sounded like the muffled cries of a baby. Like a baby whose mouth was covered.

Opening her eyes took effort and there was pain from the back of her head. But after much struggle, she managed to raise her eyelids.

Impressions assaulted her like blows: light, as from a fire, and a large table between her and the fire. On the table was a square tray? Well, a square container, and in it an indistinct form.

Doing something to the tray was a...creature? The silhouette was not right for its being a human. It consisted of a tiny head, sunk in massive shoulders, and arms like an ape. She couldn't tell from her position if it had legs.

The creature was singing, "Chicken dinner. Chicken dinner for me. Hush little baby, chicken dinner you'll be."

In between words there was a clacking, as of...teeth, and a slurping sound.

Unsteady, her legs feeling like rubber, Al dragged herself to kneeling, then reached, and grabbing the edge of the table, rose to standing.

Her eyes had by then adapted to the lack of ambient light, but the horror of the scene before her was so grotesque it took a moment to catalogue everything.

Bug, hands and feet tied together and his beak tied shut with twine, looked at her with pleading, tear-filled eyes. There was a bunch of parsley in each of his little tufted ears. He was both trying to cry, and struggling against his bonds. Albinia realized he was also tied around his middle to an oversized pottery pan.

The creature who'd clearly put poor little Bug in this position, was...horrific was the first adjective that came to mind, but it was somehow inadequate. Disgusting, while true, didn't fully cover it, either.

It was indeed pin-headed with the head sunk between its shoulders, in a way that suggested a malformed neck, or malformed shoulders, or something seriously wrong about the skeleton of such a being.

Add to that a green-bluish skin, eyes that were yellow slits. A disproportionately large mouth, with a series of very sharp teeth that didn't so much meet as interlink and cross—the clacking sound—and let saliva slip between them—the slurping sound.

It continued singing, "Baby in the oven, sleep baybee. Chicken dinner, tasty dinner you'll be," as it picked up the Bug pan in his overlong, deformed arms ending in spindly six-fingered hands.

And yes, Al was now quite sure it was male, as she could see that portion of his anatomy as he moved. She had never seen any human naked, of course, but living in the country, she was privy to the love life of cows and bulls, and at any rate, many in the village had dogs.

She had never looked close, but on this particular creature, you didn't need to look close, as that part of him was overlarge, and not covered by anything.

He must have seen where Al was looking, because he slurped, clacked and leered at her, "Chicken dinner for my wife and me, once we eat, my wife she'll be."

Al could have paused and shuddered. She realized the implications well enough, but she supposed she was in no way a delicate female. Or at least that was what her mama would say, Al was sure.

Instead, she was more worried with the idea this crazy thing was going to put poor Bug in a roaring fire. She hadn't taken Bug from the middle of Fairyland for that. She'd rescued him. It was her duty to protect him. He was her charge, she'd look after him. She could not let him get eaten. Or cooked, at any rate. And alive at that.

She started to lurch towards the creature, but something about his singing of chicken dinners got caught in her mind and gave her an idea. Reaching a free hand to the bag of plenty, she withdrew a large roast chicken, which she threw directly at the monster's head in a way that would make her brothers proud.

It hit on the snout, between the eyes and the horrendous mouth.

That was when she remembered she had the satchel, not a bag of plenty. But it had acted like the bag of plenty. Well, she was not going to pursue the mystery. Not now, at any rate.

The creature startled, the dish with Bug fell on the ground, and there was a breaking sound, then a scrambling sound.

Bug, still tied hands and feet, made use of his little wings, jump-flying over the table and into Al's arms.

Al held him against herself, as if her life depended on it.

The creature was eating the roast chicken, bones and all, crunching and slavering.

There was a knife on the table, though it was more of a rusty spike.

Al used it to cut Bug's hands and feet free. She gave silent thanks that the creature's notions of cookery were not exactly practical and didn't include killing his food before cooking it.

The creature, having consumed the chicken, looked towards them. "Chicken dinner, chicken dinner for me, shush baby, chicken dinner you'll be."

Bug had removed the tie from his beak, and screamed loudly. Al reached into the bag of plenty that shouldn't be a bag of plenty, and threw another chicken at the creature.

Then she looked desperately around. Up there, way above her reach, shone a round hole, through which she could see blue sky. Up, there was the path.

The only way to get there was by climbing a scabrous vertical expanse that seemed to be what remained of a stone wall, long buried and encrusted with dirt.

Well, there was nothing for it. She'd start climbing.

"Hang on, Bug," she said. "I'm going to need my hands and feet."

He threw his little arms around her neck, looking in horror at where the creature was devouring the roast chicken.

She dug her fingers and toes into the dirt, and started climbing.

Memories

MICHAEL HAD BEEN WALKING the path for quite a while, and was starting to feel...not bored, exactly, but strangely apprehensive. Normally, when walking a path, it was a good thing if nothing happened to one.

But on this path, at least from what he understood, things were supposed to happen. You were supposed to encounter challenges, defeat obstacles, find ways to change the world and yourself, so that you could, at the end of it, unwind the path and the little world in which it existed, and escape the path and the world.

It occurred to him that all magical paths had to be part of Fairyland. He didn't like that.

He looked around, and on both sides of the path, rolling verdant fields stretched. He thought, of course they did, and of course, in the distance, between clouds and sky there would be the suggestion of a castle atop a mountain.

In the way of Fairyland your thoughts shaped the reality around you.

Michael didn't remember Fairyland. Not in concrete memories. Or he tried not to in his awake, fully conscious state.

But now alone, and walking a path that was not truly real, and might very well be part of that dread, sanity-challenging place, he couldn't help it coming to mind.

He'd been in his workshop, the one that Seraphim had built—or allowed Michael to have built—at the back of the house, trying to create a magical orrery, one that would replicate the movements of the planets. Each planet had been created from a polished semi-precious stone. Earth's continents and deep blue sea, her tall mountain chains and deep chasms, had taken Michael weeks to sculpt, let alone the deep red of Jupiter's fires, or the ring of magic circling Saturn.

As for Earth's moon, of course Michael hadn't sculpted the vast herds of moon cattle, with their glowing horns, nor the *vaqueros* imported from Earth to tend them, and sell their meat and milk to Earth at fabulous sums. He hadn't sculpted them any more than he'd sculpted the people of Earth—and that would have been a hopeless endeavor—but he had sculpted the deep blue waters of Mare Crisium and the dark green of Mare Serenitas. And he'd taken time with the massifs, particularly Mons Huygens, from where the New Year's celebration and countdown was broadcast every December 31st.

He had to be precise with the moon for the same reason he had to be precise with Earth.

While Mars had two large cities, and a vast population of convicts and desperadoes, very few people from Earth ever visited Mars, and there were very few shows transmitted to crystal balls from there. But the moon and various points of the Earth everyone knew, many people visited and there were books and treatises written about them, which everyone had read.

Everything was in place, suspended from fine, magically-spun and strengthened gold filaments, and those in turn from the mechanism above, which was bronze, but shone with magic, so it could be confused with gold.

He was about to set it in motion, a magic greater than any he'd ever invoked. He had to set it in motion in such a way that it would continue going of its own accord, after he wasn't even near it, much less feeding it from his own magic.

It would be something that would run from the background magical radiation which inhered to any place long inhabited by man.

He knew he could do the magic. He'd researched it for months. And created his spell carefully.

And though young Michael rarely listened to the complaints of the family, he also knew that if he could get this to work perfectly, the price it would fetch from some very rich person who wanted to ornament his library might rescue the whole family out of impending calamity. And maybe Seraphim would not need to marry for money.

He had stepped back and cast the spell. Only between casting and activating, the spell had bloomed unnaturally, as another force took over and tore it wide.

And through the opening had come... He still shuddered at the memory. An army of goblins, long-armed like apes, with greenish-blue skin, and repulsive teeth and eyes. They'd grabbed him and carried him to Fairyland, while leaving a fairy in his place as a changeling, fashioned to resemble him.

He'd fought, of course, but there was an uncountable number of them. They'd bound him and gagged him, and taken him...

After that—

Michael was convinced that captivity in Fairyland might not have been as injurious to practically anyone else as it was for him.

It was the fact that in Fairyland he could not apply logic or mathematics, because everything distorted and upended that made it so horrible. It was like losing one of his fundamental senses. No. Worse. He'd have dealt better with being suddenly blind.

It could be all seasons in one day, but out of order. Or terrain that suddenly devolved, so you were walking down on the sky and looking up at the dirt.

Or worse. Much worse. At one time, they'd marched through a plane of numbers. Not written numbers, just the concept of numbers, with no solidity nor form, and they themselves had lost form and body in it, till they were just mathematical descriptions of themselves.

It was—literally—maddening.

But the most horrific thing was being presented bound and gagged to the old king of Fairyland, who had penetrated Michael's mind, and commanded it as his own, and shown him horrific thoughts and dreams, while he mined Michael's magical power, leaving him depleted and broken. It had taken him a long time to recover. And his power was not the same, still. Might never be the same.

He blinked, ridding himself of the memories, and around him, the path, the sides of it that had for a moment been concepts of numbers, became verdant slopes again.

Michael sighed. The truth was he was very much afraid that he'd find himself in that place again. And it might very well happen—even if his half-brother was now the king of faery. Fairyland had a logic of its own—if he so much as stepped out of the path.

He again verified that his feet were indeed on the neatly cobbled pathway, and that he had a good three feet of path on either side of him.

Above, the sun shone, with the occasional bit of fluffy cloud floating by.

He took another deep breath.

And suddenly, from in front of him, running full tilt and trumpeting, came an oversized swan.

Michael smiled, and wondered which of Al's brothers this was, and shaped his mouth to a welcome.

The swan attacked him, feet and beak tearing into him, while the wings slapped his face.

"Stop," Michael screamed. "I am a friend of Al's," but this only made the attack redouble.

Which was why he reached out and grabbed the creature by the neck.

Done

ALBINIA'S FINGERS DUG INTO the dirt of the hole's walls, causing it to crumble faster, but she was making very little progress.

Bug clung to her in terror, his claws digging at her clothes and flesh. She looked up at the hole where sunlight showed on a blue sky. It might as well be as distant as the moon, as she stripped skin from her fingers, but it didn't seem to get any closer.

And suddenly claws closed around her ankle, and a goopy, grating voice said, "Chicken."

Albinia lost her mind. She'd not left the path. This could not happen to her. She and Bug were not going to be eaten, because she hadn't left the path. She'd fallen. This was not the same as leaving the path. You were supposed to be safe while on the path. She was not supposed to be hurt while on the path.

"This is against the rules," she screamed. "I call to the power of the path. I call to the power of Fairyland. I was on the path."

Nothing answered. The claws closed around her ankle pulled down. "Chicken. Yum chicken."

"I did not leave the path. This is not lawful. I claim protection of the path. By the higher power of Fairyland, I demand this be set right."

Out of nowhere, an immaculately groomed hand reached out to her. She noted no more than that it was very clean and masculine. It held her hand that was scrabbling up, and pulled at it.

It was the strangest thing. That hand, grasping hers, seemed to cause her to float up the hole. Or perhaps float wasn't the correct term, because it was more forceful, as though the hole itself ejected her upwards. The claws around her ankle let go.

She found herself, Bug still clinging to her—being tossed wasn't the precise term?—perhaps floated over to the side of someone standing on the path.

As she landed, surprisingly softly on her behind, the hand reached down again, and took Albinia's much-worse-for-wear bag of plenty, and deposited it beside her and Bug.

Bug still clung to her, shuddering, but he stopped screaming. It seemed to Albinia that, like her, he was looking at the man standing on the path, waiting to see if he was friend or foe.

From the back, Al thought there was something familiar about him, but she couldn't say precisely what. He wore a dark coat, and dark pants, which looked nondescript and not particularly well cut, the sort of clothes favored by upper servants, or valets, or at least that was her impression from people she'd seen pass through or accompany her mother's occasional guests. He had dark curly hair. Beyond that, she could see nothing much, and certainly not his face, because he was...

Well, what he was doing was unbelievable enough, and she lacked words to explain it, anyway, but... If she had to try, it would be that he reached down and plucked the hole from the path, and the tunnel attached to the hole, as though the whole of it were a sock that had been pushed down through the path surface.

And as he pulled it, he...folded it. It shouldn't have been possible, because he was a normal-size, normal-looking man, but somehow, he was folding the thing as he pulled it.

From inside the tunnel, which from the outside didn't look at all like a hole dug in the dirt, but exactly like a sock, if a sock were massive, and made of a slick, stretchy and unwholesome material, came a high and sharp whine mingled with the occasional "Chicken."

Al felt herself shudder in unison with Bug.

But the man continued pulling and folding, so in a few minutes he was holding ...a much folded version of the tunnel, about the size of a shoebox. And then he folded it more.

Behind it, the path healed, and looked perfectly whole.

The man appeared to use a lighter, or make fire somehow.

He dropped the hole, on fire, to the path, and said, "Yuck."

Then turned around. Behind him, the hole melted, till nothing remained but a sort of greasy spot.

"My pardons, Miss Blakley," he said. He still looked strangely familiar. "And thank you for bringing this to my attention. I hate this type of creature and its lair traps. It was started by my predecessor who— But it doesn't make much difference, does it? You did the right thing in calling me."

"I," she said. "I called you?"

He waved a hand, and a little pram appeared, much like the one that she'd lost in the hole. "Come," he said. "You see, there is a pram for...what do you call him? Oh, yes, Bug. A silly name for the size he will be, and the position he'll hold, but I dare say he won't mind."

The man reached out for Bug, and for a moment Al thought to hold on, but Bug gurgled happily at the man, who settled Bug in his pram and closed the belts.

"Anything I can do for you to make up for this horrible experience?" he asked. He smiled at Albinia.

Al blinked. This whole time, at the back of her head, she'd been thinking he looked familiar, but now she looked into his jade green eyes, and something clicked.

"You are Lord Michael's brother," she said. And then thinking of what he'd done with the hole and the creature in it, her eyes cut to the grease spot on the ground, and her voice failed her almost utterly. "You are the king of Fairyland."

Trumpeting Away

MICHAEL HAD ONE HAND on the goose—no, swan's—neck, when he realized he wasn't going to be able to get out of this position while the swan was determined to attack him.

Reaching into the bag of plenty, with one hand, he thought fast.

The thing about magical machines was that the components existed. He'd made them and bespelled them before, and therefore he didn't need to invent each new component anew. Therefore, he could summon them to the bag of plenty.

At any rate, should he try to do it, he was likely to run afoul of the need to make the part, then spell it. While he was summoning magic and infusing the part, the swan would attack him.

In fact, just as he pulled the first piece out of the bag, the swan broke out of his one hand's unsteady hold, and tried to rip off his nose.

Michael dropped the part, reached into the bag again and brought out a bespelled rope. The thing was that he'd started making bespelled ropes for their goose herder some two years ago, since geese were almost impossible to truss up for market.

You could walk them to the market, but once you had a paying customer, handing them the goose was likely to result in a lot of honking and some injured humans.

Because Millie the goose herder had brought the problem to Michael, as most of the household did their little problems—not wanting to impinge on Seraphim's time or magic, since the Duke, as the household referred to Michael's older legitimate brother, was busy—and Michael invented something. A rope bespelled to restrain poultry was just that. And since then, he'd found himself making a dozen or so of those a month, because the poulterer also found it useful to deal with certain aggressive roosters. Apparently, it could even subdue turkey-cocks.

Now he summoned the rope out of the bag of plenty, touched it to the swan, and hoped it worked.

It worked, as it always did, very rapidly and literally by magic. A blur of movement, a loud trumpeting, and the swan was trussed up, as if for market.

His feet were tied together, his wings roped around twice. And there was a rope around his neck, making it impossible for him to move without strangling.

For a moment, the bird looked absolutely stunned, as though not believing this could have happened. And then, suddenly it flopped over.

After the first two attempts at flapping wings strangled him, he remained still. But not silent.

Michael ignored the trumpeting as he assembled his tiny machine. It was based on an idea he'd had years ago for a present for Seraphim. He thought he'd put a muzzle-translator on Seraphim's horse, and allow his brother to speak to his favorite mount.

It had been a good idea. Michael was still sure of it. How was he to know that Incitatus would be the kind of beast no one wanted to listen to?

It had taken almost no time of Michael putting the muzzle on him, to realize that inside the big black horse there lived the kind of mind most exactly replicated by an old and crotchety gardener, like Mr. Rollon, at their country estate.

It was all about how his hooves hurt, the shoes weren't quite right, people were too heavy, and didn't pay enough attention to him, and why did that ingrate, the dark-haired one, never bring him apples?

Thinking that the last thing Seraphim needed was to endure from his horse the complaints he heard often enough from older retainers, Michael had removed the translating muzzle and hid it in his workshop. He thought—and might be right—that what he'd done wrong was that the muzzle couldn't possibly translate as it would a human mind—which is what Michael had designed it for, knowing no other type of mind—and so what came out of the horse's mouth was passing thoughts, the kind of in-the-now-consciousness one would expect. Just before he'd removed it, in fact, the horse had devolved to, "What's this thing?" over and over again, which seemed to lend credence to the theory.

But Michael remembered the pieces very well. Rebuilding the machine was child's play, as he pulled this and that component in smaller size, and made it into what looked like a tiny muzzle for a deranged bird, with straps to hold it in place.

The bird stared with wide eyes, and trumpeted more emphatically.

Putting it on the creature was harder than it had been on the horse, because the swan snapped his head this way and that, trying to get at Michael's fingers.

"Stop, you idiot," Michael said. "I just want to talk with you."

This got him a malevolent look, but the swan did stop thrashing around, to stare at him with a long and dubious intensity which allowed Michael to strap the thing on.

Then the trumpeting came. It started as *blert*, but changed midsentence to, "You jacknapes, you loose fish, you rake! What have you done to Al?" As he spoke, the swan made efforts to evade the tie, so some of the words were very strangled indeed.

Michael blinked. "To Al? I've done nothing. I mean, I gave her a bag of sandwiches and a pram for Bug and she took the other path."

The swan was in the middle of a word, and stopped so fast you could hear his beak clack.

When he spoke again, his voice came out hoarse even through the muzzle. "The...other path?"

"Yes," Michael said. Quickly, he gave the swan an explanation of what had happened, that led him and Albinia to separate.

"How...long ago?" the swan asked.

"Some hours," Michael said.

"So...the distress I sensed from her wasn't from you?"

"I should hope not. Wait. Distress? I shall go back and—" Michael stood and started heading back.

"No, wait," the swan croaked. "Or at least don't leave me tied up."

Tea, Crumpets and Confusion

The King of Fairyland hesitated. Albinia knew that only because for just a moment, within the perfectly human frame of someone who looked a lot like Lord Michael, but dressed as an upper-class valet, there was something that didn't look human at all. A confusing intersection of tesseracts of light, with a suggestion of wings and an impression of sly spying eyes, and pointed ears, all of it wrapped around a core of strong magic.

Not just something that wasn't human, but something that couldn't be human. Something feral and alien, not responsive to human means of seeing the world and human logic.

She heard herself say, "Oh," as she took a step in front of Bug's pram.

And in the next minute, the man looked absolutely human again, and vaguely embarrassed. A superior servant who has made a mistake. He bowed from the waist. "Yes, I am Michael's older...half-brother. Or...our mothers were... My mother was a replica of his. A changeling formed to duplicate his mother, save for being an elf, and therefore not functioning very well in the human world. So Michael and I look like full brothers." His smile was both apologetic and strangely brittle, like glass is brittle, which can cut those who break it. "I'm sorry. I've handled this all wrong. Miss Blakley, my name is Gabriel Penn, at your service. And I am indeed, for my sins, the ruler of Fairyland. For definitions of ruler." His eyes crinkled at the corner, with the suggestion of a smile that didn't fully materialize. "Which, you must presume, include not letting myself be eaten by the forces of magic." The smile flashed, wryly, a self-mocking smile. "Some days are easier than others. But it shouldn't be a surprise that I came when you called me, should it?"

"I called?"

"You invoked a violation of the rules. At a certain level, only I can intervene. For instance, within a closed path."

"Oh. I didn't realize. It seems rude to disturb a monarch."

Gabriel shook his head. "Not when the monarch's younger brother is involved."

He hesitated, visibly, looking to one side of the path, while his face worked through embarrassment. "Miss Blakley, would it be too much to ask... That is, do I ask too much if I beg you to partake in tea with me?" He looked at Bug. "You and your utterly charming companion, of course."

Albinia tried to parse what she'd just heard. First, monarchs didn't ask commoners to tea, did they? Second... Second, this was an elf, which was to say a faery, which was to say—

"Your Majesty... Don't misunderstand me. I don't wish to give offense. I realize your nature is your nature, and independent of who you are or—" She almost said *were as a human,* then decided not to step into such eddies. "Milord, the problem I have is this: even the merest babe knows what it means to partake of faery food, and it might terminally interfere with my intent to make it through this path and free my brothers and father."

He looked puzzled for a moment and said, "Your brothers? And father? But—" Then gave the impression of having stopped himself forcibly. He grinned, this time, seeming to give way to genuine amusement. "Miss Blakley, as you said, you're on the path and protected by the laws of the path. If I remove you from the path, to feed you tea and crumpets, then you cannot be harmed. So I cannot give you food that harms you."

"Yes, but if I consent to be removed from the path, then I—"

The king of Fairyland sighed. "I see," he said. "You can't consent." His sigh seemed to invoke a gusty wind which, inexplicably, had glitter floating in it, in colors ranging from pale golden to silver, and a few other colors unknown to the human eye but suddenly visible.

Albinia felt herself lifted off her feet and made a little exclamation of surprise. Bug gave an entirely delightful childish peal of laughter and suddenly...

They were in a very proper drawing room. Albinia felt different and looking down on herself, realized she looked like she'd had a bath and was wearing quite the most beautiful day dress she'd ever seen, let alone worn. It was white silk—Mama would say it was entirely improper, since young ladies could only wear muslin. Her hair was a red curtain over it, and around her. There was a green velvet sash around her waist. And the lace on the silk would cost more than her papa's whole manor. But what struck Al most of all was that the dress was high in the bosom and had sleeves. It was an entirely appropriate dress for a Miss not yet out, which was, of course, what she was.

And therefore, whatever else the king of Fairyland was, he had a good eye for the nuances of female social status. Well, maybe not as to wealth, but what could you do to convey that to a creature who could create silk out of nothing?

In all her finery, Albinia stood in a perfectly appointed sitting room, by a deep blue, velvet loveseat. Bug wore a perfectly tailored—it left his wings free—little sailor suit, his little back paws free, and looked lost in the depths of a huge armchair, clacking his beak and humming a little song.

"Miss Blakley, if you'd sit down, please."

She looked in the direction of the voice. The king of Fairyland, now wearing a very nice jacket and pants, more what she'd expect his brother the Duke to wear, smiled at her. He stood by a crystal tea tray, which took up most of a small table. At a glance, Albinia saw three kinds of cake, a pile of different sandwiches, and three teacups. Her stomach rumbled loudly and embarrassingly. She'd had the sandwiches, of course, but she hadn't had time to eat.

The left corner of the king's lips climbed fractionally. "Just so, Miss. So I'll serve if you'll let me."

"You brought me here— You didn't— You—"

He sighed, this time without any magical effects. "Miss Blakley: you didn't consent to being taken here, or to being fed by me. Which means the food won't harm you. It is not of Fairyland, but... I've got it from someone I trust on Earth. But beyond all that, even if it were faery food, by my very rules I couldn't keep any magical properties in it. Take a deep breath, Miss. How do you take your tea?"

She told him, without thinking, and he mixed it, and filled a small plate with all manner of beautiful food that made her mouth water. He set it on a little table that turned out to be at her elbow when she sat down.

The tea was warm, and milky, and immensely soothing. The sandwiches were some of the best she'd ever had. The only thing to rival them was when her mother invited Albinia to come in to one of her parties, with grown-up guests. And then Albinia's nerves didn't let her fully enjoy them. She wanted to giggle suddenly, to think that tea with the king of Fairyland was easier than tea with Mama. And yet, it was true.

Gabriel Penn turned to Bug and asked him what he wanted, and though Bug said nothing, the king bowed, as though he'd received orders.

He waved his fingers, and Bug had a bib around his neck, protecting his beautiful sailor suit. And then the king arranged a few slices of cake on a plate, and set the plate and a glass of lemonade, sweating as if to show it was cool, on the table near Bug's chair.

Bug made a sound of delight, and sipped at the lemonade so carefully, he belied the need for a bib.

The king laughed with true joy, then prepared himself a cup of tea, and sat in an armchair, facing Albinia.

He took a sip of his tea, and closed his eyes, as though this were ambrosia, a wonderful treat rarely enjoyed. "Sometimes I forget what real food is like," he said. Then smiled. "Now, Miss Albinia, and my royal friend," he bowed to Bug. "I'm delighted to have you here for the moment. I must make sure you're properly provisioned with non-dangerous food when you leave here. You shouldn't walk Fairyland with inadequate food and no drink. Michael should know better." Then he suddenly started, and pointed at the little satchel which, still scruffy and stained, sat on the floor by the sofa. "Forgive me, you do have a bag of plenty."

She frowned at him. "I didn't," she said. She told him how they'd decided and that she gave the bag of plenty to Michael, because he might need it for machinery. "And I just took a satchel of sandwiches and—" She shook her head. Her mind was a muddle. "But then when Bug needed rescuing, and I needed a roast chicken, I forgot the satchel wasn't a bag of plenty, and I reached in, and... It worked." She looked at the king, who wore an expression as though he were both curious and patient, like a teacher waiting for the student to come up with the right question. "Your Majesty, I don't understand. How could it suddenly be a bag of plenty?"

He raised an eyebrow at her. "You don't? But you obviously made it a bag of plenty."

"I did?" Albinia asked, wondering if all elves were insane. "I'm a reasonably good witch, but I have no such power. And unlike my Papa, I don't even know the formulae."

The king opened his mouth, then closed it, then opened it again, closed it again. He sighed. "And yet you did. Please trust me."

"You won't explain it to me?" she asked.

"I'd much rather not, Miss Blakley. Not just now. It will profit no one." He sat his cup of tea down. "And you'll forgive me for bringing you here. It is part of my condition, my...position...that I can see the past I didn't live and the future, though perhaps not all of the future, and yet—" He tilted his hand sideways. "You're both very interesting people, with special fates resting on your shoulders, and because your fate is entangled with my brother's," he said to Albinia. "And yours with most of Fairyland and its fate," he bowed to Bug. "I thought much could be achieved by meeting you and finding out who you really are and your potential."

Albinia blinked. "Did you say royal? And how could Fairyland depend on Bug? He's a baby."

"Indeed he is. He's the prince heir of the—" Gabriel made a sound that Albinia's tongue could never imitate, and in fact her mind could not quite follow. "Pardon me, you'd say the gryphons. Though it's more complex than that, you know? The gryphons, by their nature, are the chief of all the magical creatures."

"But they're part of Fairyland and therefore—"

"Oh, no. Not really. They have their own kingdoms inside mine, because mine is the only place where the high magic allows them to survive, but they're not—" Another strange sound, and Gabriel Penn, very much human all of a sudden, appeared aggrieved. "I beg your pardon, Miss. My mind has got used to thinking in a language not English." He frowned. "They're not subjected to me. They have their own power, their own agenda, their own destiny. And Bug's destiny is a great one.

"Which is why your naming him Bug amused me so much."

"But that's just the name I call him," she said, in some exasperation. "Surely his parents—"

Gabriel shook his head. "No, you see, that's the thing. His parents were killed before he emerged from the egg, and then he was kidnapped. I'm not sure by whom, though I have some ideas. I suspect, before you are done, the whom will be solved, and that you'll keep him safe, meanwhile. He has some years to go before he can reign, but the truth is, you gave him his reigning name. I have no idea what the gryphons will make of their king being named Bug, but right now, he's as cute as one."

He replenished Bug's cake.

"And you, Miss Blakley, are a force of nature, and will therefore permit me to tell you that you—and my brother, also—are being used as chess pieces by forces not entirely human. It is in the best interest of both you, and my brother, and... Well, frankly, in mine, also, that you finish walking this path, and achieve your goals. But I don't fully understand. Why do you say you started on the path to free your father and your brothers? What made you think you could?"

"Well," Al said. And paused. It was really startlingly clear, and she couldn't think why this creature was so confused. "Someone had to. The boys are— They need someone to look after them."

"Yes," the king said, and sipped his tea. "But why you? You're younger than all of them, and less trained, and if you forgive me saying it, your mother—"

"My mother isn't theirs, yes. Also, Mama is...difficult."

He inclined his head. "So why?"

"Because I had to. Because..." She became aware of being flustered, and waved her hand around. "Someone had to and I was someone."

On The Way Somewhere

MICHAEL BACKTRACKED, AND PULLED his pocket knife from his pocket.

From the swan, there came a confusion of protests. “I didn’t— Please don’t—”

But just after Michael opened the pocketknife, he realized he was being stupid. He closed it, put it in his pocket, while the swan babbled, and then touched the rope and whispered the word that made it release. He kept it in his hand, though, in case the swan got aggressive again.

Instead, the swan took off running, back along the road, and Michael followed, at some speed.

They never got to where the road bifurcated, though. They got to the place where they could see the road, just in time to see Albinia, with Bug in his pram, talking to a tall stranger. “Oh, hell,” Michael said.

The swan turned to him and managed to make a trumpeting sound that didn’t get translated. Thinking about it, Michael wondered if back when he’d created the translator he’d made it so that it couldn’t translate curse words. He had a vague idea that was true. In which case, the interrogative trumpet sound meant, “Hell?”

Michael wondered what to say. If he said, “My brother,” he judged that it would probably cause the swan to attack him again. It would take much longer than he probably had between the word and unhinged trumpeting and wing buffeting to explain that while Gabriel was in fact his half-brother, and in many ways raised as a full brother in their rather unconventional household—certainly with the right to scold the younger siblings or—on one signal occasion involving a magic tripwire that caused the kitchen to fill with false ghosts, to get revenge on a cook's assistant who'd denied Michael raisins—give them a swat, he wasn't here by Michael's request. In fact, Michael had a very good idea, he thought, as he saw Gabriel speak calmly to Albinia, that Gabriel was here to extract him from the path, and take him home in disgrace, under the smug assumption that Michael was about five years old and incapable of looking after himself.

So instead, he said, "He's the king of Fairyland."

Things then happened very fast. Like that, the swan screamed, "No!" and "Albinia," and tried to jump off the path, leaving to Michael the awkward resort of grabbing him by a place he couldn't just run and leave feathers behind. Which caused a lot of strangled, "Unhand me, you loose fish, you rogue, you—" at the same time that Albinia, the pram and Gabriel all...vanished.

The effect was very pretty, leaving behind floating lights and a distant sound, like the memory of bells. Yet, it was all completely and thoroughly horrifying, because Michael felt bereft. He screamed "No!" and let go of the swan, who, fortunately, had apparently lost his suicidal intent to get off the path and cut to the other path and attack the king of Fairyland.

The swan made a series of trumpeting that sounded very much like they were language no properly brought-up young gentleman should know but which the muzzle, of course, would not translate. Then sat disconsolately down, not in the way of a swan, but in the way of a human, by dropping heavily on his behind.

Which matched Michael, who had dropped on his behind in the path. But seeing the swan so completely disconsolate, he hastened to say, "The king won't hurt her. He is—"

"Oh, you have no idea what he is. I could tell you things..."

Now that was going too far. Michael knew that since Gabriel had taken over control of Fairyland, he'd become...slippery was the way to put it. Something not quite human.

Michael could feel it, of course, and it disturbed his innate sense of who his brother was, but one thing he was sure of. That he knew more about Gabriel than this complete stranger was a given.

He reached for the swan's neck, only to have the swan pull his neck out of reach with another string of trumpeting.

"Gabriel is my brother!" Michael said forcefully, and dropped his hand, because it wasn't a good idea to grab the swan by the neck. "He's not evil. He would not hurt Albinia. At worst, he will take her out of the path and somewhere safe."

The swan blinked slowly, which was very odd for a bird, even for one that was actually a young man under a spell. "Gabriel?" It came out somewhat croaky through the translating muzzle. "His name isn't Gabriel! Who is Gabriel?"

"Gabriel Penn," Michael said. "He's my half-brother."

"Did he...inherit recently?"

"Yes. From his uncle."

"Oh," the swan said.

"So, you see, I grew up with Gabriel. Gabriel is my older brother. I've known him since I was born. And he's not going to hurt Albinia. He doesn't hurt young women."

The swan was quiet a long time. Then he said, "Well. Let's hope you're right. But I'll stay here till she returns."

"Let's go to the other path," Michael said, all nervous energy. The swan looked at him and muttered something which came out too low to be understood through the muzzle. "Beg your pardon?" Michael said.

"I said," the swan said, pulling up to his feet. "If we can."

"Why would we not be able to?"

"Well, Lord Michael, you see, this path is strange. I should know, as I've been walking it for a good five years now."

Michael blinked. He hadn't asked Albinia how long her brothers had been missing, but he had the impression the last one of them had vanished mere weeks before. After all, Albinia herself was...well, if they'd disappeared five years ago, she probably wouldn't be searching for them only now. He got to his feet, as well, and walked beside the swan, trying to work out how to phrase his query.

"Oh, I know we didn't leave five years ago. I certainly didn't leave Papa's cottage to walk the path five years ago, according to your time, because Albinia would be twenty and that she certainly is not, from both my mind picture of her and the fact she took to the path with a—" The swan swallowed, a weird sound, like a person swallowing in confusion and embarrassment, if the person were stuck with a swan's vocal cords. "You'll forgive me, but if Albinia were twenty, she wouldn't be walking the path with a stripling. At least I hope not."

Michael grimaced. He was used to that kind of derision from his own older siblings. And of course, what he immediately wanted to say was that stripling or not, he'd agreed to take risks and walk the path to free total strangers. Instead, he remembered Seraphim telling him that when someone was very rude, the best set down you could give him was to behave with irreproachable politeness yourself, and correct them that way. They would feel the reproach all more keenly for only being implied in what was said.

"Miss Blakley," Michael said, drily. "Is fifteen. And I am seventeen. And you, sir, I presume must be her oldest brother." He tried to remember if Albinia had told him her oldest brother's name, but he couldn't remember it.

The swan made a cackling noise. "Very well played, sir," he said. "I am Samuel Blakley, at your service. I imagine you need to have quite a spine, if you're undertaking to court Al."

And that confused Michael enough. "Court—"

"Pardon me. I assumed," Samuel said.

Like that, they were at the point where the path bifurcated. Michael stepped forward boldly to the conjoined place, to take the other path.

His foot hit something. He looked down. He couldn't see anything. It was rather as though the clear air had hardened and wouldn't allow him through.

"I told you," Samuel said, and his voice had a lugubrious sound, like he'd predicted terrible things that had now come to pass.

"If you know so much and have, as you said, felt as though you walked this path for five years, how come you have not made your way out?"

"Ahah," Samuel said, and leaned nonchalantly against the invisible barrier, managing to convey in his body language that he was a young man of good birth, having a conversation with a younger peer. Which was rather a miracle for a swan. "I see you're ready to give me pepper, sirrah! Well, and properly taken. You see, I could not even overcome the first challenge, to continue down the path. I have been walking this stretch of road for five years."

Michael was about to ask how that was possible, and what could one even eat while caught in a stretch of road on Fairyland, when there was a twinkling of lights from the place where Albinia had disappeared.

Immortals

THE KING OF FAIRYLAND took a big bite of his cake. It seemed to Albinia that she'd discomposed him, though she had absolutely no idea what she, Miss Albinia Blakley of Wulffen Downs, a small manor on the coast, could have done to discompose a creature who ruled an entire world of magic.

He looked at her, while keeping his face turned down, and moving only his eyes. It was something she'd seen Michael do, to look at her, she presumed, without being observed.

Which was frankly silly. It was as though they believed unless they looked at her full-on, she wouldn't see them. Also, wouldn't the king of elves be able to throw an illusion so she didn't see him looking at her?

Instead, he sat there and ate his cake, then just crumbled the remaining piece on his plate, while looking at her. And she realized she felt particularly aggravated at him, because when Michael had pulled that same surreptitious under-the-brow look at her, she'd thought that he had been looking at her because...well, because... He found looking at her pleasing. But if the king was looking at her that way, it obviously wasn't for the same reason, so why would he do such a thing?

"Your Majesty," she said, thinking she was being bold as brass, and that Mama, could she hear her, would give her a very thorough set-down. "Is there something wrong with my rescuing my brothers and father from their magical prison? Something that gives you pause?" She cleared her throat. "Because you look displeased."

He looked up. He was blushing, which she found very strange, and he set his cake plate down at a little table at his elbow and stood up.

Remembering some old etiquette about not sitting if the king was standing—or was that not sitting in the presence of a king? She couldn't remember. Her Mama hadn't been very clear on royal court etiquette, much less Fairyland royal court etiquette. Terrible oversight—Albinia made to set her own plate down.

The king waved down her attempt. "No, please, remain sitting. I just think better on my feet." He cackled, a self-deprecating laugh. "Considering for most of the parties of my youth, I stood, ready to help a guest or the other, unless it was a family party, and even then I normally stood because I never felt that my family quite accepted me. Not that they did or said anything to make me feel unwanted, but—" He shrugged. "It does not matter. You asked—"

He paced from one end of the room to the other. Albinia noted that Bug, between bites of cake, followed the king's movement with interest.

The king turned to face her, and took a deep breath. "Miss Albinia Blakley, to confirm: your brothers are the seven sons of Tristram Blakley? Am I correct?"

She nodded.

"And your father is Tristram Blakley, of Wulffen Downs? Made into a werewolf and imprisoned on a magical cottage built out of a tower at the beginning of a magical path by his second wife?"

"Yes, Your Majesty. I thought you knew?"

He let out air, in a long-held gust. It seemed to her that whatever she'd said had greatly relieved him. But that was silly, since all she'd done was confirm her identity. "I did know," he said. "But because of various... Because of the way magical paths work, I was afraid you had got confused somehow."

She smiled indulgently, then finished the last bite of her cake, which felt very rude and greedy. On the other hand, if Bug could finish his cake, so could she.

"Beg your pardon," the king said, and refilled her teacup. "I should not have let your cup go empty. But you see, I was afraid that something had got...confused, and that you didn't know who you were rescuing. Magical paths play tricks with your mind."

Albinia nodded, in some confusion. They sure did. And now she was wondering if they had played tricks with the king's mind. He still looked jumpy. Just not as though he expected Albinia to be the advanced wedge of an anti-king revolution in Fairyland. Which she now realized was what he'd looked like before.

"Very well," Gabriel said, and turned away for a moment. He went to the door of the room and opened it, something she was sure was quite superfluous. He spoke to someone on the other side, and she couldn't hear what he said. Not that he was whispering, but because she was sure there was some kind of veil in the way.

He received something from the unseen person—fairy? Creature?—on the other side of the door, and came back to her.

This time, he sat on a chair to the other side of her chair from the little table that held her tea. He sat in effect between her and Bug's chair, and it confused her, because she'd been sure that her chair was right next to Bug's, but apparently not. Apparently, there was room and another chair that matched her own. Either that, or—Albinia thought—the king had magically made a space appear between the chairs, so that he could magic yet another chair between them. She didn't know if it was possible, but why should it not be, given he commanded all magic and magic was the very fabric of Fairyland?

"I am sorry," the king said. "I can see I have discomposed you, and it was never my intention." He leaned over towards her, smiling a sickly sweet smile which didn't seem quite natural. He proffered a small cardboard square, whose lettering read, "Gabriel Penn" and then other letters which seemed to move as she looked at them. She had an idea they were the magical writing of Fairyland. "This is my card, and it has magic on it."

"I deduced as much," she said, taking the card with her fingertips, and leaning away from him, because he seemed uncomfortably close.

"The magic means that any time you clutch it and think of this room, you and Bug will be transported here." He paused a second, but she didn't know what to say, and he continued. "This should not be used to get you away from uncomfortable situations, because if you try to escape your challenges, you will never finish walking the path. Also, if you transport here, even if you are at peril of death, you should know that the magic will return you to the same place, at the same time from which you departed. So it will not rescue you."

"Sir, I don't intend rescue. I'm supposed to rescue others, not—"

Something flickered in his eyes, and she wasn't sure what. Amusement, she thought, but also something like pity and...kinship? Affection? "That much I know, Miss Blakley, but all the same, let me explain: it is easier to provision you this way. Any time you are transported here, you will find the table—" he pointed at a large table against the wall, which she was quite sure had not been there before, "—laden with food. And if something is missing, you have only to say what you want, and it will appear." He pointed to a screen, which she was also quite sure hadn't been there before, because it was a beautiful piece painted with what appeared to be scenes of dancing winged fairies. "And behind there, you will find clothes for both you and Bug, should your present clothes become unwearable and should you somehow lose your bag of plenty. And I'll make sure there's also prams, in case Bug's gets damaged. So you can come here to replenish. And maybe to nap, if you really need sleep, because no one needs to walk the path of Fairyland sleep-deprived."

He was looking at her beseechingly with eyes that were so much like Michael's, it embarrassed her. "Thank you," she said. And this time she did put the plate and cup down. She put his card in her pocket, and there touched something which she remembered from feel was the charm her brother had given her, in case Michael became amorous or something. It seemed very strange to find it now. Particularly since she'd put it in the pocket of quite a different frock. She stood up. "I don't know why you're taking such an extraordinary amount of trouble for me. Surely you don't make it so easy for all those who walk the path, do you?" She was very sure he hadn't done so for her brothers, or doubtlessly they'd have freed themselves.

He busied himself with wiping Bug's beak, and removing the bib from Bug's neck, then sitting Bug in the carriage and strapping Bug in.

Then he looked up at her, and there was a blush on his face again. "No. No. You're the first one for whom I've done that. Let me say, without explaining, please, that I have a great deal invested in seeing you succeed in your mission and rescuing your family from Fairyland, as well as my little brother Michael, who will otherwise become foolishly trapped."

She nodded, though it made no sense at all. He opened the door to her. It was the same door he'd opened to talk to someone, she still didn't know who or what, but through it, she could see the path.

He held the door open, and she started to push the pram through the door, when he held her upper arm. "Let me say also, Miss Blakley, that I know something of the trials of immortal creatures, particularly those partnered with mortals. If you should ever feel... Oh, not now, but in the centuries ahead, that you need to talk to someone who understands, feel free to keep that card. Assuming you survive the path, which you see, I am betting on. Anyway, you have only to come to the room and say my name and I—"

She hadn't understood much of any of it. But she knew an improper attention, as Mama would call it, when she heard it. She reached for the charm against importuning that Geoffrey had given her.

The king cackled and grabbed her wrist. For a moment, she was scared, but then she saw his face, and he was amused. "Miss Blakley, don't be foolish beyond permission. I'm not making an improper declaration. For one, you're a third my age. For another... Well, it doesn't apply. And if it did, Michael would draw my cork. Magical king or no magical king. You could say I think of you quite as a sister. A much younger sister. Just...remember what I said and keep my card. We both might have reason to be glad of it."

And quite without time to think about it, Albinia nodded. And emerged from the king's room onto the path, where Michael and a swan stood, pressed against...well...nothing, but nothing that appeared to be solid, for all the world like children looking in a sweets shop's window.

Gifts to a Lady

Michael wasn't quite sure what happened next, except that the swan went insane, screaming and thrashing as if Michael's automated shaver were after him.

Michael took a step back, then realized what Samuel was attacking was in fact the barrier between them and the path that Albinia was on. It didn't work, so if Samuel wanted to reach her, he would have to cross an expanse of grass, which was not recommended, since it was not on the path.

And the thing that Michael couldn't understand was what Albinia's brother had gotten so exercised about. After all, Albinia looked well. Her hair looked as though it had been combed. She looked clean. She had a pram, one, in fact, that looked better than the one that she'd had Bug in before. She had the satchel on her arm. And she wore a very nice dress. Very nice. Michael was not an expert on young ladies' haberdashery and dress, never before having taken an interest in what any young lady was wearing. In fact, if you had asked him his opinion before now, he'd have told you that any young lady would look far more attractive for some machine oil stains, and maybe an oily rag and a screwdriver in her hands.

But something in the dim recesses of his brain must have registered the appearance of young ladies in his circle. The dress they'd loaned to Albinia in his townhouse—likely Caroline's old clothing, now that he thought about it—had a look of being out of fashion, and had probably been stored for a while before being brought out for the emergency. The dress she'd gotten at her father's house was practical and solidly middle-class. It was the sort of dress Michael might see while riding across the village near his estate, or perhaps even on one of their maids on her day off. Or perhaps on a multitude of young ladies in London. Not shabby. Not old or ragged. But the sort of respectable, unremarkable, workaday stuff that young women might wear when they couldn't afford to get a very expensive dress dirty or destroyed.

The dress Al wore now, though, was silk, unless Michael deeply mistook his eyes. And it was... Well, the kind of dress young ladies might wear while visiting his Mama the duchess, or being introduced to Seraphim's wife, the Princess Royal. Not, of course, the absurd dresses used for a presentation to the Queen, but very nice stuff indeed.

He reached for Samuel, the only way he knew was likely to get his attention, though he hated to grab him by the neck. But he couldn't allow the young man in swan shape to tear himself to shreds against the barrier. He was Al's brother, and Michael didn't want Al upset at him.

He grabbed Samuel's neck, cutting off a squawk. It was saying something that the translator hadn't translated but as squawks. He was either too angry to vocalize words, or he had descended into rank profanity. "Stop, you madman," he said.

He could tell, from the corner of his eye, that Albinia was confused by Samuel's agitation; she'd turned, the smile dying on her lips, staring at them as though they had both grown second heads.

Samuel made weak efforts to free himself, then let out an indignant half-choked squawk, and glared at Michael.

"I'm going to let you go," Michael said. "And I expect a rational explanation of your behavior, including why the sight of your sister drove you into a frenzy."

"My sister!" Samuel said scathingly as soon as he was freed. He shook his wings, and ruffled his neck feathers, in a way that Michael felt would have been adjusting his neck cloth and shrugging, had he been in human form. "My sister, indeed. And the king of Fairyland, who, if I'm not mistaken, is your brother."

"Indeed," Michael said. "I told you. Gabriel is our brother, or at least half-brother, born of... Well, an elf who had become my mother's changeling."

The swan's glare turned odious, as if Michael had admitted to eating babies in ragout. "Well, Lord Michael." The "Lord" was emphasized so that Michael could imagine it written in particularly black ink and almost breaking the quill in the tracing. "It is no use thinking that just because you're of a noble family and your brother is the king of Fairyland, my family will stand by while he debauches my sister and makes her his doxy."

The declaration was of such monumental insanity that Michael stared at the swan, eyes wide, and took two steps back, his hands out, in the gesture one would use to appease a lunatic.

The man might not be aware that Gabriel was not in the petticoat line. In fact, Michael himself only knew because he was very good at overhearing the gossip of his older family members when they didn't realize he was present. But even if that weren't the case, Gabriel was much older than Al. And while Michael thought Al was one of the most beautiful young ladies he'd ever seen, in fact, only the second ever to catch his eye, he didn't think she was quite... Well, for one, it was obvious she was not old enough to be out, much less to be married.

But supposing that Samuel had some reason to believe that Gabriel had debauched Albinia, whatever that could mean, what did he propose to do about it?

As Michael put his hands up and out, open, in the universal sign for "I have no weapons," he was thinking that even if Samuel had a legitimate grievance against Gabriel, how could he possibly settle a debt of honor? Saying that Michael's family was noble was true, of course, but for the love of all that was sane, that wasn't what stood between Samuel and exacting vengeance. No, the material point was that Gabriel Penn was an elf, and the king of elves.

Even in the days when he was, to the eyes of the world, Seraphim's valet, his magic had been such that even Seraphim trod warily around him. And when Michael was a mere rank apprentice in spells and protections, he could tell that Gabriel's magic was different: slippery, strong, impossible to easily confine. Against it, what did Samuel think he could do?

But more importantly... Michael cleared his throat, and his voice came out hesitating and small, "Uh... Beg your pardon, but why are you assuming Gabriel did anything of the kind?"

The goose glared. "Giving her expensive gifts!" he said, witheringly. "And then, with meaning that seemed to have required clenched teeth, were he in human form: "A dress."

Michael sighed. He was vaguely aware of societal expectations around such things, only because Mother kept telling them to Caroline, who, like Michael, had very little patience for irrationality and would probably have put herself... What would Mother call it— Oh, that was it, quite beyond the pale, if Mother didn't repeat her instructions. Apparently, young men or, really, any non-related men, from the time they were in pants, were never supposed to give anything to a girl or woman unless they were engaged to be married. Not even correspondence. By that principle, he'd already heavily transgressed against Al by giving her a bag of sandwiches, but surely on the path, such things could be excused. But all the same—

"Samuel," he said ponderously, realizing that making him see sense would be difficult. "I think the expensive dress was not so much a gift as a wave of the fingers, and a casual expenditure of magic to the king of Fairyland. And I don't think Gabriel even thought much about it, beyond evoking something suited to a young lady of quality. He used to be a valet, so he has some idea of clothes, but I doubt he thought much of it at all. He's an elf, Samuel. You can't hold elves to our societal rules."

The neck feathers ruffled again, and the beak opened and closed. The swan managed to say something that sounded much like, "Umph. He's still half-human."

Michael sighed. "I'm not sure he is. Not anymore. Some humanity remains, but becoming the king of Fairyland made him different. More magic than being, if that makes sense."

Michael spoke uncomfortably, because it made him uncomfortable. He didn't like the idea that someone who had been his family member was now something else, something alien and cold. Two people who used to be part of his family, at that, because even if Seraphim hadn't changed intrinsically and in himself, he had changed, deeply. And like Gabriel, he'd become colder, more distant, even if still human. And transgressing against the rules of either of his older brothers could bring repercussions far worse than a good talking-to, or being sent to bed without dinner.

He sighed, realizing he'd refused to obey either of them, as he was fairly sure their presence in his dream had been true ones, magically conjured by them. He was going to be in so much trouble.

"What's more," he said, embarrassedly. "Gabriel is not...well, he's not in the petticoat line."

To Samuel's suspicious look, he said, "Look, I'm not a hundred percent sure what it means. It's not something the family speaks of freely, and I get the impression it's one of those things we should keep secret. But Seraphim says Gabriel prefers the company of men, and the new Earl of Sidell is his particular friend."

"Oooooh," Samuel said, managing to make the sound have at least five syllables. "Knew fellows like that at Cambridge. Or rumored to be. But then—" No longer maniac, but looking very confused, he waved his wings about, giving the impression of opening his hands in turn—were he in human form—towards Michael. "What did he want with my sister? And why did he take her off the path?"

Michael shook his head. He realized at the back of his mind it had been bothering him, also. "You know, I have not the slightest idea," he said. Then he sighed yet again, "But you know, Albinia is looking at us and probably wondering what came over us to nearly brawl on a path of Fairyland. So please turn and wave at her so she can go on her way."

"But what if he did something nefarious?"

Michael shook his head. He knew he was going to lie. Or, rather, he was going to tell the truth about what Gabriel had been when he was fully human. But the problem there was that Michael himself had been a prisoner in Fairyland. And he knew the place itself was...twisted by human standards. Its magic would probably drive a human—any human—insane. And Gabriel was not even fully human. Surely something remained of his half-brother, but how much, he could not tell.

However, that wasn't what Samuel needed to hear. Michael was starting to understand what Seraphim meant when he sighed deeply and talked about "diplomatic truth" as opposed to strict truth. Something about the king of France not needing to know strictly why Seraphim had arranged for new charter lines to the Americas, because it would only make him retaliate, when Seraphim didn't intend to do anything with the French possessions in Canada.

Aloud, he said, "I don't know what it was, Blakley, but it can't have been bad. No, really, remember he is my older brother, and in fact tried to protect me by keeping me away from the path. Perhaps he was trying to convince her to take Bug and desist from path-walking."

Samuel made some sound of debt.

"Come now: if anyone could extricate her once she started on the path, it would be the elf king. Now, let's walk our own way and tell me what has stopped you this long on this stretch of road. Presumably your brothers got past it, or they would be here, too?"

"I don't know," Samuel started. "I've thought of it and wondered if perhaps they went off path and are lost in the—"

Both of them whirled at Albinia's scream.

She wasn't even that far away, but they couldn't see her. It was very odd.

Al, and Bug's pram, with Bug in it, presumably, weren't on the path anymore, but there was something like the translucent shape of them in the air above the path, flying away from the path and from them.

Suddenly, the pram fell tumbling from the height, and it was easy to see it was empty. It became fully visible as it fell, and crashed to pieces on the path.

Michael realized that he was beside Samuel, trying to tear down the magical barrier.

Claws in the Air

ALBINIA STARED AT THE boys having what seemed like a terribly emotional argument, and couldn't make heads or tails of it. It was the strangest thing watching this, because she could not hear them at all, just see Samuel make gestures she mentally translated to the gestures he made as a human when he was very angry. And Lord Michael looking discomfited and appearing to do his best to speak calmly.

It was hard to read Lord Michael's expression at this distance, but it seemed to her that he was making all the gestures and faces of someone dealing with a dangerous lunatic. She chewed the corner of her lip, and told Bug, who was making questioning sounds, not quite words, "Well, I don't fully blame him, you know? Sam can come across as a complete lunatic when he's not thinking and is in the grip of some emotion. He once chased Edmund for hours because Edmund had stolen his fishing net to catch an injured bird."

She shook her head, a little worried. She wasn't exactly like Mama, who was always afraid of giving a less-than-couth impression to "people of quality" but really, did Sam need to make her entire family appear as though they were mentally unstable? She didn't know exactly why, but she couldn't stand the idea of Lord Michael thinking badly of her and her family.

But after a moment, they seemed to calm down. Their conversation looked like a normal conversation, now, though she could tell that Michael was embarrassed, but she couldn't have told why she thought that, or what specifically gave it away.

She hoped that Samuel hadn't been all worried about Michael dishonoring her, or something. Boys were soooo strange.

When they both turned and Michael gave her a sickly smile, and waved, while Samuel waved a wing, in the most unnatural position for a swan, she turned to walk the path.

She wished she was with them because— Well, for the same reason she'd come here. If you left boys alone too long, they were likely to come up with the strangest ideas. It was like their brains weren't wired for practical life decisions at all.

And now, she realized, this strange adventure had her sounding like Mama on the subject of men. When Mama wasn't haranguing Al about the fiendish masterminds men were, and how they could seduce the best protected of maidens without even trying, and stealing her virtue, she was making comments about how men wouldn't be able to survive without women, and could barely be trusted to get their own clothes on the right way.

Still, even if Mama said it, Al realized it was probably true. Because that was exactly what Papa and her brothers were like, and while Lord Michael seemed more capable, she suspected he went a little silly around his machines.

And his spells. After all, Papa said Lord Michael was a genius. She smiled in her turn, looked back, and waved to them.

The day was beautiful, and on either side of the path were fields of fragrant flowers. But this time, she wasn't going to be lulled into a false sense of security, and she wasn't—

Something grabbed her. She had no idea what it was, because it was invisible. No. Correction. She didn't know what it was except for the very large, very intensely yellow and scaley three-fingered claw grabbing at her ankle and pulling her up in the air.

The pram lifted with her because she was holding it. In fact, in the first reaction to feeling herself lifted, she'd grabbed the pram with both hands.

But she heard Bug squeal in fright as the pram tilted at a crazy angle, and let go of the pram with one hand to reach for Bug's leg and grab him about the ankle. Just in time, as the belt around Bug seemed to have come undone, and the pram went completely sideways, and would have dumped him.

Bug started crying fully, as he had beside the path, his voice that of a human baby in deep distress, and Albinia, without thinking, let go of the pram to grab him about the middle with her other arm, and hug him to her.

The hug was probably not as comforting as she wished it were, because by now, Albinia was fully upside down, her skirts around her ears, probably showing her ankles, not to mention her underwear, to the world. What was worse was that she couldn't see anything for the cloud of silk around her face.

She heard the pram hit the ground with force. She felt them climbing higher. She wondered how high they were, and whether everyone for miles around could see her underthings. Her face felt very hot. She thought how horrified Mama would be. Then realized the only people she could possibly be shocking, the only more or less fully human people who might have a view of what was happening, were her brothers and Lord Michael. And maybe Papa. And except for Lord Michael, "fully human" was a stretch to apply to any of them.

And suddenly she was laughing, loud and, even to her own ears, hysterically.

Bug stopped crying, and she could feel his little body tense in her arms.

With an effort of will, she stopped laughing, and swallowed hard. She felt as if her throat was raw, whether from laughing or from being transported, very fast and what felt like very high up in the air indeed. It was hard to summon a thread of voice, but she managed it, and said, "It's all right, Bug. We'll figure it out. I won't let anything bad happen to you. I promise."

She had absolutely no idea how she could keep such a promise, but if she had any say in it, she meant to. "I will protect you," she said. "To the best of my ability." Unsaid was that she wasn't quite sure how good her ability was against threats like the ones she'd been facing. Sure. She'd kept them alive so far, but how long would she be able to do it?

It seemed to her like Bug had calmed down, and later she wondered if he'd gone to sleep, because his breathing became slow and regular. And then even later, there was a little trill that might be a baby snore.

She wished she could sleep. The claws around her ankles—there was one around each ankle now—hurt. They clasped her so tightly that she was sure they would leave an imprint. And she felt as though her legs were half-frozen and quite asleep, having lost all blood circulation.

She also imagined she looked a fright, but that couldn't be helped, could it? Still, worrying about how much of a fright her clothes and hair were was, after all, a good way not to worry about where she was going or what might wait there.

She wondered if the king of Fairyland's card had dropped out of her clothes. Or the anti-molestation charm. Not that she intended to do anything about it just now, because applying such strong magical remedy would probably cause her and Bug to tumble through the air, suddenly free, and dash herself upon the path, just as the pram had.

On the other hand, she would like to know she had it for later. Because she remembered all too well the dank cave under the path, and the creature who wanted to cook and eat Bug. Surely it couldn't be that bad this time, could it? But the back of her mind told her that it could very well be worse.

After what seemed like an unimaginably long time—but frankly could have been minutes in the darkness of her upended skirts, and holding a little sleeping gryphon. How would she know otherwise?—she felt them losing altitude, and then felt herself being gently set down.

The gently part was good, as she was put headfirst, on a definitely hard surface. The claws gently allowed her to pivot, until she was lying on it on her back with Bug in her arms.

Whatever it was, it felt cold and hard like stone. The claws let go, and she heard wings flying away. Giant wings.

She let go of Bug and tried to free them from the mess of her enveloping and upended clothes. It was easier said than done, since—she wouldn't have known, since she hadn't put these clothes on. They were magicked on her—she appeared to be wearing at least two layers of petticoats, a dress and an overdress, the sort of clothes that usually necessitated a lady's maid to don.

She managed to free her head from the last layer of petticoats and blinked. She was, as far as she could tell, lying down in a balcony carved entirely of alabaster, and near a glass door. Above her rose what looked like multiple white towers.

With immense effort, which included massaging her legs that had gone all pins and needles, she managed to collect herself and sit down, pulling her skirts down, so she was fully decent. Bug sat up on her belly and looked at her, opening and closing his beak, while he blinked his little eyes in confusion.

While she didn't have much experience of babies, she was very sure there would be a monumental scream erupting any minute, and she really didn't want that.

For one, she didn't know where she was, nor where the owner of what looked like a magnificent palace was. Or what he was. It was entirely possible she was trespassing and she didn't wish to call attention to them.

She felt for the king of Fairyland's card on her sleeve. She'd take herself and Bug there for a few moments. They'd recoup, and then—

She closed her eyes and thought of the room where the king had received her. Really thought. Really hard. Nothing happened. Absolutely nothing. And that wasn't right. Had the king been toying with her? Had he lied to her? No. She'd felt the magic in the thing. She could still feel the magic in the thing, but now it felt somehow damped, stopped. Like...like someone had thrown a blanket over it.

But who could do that to the magic of the king of Fairyland?

"No, Bug," she said, as she heard him draw in a deep breath. She put as much authority into it as she could. "No, Bug. We must be silent. Al will take care of you, but you must not cry."

It hung in the balance for a moment, his blue eyes blinking, full of tears, and the little beak click-clacking. But he didn't scream. And she took a deep breath.

Her legs still hurt and felt very cold, but she had to stand. She and Bug had to find out if there was anyone in this palace who could help her. Or of course, if anyone in this place intended to eat her or Bug.

She stood, shakily, holding on to what felt and looked like a very elaborate white marble banister. She stood for a moment, till she could trust her own limbs. Then she bent and carefully picked Bug up and turned to the glass door. If it were locked, she might have to break one of the panels to reach in and unlock it.

But the beautiful handle, in the shape of a...gryphon in flight? Moved under her hand, pulling down, and allowing her to open the door.

A step inside, and she realized she was in the most beautiful bedroom she'd ever entered. It was prettier and grander than even the Ainsling townhouse.

There was a massive curtained bed, with gossamer curtains in tones of pale green, that fluttered in the breeze from the open door. The bed itself was covered in a green silk counterpane, and had a multitude of fluffy, green silk-attired pillows at the head. After her ride, Albinia felt like dropping into it, and resting a long time. But who knew whose bed it was or how annoyed its owner would be? She'd heard enough fairy tales in her childhood to know one didn't flop uninvited into an unknown bed. She could be turned into something horrible or sleep for a thousand years or something. Though to be fair, young ladies seemed to have a dispensation from such rules. But as for young ladies and a baby gryphon, that was a completely different idea. And the young ladies who could safely lie down on beds were also usually princesses and very pretty, while she was neither.

The baby gryphon was trying to fight free from her arms, but she ignored him. There were bedside tables, two, with spindly golden legs topped with marble. And there was a vanity, with a lot of bottles and boxes atop of it, and quite the largest mirror Albinia had ever seen, hanging on the wall over it. Next to the vanity was a frilly green chair, with another table—smaller—next to it. There were books on the table. A vast wardrobe, with many doors, took up the opposite wall entirely.

She held tight to Bug as he tried to squirm out of her arms, and opened one of the doors. Inside it were dresses. She opened all the doors. Many, many dresses, of every kind that Albinia could identify, from day dresses to ballgowns. She'd never seen a ballgown in reality, but she'd seen enough drawings in the pages of *La Belle Assemble* to identify them. There were also capes, muffs, gloves, shawls, and, in the last compartment, a lot of boots and shoes.

The thing is, they all looked one size. And, unless she was very wrong, they were all her size.

She was so shocked, she didn't react as Bug managed to get out of her arms and headed straight for the bed, where he sat up, making cooing sounds of approval.

She turned and looked at the rest of the room. It looked to her like there was a note wedged into the mirror frame, at about her eye level.

Walking across, she saw there was indeed such a note. And getting close enough, she could read it. It was written in a most elegant hand, and it read,

"Your Highness, we apologize for the inconvenience of your mode of travel, but hope you understand the honor you give us in being our guest.

We only want to make you happy and provide you with everything you could hope. In fact, if anything is lacking for your present comfort, do not hesitate to let us know. We hope you consider this, henceforth, your own home."

The letter wasn't signed. What's more, Albinia was fairly sure it wasn't to her. Someone had been sent to kidnap a princess—something that probably happened every day in Fairyland—or sent a semi-sentient fetch to kidnap a princess, and because of the finery, the king had given her, she'd been mistaken for the princess.

"Oh, bother," Albinia said aloud. And hurried to Bug, who was bouncing wildly on the bed, ready to pick him up and leave, if necessary, by climbing out the balcony. Sure, they were a floor up, but she was almost sure there was a tree nearby.

There was a knock on the door.

His Sister's Keeper

ALBINIA DID THE ONLY thing she could think of. She grabbed at Bug, held him tightly, one hand closing his beak, and dove under the bed, beneath lustrous satin ruffles.

There was a moment of shock, because whatever else she expected, she counted on some dust under the bed. Even in Mama's very well-run house, where the house servants lived in fear of Madame, there had been a little dust in less seen places, which never got cleaned but once or twice a month.

Here, the carpet under the bed, part of the same immense and plush rug that covered the rest of the room, was as clean as the visible parts. There was a faint smell of lavender, but neither Albinia's nor Bug's sneeze reflex was triggered, which, considering Bug was making strenuous efforts to squawk, was good.

Hiding under the bed, Albinia was nearly deafened by the beating of her own heart.

She heard the door open, very carefully, and someone slip in. And she tried to stay even quieter, which meant moderating her breathing.

The door closed, and a throat cleared. "Al?" a male voice asked at the curious junction of whisper and careful low-voiced enunciation. "Al? Where are you?"

It was Edmund.

Albinia started to move towards the edge of the bed, then wondered if it was Edmund, truly, or only his voice. She'd lost the little trowel that would tell her who was friend or foe, and she didn't know whose palace this was, nor what their abilities were, after all, or what they might be capable of. She knew that whoever owned this place surely had enough power to block the king of Fairyland himself, so he was dangerous. She'd stay quiet. But she must have made some scoff sound as she shifted, because the steps bent towards the bed, the ruffle lifted, and Edmund was there, his face upside down looking at her and blinking in some astonishment.

"Albinia," he said, sounding shocked, even though his voice hadn't raised above minimum sound. "And is that the crown prince that was kidnapped?"

Albinia gave up. If it was an imitation of Edmund, someone had gone through an extraordinary amount of trouble to make sure he looked and sounded like himself. She sighed and shuffled from under the bed, still keeping Bug's beak closed as much as possible.

She emerged, feeling worse for the wear, blinking in light that suddenly looked too bright, and assessing Edmund. He was almost certainly not a semblance of Edmund, but the real thing. The trick was that if he were an image of the brother she knew, he'd be unchanged from the last time she'd seen him, and that was not true.

He was undoubtedly Edmund almost two years older. He'd grown. There was a darker shadow of beard on his skin, no longer the "does he have facial hair or not?" of his younger days. He looked, for lack of a better term, more manly. Which, in Albinia's limited experience of men, meant a lot more like Papa or Samuel. But he was attired in the most ridiculously extravagant fashion, in a suit of clothes that looked more Elizabethan than present day, and was, to make it worse, a bright pink satin, worked all over in an embroidery of seed-pearl arabesques. He also wore a gold chain around his neck, the links too large and gaudy for anyone's taste. From it hung a stylized gryphon in flight, much like the handles on the furniture. His hair was grown and tied back, a lot of it, and blond rather than Papa's mouse-brown. Al understood that the boys' Mama had been a blond beauty. But the eyes were the same that Albinia remembered, the keen blue-grey eyes of the brother who had taught her to be observant and careful and quiet while watching birds. The brother who'd taken her on daylong adventures along the cliffs, patiently explained everything, and never complained at the slow pace or inane talk of a much younger sibling.

Those eyes were watching Bug with extreme fascination. "Is it really the crown prince?" he asked. "It looks like him. Or rather, it looks like the paintings of his father as a baby."

"The king of Fairyland said he was the king of the gryphons," Albinia said, shocked that her voice was in a normal tone. Edmund looked at the door, waved his hands frantically, then, almost as an afterthought, dropped something magical over them.

Albinia wasn't quite sure what the something was. It felt like a blanket made of magic, soft and dampening.

She looked up at where the unseen-but-real-magical-object was.

"No one will hear anything we say. More importantly, no one will hear him, if he gives vent, which I think he's about to do?"

Al let go of Bug's beak, and was treated to an indignant squawk, and a frown, but no more, as Bug was fascinated by Edmund. He clicked his beak at Edmund, smiled at him, then jumped from Albinia's arms to his and hugged him.

This was not exactly a surprise, as every bird ever seemed to think Edmund was very interesting and impossible to ignore. In fact, the only surprise was that gryphons, despite their nature as part-bird, part-lion, supposedly human shifters, and all sentients responded the same way. Then again, Bug being young probably made him more like a bird.

"Winning little thing, isn't he?" Edmund said, smiling, and ruffling the little tuft of feathers standing up between Bug's ears. "But he—and we—will be in big trouble if he's found here."

"But why?" Al said. "Why would Bug be in trouble, or us, for that matter? And where are we?"

"Lord, Al. Bug? You named him Bug?"

"There's no reason to make much of it. I didn't think I was naming him. Just bestowing a nickname. The king of Fairyland has already been suitably shocked."

"The king of—" Edmund dropped onto the bed, as though his legs had lost the power to support him standing. Bug took the opportunity to ruffle at his hair, in what was obviously a return gesture, all the while babbling comfortingly. "Al. Little sister. I think it's time you told me exactly what kind of trouble you've been creating."

This was just the sort of unfair pronouncement that Albinia despised from her older brothers. After all, it wasn't as though she'd gone looking for her father and disappeared. Or, for that matter, as though she were to blame for her father going missing. She'd only come on this wild goose chase—swan chase, as it might be—to help her siblings. And yet, they'd treated her as though she were still the toddler who, by accident or willfully, messed up their more grown-up pursuits.

She started to open her mouth to defend herself vigorously, and then stopped. There had been enough to her adventures to tell her they might not have much time. And besides, Edmund had dropped a silencing charm in a place where the spell the king of Fairyland had given her didn't work. All of which went to ring alarm bells, and silence the younger, aggrieved Albinia, and her justified upset at her brother's unfair accusations. Whether Edmund thought she was to blame for this or not was of remarkably little import. What mattered most was that she had in fact been caught in some very strange adventures, and was now in a place and a predicament which she couldn't fully understand.

From what she had seen of this land and its perils, not understanding something like this could get her or Bug roasted. Or worse.

She told the sum of her adventures as fast and succinctly as she could. She noted that Edmund's eyebrows rose at her falling in with Michael Ainsling, and even more when she explained about the letter that Papa had sent Michael. He did chuckle at the parts that involved Papa, as though this were an old and accustomed tale, and something he was quite familiar with. Since Papa had left before Albinia had been born, it was not for her, and some of Papa's behavior had seemed unnatural and hurtful, but perhaps it was just his way.

Bug fell asleep in Edmund's arms, one little hand clutching at Edmund's neck ruffle, as though to prevent his falling.

Edmund almost spoke up when the king of Fairyland came into the tale, then looked more puzzled than anything.

"May I see the card he gave you, Al?" he asked, when she was done with her tale. She handed it over, somewhat reluctantly. He held it in between his fingers, and frowned. "Nothing bad about it, and no traps. Very well. You may keep it, in case things get fraught enough."

Al huffed at being given permission when she'd not asked it, and Edmund smiled, showing that he'd at least grown enough to be aware of when he was irritating.

"I can't explain. There are in fact many things I can't explain to you, Al." And in response to the frown she felt forming on her face, he sighed. "Yes, I'm aware it is not fair, and it is not really playing the game, and furthermore, it is possibly dangerous. But not as dangerous as it would be for you to know the truth right now. There are levers the people here could manipulate, and things they could get from you if you knew them. And I'm not yet at the point I'm willing to risk that." He freed a hand from holding Bug and held it up, in a demand for silence. "No, listen, Al. For good or ill, this is how it stands. You cannot tell them what you do not know, and your knowing only the essentials will keep you and this little one safe.

"In fact, securing his safety is the most important thing, as it might be the hidden card we all need to break this deadly game."

"Deadly game?" Al asked, confused.

Edmund sighed again. "This is the palace of the king of gryphons. His Majesty, Aodh the Bright, was killed with his wife, Muirn the Fair. They were attacked and killed, and their egg was stolen from the royal nursery, and the hatchling, days from emerging, was counted as lost. From the feel of magic around him, and from his features, I'm sure this is him."

"But then—" Al tried to order her thoughts. Since her talk with the king, she'd thought that there was a high possibility that Bug was a very important personage, though why this should apply to her, too, was beyond her understanding. Perhaps the foster mother of a gryphon king was a sort of princess in their strange lands. What was it the king of Fairyland had said of them? "Of fairyland and yet not." Yes, that must be it. And still, she didn't understand. "If this is Bug's palace and Bug's court," she said. "Shouldn't he be announced? Won't they want to...crown him, or acclaim him or whatever it is gryphons do?"

Edmund looked thoroughly miserable. "In effect, why not tell them so they might kill the fatted calf and ring the bells in joy and all that? Well, little sister... When I said the royal family was killed, what you should be asking is by whom, and therefore who is in control of the palace."

Al's mouth dropped open. She'd been thinking of the whole thing as though they were in a mythical fairy tale, where monarchs were of course sometimes killed, but none of it meant much of anything, not in the long run. And the guilty parties were evil sorcerers, or a magical force, or something of the kind.

Though of course, in thinking about it, it made sense that the politics of Fairyland would mean someone would kill someone else, and it would all be the same as in the non-magical world. There would be some sentient entity who plotted against the royals and had brought about their downfall. It wasn't some impersonal force, but a personal one. And yes, there would perhaps be some magical rules involved, but even in the human world there usually were those, if she understood the whole plot with the vanishing princess of Britannia, now the wife of Michael's older brother, and how she'd been restored.

"You mean," she said. "The revolutionaries are in control of the palace?"

He nodded slowly and solemnly.

"And you're with them?" she asked, looking him up and down significantly. It was clear he was dressed for a royal court, and therefore he must be known and favored here. Surely.

He sighed again. "You could say that, though remember, Al, mostly I am on your side, and the side of our family. I came as you did, to free everyone. But birds do love me, and I got kidnapped. And they... They have been very nice to me, I think because they know I'm related to you. The new... Well, he calls himself king, though this little fellow here explains why he hasn't been able to command the powers of the king of gryphons, or sit on the ancient and sacred throne... Well, King Cormac, as he styles himself, would very much like to earn your hand in marriage, and I couldn't stop him from kidnapping you so that he could woo you at leisure."

"Woo me?" Al stared. "Me?"

"Well, yes. He thinks if you marry him, he will have the powers of the king fully. And I'm not sure he's not right, this little guy notwithstanding." Edmund sighed again, and it seemed to her as though he carried the weight of the world on his shoulders when he did so. "So, I could not stop him, and it occurred to me, with all the forces arrayed against you, there was possibly no safer place. And I very much doubt you'll fall for Cormac, because you're too sensible for that. And—all of this to say, Al, I have no idea how Cormac, who is, his ambition notwithstanding, a very sharp fellow and as shrewd as he can hold together, missed that you had this little fellow with you. How did he not see him?"

Al shook her head. "Perhaps the king of Fairyland did something?" she said. "It didn't seem to me as though he told me everything. Maybe like you, he thought my ignorance would protect me." She glared at her brother.

He almost smirked, then looked serious. "Well, perhaps so. And perhaps it will. But the truth, Al, is that we're now in no end of trouble. If this little one is discovered, he'll be killed. Yet, he's bonded to you, and we can't entirely rip him away. Birds—young birds—" Edmund looked down at the bundle in his arms. Bug was snoring softly, a high, musical sound. "Attach to their caretakers, and can pine themselves away if removed. And yes, I know they aren't fully birds. But when very young, they seem to react like them. We will have to get our other brothers to help." He paused. "Well, all except Samuel, of course."

"Our other brothers? They are here?"

"Yes. Cormac has been collecting us. All except Samuel, who he hoped would free—" He paused. "Well, that's neither here nor there, if Ainsling has got involved. The situation is not at all what I thought, little sister, and it could all tip into insanity at any minute."

Kingship and Kinship

THERE WAS NOTHING FOR it but to wait until Samuel calmed himself enough to be talked to. Not that Michael himself was calm. There had been a giant gryphon, and he'd swooped down and grabbed Albinia by the ankle.

For a sickening moment, as the pram crashed onto the path, Michael was sure that Bug would be dead in the debris. But once he could focus on it, he realized it was just the pram, and there was no living creature in it, nor even the remains of a once-living creature.

Instead, he focused on Albinia's form—upside down. How the poor girl would be mortified—as it retreated from view in the blue sky, the gryphon holding her winging desperately, at a great pace.

It seemed to Michael that this could not be the normal mode of flying of gryphons. Like condors or other large-winged beings, they seemed built for soaring. But this one seemed rather in a hurry, and he feared what waited Albinia at the other end. He wanted, more than anything, to intervene, but it seemed hopeless.

Probably. Samuel was still beating at the barrier and screaming, and that was surely also hopeless, but—

Michael cleared his throat. "Gabriel," he said aloud, and felt somewhat relieved that Samuel didn't react. But then again, nothing did. The clear air of the path didn't part, and Gabriel Penn, his older brother and king of Fairyland, did not materialize.

Well, and there was a reason for that, Michael realized. When he'd called his brother, he'd called him as his brother. And that, while important—he was sure some part of Gabriel remained human enough to care for his human family, else, why would he have had the talk with Michael, in Michael's dream?—was not an invocation. And Michael was also, as a young son, all too aware of how his importance was seen by his family. Shuffled to one side, and forgotten until it was absolutely necessary to attend to him.

He chewed on his lip and looked at Samuel. Bringing Gabriel here was dangerous, in the sense that it might very well set Samuel off again. On the other hand, it was the only thing he could think of for helping Albinia. If she could be helped. He couldn't leave the path himself, of his own volition.

If he understood the rules of the path, and he thought he did, then if he left the path voluntarily, he'd be throwing himself fully into the tender mercies of Fairyland, which, even if his brother was king, he had no great wish to experience. Further, Gabriel might not be able to help him if he did that, because, so far as he knew, there were competing rules and jurisdictions in Fairyland, and one or the other might be topmost at any given time. The king was king because in the ultimate instance, he could intervene, and because the king's personality influenced all of Fairyland. But some petty monarch of the glade, or some nymph or dryad might have more power over a rock, a tree, a particular place.

On the other hand, Michael was sure if you were taken from the path against your will or without your volition, you were not under the rule of faery. And therefore, they had no ultimate power over you. Of course, what that meant when some of the creatures could still kidnap, threaten and perhaps kill you was not very clear.

What was clear, though, was that the king should be able to restore one in such a predicament. Michael took a deep breath. "I call on the king of Fairyland, by the law of the path, to correct a breach."

He never saw Gabriel appear. There was no light, no explosion, not even the feeling that the air opened up. It was just that where there had been no one, there was now Gabriel, wearing the clothes he'd so often worn around the house: the somber, dark, correct but not showy outfit of Seraphim's valet.

He raised an eyebrow at Michael, and his expression was much what it had been when Michael treated him as a servant, even when he'd technically been one. "You rang?" he said, his voice echoing with irony.

But Michael wasn't about to indulge him. He didn't know if Gabriel's feelings had actually been offended, or whether the king was simply trying to be facetious to put Michael at ease. And it didn't matter in the slightest, as far as Michael was concerned.

He made his face stern, and spoke with absolute correctness as he would if Gabriel were a stranger, a dangerous creature of magic and tradition. "Albinia Blakley has been taken from the path against her will. I demand you restore her."

There was a moment, just a moment, when he saw a flicker of confusion and surprise in Gabriel's eyes. This moment made everything in Michael totter. Gabriel was connected to all of Fairyland. He was sure of that. He had heard the conversations between Seraphim and the Princess Royal. And that part was true. So how could Gabriel not know that?

Gabriel's eyes went, as though unwilling, to the other path, and lingered on the smashed pram. Samuel had stopped beating on the barrier and screaming. He'd gone eerily silent, but Michael wasn't going to look. Because he was too busy looking at his brother, and reading the changes in his expressions. Which were terrifying enough.

Particularly when Gabriel pursed his lips and then said a swear word, one that was just outside Michael's vocabulary.

"You didn't know she was gone," Samuel said, in an accusatory tone. "Some king."

Gabriel looked at Samuel for a moment, then made a hand gesture, and where the swan had stood, now stood a young man, still wearing the translator muzzle and nothing else. Gabriel made another sound, one of exasperation, and waved his hand again.

Michael was almost sure he recognized the outfit that Samuel found himself wearing as the copy of an outfit—trousers, shirt, waistcoat and superfine driving coat—that had been in Seraphim's wardrobe. All of it was in dove-gray and well made, including the embroidery on the waistcoat. There were also super-polished hessians, topped with a border of silver, and silver tassels. It was all completely out of keeping with what he'd seen of the Blakley family attire.

The strange thing being that Samuel didn't even react, but just looked down at himself, then back at the king of Fairyland.

He removed the translator muzzle tied around his face, though Michael noted it had changed sizes and didn't cut into his face. Then he sighed, and asked, "How can I get my sister back?"

Gabriel looked angry. Not at Samuel or even at Michael, though Michael took a step back before he realized that. The truth was that he'd rarely seen Gabriel angry. Truly angry. And this was true anger. A look of suppressed rage that, had it been on anyone else, would presage either fisticuffs or a duel at dawn.

But what Gabriel said was perfectly civil. He looked at Samuel, then back at the pram on the path. "No, I did not know. And the number of...laws that have been violated to allow that would be hard to explain. Not legal laws." Another look at Samuel, then an intent look at Michael. "By laws, I don't mean my decrees, or even rules agreed upon by my people. This is more akin to violating the law of gravity." He frowned. Then turned, and walked through the barrier on the path as though it weren't there. Michael didn't try to follow, but Samuel did, only to hit the barrier full-force. Michael ignored that, and Samuel's exclamation.

Instead, he watched as Gabriel righted the pram, and touched the broken wheels, the bent frame. The look on the face of the king of Fairyland grew even more thunderous, which should be impossible. Then he returned, striding firmly back to Michael's path.

"I think," he said. "I see how it was done, and why. She should not be in immediate danger. You two have two choices: you can desist from walking the path right now, and come with me, become in effect guests at my palace, while I deal with the current situation. Your other option is to continue walking the path, in the hope of overcoming the challenges and reaching the end. Because if you reach the end, Michael, you can demand Albinia's restoration, since she started the path with you." He frowned. "Whether that will also restore Bug or not, or how it would be in the circumstances, I do not know, because I do not have visibility into where she is, though I know who took her."

As Michael started to open his mouth to respond—and say he'd been the guest of the king of Fairyland once, and wasn't willing to repeat the experience, even if the king had changed—Gabriel held up his hand. "Before you respond, either of you, I want to make it clear that the path is about to get more perilous than you or anyone else on starting could have bargained for. I think we are looking at full war in Fairyland, where parties can declare for or against me, and for or against any of the other parties in this dispute at will, without notifying me or you or anyone else. There will be magic at war with magic, and the events will be quite uncontrollable. I'm not even sure what reaching the end of the path will mean at this point."

Samuel was frowning. "Do you mean to say," he asked in an unbelieving voice, before Michael could speak. "That the law of the path won't be obeyed? That Fairyland might openly refuse its laws?"

Gabriel nodded. "That is the very gist of it. The only thing I can do for you, and I've done it, should you continue the path or not, is to do what Albinia Blakley set out to achieve. You and your family are fully free of the curse of shape-changing laid upon you. Since the law isn't being respected, I have no reason to uphold a minor part of it.

"The bad consequences are that the witch who laid the curse has just felt it, and is likely to come looking for you. On the other hand, your father, when he realizes the curse is lifted, is likely to come to your aid, as well. If you're smart, you'll let those two fight it out."

"But if the curse is lifted," Michael said. "Why can't we abandon the path and go look for Albinia?"

"You can do what you very well please," Gabriel said, but sounded like he was telling Michael to go to the devil. "But the thing is that while the rules are being violated, if you stay on the path and meet the challenges, you can still get Miss Blakley back in a...lawful way. If you do not, on the other hand, I'll truly have no control over your fate, so if you abandon the path, both of you will be taken to my palace and kept safe as guests. You, Michael, because I will not have Seraphim descend upon my realm intent on rescuing you, and getting enmeshed in battles magical. And you, Master Blakley, because I will not give the other side more hostages in order to persuade your sister to do the unadvisable."

"My sister? The unadvisable. What can she do?"

"Can't you imagine?"

"No," Samuel said. "I cannot. She's a half-competent witch, but that's all. Her mama wouldn't allow her to be more."

"No, her mama wouldn't. But she's away from her mama. Bend your mind to what she can do."

Samuel frowned. "Enchant a quantity of sweets? Bespell birds to come to the hand? Those were the only strange spells I ever saw her do. Hardly world-shattering."

Gabriel opened his mouth, then closed it. "You truly don't know? I envy you. Again, if you want her restored to you, as you've known her, you'd best finish the path. If, on the other hand, you trust her to extricate herself ably on her own, then you should come with me."

Michael's head ached. He was almost sure the warnings that Gabriel was giving meant that Albinia was a strange and magical creature, the sort of being like... Well, like Gabriel himself. But Michael had met Tristram Blakley and didn't find him particularly formidable, and certainly not eldritch. So how could Albinia be something strange?

Perhaps her mother was elf or half-elf? Or perhaps some other peculiar breed of Fairyland. He'd heard strange things about dragons. In fact, he'd heard stories that made no sense about dragons. And all creatures of Fairyland were shapeshifters, as well. He knew his sister's fiancé appeared as a rather shy young man in Michael's world, for instance.

It was just like Gabriel, too, not to explain. He'd always been like that. Michael used to think it was just his pleasure in lording it over a younger, and therefore more ignorant brother, but right then he was not so sure of it.

There were things, he knew, in the realms of magic, which could be affected by mere knowledge of them. Still, he said, "Instead of envying us our ignorance, you could enlighten us."

"I don't doubt I could, but in this war I'm waging, it would not be advisable."

"You're not at war with us," Samuel said.

"For now, I'm not."

And that was the problem. Michael wished to say that Gabriel had become infuriating since becoming the king of Fairyland, but the truth was that Gabriel had always been infuriating, possibly because he was half-elf, half-not, or possibly because he was half-family, half-not, half-gentry, half-not.

The king of Fairyland might be at war with Fairyland, or portions of it, but Gabriel Penn had been at war with the world long before that.

"I thank you for the invite to your palace," Michael said. "But having enjoyed the status of guest of the king of Fairyland, I would prefer not to experience it again."

For a moment, the anger and smoldering irritation in Gabriel's face was displaced by stunned disbelief. "Michael!" he said. "You can't possibly think that I am that...creature."

"No," Michael said. "But if you are at war, I don't know who might suddenly succeed you. If the path affords some protection, however slight, I will stay on the path and take my chances. Perhaps thereby, I might at least rescue Albinia from this debacle."

Samuel stepped up beside Michael. "Well done, Lord Michael. I'll stay on the path, too."

Gabriel nodded. "Very well," he said, and waved his hand again. The path that Albinia had been on disappeared. The path was now just one. "So you have chosen. So might it be."

The Young Princess

BEFORE ALBINIA COULD EVEN think of what to tell Edmund, there was a knock at the door.

Edmund looked at the door, shook his head, tiptoed to the closet, opened it, reached in and it seemed to Albinia he opened the back of it. He stepped through, still holding Bug, and first the back panel, then the door closed behind him.

Albinia wanted to scream. Had she just let Bug be kidnapped out of her arms, without even complaining? She was fairly sure the person who had just left was her brother, Edmund, but was she sure he wasn't bespelled or otherwise in the service of evil? No, she was not.

But then the thought came to her that not even bespelled Edmund could be convinced to do something bad to a creature that looked much like a bird, and she felt a little better.

Still, her voice shook as she raised it and said, "Who knocks?"

Which was probably just the right touch, she thought, in retrospect, since in fact, if she had been dropped into this place all alone and not known where she was or what was expected of her, she would be very nervous and possibly upset.

Then again, she was nervous and upset, and confused, besides, about this whole thing.

"May I come in, Your Highness?" a female voice asked.

This dispelled Albinia's hope that the visitor was another of her brothers. Her voice shook even more as she said, "Ye— Yes?"

A bevy of maids came in. It was a word that Albinia had never thought to use about servants. Not that she and Mother had ever had personal maids, as such. Mother used spells to do the same turn. But when she dreamed of having a lady's maid when she grew up and hopefully got out from under Mother's thumb, she never hoped for a bevy of them. A lady's maid, perhaps, and a maid of all work, and maybe a cook.

But at least fifteen maids walked in, all attired in dresses of the finest cloth, if truth be told, better than her own at home. Granted, those dresses were pale blue and plain cut, surmounted with little white aprons, denoting the profession of the wearer. The caps on their heads were also white and ornamented with a little frill.

As they walked in, they stopped in a line and all curtseyed and lowered their heads at the same time. They looked like nothing so much as birds to Albinia, who had trouble not saying so, and also not curtseying back. They were acting like she was by far their superior, which denoted she shouldn't curtsey to them, in fact.

Instead, she took in their appearance. They were all uniformly more beautiful and older than she thought any single group of palace maids, even if this were a royal palace of sorts, should be. Pale-skinned, blonde, and all had regular features and large eyes. The only obvious differences, without looking at the details, was that some had blue eyes, some brown, and there was one, slightly taller than the others, with bright green eyes, like light on ice.

"Your Highness," they said in perfect harmony, as though they'd rehearsed it for months.

"Yes," Albinia said. "What do you wish?"

There was a moment of confusion. The girls, each looked to the other, and momentarily they all started speaking at the same time. Then the taller one said, "We are here to serve you, Your Highness. We thought you might wish to change out of your ruined dress, and perhaps dress into something suitable to meet the king, Your Highness."

"The king?" Albinia said, judging that this would be exactly how she'd behave if Edmund had never told her anything.

A smile bloomed on each little face, also on cue, as though commanded. "Oh, yes, Your Highness. King Cormac." The smile had a hint of that not-quite-malice but intent interest that young girls have when trying to arrange a relationship for one of their own. Or watching the relationships of those they consider famous and important.

"Who is this King Cormac?" Albinia asked. "And why should I meet him?"

They looked shocked, as if their faces were the face of a single being. "Why, Your Highness, he is the king of the Gryphon kingdom, Protector of the Winged, Might of the Air, Lord of the Suspended Isles."

While the untutored Albinia, say the same girl who had entered the path full of her own purposes and little caring what she faced or why would have responded to that long list of titles with a puzzled look and possible confusion, Albinia did know better. It didn't do her any good to—rightly—say she knew nothing of such honors or titles. Because these lists of honors and dignities clearly were important in this palace where she was an utterly unwilling guest. But being an unwilling guest meant she was at their mercy, at least to an extent. Which in turn meant she probably should not offend them or not too openly.

Also, she reminded herself, they had power over her brothers, who were also more or less unwilling guests here. And besides, Edmund had Bug, and if something happened to Edmund, something would happen to Bug. It was utterly ridiculous to be so attached to the little gryphon, but she was, in fact. And since according to the king of Fairyland Bug was the true king of the gryphons, she was probably dealing with an impostor.

She said the only thing she could think of: "Oh," but she strove to infuse it with a sense that she was immensely impressed, and she must have succeeded because the bevy exchanged looks, and smiled a little, as if very pleased at her reaction.

Though it seemed to Albinia that she caught something else, just a hint in the eyes of the green-eyed maid.

And that's all she had the time to think before she was submerged in a confusion of activity.

A hip bath was brought in and a line of footmen all attired in very good black suits—at least as good as the one the King of Fairyland had worn—came through, one after the other, carrying buckets of water and pouring it into the hip bath.

Albinia would have laughed at such a backward process in a palace that must be suffused and penetrated through with magic, but while the line filled the bath, her attention was claimed by the bevy, showing her a plethora of dresses, and demanding she choose one to wear.

Albinia had never in fact chosen her own clothes to wear, not even from the limited selection in her mother's house. The only time she'd put on something of her choosing was when she'd stolen Geoffrey's outgrown suit and donned it. Which was to say, at the beginning of this highly inadvisable adventure.

In fact, she'd never chosen so much as the color of ribbon she wore in her hair.

But now she was expected to choose from at least twelve dresses, all in different colors and with different levels of ornamentation, and she blinked in confusion.

As an alternative to what she felt like doing, which was to run screaming from the room, she chose the plainest of the dresses, because it was more like what she was used to wearing.

It wasn't much like any other dress she'd ever worn, mind, in that it was made of silk and spring-green, but it was like her dresses in not being entirely surrounded and choked by lace and frills.

It seemed to her this choice disappointed the bevy, and this pleased her, if for no other reasons but to be contrary.

Then there was the picking of the shoes, and she blindly pointed at a pair that looked like it wasn't so pointy it would crush her toes.

The footmen were done and bowed before leaving, in an orderly line.

Which was when Albinia realized the bevy expected her to undress in front of all of them.

Oh, dear. She'd allowed Lord Michael's housekeeper to help her into a bath, but that was one middle-aged, motherly woman who had retreated once Albinia was in the bath..

These were a lot of young women her age or a little older. They would be marking all her imperfections and possibly giggling. And probably trying to "help" her wash.

No one had told her there would be tests of fortitude, Edmund least of all.

The Deposed King

"YOU NEVER TOLD ME why you were in that place on the path, unable to advance, for however long it was for you. Months, as far as I can tell, by the reckoning of the time outside," Michael told Samuel, as they resumed the path.

He felt very kindly towards the man, which would have surprised him very much when he'd first met him in the shape of an irate swan. He still thought Samuel Blakley was a hothead and possibly a little insane. On the other hand, Michael could attest to the fact that having dealings with Fairyland made people a little insane, and also that being a hothead was not a crime, particularly when one's siblings were involved.

Samuel sighed. He looked a little abashed. "A little ahead here, not sure how far, there will be a palace sitting astride the path. In the palace there resides a deposed king, sent to Fairyland by an evil magician. To cross through his palace, he demands a task of us."

"Oh?" Michael said.

"Oh. You see, when he was transported, all of his private lakes, preserves and forests were transported with him. And to free him from his enchantment and return him to his rightful kingdom, he requires that we kill and cook all the game in his forests, and the fish in his lakes, and harvest all the crops in his fields."

"A standard magical challenge, then?" Michael said.

Samuel sighed. "Yes, it is, isn't it, one of the old fairy tale challenges. You do it all with some spell, of course, or perhaps just an insane amount of work that would take you months or years."

"But you didn't do it," Michael said, stating a fact. "I wonder why."

Samuel bit at the corner of his lip. "I can't rightly explain it. At first, I thought if I went into the forest to hunt the birds and the animals, I would be breaking my connection to the path, but that is not of course true, and once I thought about it, I realized it wasn't true. Any place you're required to go to fulfill a task given you on the path is a part of the path and will therefore be safe to be on. But—"

"But?"

"You'll see. There is something...a sense of something wrong. And the king seemed...odd. Like he wasn't fully present in his form, like the whole thing from the way he looked to his palace was a pretense. And when I asked him what game he wished cooked, he included insects, as though he weren't sure how humans lived and ate. It was like—"

"I see," Michael said. In fact, he thought he saw. Samuel had gotten scared. Surely, he knew at least some of the spells to perform the task necessary. But on the other hand, he more than likely had never performed them. Even highly magical families didn't hunt and harvest their crops by magic. That's what they had keepers and farmers for. It was a task that demanded too much granular discernment for your basic spell, anyway. No. Samuel had probably started the task, and gotten scared that he couldn't do it. Or perhaps tried to remember the spells and couldn't.

Well, Michael had no such fears. He knew that he could perform the task. Not strictly with magic, as such, truth be told, but with some of his magical machines. He could create machines on the fly and make them work to do all that harvesting and hunting and cooking in mere days. Having Samuel stand by to hand him screwdrivers and pieces would only make it quicker. They would be fine.

As they walked along the path, the weather changed. Or perhaps weather wasn't the correct term for it.

Above them, inky black, semi-translucent shapes moved, projecting strange shadows onto the path: shadows that looked like horses and fully armored men riding them, and things that had no name but had unsheathed swords and lances ready to strike, and rushed headlong.

From the other side, other shadows, less inky black and more blue-bright seemed to come, all of them as bellicose.

And above, too, great winged things flew with a sound like unfurled sheets in the wind.

Michael looked up, but most of the time could see nothing. Everything was hidden by the inky black not-clouds. Though he thought, momentarily, he recognized the vast and red shape of a dragon.

Samuel grabbed his arm and pointed to the left. There, running by the side of the path, completely ignoring them as though they weren't even there, was a troop of armed centaurs, galloping to some battle horn that sounded from beyond a massif of trees that seemed half enshrouded in fog.

Michael felt Samuel's hand shake and said, "It's just centaurs." He said it in as matter-of-fact a tone as he could manage. "My sister is engaged to be married to one."

Samuel made a low chuckle, and looked at Michael disbelievingly, and Michael didn't tell him he was not in fact joking.

He didn't tell him, because suddenly—though he'd been quite sure the road wasn't rising before—they were at the top of a rise in the road, and from there they saw another rise, upon which sat what looked like a beautiful fairy tale castle that had fallen into some disrepair.

Not to the point that things were coming apart, but it looked like its magnificent spires were much in need of a coat of paint, and its crenelated walls had become gray with dirt.

There were no flags or pennants flying, which seemed odd to Michael, because even if the king had been defeated, particularly in a magical battle, he would still be entitled to his own family's pennant and he'd never heard of a king not interested in flying the flag of his own kingdom, as though to proclaim that he was still very much the rightful king of the lost domain.

So it was with some dread and foreboding that he walked down to the vale, and then up the path to the castle's entrance, beside Samuel.

Samuel also didn't say anything, but perhaps in his case he was remembering his previous inability to win against the challenge.

Above the dark and slightly brighter, shapes kept moving and projecting ominous battle onto the path. Was faery already at war? Gabriel hadn't said he was going to war, only that he might have to go to war.

He sighed. It was what it would be.

The closed portcullis to the castle opening at their approach, and the drawbridge dropping over a turbid and muddy moat, did not reassure him.

Durance Vile

THE ENTIRE PALACE, LYING astride the path of Fairyland, looked like a forgotten residence, with vast echoing rooms devoid of all furniture, or else with what furniture remained shrouded and ghostlike under sheets.

Samuel and Michael walked through, and it seemed to Michael as though he were walking on some thick material that cushioned his steps, even when looking down he saw only stones. The back of his neck prickled with unease, but he kept his face impassive to hide it.

They walked through salon after salon. In one, there were bare bookshelves, besides the ghostly-shrouded furniture. He stared at it, feeling as though he'd seen it before. Had he?

Samuel cleared his throat and looking at him, Michael momentarily and unexpectedly met his eyes. Samuel gave an embarrassed grin, but his eyes showed fear, and suddenly Michael liked Albinia's brother a whole lot more than before. "Buck up, old man," he said. "I believe someone is trying to make us afraid."

The last syllable was not pronounced before, seemingly out of nowhere, there came a loud roaring, as though a lion were very nearby. Both Michael and Samuel stopped. But Michael's mind was of a kind that he couldn't long be scared by that sound, that sort of ridiculous effect.

He managed a chuckle. "Oh, really," he told Samuel. "I hate it when magical entities try to scare us by stupid means."

Samuel managed a sickly smile, but said, "Something doesn't want us to meet with the king?"

Michael lifted an eyebrow. That was certainly possible. They crossed the doorway of the room, walking into a hallway between the empty bookcases and were suddenly in a room lit by so bright a light that for a moment, for just a moment, Michael could see nothing.

And yet his mind retained a sense of having seen something: an image of a structure composed of glowing light points and light bars connecting the points, and inside it, something dark and raging.

He blinked.

They were in a vast throne room, echoing and immense. They stood at the beginning of a long red carpet, which traversed a vast marble expanse and at last climbed the steps of a platform, on which an immense throne was placed. The floor, the steps, everything, were the purest white marble, so clear and perfect it seemed to glow. More marble, in cylindrical columns, upheld a distant ceiling.

The throne itself was marble, though draped with a red cloak, upon which sat the most inoffensive man that Michael had ever seen. He looked like someone you might glimpse pruning roses, or perhaps planting them in some little cottage by the road.

Samuel started to bow, but Michael grabbed the back of his jacket and held him firm. To Samuel's surprised look, he whispered, "Never bow to anything in Fairyland. You don't know what it is, and bowing might be taken for agreement to its power and supremacy."

When Samuel answered with a dubious nod, Michael momentarily wondered why no one had taught the young man this, then realized that perhaps he and his family had gotten a little more instruction on Fairyland and its dangers, on account of Gabriel living with them. And Gabriel, before inheriting the throne of Fairyland, being even less trusting of faery than...well, than anyone else who'd had experience with it. Because his own experience was intimate and close up, and often from inside his own mind.

Instead of bowing, they walked in, side by side, bold as brass. No asking permission. No bowing. This deposed king was impeding their voyage. And he needed something from them, whatever that might be. They needed nothing from him, except that he stop obstructing them.

Closer up, Michael could tell the king had sparse brown hair and twinkling blue eyes that kept blinking, helplessly, in a confused way.

Thinking through everything that he could say and what it might mean in faery, Michael came up with words that gave nothing and stated the essential. "We crave passage on the magical path," he said. "And you obstruct it."

The man on the throne blinked at him, and gave a simpering, hesitant smile. "No problem at all," he said. His voice was odd. A whining sound, as though a punctured balloon, letting out air, were modulated through his mouth. "Provided you pay my price, young magician. If you kill and cook every animal in the woods that surround my castle, and you harvest all the grain from my fields, grind it and make it into bread, I will resume my kingship in my rightful kingdom and cease obstructing you."

Michael opened his mouth to demand to see these woods and fields, but Samuel was—very oddly—rubbing the middle of Michael's back.

Michael looked annoyedly at his companion and met—only—an unwavering stare as though Samuel were trying to speak through his eyes. And Michael realized the rubbing was actually forming...letters?

It paused, then restarted, and Michael spelled out in his mind the message conveyed by Samuel, "He wasn't like this before."

Michael actually took a step back as he thought. Complying with the king's demand would be a little time-consuming, but not difficult. He'd need to go into the bag of plenty and get enough pieces to build large machines, and set them loose on these woods and fields.

But the idea bothered him. Why did this king want all that food? There were no armies of servants ready to eat. And supposing he returned to his rightful kingdom, surely his servants had other food and had been eating, anyway, while he was away? And what rightful Lord wanted to denude his woods and fields utterly? In Michael's experience, Seraphim went through great trouble to preserve the animals on his land, so they could reproduce and continue to thrive. Hunts were careful and controlled.

Also, exactly what did it mean to kill and cook every animal in the woods? Did this also include insects and worms? And other small, non-edible life forms? And what kind of grain was in the fields, and why did it all have to be made into bread?

At some level, Michael thought, it sounded like this man had absolutely no idea what woods and fields contained. And while that might be possible, it would require the king of a vast kingdom. One so isolated, he never left his palace. Even King Richard knew what was in woods. Most kings did, being hunters.

He frowned at the king. "I require a moment with my associate," he said.

He pulled Samuel to a corner of the throne room, off the red carpet. If this were a natural room, it would be so designed that anyone on the carpet, approaching the throne, would be easily heard by the person on the throne. On the other hand, the edges of the room were safe. However, the back of his neck prickling was giving him the strong impression that no, this was not a natural room. None of this was natural. And he was starting to wonder if the creature on the throne was truly human.

So as he pulled Samuel, he pushed out a silence spell that he had learned when he was very young. He hadn't learned it precisely from Gabriel. He had in a way created it under Gabriel's tutelage, so that he could avoid his older brother's supervision, when Gabriel was given the invidious task of supervising Michael.

He pushed the shield into place and felt resistance, which further made his hackles rise, because it seemed exactly like the sort of thing Gabriel did to try to penetrate the shield. Not that he'd ever managed it.

It felt like faery magic.

"I don't think that's a real person," he said. "I think it's something magical pretending to be human. I don't like any of this."

"Well, he wasn't like this last time I came by," Samuel said. "He was a tall, blond man, very commanding."

From the throne, the voice emerged again, whining like a balloon losing air. "I don't see why you need to discuss it, young magician. You can do it easily with your magical machines."

Suddenly, Michael wanted to throw up or run. Memories assembled in his mind, creating a picture he did not like at all.

The Gryphon Throne

THE BATH WAS EASIER to get through than she expected. All the maids seemed to be in dread fear and awe of Albinia, so none of them dared so much as look up. It was strange to have them help her into the tub, and hand her shampoo and soap, all without looking up.

Even odder when they poured porcelain buckets full of warm water over her head without looking.

She was helped out of the tub, wrapped in warm, luxurious towels, then helped to dress, all without the maids looking directly at her, until she was fully dressed.

At which point, they led her to the vanity table in front of the mirror. The green-eyed maid then did look at Albinia as she deftly piled Albinia's red curls up in a hairstyle that Mama would doubtless stigmatize as much too adult and grand.

When she was done, Albinia stared in the mirror at a fancy court lady, someone she didn't recognize.

She'd no more stood up, wondering if the whole pile of hair would fall if she moved, when someone knocked at the door, and when a maid opened it, a young man appeared. Attired in an improbable suit of blue velvet, worked all over with gold embroidery and with amazingly curled, shoulder-length golden hair, he bowed at an improbable angle, that looked like he would tip over.

But he managed to straighten himself up, as he made a gesture with his right hand, describing circles in the air. "Most High and Gracious Princess,

Albinia, Lady of the realms of faery and light, of magic and power, you are waited in the throne room."

She nodded, while her mind tried to process.

The whole princess thing still bothered her, but she imagined she would have to go along with it. Of course, part of the problem is that she had absolutely no idea how a princess would act. So she opted for acting like Lord Michael when he was in his nose-in-the-air persona. Though she'd come to suspect he was actually absentminded or avoiding interaction, it would do.

Holding her head up high, she said, "Very well. You may lead me."

She expected the man to turn around and lead her, but this apparently was not to happen. Instead, he walked backwards, still bowed.

It was quite fascinating to watch, and a little strange. He walked backwards, flawlessly, while looking down at the floors.

Albinia found herself wondering if he had memorized the floors of the palace, so he could afford to move around this way. What would the training consist of? Years of walking half-bent and being quizzed? *Very well, young man, you are now in a tiled floor with yellow rugs, where are you?*

She found herself smiling at the idea and wished that Lord Michael was there so she could tell him. She sighed, and the young man looked up. "Most Gracious Princess, am I not going fast enough?"

"No, no. You are quite fast. Please continue," she said, and vowed to control her expressions of exasperation. On the thought, a point of interest arose, as the man, walking backwards, approached a huge double, golden door. But the doors were apparently bespelled, because they opened before the approach of his velvet clad behind.

They creaked ponderously on their hinges and flattened themselves to the side, as they continued. Which is when Albinia heard the steps behind her. She was not only being led by this ridiculous creature, she was also being followed.

Turning around, she saw all her maids following her. She wasn't sure they'd seen her, though, because as soon as she turned around, they all bowed. She had a moment of pure mischief where she wondered if she started walking the other way, would the door to the room open before the maids' ruffled derrieres?

But it would be childish to do that, so instead she turned around and followed the backing valet, while trying to ignore the *pit-pat* of maid steps behind her.

Past the doors was another seemingly endless hallway, with doors at the end. When those doors opened, she followed the valet into a vast room. The largest room she'd ever seen. Why, you could fit all of Father's manor into this one room.

It was opulent, too, to the point of blinding. Without turning to look, she had the impression of elaborate tapestries, and golden statues, and right there at the end, stairs, leading up to a throne. On the throne sat...

He was young, and handsome, and wore the highest fashions and a crown on his head. For some reason, Albinia had thought the would-be king of the gryphons would be a gryphon, but this was a human. Just a little older than Lord Michael.

The valet turned around and approached the throne in the same kneeling posture. Albinia was sure she was supposed to bow, particularly when the valet fell to his knees and announced, "The princess Albinia Blakley, Your Majesty!"

But Albinia was herself. She stood, head high, looking at the king, who smirked at her.

Two heralds from either side of the throne stood and announced, "His Majesty King Cormac, king of the gryphon kingdom, Protector of the Winged, Might of the Air, Lord of the Suspended Isles."

Albinia looked up at the blond, curly-haired king—was he really a king? Wasn't Bug the king?—and inclined her head in greeting more than fealty.

He danced down the steps from the throne. There was something about him, something that seemed to shimmer and gave the impression of slipperiness. Albinia frowned slightly and tried to look impassive as he approached her and said, "Princess. It is not often I meet my equal."

Old Enemies

MICHAEL STOOD ROOTED ON the spot as he stared at the thing on the throne. It had dropped its human aspect, or else, knowing what it was, Michael's eyes now saw it better.

Interacting tesseracts, like the ones he'd occasionally seen within Gabriel, danced within the creature, woven with a dark thread of something not quite substantial. He'd long since learned the tesseracts appeared when Gabriel forgot his human side, but he didn't think the being before him *had* a human side.

This was the same, but different. He couldn't explain it. It was unsettling in Gabriel, mostly because it was a measure of how much he was becoming the king of Fairyland and going away from the familiar figure of Michael's childhood, the half-brother who'd watched over him as much as Seraphim had.

These tesseracts were unsettling...in another way. The light swirled and changed in an oily way, and in the center of it all there was a sort of pulsing, something like a light under cloth.

Images crawled from Michael's memories of being caught in a web of energy while something riffled through his thoughts, his emotions, like a hungry scavenger.

And on the thought of it, before he could make a sound, ropes made of thought—which was a really bad description, but the closest he could conjure for the situation—came and wrapped around him, holding him immobile.

Aloud, he said, "You. I have no intention of doing what you want."

The thing on the throne, wavering madly between greasy light infusing tesseracts of dirty gleaming evil, and a man who looked less insignificant and considerably more insane than he had before, cackled. "Too late," he said. "You already have."

Michael opened his mouth to rebut, but the thing laughed. "Oh, you think I wanted you to fulfil the task? Not a chance of that. I knew exactly how stubborn you were. Remember, I played for months with your mind. I know the limits of how much I can force you to do. No. You are the bait, Duke's son."

And Michael saw it. Saw it clearly and with a sudden sinking feeling in his stomach.

If he was bait, it could only be for his brothers. He managed to stare the thing in the eye—when it had eyes—and strove to make his face stone, like Seraphim when he was seriously displeased by something that Michael had done, but at the same time also scared that something would happen to Michael. It had taken years for Michael to see the fear behind stone-faced disapproval, and he hoped his face was as effective. "I will never call them."

"Oh, won't you?" the deposed king of Fairyland asked.

Through Michael's mind, the memory of precisely who this was roared: Gabriel's uncle who had tried to kill him more than once, the creature who had used Fairyland as a blunt weapon to attack and despoil the worlds of men, the corrupter of the innocent, whose tendrils in his own world had almost destroyed Michael's family.

It snickered. It snickered like a naughty boy who has caught an animal unawares and is about to torture it to death. "Well, then, I guess I will have to make you."

Then there were pincers of power in Michael's mind, moving things around.

Into his memories of childhood, the innocent games with Caroline, the warm images of his childhood pony Buttercrumb, the gentle, well-lit corners of his mind where he spent time hiding when reality became harsh suddenly turned. Caroline grew to ten feet tall and chased him through the garden, to stomp him with her boots. Buttercrumb grew carnivorous teeth and chased him with an evil look in his eye. The barber robot could not be killed, and kept trying to kill him, while maiming everyone else in the household.

And all of it was Michael's fault. All of it. His past drowned in an endless morass of guilt and regret.

Michael tried to assert the reality, the memory of what had actually happened, but nothing worked.

It felt like his mind was not his own, like the memories had changed, really changed, and the real world would now be like that, too, a place of endless nightmare and suffering.

Except Michael remembered this game. He remembered none of it was real.

He remembered something Gabriel had told him when he had come back from Fairyland. "It's all games, Michael. All illusions and games. They can't actually change your mind or play with your memories. I'm more susceptible because part of me is of them, but you? You they can't touch. They can only pretend to and play over your fears and your horror. They can make you wish you could clean your thoughts with a good scrub sponge, but the truth is they're not your thoughts. They're the thoughts of the evil in Fairyland. It's old, thorough, and very proficient evil. And it can't vanquish you, because you are a son of Adam, and you can't be conquered by the shadow world. But it can make you feel it did.

"They took you because you're a child. They delight in taking children. Children don't know any better, and don't realize that the horrors they're being shown are not actually in their minds."

Well, Michael wasn't a child anymore. And the horror stopped here, now.

He shook himself. He wished the ropes of thought away. They were the ropes of his thought, he realized. The thoughts and fears of his childhood and the memory of the horrors that had been inflicted on him while prisoner in Fairyland had combined to paralyze him.

But he wasn't a child. For years now, he'd wanted to stand up for himself, to make his brothers recognize him as the adult he hoped to be.

Well, it started now.

He tried, but nothing happened. And he could feel the tesseract-fractured thing laughing.

Almost reflexively, his hand went to his pocket and found the beautiful snuffbox the servants at his estate had given him. With immense effort, his mind in turmoil, he pulled it out. Perhaps he could throw it.

He flicked the lid up.

A cloud of something blazingly bright poured out, scintillating in the air.

Like that, the ropes, the feeling of being tied down, and the feel of something greasy and dark binding him vanished.

It was a defense spell, he realized. The staff had given him a defense spell. The box fell from his nerveless feelings as relief overtook him.

He stood straight, and mentally slapped away the mind of the king of Fairyland. "Sickly, dark nonsense," he said, and was pleased his voice sounded every bit as haughty as Seraphim in his *Duke* moments. "Stop it. That's not me, and none of it is real."

He dusted his clothes, and advanced towards the throne. "Stop this nonsense right now, you trickster, you fraud. Be gone from the path and let us continue."

For a moment, the creature looked as though he would fight back. There was a glimmer in his eye, something like the low animal cunning of a feral dog who intends to bite.

But Michael advanced. He wasn't sure what he intended to do, just that he'd had enough and he'd do something.

The creature turned to dark tesseracts again. "No," it said, and it was the petulant sound of a child at bay. "I will not. You will stay in this palace until you call for your brothers to remove it."

Michael laughed. "Not likely. You can't obstruct the path."

"Oh, no? Who are you going to call? Are you going to invoke the law of the path and call on the king of Fairyland?"

Michael realized that was a trap and frowned. And then out of nowhere an idea came. It wasn't real, and he didn't think that she would scare the creature, but he'd seen Albinia come up with the strangest ideas and pull them out of the most fraught situations, so why not this? And anyway, maybe Albinia would tell him whom to call.

He felt in his pocket and found the magic glass he'd put there. Did she still have the other end of it? He pulled it out and waved it around. "I will do worse," he said. "I will call Albinia Blakley."

To his surprise, this startled the creature. The king was back. "And what can she do, do you think? Your little friend?"

Michael knew Al was neither little nor harmless. Why, she was the most resourceful person he knew. He lifted the glass to his face. "Al, Al, who should I call to get me out of this? The deposed king of Fairyland is holding me prisoner and I will not expose my brothers to him."

"No," Samuel screamed. Michael had quite forgotten he existed. "No, you fool. Don't bring Al into this!"

It was too late. From the glass square, there was movement, and then Al, wearing the strangest, most elaborate coiffure. "Michael? Michael! I'll come to save you."

Which was not at all what Michael wanted. And only brought her into danger.

The binds came back and wrapped about him, the mind tendrils of the evil old king. The snuff box was on the floor, bright and open, and probably quite out of spells, or at least out of his reach. He tried to yell that Albinia should not come, but the square of enchanted glass shattered in a hundred pieces, and he felt magic binds crush him.

He'd been wrong all along. It wasn't a trap for his brothers, he realized. For some reason, the king of Fairyland wanted Al.

But why?

The Suspended Isles

ALBINIA HAD REACHED THE seventeenth fountain when she realized that if King Cormac compared her eyes to spring grass one more time, she might actually scream.

This would be, she reflected, extremely unwise. She was, after all, a prisoner on a floating island in the sky, surrounded by the pretender king's guards, with no clear means of escape. Screaming at one's captor, no matter how insufferable his poetry, seemed like poor strategy.

He'd already solved one of her confusions, which was why the gryphon court all appeared to be human. Apparently, gryphons were shape-changers. After toddlerhood, they could take human form when they wished.

Cormac had assured her that he'd never take magical form when inconvenient. Whatever that meant. He'd also praised his own non-human form by telling her he was a big, golden, "perfect" gryphon. Whatever that also meant.

Now he was back to praising Albinia. "And your hair," Cormac continued, oblivious to her inner turmoil, "is like the sunset over the copper mines of—"

"Your Majesty is too kind," Albinia interrupted, because she truly could not bear to hear what copper mines had to do with anything. Certainly not with her hair. So she had red hair. Must he go on about it? She kept her voice level and her face pleasantly blank, the way she'd learned to do when Mama was in one of her moods. "But surely you have more important matters to attend to than walking with me through your gardens?"

Cormac smiled. It was the smile of a cat that has cornered a mouse and is in no particular hurry to finish it off. He was handsome, she supposed—golden-haired and fine-featured, dressed in his improbable blue velvet suit worked all over with gold embroidery. But there was something in his eyes that made her skin crawl. A calculating quality, like he was always measuring, always planning.

"Nothing is more important than ensuring my future queen is comfortable," he said smoothly.

Albinia's stomach turned. He'd been at this for hours now—ever since the fountain walk began. Gentle suggestions that she might find ruling at his side appealing. Carefully worded implications about her importance, her bloodline, her destiny. None of it made any sense.

"I'm afraid Your Majesty is mistaken," she said, for perhaps the twentieth time. "I have no interest in queenship, and furthermore, I am not of royal blood. I'm the daughter of a country squire who is an inventor of some fame, nothing more."

"Ah, but are you?" Cormac's smile widened. "Are you truly?"

Before Albinia could ask what he meant, her mind clicked and she realized something.

She was being hexed. Or whatever you called it when someone got into your mind and bespelled you to believe something.

Cormac was trying to enchant her into believing herself in love.

Albinia had excellent spatial memory. She imagined herself floating above them, and retracing the path around and around the various fountains with their mini-gardens. As she half-expected, the design was one she knew: a magical diagram that would bind someone's mind and will within it.

She realized its trefoil design was almost complete, and Cormac's low recitation of praise and pretended love was a spell. It had taken this long, and he'd been walking this slow because she was resisting and her power was stronger than he expected. Which was silly. She was just a middling witch and half-taught. But somehow, this would-be king found her magic and will hard going.

And yet he was about to imprison her forever.

He turned around, eyes shining. "Albinia Blakley, Princess of the faery realms, would you do me the great—"

He was about to take the last step and it would be done. She couldn't run. She couldn't speak. She tried to shake her head, but it did not work.

She remembered the charm her brother had given her in case Michael—Michael!—tried to importune her. For a miracle, her hand moved, and reached into her pocket. She grasped the charm tight and inserting her finger in the loop, broke the thread to activate it.

Something exploded. The king was thrown backwards and on his behind against a statue, on a very nice rose bush.

Something else happened. An impression like ripping fabric, like fabric was torn and like a binding on her was broken wide. Not the spell Cormac had tried to lay on her, but... Something old and strong.

Al! her pocket screamed.

Lord Michael's voice. Distant, desperate, but unmistakably his.

She put her hand to her pocket and pulled out a piece of glass she thought she'd lost. Michael appeared on it, looking scared and pained. He said something, but she couldn't hear him, just retained the idea he needed her.

She felt for him, and felt him on the path. "Michael?" she said before she could help herself. "Michael! I'll come to save you."

"No," Cormac said sharply. He stood up faster than he should be able to. And suddenly his hand was on her arm, gripping hard enough to bruise. "No, you're not going anywhere."

The pleasant pretense dropped from his face like a mask. What remained was cold and calculating.

"The little Ainsling boy, all alone and in trouble. How presumptuous of him to call you! You will not go."

Albinia tried to pull her arm free, but his grip was iron. "Let me go."

"I think not. You see, I've invested far too much effort in bringing you here to simply let you fly off to rescue your sweetheart." He tilted his head, studying her. "Though I confess, I'm curious. Does he know?"

"What? He's not my sweetheart, so there's nothing for him to know!" Albinia said, though she felt her face blazing red.

"Don't pretend to be a fool," Cormac said. "Does the Duke's son have any idea what you really are?"

"I don't know what you mean," Albinia said, but her voice shook. Her power unfurled immense, incontrollable. Where had it come from? Who was she? Something was very wrong. Her voice shook as she spoke. "I am Albinia Blakley, nothing more."

"Does he know about your bloodline, my dear?" Cormac's teeth flashed. His fingers dug into her arm. "Your magnificent, terrible bloodline." Cormac's eyes glittered. "You must know you're not Tristram Blakley's daughter. Oh, perhaps your mother deceived him into thinking so. But you know the truth, don't you? You and I both know the truth, don't we? You're the daughter of the deposed king of Fairyland. You have all the power of faery. And if I marry you, your blood will legitimize my claim to the gryphon throne and give me power like no king had before." The look in his eyes was of a famished man seeing a cake.

The words hit Albinia like a physical blow. Daughter of the deposed king? That couldn't be true. That couldn't possibly be—

But somewhere deep inside, a small voice whispered that it made a terrible kind of sense. Her power. This terrible power that had somehow been unleashed. Her mother's paranoia. The way Mama had always kept her isolated, controlled, watched.

Mama! She realized the charm was designed to break bonds on her. And it had. Mama had been taking her magic and using it. Hiding it from Albinia herself!

"I see you're beginning to understand," Cormac said softly. "Your mother slept with the last elf king of Fairyland until he abandoned her. She was already carrying you when she seduced Tristram Blakley into marriage. A clever woman, your mother. She gave you legitimacy, a respectable name, a place in the world. All while hiding what you truly are so the mortals wouldn't get ideas."

"No," Albinia whispered.

"Yes. And now you're going to marry me, and together we'll—"

"Al!"

The shout came from behind them. Albinia turned her head—as much as Cormac's grip allowed—and saw Edmund running toward them across the fountain gardens. In his arms, wrapped in a blanket, was Bug.

Relief and terror warred in her chest. Edmund was here, Bug was safe, but they were also in terrible danger. Why had they come here?

"The concealment charm broke," Edmund said. "Albinia, we must run."

The bond Cormac tried to create, Mama's bonds on her magic—how strong *was* that charm, to break every binding in the vicinity?

Cormac looked like a man seeing the impossible. His face went white, then red with fury. "Who are you carrying, Blakley? That can't be the spawn of my enemy. That's impossible. That creature should be—how did you hide—"

He released Albinia's arm and strode toward Edmund, one hand raised. Albinia could see magic gathering around his fingers, crackling and dangerous. He would hurt Bug.

"Guards!" Cormac shouted. "Stop them!"

Edmund skidded to a halt, breathing hard. He was still wearing the ridiculous pink suit from court, now rumpled and torn. Bug peeked out from the blanket, his little beak opening in distress.

"The court saw Bug. I came to you. Al! Run," Edmund panted. "Al, you have to run. He knows—he knows what Bug is—"

"The true heir," Cormac snarled. "The crown prince of the gryphons. I should have killed you when I had the chance, but I thought you were lost, gone, safely disappeared while still in the egg. How—"

He stopped, his eyes narrowing as he looked at Edmund. "You. You've been hiding him. All this time, using bird magic to keep him concealed." His laugh was bitter. "Of course. The bird-charmer brother. I should never have let you into my court." His hand remained raised and magic gathered.

Albinia felt for his magic and ripped it from his hand, then shoved him hard with her own power. He went flying backwards.

She grabbed Edmund's free hand. "Run to the edge," she said. "The island's edge. Now." She didn't have a plan so much as a feeling of what she must do.

Get to the edge. Find a way out. Rescue Michael.

They ran.

Behind them, Cormac shouted orders. She could feel his guards responding, materializing from behind fountains and hedges. The fountain gardens that had seemed so open and peaceful suddenly became a maze, a trap. His guard had always been there, waiting.

Albinia pulled Edmund through a gap between two circular gardens, her skirts tangling around her legs. She cursed the elaborate dress, the piled-up hair, the delicate slippers. None of it was made for running.

Bug was crying now, high wailing sobs that tore at her heart. She wanted to comfort him, but there was no time.

They burst through a hedge—Albinia felt branches scratch her face and arms—and suddenly they were in a different part of the gardens. One she hadn't seen during the hours of walking with Cormac. They ran down a slope with sparse bushes. Maybe there was a field or something. Perhaps—

And then she saw the rest of the landscape. Ahead, the palace grounds simply...ended.

They skidded to a stop at a stone balustrade, ornately carved with gryphons in flight. It stood at the edge of the island, as though to prevent the unwary from knowing it was happening. Beyond it was open air—they were on the edge of the floating island.

But there was also water.

A river flowed along the edge of the island, wide and rushing, disappearing into an endless plunge a hundred feet beyond them, its source some magical spring deeper in the palace grounds. The water rushed past them with tremendous force, heading toward the island's edge, where it ran around for a moment and then simply...fell off. Disappeared into the sky, presumably to fall as rain on the lands far below.

"We're trapped," Edmund panted. He turned to her and clutched Bug tightly, sweat on his brow. Behind them, they could hear shouting, the sound of many feet running.

Albinia stared at the river. At the white foam and the dark, rushing current.

And at the shape she could just barely see beneath the surface where the river curved around the suspended isle. Something large and sinuous, with a mane that flowed like seaweed.

"No," she said slowly. "We're not trapped. Not quite. Not yet." She had all that power. All that lovely immense power. *Princess of Fairyland!* She'd put it to good use.

"Al, what are you—"

"You have to trust me," she said. She looked at her brother, at Bug clutched in his arms. She remembered Michael needed her. Her delay in rescuing him was a constant ache in her chest. He needed her. He'd called for her. She would go to him.

But first, she had to make sure Edmund and Bug would be safe. She could weave a new concealment with all her power.

"I need you to stand very still for a few moments," she told Edmund. "Don't move. Don't speak. Just trust me."

She began to pull power, drawing on every trick Mama had taught her about binding and controlling. Pulling reality. But she wasn't binding the creature in the water. Not yet.

First, she needed to make sure her brother and the baby legitimate king of the gryphons could survive what was coming.

The guards burst through the hedge behind them, swords drawn. Cormac stepped through after them, his face twisted with rage.

"It's over," he shouted, loud enough they heard him. "There's nowhere left to run."

Albinia smiled. It wasn't a nice smile. She felt her power sparkling and deep, alien and yet part of her. It had always been part of her.

She couldn't port into the In-Betweener from here. But she'd find a way out.

"You're quite wrong about that, Your Majesty," she said. "I'm not running. I'm answering a call." And she began to weave the most complex spell she could even ever dream of.

Ride, Witch, Ride!

THE SPELL ALBINIA NEEDED was not one simple enchantment but a layering of protections, each interwoven with the next like the threads of a tapestry. She'd never attempted anything this complex, and certainly never under pressure, with guards advancing and a would-be king shouting threats behind her.

But she'd watched Michael work. She'd seen him build intricate magical machines with dozens of moving parts, each one precisely calibrated. And she'd watched Michael assemble his path-finder from components pulled from the bag of plenty, each piece fitting exactly into place.

Magic could work the same way. It had to. She could sense it, and sense, also, her magic, levels and levels of magic, unplumbed which she'd never used or even felt before. Glorious magic. Power she had never heard the like of.

She held out her free hand toward Edmund and Bug, palm forward. "Don't move," she said again.

"Al, what are you doing?" Edmund's voice was tight with fear. Bug had stopped crying and was staring at her with enormous blue eyes, his beak trembling.

"Making you safe," she said.

The first layer was the simplest: a don't-look-here charm, the kind pick-pockets used in crowded markets. She'd read about them in one of the books Mama had forbidden but which Al had abstracted from the home library, anyway. The charm made people's eyes slide past its target, finding anything else more interesting to look at.

She whispered the words and felt the magic settle over Edmund and Bug like a veil.

But that wouldn't be enough. Not nearly enough. Surely, a gryphon would have enough magic to see past such a thing, much less a gryphon king, even a usurper.

The second layer was harder: a true invisibility, not just misdirection. This required understanding how light worked, how it bent and reflected. She had learned it from Samuel when he was studying it with his tutor. She recalled her brother drawing diagrams in the air with his finger. Light could be bent. Redirected. Made to flow around an object rather than bouncing off it. Her brother had shown this with lenses, but magic could be a lens, too.

She pulled the magic through her intent, shaping it with her will and her understanding. The air around Edmund and Bug shimmered, then cleared. They were still there—she could feel them—but she couldn't see them anymore.

Edmund made a startled sound.

"Shhhhh," she said to the empty air where he stood. "I'm not done."

The guards were getting closer. They'd now have a clear view. She could hear Cormac ordering them to surround the area, to cut off any escape.

The third layer was the most difficult: a ward against finding. This was the kind of magic Mama used, dark and binding, the magic that had kept Papa and the boys trapped for years. Albinia hated it, hated the oily feel of it in her mind. But she needed it.

She thought of Bug, precious and small and the heir to a magical kingdom. She thought of Edmund, her brother who loved birds. And she thought of Michael, calling for her, needing her.

She couldn't save them all unless Edmund and Bug were protected first.

The magic fought her. This kind of binding wanted to trap, to control, to hurt. But she bent it to her will, forcing it into the shape she needed. Not a cage. A shield. A protection that would make Edmund and Bug unfindable by any means—magical or mundane—until they were truly safe.

The effort made her nose bleed. She felt the warm trickle and ignored it.

"Al—" Edmund started. She could still hear him, very faintly, but he was resonating through the spell. No one else would be able to hear him.

"No," she said sharply. "Listen to me. This binding will hold until you and Bug are safe. Do you understand? Until you're *safe*. Not until danger passes. Safe. Now run."

"But you—"

"I'm going to Michael. He needs me." She could still feel the pull, constant and urgent. "And you need to protect Bug. Get him back to his throne. His people need to know their true king lives."

"You can't go, Al. They'll hurt you."

"No. They won't. They can't. I must save Michael."

"The guards are coming," Edmund said, his voice shaking. "Al, they're—"

"They can't see you. They can't find you. Go. Somewhere. Trust the spell. Trust me." She paused. "And take care of Bug. Tell him...tell him I will come back for him when I can."

She heard a rustling sound and felt something small and warm press against her leg for just a moment. Bug, hugging her ankle. Then Edmund must have pulled him back.

"I love you, little sister," Edmund said softly. "Do not get killed. Please. Don't get killed."

"I love you, too. Please stay well."

She turned her back on the spot where Bug and Edmund last stood, and walked toward the river's edge.

The guards had formed a semicircle behind her, cutting off retreat. Cormac caught up to stand in their midst, his handsome face twisted with fury.

"There's nowhere to run," he said. "Give me the child and I might let you live."

Albinia smiled. Her nose was still bleeding, and she could feel magic thrumming in her veins, making her hands shake and her whole body vibrate. "I'm afraid I can't do that, Your Majesty."

"Can't? Or won't?" He took a step forward. "You think I don't know what you just did? Some clever binding to hide them? I'll break it. I'll tear it apart and find them and—"

"You're welcome to try," Albinia said. She was at the river's edge now, her back to the rushing water. "You see, I learned from the best. My mother might be a terrible person, but she knows how to make a binding stick."

She didn't wait for his response. She turned and dove into the river.

The current seized her immediately, tumbling her end over end. The water was cold, and far stronger than she'd anticipated. She fought to orient herself, to find which way was up, but the river was in control.

And then she felt it. The presence in the water. Large and ancient and hungry.

The kelpie.

It rose from the depths of the river, moving towards her, hungering for her flesh, and Albinia's first clear sight of it drove breath from her lungs.

It had the shape of a horse—a massive black stallion with a mane that flowed like underwater weeds and eyes that glowed a sickly green. But there was something wrong about it, something that screamed *predator* in a way no natural horse ever could.

Its teeth, when it opened its mouth, were pointed. Rows of them, like a shark's.

Water horses, the books had said, were beautiful and deadly. They lured the unwary to mount them, then dove deep and drowned their riders, feasting on the corpses at their leisure.

Albinia had no intention of drowning. She had no intention of being eaten. She would not let it happen. She resurfaced, took a deep breath.

With intent, she pulled power, fighting to focus despite the cold and the current and the terror. The binding she needed was similar to the one she'd used on Edmund and Bug, but reversed. Not protection, but control.

The kelpie lunged at her, jaws open wide.

Albinia spoke the first word of the binding.

Her magic lashed out like a whip, wrapping around the kelpie's neck. The creature screamed—a sound like grinding metal and breaking glass—and thrashed like something dying. The river around them churned into foam.

But the binding held.

Albinia spoke the second word, then the third. Each word was a nail driven into the spell, fixing it in place, making it solid. She was using Mama's magic, the cruel controlling kind, but she was shaping it with

Michael's precision. Each syllable had to be perfect. Each thread of power and binding had to be exactly the right strength, no more, no less.

The kelpie tried to dive, to pull her down into the depths. But the binding forced it to surface, forced it to obey.

Albinia spoke the seventh word, the ninth, the twelfth. The spell was complex, multi-layered, designed to bind a creature of pure malevolence to her will without breaking its spirit entirely. If she broke it, it would die. And she needed it alive and strong enough to carry her.

The final word left her lips like a blade.

The binding snapped into place with a vibration she felt through her bones.

The kelpie went still, its green, glittering eyes fixed on her with pure hatred. But it couldn't attack. Couldn't flee. Couldn't do anything but what she commanded.

"Take me to the ground," Albinia gasped. "Now."

The kelpie's body moved without its consent, rising through the water until its back broke the surface. Albinia grabbed its mane—the strands felt like wet silk and river weed combined—and pulled herself up. She straddled it, tightening her legs on its body.

The effort left her shaking. She was soaked through, her elaborate dress dragging her down. Her hands were already cramping from maintaining the binding. And she hadn't even started the real journey yet.

From the shore, she heard Cormac screaming orders. Arrows hissed through the air. One grazed her shoulder, and she gasped at the sudden pain. But she had no time for pain. No time for delay.

"Go," she told the kelpie. "To Michael. To wherever he's calling from. Now!"

The kelpie's muscles bunched beneath her. And then it was running, galloping across the surface of the water with impossible speed.

The river's edge approached. The place where the water fell off into nothing. Arrows flew but fell short of them. The frustrated pretender to the throne of the gryphons screamed.

They didn't slow down. The kelpie leaped.

For a moment, they hung in the air. Albinia had time to look down and see the world, the real world, not the suspended isles, spread out far below—forests and fields and distant mountains, all impossibly small.

Then they were falling.

Albinia screamed.

The kelpie screamed, too, a sound of pure rage and frustration. It wanted to kill her. Wanted it more than anything. It hungered to bite her, to tear her apart. The binding was the only thing stopping it from twisting in midair and tearing her throat out with those terrible teeth.

She could feel the creature fighting her control, testing every strand of the binding for weakness. And she had to maintain her focus, had to keep the spell intact, even as they plummeted through the sky. She bent will and strength to it. It was all she could do. And she would survive this.

The wind tore at her, ripping the careful hairstyle apart, sending her red curls whipping around her face. Her hands were locked in the kelpie's mane, holding on for dear life, her legs locked around its cold, pulsing body.

And then, impossibly, they weren't falling anymore. They were running again, but not on water. On air itself.

The kelpie's hooves struck something invisible with each stride, making ripples spread out across the sky like disturbed water. It was galloping through the clouds, between worlds, cutting through reality itself to answer the call that had brought them here. To obey her order and the binding on its very being.

The binding required maintaining. She had to keep it going. Albinia could feel her power draining like water from a cracked cup. Every moment of the ride took more from her: more concentration, more strength.

The kelpie tried to buck her off. The motion was sudden and violent, and only her death grip on its mane kept her in place. She renewed the binding, speaking the words through gritted teeth, but her voice was getting weaker.

Blood was running from her nose again. She could taste it, coppery and warm. Her vision blurred at the edges.

The kelpie tried a different tactic. It dove toward a cloudbank, thick and white and deceptively soft-looking. But Albinia had read enough to know that hitting clouds at this speed would be like hitting water from a great height. It would shatter her bones.

"No," she gasped, and yanked on the binding. The kelpie screamed in frustration but pulled up, skimming the surface of the cloud instead.

The moisture soaked her further. She was so cold now that she couldn't feel her feet anymore. Her hands were white-knuckled claws locked in the kelpie's mane.

How much farther? How much longer could she hold on?

The kelpie sensed her weakness. It tried to throw her, this time with a twisting leap that nearly succeeded. Albinia felt herself sliding, losing her grip. For one terrible moment she was sure she would fall, would plummet through the sky and die without ever reaching Michael.

But she wouldn't let that happen. Michael, Edmund and Bug needed her.

She pulled more power, drawing on reserves she didn't know she had. The binding tightened, and the kelpie shuddered beneath her. She could feel its hatred like a physical thing, beating against her mind.

Her vision was tunneling now, going dark at the edges. She couldn't feel her hands anymore, couldn't feel anything but the desperate need to maintain the binding, to keep going, to reach Michael.

I'm coming, she thought. *I'm coming, just hold on, I'm—*

Reality shifted.

They burst through something—a barrier, a membrane between worlds—and suddenly they were somewhere else entirely. A dark forest, a stone path, a palace in the distance.

The kelpie tried to kill her one last time. It reared up, attempting to throw her into the trees where branches could impale her.

It couldn't, because Albinia was already falling. She lost her grip, lost the binding, lost everything.

She hit the ground hard enough to drive the breath from her lungs. Pain exploded through her body. She tried to move, tried to stand, but her limbs wouldn't respond.

Through blurring vision, she saw the kelpie rear above her one final time. Free of the binding at last, it could kill her now. Could finish what it had wanted to do from the beginning.

But just as it reared and nickered in triumph, Albinia found somewhere a last spark of power and consciousness, and sent out a flash to sting the beast's nose.

It was nothing. It was like the fireball she'd flung at Papa.

But as it hit, there was a smell of burnt fish. The kelpie screamed. Suddenly, it turned and fled, galloping back toward whatever realm it called home with all the strength it had left. Perhaps even a creature of malevolence knew when to count its blessings.

Albinia laid on the cold ground, every part of her body screaming in agony. Her magic was depleted, her strength gone. She couldn't have stood if her life depended on it.

But she'd done it. She'd answered Michael's call. She'd made it. Except...she hadn't. She must go to him. Really go to him.

She laid there for a long moment, trying to gather herself. The pull from Michael was still there, but different now. Closer. More urgent. And beneath it, she could feel something else—a wrongness, a dark and oily magic that made her skin crawl even from a distance.

He was in trouble. Real trouble. And she was the only one who could help.

Albinia pushed herself up on her elbows. The world spun violently and she had to close her eyes until it stopped. When she opened them again, she saw the palace Samuel had described—the one that sat astride the path, blocking progress.

It looked abandoned and wrong. The white marble walls were gray with neglect, and there were no flags flying from its towers.

She had to get there. Had to reach Michael.

Her first attempt to stand failed spectacularly. Her legs gave out immediately and she crashed back to the ground, crying out at the fresh pain.

"No," she said aloud. Her voice was hoarse and weak. "No, get up. Get up, Albinia."

She tried again, using a nearby tree trunk to pull herself upright. Her hands were shaking so badly, she could barely grip the bark. Her dress was soaked through and torn, hanging heavy and useless around her legs.

One step. Then another. Each one was agony.

She thought of Edmund and Bug, hiding invisible and unfindable on the suspended isle. Waiting for her to make everything right. She thought of her brothers—all of them lost somewhere in this terrible place. She thought of Michael, calling for her, needing her.

She took another step.

The path was farther than it looked. Or perhaps she was just moving impossibly slowly. Either way, it felt like hours before she finally staggered onto the red carpet that led through the palace gates. She knew it had probably been minutes.

The portcullis was raised, the drawbridge down. As if something inside was expecting her.

That thought should have terrified her. But she was beyond terror now, running on pure stubborn will.

She stumbled through the entrance, into a vast echoing chamber. Her footsteps—uneven and dragging—sounded impossibly loud on the marble floor.

The palace was like a ghost of itself. Furniture shrouded in white sheets. Empty bookshelves. Dust and silence.

But ahead, she could see light. Bright, unnatural light, pulsing like a heartbeat.

She followed it, one agonizing step at a time.

Through empty salons and abandoned halls, leaving a trail of water and blood behind her. Her nose was bleeding again, and she thought she might have cracked a rib in the fall. Breathing hurt.

None of this mattered. She kept going.

The light grew brighter, and she heard voices. One she recognized as Michael's, sharp with barely controlled anger. The other was unfamiliar—a whining, strange sound, like air escaping a punctured balloon.

The throne room doors stood open.

Albinia dragged herself through them and stopped, swaying on her feet.

The room was immense—all white marble and soaring columns. At the far end, steps led up to a throne where sat the most ordinary-looking man she'd ever seen. He looked like someone who might prune roses or tend a garden.

But this was an illusion and a thin one at that. Even through her exhaustion and pain, Albinia could see the wrongness. The way he flickered at the edges, like he wasn't quite real. The greasy darkness that clung to him.

And standing before the throne, she saw Michael.

He was caught in something—magical bindings she could just barely perceive, like ropes made of thought and nightmare. His face was pale and set, jaw clenched with the effort of resisting whatever the creature on the throne was doing to him.

Samuel stood off to the side, unbound but looking uncertain and frightened.

The creature on the throne hadn't noticed her yet. It was too focused on Michael.

"Face it. I have won. Albinia will join me. You must give up. It's so simple, young Ainsling. Why do you resist?"

"Because," Michael said through gritted teeth, "I will not be your pawn. Not again. Never again. And Albinia joining you? Why should she?"

The creature laughed, and the sound made Albinia's skin crawl. "You think you have a choice? I've been inside your mind, boy. I know every fear, every weakness. I can make you—"

"No," Albinia said.

Her voice was barely above a whisper, but somehow it carried through the vast room. Every head turned toward her.

She stood in the doorway, a bedraggled mess of torn silk and tangled red hair, soaked to the bone and swaying on her feet. Blood ran from her nose, warm on her lips, and mixed with river water, dripping onto the pristine marble floor. But she was standing. She'd made it.

Michael's eyes went wide. "Al?" His voice cracked with shock and what might have been relief. Or horror. "What happened? How did you—"

"You called," she said simply. "I came."

"I didn't mean you to come. I just—"

The creature on the throne went very still. Then, slowly, it began to smile. "Well, well, well," it said. "This is unexpected. Though perhaps.. .perhaps it shouldn't be. You are worthy, girl. Chip off the old block."

It rose from the throne, and as it did, its form flickered. For just a moment, Albinia saw what it truly was—tesseracts of greasy light wrapped around something dark and pulsing and wrong.

Then it was a man again, walking down the steps toward her.

"Hello, daughter," said the deposed king of Fairyland. Somehow, Albinia knew that was what he was. Knew it at a gut level. The one who'd created the creature who tried to eat Bug. The one— The one who *sired* her? Not her father. Her father was— She thought of Tristram's cold treatment of her. She had no father.

Albinia's legs finally gave out. She would have fallen, but Samuel was suddenly there, catching her before she hit the ground. His arm felt very warm around her. Or she felt very cold. "I've got you," he said quietly. "I've got you, Al."

She clung to her brother's arm, trying to focus through the haze of exhaustion. The creature was still coming toward them, still smiling that terribly ordinary smile.

"Daughter?" Michael's voice was sharp with confusion and something that might have been betrayal. "What does he mean, daughter?"

The deposed king laughed. "Oh, he doesn't know yet, does he? How delicious. Shall I tell him, or would you like him to discover the truth for himself, my dear?"

Albinia looked at the creature approaching her. At the darkness that clung to him. At the wrongness of his existence. And somewhere deep inside, in a place she'd always tried not to examine too closely, something recognized him. Not just as the previous, evil king of Fairyland, but as part of her.

"No," she whispered.

But she was very much afraid it was true. She remembered what the gryphon pretender had said. She thought of her immense power. The power of Fairyland. She felt nauseated and somehow even colder.

Father and Daughter

ALBINIA COULDN'T BREATHE. IT wasn't just exhaustion or the possible cracked rib which hurt like fire all this time, but could be ignored, or the magic depletion making her chest tight. It was the word echoing in her ears, impossible and terrible.

Daughter.

"No," she said again, louder this time. "Not yours. Never yours."

The creature—she refused to think of it as a man, refused to think of it as anything with a real claim to the word *father*—tilted its head. Its smile widened.

"Are you not? Look at me, child. Really look. Don't you recognize yourself?"

Samuel's grip on her arm tightened. She could feel him trembling, though whether from fear or rage, she couldn't tell.

"Don't listen to him, Al," Samuel said. "He's the deposed king. He's been twisted by—"

"By what? By betrayal?" The creature laughed. "By being cast down from my rightful throne by my own nephew and his allies? By being cut down from sustenance and power from Fairyland and have to scrounge for scraps? Yes, I suppose that does twist a person. And not to be able to find one's own daughter, hidden by her willful mother! She promised I could use you to recover the throne, then she said you disappeared. But she was still using your power!"

It waved a hand, and suddenly the air before Albinia shimmered. Images formed—visions pulled from memory or magic or both.

She saw a village. Poor and hardscrabble, the kind of place where people scraped by on little and hoped for less. And in the center of the village green, on Midsummer's Eve, she saw a young woman. Dark-haired and pale-skinned, wearing a dress that had been mended too many times, standing before a makeshift altar of stones and flowers. A stunning young woman who didn't fit in this terrible place.

The woman was younger than Albinia had ever seen her mother, barely more than a girl, really. But there was no mistaking those cold, calculating eyes.

"Mama," Albinia whispered.

The vision-Augusta was speaking, her hands raised to the sky. Albinia couldn't hear the words, but she could see the magic flowing from the girl's lips, desperate and hungry, and she could read the sigil on the ground. A summoning. A calling for power, for someone to hear her, to give her what she needed to escape the poverty and obscurity of her birth.

And something answered.

The air above the altar split open, and through it came...wrongness. Beauty and terror combined. The deposed king stepped through, and in this memory he was still magnificent. Still crowned and powerful, still burning with the unchallenged authority of one who had never known defeat.

He looked at the girl who had called him. And he smiled.

What happened next made Albinia want to look away, but she couldn't. She watched as her mother fell under his thrall, as whatever will she'd possessed was subsumed by his. It wasn't love—Albinia could see that clearly. It was possession. The king taking what he wanted because a mortal girl had been foolish enough to invite him in.

The vision blurred, moving forward in time. Weeks, perhaps months. And when it cleared again, Augusta was different. Harder. The softness of youth had been burned away, replaced by something cold and calculating. She was no longer in the village—she'd left, or been driven out. And she was alone.

And pregnant.

"She called on me for power," the deposed king said, his voice full of dark amusement. "A foolish girl who thought she could bargain with the king of Fairyland. I gave her what she asked for. A child she could take power from. And I took what I wanted in return."

"No," Albinia said, but her voice was weak. She could already feel the truth of it settling into her bones like ice. She wasn't denying it. She was just riven by utter pain and shame. For herself, for Mama, for the whole human race.

"Yes. And when I was done with her, when she realized what she carried, she needed legitimacy. Needed a name, a place in the human world where you could grow up safe from those who might see you as a threat. Or who might see you as the bastard half-faery child you were and cast you out. Send you to one of those orphanages. Or use you for their pleasure. And she'd promised me you'd come back to me, when your power was full grown. To use for my purposes. Which I need more than ever now." The vision shifted again, and now she saw her mother—older now, harder, but with a veneer of softness carefully applied—approaching a man in a magical book shop. A thin man with unruly dark hair and ink-stained fingers, completely absorbed in some magical diagram.

Tristram Blakley. The man she'd thought was her father until today.

"A widower," the deposed king said. "With seven young sons. A brilliant inventor, but utterly useless at practical life. Perfect for her purposes."

Albinia watched as the vision-Augusta smiled at Tristram, spoke to him. She couldn't hear the words, but she saw the magic woven through them—subtle, insidious. Not quite a love spell, but close enough to make no difference.

"She made herself indispensable," the king said. "Made him believe he couldn't manage without her. Made him believe she loved him. And when she was certain of him, when the boys needed her too much to question—"

The vision showed a wedding. Tristram looking dazed and happy. Augusta looking triumphant. And between them, barely visible, a slight curve to Augusta's belly.

"She was barely pregnant when they married," the king said. "Barely showing. And then, before you were born, before anyone could count months and question, she could already reach your magic and use it—"

The vision shifted one final time. Augusta, standing in Tristram's workshop, weaving magic. Dark, cruel magic. A binding that wrapped around Tristram like chains, then lifted him up and away, depositing him in a pocket universe of his own creation. He fought against it, Albinia could see, but Augusta's magic was too strong, too ruthless. Within moments, he was gone.

"She sent him away," Albinia whispered. "Before I was born. Before he ever knew I existed."

"Indeed. And told everyone he'd simply disappeared. Gone adventuring, perhaps. Or been taken by fair folk. Who could say? Eventually, she had him declared dead." The king's smile was cruel. "She gave birth to you in his manor, surrounded by his servants and his sons. Everyone assumed you were his daughter. Why wouldn't they? You lived in his house, bore his name, were raised with—or shall we say, by—his children."

The visions faded, leaving Albinia staring at empty air. She felt hollowed out, like someone had reached inside her chest and scooped out everything that made her who she was. Everything she'd believed about herself, about her family, about her place in the world—all of it was a lie built on manipulation and cruelty. She wasn't part of her family.

She wasn't Tristram Blakley's daughter. She'd never even met him until she came to the pocket universe, and then he'd greeted her with confusion and distance, because of course he had—she was the child of the woman who had destroyed his life. The boys weren't her brothers. Not really. They were the sons of a man who'd been tricked and trapped, and they'd been stuck helping to raise a child who wasn't part of their family at all.

And she was the daughter of this creature. This twisted, terrible being who ruled through fear and power and saw people as nothing but tools to be used and discarded.

She couldn't look at Michael. She was afraid of the scorn she was sure she'd read in his face.

"I can see you're thinking through it," the deposed king said. "It's a lot to take in, I know. But you must see now that if you fulfill your glorious—"

"See what?" Albinia's voice came out harsh, cutting through his smooth words. "That my mother is a monster? I already knew that. I've lived with her my entire life."

"That you and I are the same," the king said, as if she hadn't spoken. "That we're meant to rule. That all these lesser beings—" he gestured dismissively at Michael and Samuel, "—are nothing but tools to be used. Means to our ends."

Albinia looked at Michael. She couldn't help it. She had to know. He was still caught in those magical bindings, invisible ropes of thought and nightmare holding him immobile. But his eyes were on her—not frightened, not disgusted, just watching. Waiting to see what she would do. She saw trust there, and something else. Something that made her chest ache in a way that had nothing to do with her injuries.

Samuel's hand remained on her arm, steadying her even though he must be exhausted himself. Even now, even knowing what he'd just learned about her true parentage, he hadn't let go. He was still there, still supporting her, still her brother in all the ways that mattered.

"Your mother kept you hidden, raised you among mortals, took your magic, denied you your birthright. But you don't have to let her theft stand. You can choose differently. You are due power and adulation. You can stand with your father, your true father, and together we can reclaim what's rightfully ours."

"Reclaim," Albinia repeated flatly, testing the word. It tasted bitter and wrong. "You mean steal. You mean destroy everyone who stands between you and power."

"The throne of Fairyland. The power that should be yours by blood." He stepped closer, and she could feel the wrongness radiating from him like heat from a forge. "You felt it, didn't you? You tasted it when you controlled the kelpie. No mortal power could allow you that force. When you bound your brother and the gryphon prince with magic that even I would struggle to break, you were using Fairyland magic. You're powerful, Albinia. More powerful than your mother ever was, and she was formidable, as powerful as I once was in the glittering days of Fairyland."

He was right, and she hated that he was right. She had felt it—the magic responding to her will in ways it never had before. The ability to weave complex bindings that should have been beyond her skill level, beyond her training. The raw power flowing through her veins like liquid fire. Mama had kept it hidden before and Geoff's misguided binding breaker had destroyed that bind.

"And with me to teach you," the king said, his voice dropping to an intimate murmur, "with my knowledge and your raw power, there's nothing we couldn't accomplish. We could destroy those who wronged us. We could make them pay for every slight, every betrayal. Starting with the *Darkwaters.*"

His attention shifted to Michael, and Albinia saw hunger in his eyes. The hunger of a predator who has finally cornered prey that has eluded him for too long. "This one's brother sits on my throne. Stole it from me. A half-breed mongrel with no right to rule, and yet he wears my crown. But with you by my side, we could crush him. We could reclaim Fairyland and reshape it to our will. Make it what it was always meant to be."

Michael's jaw clenched, and Albinia could see the muscles in his neck standing out with the effort of resisting whatever the bindings were doing to him. But he stayed silent, unable to speak through the magical constraints. Albinia thought of the kindly king of Fairyland. She thought of the creature on the path, the one that thought Bug was chicken. The new king said the old king had liked them.

"And then," the king continued, turning back to Albinia with that terrible smile, "we could deal with your mother. Make her pay for her betrayal of you and of everyone you loved. Make her understand what it means to cross us. Make her suffer as you've suffered, trapped and powerless, for all these years."

Us. As if they were a team, as if Albinia had already agreed to become his accomplice in revenge and cruelty. As if blood alone was enough to bind her to him and his twisted purposes.

"You're my daughter," the king said softly, and there was something almost pleading in his voice now. "My blood. My heir. The only thing the Darkwaters didn't manage to take from me. You belong with me, not with these...mortals." He said the word like it was something distasteful, something less than worthy of consideration. "You're better than them. Stronger. More. Why chain yourself to weakness when you could embrace what you truly are?" A feeling of power within her reach, a feeling of grandeur and glory swept down upon her.

Albinia looked down at her hands. They were still shaking from exhaustion and magic depletion, still bloodstained from the kelpie ride and her injuries. These were the hands that had woven protections over Edmund and Bug, protections that even now kept them safe and hidden. The hands that had controlled a kelpie through sheer stubborn will and refused to let go even when every instinct screamed at her to give up, even as her body suffered to the edge of breaking. The hands of the deposed king's daughter, yes, but also the hands that had helped Geoffrey find his lost things, and soothed Bug's tears, and reached out to catch Michael when he stumbled. The hands that had held Edmund's fallen nestlings as he fed them with an eye dropper.

"I know this is difficult," the king said, his tone turning understanding, sympathetic, even. "I know your world is upended. You thought you were something else. Someone else. You had no idea of your great destiny. But now you know the truth. You're mine. And together, we'll make them all pay. Your mother. The Darkwaters. Gabriel Penn, that half-breed pretender on my throne. Everyone who stood against us, everyone who thought they could cast us down and forget about us."

He held out a hand to her, and she could see power crackling around his fingers. Could feel the welcome he extended. Could even see that in his own way, he was sincere. "Come. Stand with your father. Claim your birthright. Stop pretending to be something small and weak and mortal, you who are woven of the magic of the stars and the power of eternity. Take my hand and let's rule together."

Albinia stared at that outstretched hand. Part of her wanted to take it—not because she agreed with anything he was saying, but because it would mean an end. And end to running, to working, to struggling. She was so tired. So exhausted from the ride, from the fighting, from the constant struggle to prove herself and protect others and be strong enough. To escape Mama, to protect the boys, to save her—the man she'd thought was her papa.

This evil thing was offering her answers, an identity, a place to belong that didn't require her to be anything but powerful and safe.

Even if that place was at the side of a monster who saw love as weakness and people as tools. Even if accepting his hand up meant becoming everything she'd always despised about her mother—cold, calculating, cruel.

She looked at Michael again. He watched her with those green eyes that reminded her so much of Gabriel Penn's, and she saw no judgment there despite everything he'd just learned about her parentage. Only trust, and something warmer. He'd called for her across worlds and dimensions. He had faith that she would rescue him no matter the cost. Even now, even after learning what she was, he trusted her to make the right choice. He trusted her to save him.

Samuel's hand tightened on her arm, a gentle pressure that grounded her in reality. "Al," he said quietly, his voice pitched low. "Whatever you decide, I'm with you. We all are. But remember—blood doesn't make family. Love does. Life does. You're my sister because, because I taught you to walk, because you looked after us from the moment you could, not because of whose child you are."

The deposed king's smile faltered, and his eyes narrowed as he looked at Samuel. "Don't listen to him. He's trying to manipulate you, trying to make you doubt what you are. They all are. They fear what you could become, fear the power you could wield. That's why they want to keep you small and controllable."

"No," Albinia said slowly, her voice growing stronger as she spoke as the thoughts seemed to thaw from deep cold, and assemble themselves in her mind. It was almost like her thoughts were living entities, struggling past her shock, past her tiredness, past her fear. "I don't think they do. I don't think they're afraid of my power at all."

She looked at the creature claiming to be her father, really looked at him past the human disguise and the smooth words to what lay beneath. She saw power, yes—immense, terrible power diminished now, but with a potential that dwarfed anything she'd ever encountered. But she also saw emptiness, a void where love should be, where connection and care and warmth should exist. He didn't see people, didn't feel affection or loyalty or tenderness. There was only ambition and rage and the endless, aching need for revenge. Everyone and everything were pieces in his great game. That's what people were, both human and fey.

He didn't want a daughter. He wanted a weapon, a tool, another means to an end. Just like her mother had wanted magical power, then had wanted to secure her position, had wanted a child only for what that child could provide.

And she'd spent fifteen years being her mother's weapon, her mother's tool, her mother's possession. She wasn't about to become his. She wasn't about to trade one cage for another, no matter how much prettier the bars might seem.

"You're right about one thing," Albinia said, and she was pleased that her voice came out steady and clear. Her normal voice, not ragged with tiredness and pain. "I am powerful. More powerful than I knew, stronger than I imagined possible."

The king's smile returned, wide and triumphant. "Yes. Yes, you are. You are the princess regnant of Fairyland. Together—"

"But you're wrong about everything else." Albinia pulled away from Samuel's supporting hand and stood on her own, swaying but upright, meeting the deposed king's eyes without flinching. "I'm not your heir. I'm not your weapon. And I'm not going to help you hurt people I care about for your satisfaction."

The king's face went very still, all expression draining from it like water from a broken cup. "You care about them? These mortals? These nothings, these insects, these brief sparks that burn out almost before they've begun?"

"Yes," Albinia said, and she'd never been more certain of anything in her life. "I do. I care about them more than I could ever care about power or revenge or ruling over people who fear me. They are everything to me."

"Even though they're mayflies? Even though they're not your real family?" The king's voice was low and dangerous now, the pretense of paternal concern evaporating. "Even though every moment you spent with them was built on a lie? You're not a Blakley. You never were. You're mine."

"They're more my family than you'll ever be." Albinia felt tears prickling at the corners of her eyes, but she blinked them back. "Family isn't about blood. It's about who shows up when you need them. It's about who teaches you things and helps you grow and makes you want to be better. It's about sacrifice and care and love, and you don't even know what those words mean." Her last words were a shout.

For a moment, there was silence in the vast throne room. Then the deposed king's face twisted with rage, and the pleasant pretense was completely gone. What remained was pure malevolence, ancient and terrible and utterly inhuman.

"Foolish child," he snarled, and his voice had lost all its human qualities, becoming something that hurt to hear. "I gave you a choice. I offered you everything—power, knowledge, revenge, a throne. And you throw it back in my face for these...these insects who will die in the blink of an eye while you live on for centuries!"

"Yes," Albinia said simply. "Because they're worth it, and you're not. Power or not, you are nothing."

"Very well," he said, and reality shuddered around them as his power manifested visibly. "If you won't join me willingly, I'll simply take what I need from you. Your power will serve me whether you wish it or not. I'll drain you dry and use every drop of magic in your veins to fuel my return. It's what I always intended to do if you proved stubborn."

He raised his hands, and Albinia felt magic slam into her like a physical blow. It wrapped around her, trying to burrow into her mind and her power, trying to pull everything she was out by the roots. She'd been right about one thing: he was immensely powerful, far beyond anything she could hope to match directly. And she was exhausted, depleted, barely standing, her reserves had drained into the kelpie ride and the protections she'd woven over Edmund and Bug.

As the deposed king's magic wrapped around her like chains, trying to crush her will and steal her power, Albinia smiled.

Breaking Bonds

Albinia had learned something important on the kelpie ride, something that gave her hope even in this impossible situation.

She could yield her power as a weapon. She could push past what she thought her limits were. She was good at maintaining bindings under impossible circumstances. And breaking them was just binding in reverse.

She felt the king rifling through her thoughts the way someone might rifle through a desk drawer looking for spare change, careless and invasive and utterly without respect for what he was touching. She knew he was looking for something to use.

She screamed. She couldn't help it. The violation was worse than any physical pain she'd ever experienced. It was like having someone reach inside her skull and start rearranging things at random, pulling out memories and examining them with cruel amusement before tossing them aside.

He saw her childhood. Saw Mama's cold discipline and the boys trying to protect her from it. Saw her loneliness, her desperate attempts to be useful so Mama wouldn't send her away. Saw every small humiliation, every moment of fear, every time she'd hidden in her room and cried where no one could see. He laughed.

"Is this what you're protecting?" His voice echoed in her mind, mocking. "This pathetic excuse for a life? These people who kept you prisoner in that comfortless manor, who let that woman control you? You call that family?"

Albinia wanted to argue, wanted to explain that it hadn't been the boys' fault, that they'd done their best. But she couldn't form words. The assault on her mind was too overwhelming, too all-consuming.

He pushed deeper, looking for her power. Looking for the core of magic that made her his daughter, that made her worth keeping. And when he found—

He recoiled.

Just for a moment, but Albinia felt it. A flicker of surprise, almost confusion. As if he'd expected to find one thing and discovered something else entirely.

Her power was there, yes. The raw magical potential she'd inherited from him, vast and deep and largely untapped. But it was wrapped in something he didn't recognize. Layered over and through with feelings that were utterly foreign to him.

Love, protectiveness and the willingness to die, if needed, to protect that which was more important than even her life.

Albinia saw the fear and leaned into it for strength. She remembered Mama's magic. The cruel, controlling bindings, yes, but also the carefully hoarded power. The way to do immense things with minimal energy. The efficiency born of paranoia and the need to hide what you truly were.

And beneath that, newer still, she remembered what she'd learned from watching Michael work. The mathematical precision. The understanding that magic followed rules, and if you understood the rules well enough, you could bend them in ways that looked impossible.

The deposed king pushed against the strange layer of love and protectiveness, trying to tear through them to reach the pure power beneath. But they didn't tear. They flexed and bent and absorbed the force of his assault, diffusing it.

And that's when Albinia understood. Her father was immensely powerful. Terrifyingly so. But he'd never had to conserve his strength, never had to be clever or efficient or precise. He was like a man with an endless supply of water trying to put out a fire by throwing bucket after bucket at it, never stopping to think that a well-aimed stream would work better.

He was wasteful. Crude. Overwhelming but not elegant.

And Albinia had been raised by a woman who'd had to steal her daughter's power and hide what she was doing, to conserve it, to make every drop of magic count because discovery of Albinia's true nature meant death at the hands of outraged mortals. Augusta had taught Albinia to be precise because precision was survival. To be efficient because waste drew attention. To hide what she truly wasto hide what Albinia was even from Albinia herself—because the world was full of dangers for a half-fairy bastard child whose father was the deposed king of Fairyland. And Albinia herself was a danger to her mother, if she comprehended her own power.

The assault on her mind continued, but Albinia stopped trying to resist it directly. That was what he expected, what he was prepared for. Instead, she started looking at the structure of his attack.

It was like Michael's magical machines in a way, she realized. Composed of many parts working together. But where Michael's inventions were elegant and efficient, this was brutish and overcomplicated. The deposed king was using ten times more power than he needed, and half of it was working against itself.

There. She could see it now. The places where his magic tangled, where components interfered with each other. The weak points in the structure.

She'd learned to find weak points. Mama had taught her how to look for the cracks in any spell, any ward, any protection. How to slip through them or, when necessary, how to widen them until the whole thing fell apart. Because that was the only freedom Albinia had.

Albinia stopped screaming. She took a breath—mental more than physical, though her body responded, too—and started to work.

The first thing she did was small. Almost insignificant. She found a place where two threads of his magic crossed each other and gave one a tiny push. Just enough to throw it slightly out of alignment.

The effect rippled outward. The thread she'd pushed pulled on another, which pulled on another, which pulled on three more. The deposed king's assault faltered, just for a fraction of a second. In the manor, where money was tight, she'd unwound old clothes to use the thread for new ones. This was the same.

He didn't even notice.

Albinia smiled grimly and found another weak point. Then another. She worked methodically, the way she'd helped Aaron find his lost things—not by searching everywhere at once, but by eliminating possibilities one by one, narrowing down until only the answer remained.

Each tiny change cascaded through the structure of the king's magic, introducing inefficiencies, creating friction, making him work harder to maintain the same level of control.

And he still didn't notice. He was too focused on overwhelming her by sheer force to realize she was dismantling him strand by strand.

"You can't win," he said, his voice echoing in her mind. "You're powerful, yes, but you're untrained. Exhausted. And I am the king of Fairyland. I am—"

The binding around her mind suddenly loosened.

Not much. Not even enough for her to break free. But enough that she could think more clearly, could breathe without feeling like she was drowning.

Albinia pressed her advantage. She found the main structural supports of his assault—the key bindings that held everything else together—and started pulling at them. Not directly, which would have alerted him. But indirectly, weakening the foundations so slowly he wouldn't feel it until it was too late.

It was like the time Edmund had taught her about rock climbing on the cliffs. You didn't pull on the rocks to see if they were loose, he'd said. You tapped them gently, listening to the sound they made. A solid rock sounded different from one about to give way. Magic was similar. If you listened carefully, you could hear the places where a binding was stressed, where it was working too hard, where one good push would make it fail.

She pushed here and there, again and again.

Something in the deposed king's assault snapped. Not completely, but enough that his attention suddenly shifted. He'd felt that. He knew something was wrong.

"What are you doing?" His voice was sharp now, suspicious. "You can't possibly—"

Albinia pushed again, harder this time. Another binding snapped. Then another. The assault on her mind weakened and faltered rapidly now, like a dam with too many cracks to plug.

"No!" The deposed king pulled back slightly, trying to shore up his defenses, trying to figure out what she'd done. "That's not possible. You're just a child. You don't have the training to—"

"I have exactly the training I need," Albinia said, and her voice came out stronger than she'd expected. "Mama left me almost no power, and it taught me how to make every drop count. You're pouring yours out like water."

She could see him now, really see him. The way Michael must see his magical machines, as a collection of components and connections. The deposed king was immense, yes, but he was also thin and inefficient. Half his power was tied up in maintaining his own existence in this pocket universe, despite lacking the strength of Fairyland to sustain him. Another quarter was fighting against the very structure of reality, trying to force the path to bend to his will. What he was actually using to bind her and Michael was less than a quarter of his total strength.

And even that looked poorly organized.

Albinia reached for the bindings that held Michael. She could see them now, visible in her mind's eye as she'd learned to see magical structures. Ropes of thought and nightmare, yes, but also remarkably sloppy. The king had bound Michael in rage and haste, and it showed.

There. The key knot, the one that held everything else together. She didn't pull at it. That would just make it tighter. Instead, she found the loose end—there was always a loose end, Mama had taught her that when unravelling fabric—and started working it backward through the knot.

"Stop!" The deposed king's assault redoubled, and Albinia gasped as fresh pain lanced through her mind. "You will not—"

"I already am," Albinia said through gritted teeth. She kept working at the knot binding Michael, even as she had to shore up her own defenses. This was the hardest thing she'd ever done—fighting a defensive action on one front while attacking on another, all while exhausted and injured and barely able to stand. It should be impossible.

But she'd ridden a kelpie through the sky. A creature of evil and malice bent on destroying her. A creature of the deep waters, not the clear sky, much less the realm between worlds. Compared to that, this was merely extremely difficult.

The knot around Michael loosened. She felt it give, felt the binding start to unravel. Just a little more, just a bit farther— The binding snapped.

Michael gasped, stumbling forward as the magical ropes holding him dissolved. For a moment, he swayed, catching himself on a nearby column. Then he looked up, and his eyes met Albinia's.

"Al?" His voice was hoarse. "How did you—"

"I'll explain later," she said. "Right now, I need—" She wavered on her feet, and suddenly the deposed king's assault intensified. He'd realized what she'd done, understood that she'd freed his prisoner, and his rage was incandescent.

"You little fool!" he screamed. "You have no idea what you've done! I'll tear the power from you strand by strand, and then I'll make you watch as I kill them all—"

Michael's hand came up, and Albinia felt a surge of different magic. Clean and precise and mathematical. He couldn't see the structures the way she could—she was almost sure of that—but he could sense them. Could feel where the magic was concentrated and where it was weak. Where it moved, and where it held together.

"There," he said, pointing. "Al, hit there."

She looked where he was pointing and saw it. A place where three major bindings came together, each one supporting the others. If she could break one—

She struck, putting everything she had behind it. The binding shattered, and the deposed king screamed. It wasn't pain, precisely. More like the shock of a limb going numb, of suddenly losing something he'd taken for granted.

"Again," Michael said. He was moving now, circling around toward Samuel. "Samuel, when I break his hold on you, be ready to run."

"I'm not bound," Samuel said. He sounded shaken, but steady. "He didn't think I was a threat."

"Then help Al," Michael said. "She can see the structure better than I can, but I can do the mathematics. We can do this together. Lend her your power."

The deposed king started recovering now, pulling his scattered power back together. But it had become harder for him now, Albinia could see. He had to work to maintain things that had been effortless before. Her attack had disrupted his efficiency, forced him to think about the structure of his magic instead of just pouring it out thoughtlessly.

"You think you can defeat me?" The king's form flickered, showing those tesseracts of greasy light again sliding in something like oil. "I am power incarnate! I am—"

"Wasteful," Michael said flatly. He had moved to Albinia's side now, and she could feel his magic working in concert with hers. She could also feel

Samuel's magic pouring into her like warmth and love. Without looking, she could sense her brother's smile. "You're using at least thirty percent more power than you need to maintain any given binding. I can see the equations, and they're a mess."

"Equations?" The king laughed, but it sounded strained. "Magic isn't mathematics, boy. It's will and power and—"

"Everything is mathematics," Michael said. "And Al's right. You pour out power like you have an infinite supply. You used to. When you had Fairyland. You don't have it now. And you still act the same. But she knows how to use minimal force for maximum effect, and I know how to find the most efficient path through any system. Together, we can take you apart piece by piece. You can't even stop us."

Albinia felt a surge of hope. He was right. Together, they could do this. Her power and his mathematics, working in harmony.

"Where?" she asked.

Michael pointed. "That binding, the one that's maintaining his physical form here. It's the keystone. If we can disrupt it—"

"He'll lose cohesion," Albinia finished. She could see it now, the way the binding was tied into everything else the king was doing. Pull that thread and the whole tapestry would start to unravel.

The deposed king saw them looking, understood what they were planning. "No!" He threw power at them, trying to knock them down, to separate them. "You will not—"

But Albinia moved. She struck at the binding Michael had identified, pulling at it with all the techniques Mama had taught her. Beside her, Michael was doing something with mathematical formulae, speaking numbers under his breath all wrapped in some kind of spell. She didn't understand it, but she could see the effect—the binding was becoming unstable, its internal mathematics no longer balanced.

Samuel joined them, adding his own spell to the assault. He didn't have their precision or their training, but he had determination and he had rage. Rage at what had been done to his family, to his father, to his little sister who wasn't really his sister but whom he loved as one.

The binding shattered.

The deposed king screamed, and his form rippled. For a moment, he was nothing but those greasy tesseracts of light, writhing in space. Then he pulled himself back together, slower now. Albinia could see the effort it took.

"Again," she said.

They struck in unison, Albinia and Michael and Samuel working together. Three different approaches to magic, three different strengths, all focused on the same goal.

Unmaking a king. Dismantling his very being.

The throne room shuddered. Reality itself seemed to flex as the deposed king's hold on this place weakened. Outside, Albinia thought she could hear sounds—shouts, the clash of weapons, the roar of combat. The war Gabriel had predicted was about to begin, and they were at its center.

But right now, in this moment, all that mattered was the next binding to break. The next thread to pull. The next step in taking apart a monster strand by careful strand.

"Together," Michael said.

Albinia nodded. "Together."

Samuel shouted, "Together," through gritted teeth.

And they struck again.

The Unraveling

MICHAEL HAD ALWAYS THOUGHT of magic as something like mathematics. Clean, precise, following immutable rules. When you assembled a spell properly, it worked. When you didn't, it failed. There was a certain comfort in that predictability, even when the magic itself was complex.

But what Albinia was doing—what they were doing together—was something else entirely.

She worked like a surgeon, he thought. Or perhaps like someone dismantling a clock, removing each gear and spring with careful precision so the whole mechanism stopped functioning. She never wasted energy on dramatic displays of power. She simply found the weak points in the deposed king's magical structure and pulled them apart, one by one, with relentless efficiency.

It was brilliant. Michael found himself marveling at it even as he worked beside her, using his understanding of magical mathematics to identify targets and calculate the most efficient angles of attack. This was genius of a kind that rivaled his own inventions—not flashy or loud, but devastatingly effective.

The deposed king was powerful, yes. Immensely so. But power without efficiency was like an engine that burned through fuel at ten times the necessary rate. It might be impressive in the short term, but it couldn't last.

And they weren't giving him time to think or defend.

"There," Albinia said, her voice hoarse but steady. She pointed at a binding that Michael could barely see, a thread of magic so fine, it was almost invisible. "That one's supporting the connection to his forces outside. If we sever it—"

Michael saw the mathematics of it immediately. "It'll cascade. He won't be able to maintain command and defend himself simultaneously." He began calculating the best approach, muttering numbers under his breath. "If we hit it at a forty-seven-degree angle relative to the primary axis, the interference pattern should amplify the disruption by—"

"I don't need the equations," Albinia interrupted, but she was smiling slightly, despite her exhaustion. "Just tell me when."

"Now," Michael said.

They struck together, and the binding snapped like an overstressed wire. The deposed king staggered, and Michael felt a shudder run through the entire palace. More than that—he felt something shift in the larger structure of magic around them.

The war outside was real, he realized. Not just a distant threat but an actual battle, happening right now. Forces arrayed against each other, waiting for something to tip the balance. And what they were doing in here affected everything out there.

The deposed king's scream became less human now, more the sound of something ancient and terrible being wounded in a way it had never imagined possible. "You cannot do this! I am—I was—I will not—"

But his protests grew weaker. Michael could see it in the way his form flickered, the tesseracts of light that composed his true shape becoming unstable. Each binding they destroyed took a piece of him with it. Not just his power, but his coherence. His ability to maintain existence in this place.

"The anchor," Albinia said suddenly. She was swaying on her feet now, and Michael wanted to tell her to rest, to let him take over. But he knew she wouldn't. She'd come too far, endured too much, to stop now. "Michael, he's anchored to something. Otherwise, he'd have dispersed when he was deposed. He has a source of power that anchors him in existence. Can you see it? It's how he's maintained this pocket universe for so long."

Michael looked, really looked, pushing his perception beyond the immediate battle to see the larger structure. And there it was—a massive binding that connected the deposed king to the very fabric of this place. It pulsed with dark energy, drawing power from...somewhere. Not Fairyland. That would be Gabriel's now. Then she realized—trapped souls, the power and magic of those the king had captured magical paths over the years. All of those he'd caused to die. Humans and elves and other, stranger creatures. Their souls, their essence, even their memories stayed behind, powering his magic, giving him greater power. Keeping him tethered to existence.

"I see it," he said. "But Al, that's enormous. I'm not sure we can—"

"We don't have to destroy it," she said. "Just break the binding. Crack it. Just enough to let the prisoners escape. Burst out. Naturally, they will move towards their destination, once there's a crack."

She was right, of course. The anchor was too large, too complex to dismantle completely. But they didn't need to. They just needed to introduce enough instability that it would begin to fail on its own and free the poor souls inside.

Michael began calculating. The anchor had seven primary supports, each one reinforcing the others. But there was always a weakest point, a place where the stresses were highest. There. Where three supports came together, the mathematics showed a slight imbalance in the force distribution.

"Samuel," he called. "We need you."

Samuel looked uncertain. He was pale and shaking, whether from fear or exhaustion, Michael couldn't tell. "I don't have your precision. I'll just get in the way."

"We don't need precision," Michael said. "We need raw force. Al and I will weaken the structure. We need you to hit it as hard as you can when we tell you to."

Samuel's jaw set, square with determination. "I can do that."

They worked in concert, the three of them. Albinia found the fine threads that held the weak point together and began pulling them loose. Michael calculated the exact moment when the structural integrity would be at its lowest. And Samuel gathered his power, crude and unrefined but strong.

The deposed king realized what they were doing. "No! Not the anchor! If you destroy that, you'll—you'll collapse the entire universe! You'll kill everyone trapped here!"

"Liar," Albinia said flatly. "The anchor isn't holding this place together. It's holding you together. The souls you trapped will just go free."

"Now!" Michael shouted.

Samuel's power lashed out, striking the weak point with all the force of a battering ram. The anchor didn't break completely, but a crack appeared in it. A hairline fracture that began to widen as the stresses redistributed themselves across the damaged structure. Light poured out, blinding. Then with a sound like heavenly choirs, bright things escaped it. Glowing orbs of brilliant light. They made a fluttering sound as they flew upward.

Michael didn't hear words, but retained a memory of many voices saying, "Thank you, thank you. Bless you."

The deposed king screamed.

Outside, Michael felt some larger magical structure shudder. As though chains had bound the deposed king to various points of Fairyland. And the power he'd been feeding into those chains broke.

Whatever forces the king had been commanding, whatever allies he'd gathered, they were suddenly cut off. Michael couldn't see it directly, but he could sense it in the way the magic around them shifted. Like in an army that had suddenly lost its general, confusion spread through the ranks.

Michael got—through the old king's dissolving magic—impressions of places his magic had been tied to.

Most of it made no sense to him. But some did.

On the suspended isle where the gryphons dwelt, something changed. Michael felt it through the web of magic that connected everything in this pocket universe. A binding that had been holding steady flickered and failed.

Edmund's binding, he realized. The protection Albinia had woven over her brother and Bug. It had held until they were safe. And apparently they were safe now, because the magic released them.

He couldn't see what happened after that, but he could feel the ripples spreading outward. A revelation. A truth revealed. The infant king of the gryphons, hidden all this time, suddenly made visible to his people.

And the pretender to the throne—Cormac, twice a murderer and traitor, who had kidnapped Albinia, who had allied with the deposed king in hopes of legitimizing his false claim—suddenly finding his power crumbling beneath him, running as the knowledge that he'd killed the royal gryphons spread, being caught and accused of treason.

Michael smiled grimly. The deposed king's web of influence snapped and collapsed everywhere at once. Every deal he'd made, every alliance he'd forged, every promise of power he'd extended—all of it unraveling as his own strength failed.

There was something with the dragons. And in a far away glade in Fairyland, the sylphs escaped his binding.

"He's weakening," Albinia said. She barely stood now, leaning heavily against a column. Blood trickled from her nose again, and her hands were shaking. "Michael, we need to finish this. I don't know how much longer I can—"

"I know," Michael said. He moved to support her, one arm around her waist to keep her upright. "One more. Just one more strike, and he'll fall apart completely."

The deposed king was barely coherent now, his form shifting between human and those awful tesseracts of light with increasing rapidity. "No. No. You can't. You're mine. She's mine. My daughter. My power. Mine."

"I'm not yours," Albinia said. Her voice was weak, but certain. "I never was. And I never will be."

The throne room's doors burst open.

Michael's first thought was that the deposed king had called reinforcements, that they were about to be overwhelmed by whatever forces he still commanded. But the figures that strode through the doors, powerful and intimidating though they were, were not enemies.

Gabriel entered first, and Michael felt a surge of relief so strong, it nearly buckled his knees. His brother—his powerful, infuriating, overprotective brother—was here. Gabriel's form flickered as he walked, showing his dual nature more clearly than Michael had ever seen. Half-human, half-elf, wholly the king of Fairyland now. Behind him came elven warriors in crystalline armor, and creatures of Fairyland that Michael couldn't even name.

And beside Gabriel, striding with the confidence of someone who had never doubted his right to be anywhere he chose, came Seraphim. Michael's oldest brother looked travel-worn and furious, his dark hair disheveled and his coat torn. But his green eyes blazed with protective rage, and magic crackled around his hands.

"Michael!" Seraphim's voice carried across the throne room. "Are you hurt? Did he—"

"We're fine," Michael called back, though that was perhaps overstating things. "Or we will be. We've almost got him. Give us a moment."

Gabriel's eyes swept the room, taking in the scene with that unnervingly complete perception he had now. His gaze lingered on Albinia, and something flickered in his expression. Recognition, perhaps. Or satisfaction.

"You've done well," Gabriel said. It wasn't clear if he was addressing Michael or Albinia or both of them. "Better than I hoped. But let me finish this. You're both exhausted, and there's no need to—"

"No," Albinia said. She pulled away from Michael's supporting arm, standing on her own despite her obvious exhaustion. "He's my *sire*. This is mine to finish."

Gabriel inclined his head, a slight smile touching his lips. "As you wish, cousin."

Cousin. Because of course they were related now, weren't they? Gabriel's uncle had been the king of Fairyland before him, which meant the deposed king was Gabriel's uncle, as well. And if the deposed king was Albinia's father, that made her and Gabriel cousins of a sort.

Michael filed that realization away to think about later. Right now, all that mattered was ending this.

"Together," he said to Albinia.

She nodded. "Together."

Samuel cleared his throat. "Together."

They could see it clearly now, the final binding. The one that held the deposed king's consciousness together, that kept him from dissolving completely into the raw magical chaos of his true nature. It was damaged already, weakened by everything they'd done. But it still held.

Not for much longer.

Michael began the calculation one final time. Albinia positioned herself, gathering the last of her strength. And Samuel, loyal Samuel who had walked this path and been stuck for years trying to save his family, stood ready to help however he could.

The deposed king made one last desperate assault. Not at them, but at Albinia, specifically. He threw everything he had left at his daughter, trying to overwhelm her, to break her, to take her power for his own if he could not have her loyalty.

"You could have been great!" he screamed. "You could have been a queen! And you threw it away for these insects, these nothings, these—"

Albinia didn't flinch. She met his assault with calm precision, deflecting it, diffusing it, turning his own power back against him. And Michael saw, with a clarity that took his breath away, exactly how brilliant she was. How strong, not in the raw-power sense that the deposed king valued, though she had that, too, but in the ways that actually mattered. The strength to endure. The strength to protect. The strength to choose love over power, even when it would have been so much easier to give into power.

"Now," Albinia said.

Michael spoke the final equation, undoing the king's remaining magic. Samuel threw his remaining power into the attack. And Albinia, with the precision that had carried her through everything, severed the last strand of her father's being.

The deposed king's scream cut off abruptly.

His form unraveled. The tesseracts of greasy light collapsed inward, folding through dimensions that hurt to look at. The darkness at his core pulsed once, twice, then began to fade.

"No," he whispered, and his voice was almost pitiful now. Almost human. "I was supposed to... I should have...my throne...my power...my—"

He ceased to exist.

Not with a bang or a flash of light. Just a gradual fading, like noxious smoke dispersing in the wind. One moment, he was there, diminished and broken but still present. The next, he was simply gone, leaving nothing behind but the faintest smell of ozone and the echo of his final words.

The throne room fell silent.

Michael realized he was still holding the mathematical formulae in his mind, still ready to calculate the next attack. He let them go. His head ached from concentration, and his hands were shaking.

"Is he...?" Samuel started to ask.

"Gone," Gabriel said. His voice was quiet, almost reverent. "Unmade. Returned to the raw chaos from which all magic springs. He won't be coming back."

Albinia made a sound that might have been a laugh or a sob. Then her legs buckled, and Michael barely caught her before she hit the floor.

"I've got you," he said, lowering her gently to sit with her back against a column. "Al, you did it. You actually did it. You unmade the king of Fairyland."

"We did it," she corrected weakly. Her voice was thin and wavering. "We did it together." She looked up at him, and despite her exhaustion, despite the blood on her face and the way her hands shook, she was smiling.

"I couldn't have done it without you, Michael. Your mathematics, your precision—" She reached a hand to her brother and said, "And Samuel."

"And I couldn't have seen the structure without you," Michael said. "You're brilliant, Al. Absolutely brilliant. I've never met anyone like you. Never dreamed anyone like you. You're—" He was borne down to his knees by her weight, his tiredness, but did not let go.

Seraphim came up beside them now, kneeling down to check them both for injuries. "Michael! When I heard you'd been taken, when Gabriel told me what was happening—" He stopped, seeming to realize that this wasn't the time for lectures about responsibility and danger. Instead, he just pulled Michael into a brief, fierce hug. "I'm glad you're safe. Both of you."

Gabriel stood where the deposed king had been, looking at the empty throne. "This path in the pocket universe will collapse soon," he said. "Without his power maintaining it, Tristram Blakley's original creation will reassert itself. And since your mother's binding on it broke when you took your power back, the universe can no longer hold itself. It's wounded and cracked. Which means everyone who's been trapped here will be expelled."

"Expelled where?" Samuel asked. He had moved to stand beside Albinia, and Michael saw the protective way he hovered near his not-quite-sister.

"Back to the place they belong," Gabriel said. "Which, in most cases, means the Blakley manor. I hope your mother is prepared for quite the homecoming. I think I'll make it we come with you."

Michael saw Albinia's expression harden at the mention of her mother. And he realized that while they'd defeated the deposed king, there was still one more confrontation to come.

One more monster to face.

But that could wait. For now, they had won. Against impossible odds, against a creature of immense power and ancient evil, they had won. And they'd win again.

When It All Crashes Down

THE POCKET UNIVERSE SHUDDERED.

Michael felt it through his bones, through his magic, through every sense he possessed. Reality itself was convulsing, trying to expel something that no longer belonged. With the deposed king unmade, the enchantment that had bound this place—that had twisted Tristram Blakley's creation into a prison—was collapsing strand by strand.

"Everyone brace," Gabriel said. His voice carried the absolute authority of command, the kind that made people obey without thinking. "The expulsion will not be gentle."

"Where's Bug?" Albinia asked suddenly, trying to push herself upright. Michael helped her, keeping one arm around her waist to steady her. "Edmund had him, but they're still on the suspended isle. If this place collapses—"

"The gryphon kingdom exists within Fairyland proper, not within this pocket universe," Gabriel said. He'd moved to stand near them, and Michael was struck by how strange it was to see his half-brother dressed as he used to be—simple black suit, white shirt, the clothes of a gentleman's servant—while radiating power that made the air around him shimmer. "They'll be safe. More than safe, actually. I suspect by now young Bug has been formally presented to his subjects."

"And Edmund?"

"Will be honored as the prince's protector and given every comfort, every honor." Gabriel's lips quirked in something that wasn't quite a smile.

"Your brother has quite the reputation among the bird folk. They're calling him the Gryphon's Friend."

Before Albinia could respond, the floor beneath them buckled. Not violently, but with a slow, inexorable warping that made Michael's stomach lurch. The white marble of the throne room began to fade, becoming translucent, then nearly invisible. Through it, he could see other places—Tristram's cottage, various points along the path, forests and fields that had been part of the pocket universe for years.

And through all of it, he could see people. The other Blakley brothers, scattered across the landscape. They were in human form, all of them looking around in confusion and wonder as they felt the change beginning.

"Here it comes," Seraphim said. He'd positioned himself near Michael and Albinia, ready to shield them if necessary. His protective instincts never really turned off, Michael reflected, even when his little brother had just helped unmake a king. Even when Michael had proven himself perfectly capable. It wasn't that he thought Michael a child. It was that he protected everyone. Or tried to. He'd probably try it on Gabriel, too.

The world twisted. Reality warped.

Michael had been through the In-Betweener before, but this was different. Instead of the cold nothing of the space between worlds, this was more like being turned inside out while reality decided where you belonged. Colors inverted, then inverted again. Up became down became sideways became something without a name.

He didn't want to go back to Darkwater. Where Albinia went, he'd go. He felt a sense of amusement from Gabriel, and a flush of power to help with just that.

He held tight to Albinia, and felt Seraphim's hand on his shoulder, anchoring him. Gabriel stood apart, untouched by the chaos, watching with those too-knowing eyes.

And then, with a sound like an immense soap bubble popping, they were somewhere else.

Michael landed hard on polished wood flooring, his already-bruised body protesting the impact. Around him, others were appearing in flashes of displaced air—Samuel, looking disheveled and stunned; the other Blakley brothers, all blessedly human now, all looking like younger versions of Samuel, tumbling through in various states of disarray; and Tristram

Blakley himself, no longer a wolf, thinner and older than in his portraits but unmistakably himself.

They were in an entrance hall. A grand one, with a curved staircase leading up to a gallery lined with portraits. The Blakley family's home, Michael realized. He'd never been here before, but he recognized it from Albinia's descriptions.

Servants screamed and scattered, which was probably a very reasonable reaction, given that a dozen people had just materialized out of thin air in their front hall.

And at the top of the stairs, dressed in severe black silk, stood Augusta Blakley.

Michael had never met Albinia's mother, but he would have known her anywhere. She had the same pale skin, the same sharp features, though her hair was dark where Albinia's was red. But it was the eyes that confirmed it—cold, calculating, they swept over the chaos below with an expression that managed to combine fury and fear in equal measure.

"No," she said, and her voice carried through the hall with unnatural clarity. "No, this isn't possible. Your father said he'd claimed you. I thought that's why the power had gone. He should have—you couldn't have—"

"Hello, Mother," Albinia said. She'd gotten to her feet with Michael's help, though she swayed dangerously. Her voice was quiet, but it cut through Augusta's protests like a knife. "I believe we have matters to discuss."

Augusta's face went white, then red. Michael saw her hands move in a complex gesture, magic gathering around her fingers. But before she could cast whatever spell she was preparing, Gabriel appeared at the bottom of the stairs.

He hadn't walked there. He'd simply been beside Michael one moment and at the base of the stairs the next, as though the intervening space were merely a suggestion he'd chosen to ignore for convenience's sake.

"Mrs. Blakley," Gabriel said, and his voice was perfectly polite, perfectly civil, and absolutely terrifying in its calm. "I would advise against that."

Augusta froze. She looked at him like a bird at a snake.

Michael saw true fear flash across her face as she took in Gabriel's appearance—the black suit of a valet, yes, but also the unmistakable aura of the king of Fairyland. To Michael's ordinary sight, Gabriel looked much as he always had. But he could see Albinia's sharp intake of breath, could see the way Augusta paled further, and realized that those using their mage-sight were seeing something else entirely. He could look on Gabriel with his own mage-sight, of course, but he had a feeling he wouldn't like it.

That he'd see something he would never forget even though he tried to. Something that would pursue him in his nightmares. Something that would change his sense of the brother he loved.

Something that made Augusta lower her hands slowly and carefully.

"Your Majesty," she said, and managed to make it sound both respectful and resentful at once. "I was not aware the king of Fairyland concerned himself with domestic disputes."

"I concern myself with many things," Gabriel said. "The fate of my family, for instance. And those who have aided them." His eyes flicked to Albinia briefly, something unreadable in his expression. "Also with ensuring that justice is served and the debts Fairyland owes are paid."

More people were arriving now, though how they'd gotten here, Michael couldn't say. Elven warriors in their crystalline armor appeared in the doorway, flanking the entrance. And was that the Princess Royal's guard in celestial blue? Yes—Seraphim's wife must have sent them when she heard he'd gone to rescue Michael. How they'd been transported here was something else. He'd guess it had something to do with Gabriel, though. They were here because Gabriel wanted them here.

The entrance hall of Blakley Manor, cavernous though it was, became quite crowded indeed.

Tristram Blakley stood in the center of it all, looking dazed and overwhelmed. His sons—all seven of them, now blessedly human and whole—gathered around him, a protective circle that excluded the woman at the top of the stairs. Michael saw the exact moment when Tristram's eyes found Augusta, saw the complex play of emotions across his face. Recognition, yes. But also hurt, and betrayal, and underneath it all, a kind of weary resignation.

"Augusta," he said quietly. "I should have known. I think I did know, or suspected, but I didn't want to believe."

"Tristram, I can explain—" Augusta started down the stairs, her posture shifting, becoming softer, more appealing. Michael recognized the technique, the subtle magic woven through gesture and voice. She was trying to enchant him again, to wrap him in the same spell that had worked before.

But Tristram held up a hand, and to Michael's surprise, the enchantment slid off him like water off oiled cloth. "No," the inventor said. "No more explanations. No more lies. I've had years to think about what you did, Augusta. Years to work it out. You needed a father for your child, and I was convenient. A widower with sons who needed a mother, too distracted by my work to ask difficult questions."

"You were more than convenient," Augusta said, and there was something almost desperate in her voice now. "You were kind. You were—"

"A fool," Tristram finished. "Yes, I was that. But no longer."

Albinia had pulled away from Michael's supporting arm and was standing on her own now, though she looked ready to collapse at any moment. She was watching her mother with an expression Michael couldn't quite read. Not hatred, exactly. But not forgiveness, either. Something more complex, more painful. Almost like a judge.

"You called on him," Albinia said. Her voice was barely above a whisper, but somehow everyone in the hall heard it. "On Midsummer's Eve, in some poor village, you called on the king of Fairyland for power. And he came."

Augusta's face froze. "How do you—"

"He showed me. Before we unmade him." Albinia took a shaky breath. "He showed me everything. How you summoned him. How you fell under his thrall. How you fled when you realized what you carried. That he'd given you what you asked for, the magic you wanted, by impregnating you, by giving you a half-elf child." She gestured at herself. "Me. His daughter. His bastard half-elven child."

The servants who hadn't already fled gasped and scattered at this revelation. The brothers—Albinia's brothers, Michael reminded himself, even if not by blood—looked stunned but not disbelieving. They'd suspected something, he realized. They'd known Albinia was different, had seen the signs, even if they hadn't understood them.

"You were mine to protect," Augusta said, and now there was genuine emotion in her voice. "Mine to hide from those who would use you. Yes, I called on him. Yes, I was a fool. But everything I did after that was to keep you safe. To give you a name, a family, a place in the world."

"By imprisoning an innocent man?" Albinia's voice rose. "By trapping him in a pocket universe before I was even born? By enchanting his sons into swans and trapping them, as well?"

"The boys were growing suspicious," Augusta said. "They would have ruined everything. And Tristram—he was starting to count months, to wonder. I did what I had to do to protect us both."

"You didn't want me as a daughter. No. You protected yourself, and the source of magic you could steal. And what did you mean to do with me, Mother? My...my father said that he had tried to get me back to use me for his purposes, but you'd hidden me."

"I was trying to protect you!"

"You meant to use me. I don't know for what and I don't know how, but you meant to use me." Albinia saw her mother flinch. And she very much wished she hadn't. But she had.

Gabriel, who had been silent during this exchange, now spoke. "You did what you did to protect yourself, Mrs. Blakley. And in doing so, you allied yourself with forces you should have left well alone." He paused. "Did you know that your former lover was planning to use your daughter to reclaim his throne? That he'd got his hands on her and was going to use her?"

Augusta's face went gray. She didn't answer, but it was answer enough.

"He intended to use her power, her bloodline, to legitimize his return to Fairyland. Whether she wished it or not." Gabriel's voice was perfectly neutral, but Michael heard the steel beneath it. "She would have been a slave to his will, a weapon pointed at everyone who stood against him. Including her brothers. Including the man you forced to give her his name."

"I couldn't stop that. I thought—I thought if I kept her hidden, kept her magic suppressed— I thought in due time, she and I—I never wanted more than this manor." Her mother looked around, her eyes desperate. "I wanted both of us to be safe and well off. I wanted to be safe and well off. We—You don't know what it's like to be poor. I wanted us to not be poor. I thought—"

"You thought you could control everything," Albinia said. She sounded exhausted beyond measure. "But you couldn't. You can't. It's over, Mother."

Augusta looked at her daughter, and for the first time, Michael saw something like genuine grief in her cold eyes. "Albinia—"

"No." Albinia held up a hand, the gesture an unconscious echo of how Tristram had stopped her mother's enchantment. "I don't want to hear it. I don't want your explanations or your justifications. I just want you to stop."

The hall fell silent. Everyone was watching now—the brothers, Tristram, Seraphim, the gathered guards. Even the servants who had stayed were frozen in doorways, witnessing this family's dissolution.

Gabriel moved then, ascending a few steps so he was between Augusta and the rest of the hall. When he spoke, his voice carried the weight of absolute authority. "Augusta Blakley, you have committed crimes against your own family and against the natural order. You have trafficked with the deposed king of Fairyland, knowingly or unknowingly aiding his schemes. You have imprisoned innocents through cruel enchantment. You have deceived and betrayed those who trusted you."

"What will you do?" Augusta asked. Her voice was steady, but Michael could see her hands trembling. "Imprison me? Execute me?"

"Neither," Gabriel said, and Michael heard something almost like pity in his brother's voice. "I will do what should have been done years ago. I will remove you from this place and from the lives of those you've harmed."

He raised one hand, and magic swirled around him—not the greasy, dark magic of the deposed king, but something cleaner, brighter, though no less powerful. Augusta began to fade, becoming translucent at the edges.

"Where are you sending me?" she asked, and now there was real fear in her voice.

"Nowhere," Gabriel said. "And everywhere. To the spaces between worlds, where you can harm no one else. You'll exist there, neither in the mortal world nor in Fairyland, neither alive nor dead. A liminal state for one who lived in deception."

"No!" Augusta's hands moved, trying to cast some counterspell, but Gabriel's magic was too strong, too complete. "You can't—I'm her mother!" She rounded on Al. "Albinia, tell him—"

But Albinia said nothing. She crossed her arms. She stood silent, her face pale and set, as her mother faded from existence. Michael saw her flinch when Augusta called out to her, saw the pain in her eyes. But she didn't intervene. Didn't ask Gabriel to stop.

And then Augusta was gone, leaving behind only the faintest shimmer in the air where she'd stood.

The silence that followed tolled like a reverse bell. Then Tristram Blakley moved, climbing the stairs to where Gabriel stood. He looked at the spot where his wife had been, then at the king of Fairyland.

"Thank you," he said simply.

Gabriel inclined his head. "She would have destroyed you all, given time. This was mercy, in its way."

"Perhaps," Tristram said. He turned to look down at the hall, at his seven sons and the girl who bore his name but not his blood. "Though I'm not sure any of us will feel it as such for some time."

He descended the stairs slowly, and Michael saw how the years of imprisonment had aged him. But there was also something of the man in the portraits, the brilliant inventor who'd changed the world. He walked to where Albinia stood and stopped a few feet away, as if uncertain of his welcome.

"Miss Blakley," he said formally. "I believe we have not been properly introduced, though we met briefly in rather trying circumstances."

Albinia looked at him, and Michael saw tears forming in her eyes. "Mr. Blakley," she said, just as formally. "I apologize for intruding on you. I beg your pardon for...everything. The circumstances of my...existence. If I had known—"

"You have nothing to apologize for," Tristram interrupted gently. "You are not responsible for your mother's choices, or your father's crimes. You are only responsible for your own actions. And from what I understand, those actions saved not only my sons, but quite possibly all of Fairyland."

Samuel stepped forward then, moving to stand beside Albinia. One by one, the other brothers joined him—Geoffrey and Edmund, Aaron and Jeremy and Joshua and William. They formed a protective semicircle around their not-quite-sister.

"She's ours," Samuel said, and his voice rang firm and certain. "Blood or no blood, she's our sister. And anyone who says otherwise will answer to us."

Albinia made a sound that was half-laugh, half-sob. "You don't have to—I'm not really—"

"You helped us find things when we lost them," Geoffrey said. "You reminded us to eat and sleep and not disappear up our own magical spouts." He smiled, though his eyes were bright with unshed tears. "You're the only reason we survived your mother's rule of the house, Al. That makes you our sister."

"You're a right 'un," Edmund added. "And you kept Bug safe. That's worth more than any bloodline."

Aaron cleared his throat. "Blood doesn't make family, Al. We learned that—" He stopped, seeming unable to finish the sentence. "What matters is that you're here. You're ours. You always have been."

The twins, Jeremy and Joshua, nodded in unison. William, the quietest of the brothers, simply reached out and squeezed her hand.

Albinia looked around at all of them, and Michael saw her face crumple. "But I'm not," she whispered. "I'm not yours. I'm the daughter of a monster. I'm half-faery, half-something that shouldn't exist. You're Tristram's sons, and I'm just—"

"You're our sister," Samuel said firmly. "And that's the end of it."

Tristram had been watching this exchange, and now he spoke again. "They're quite right, you know. I may not be your father by blood, Miss Blakley, but you've lived in my house, been raised by my sons, borne my name for fifteen years. That counts for something. You've done my name credit. I'll claim you."

"But you didn't know," Albinia said. "You never even met me. Augusta sent you away before I was born."

"True," Tristram acknowledged. "But I'm here now. And I see before me a young woman of remarkable courage and ability. A young woman my sons clearly love as their sister. A young woman who risked everything to save people she believed were her family." He paused. "If you'll permit it, I would be honored to truly be your father. Not by blood, perhaps, but by adoption. To protect and guard you and in time perhaps love you as my own."

Michael felt his throat tighten at the quiet dignity in Tristram's words. *This was what family should be,* he thought. Not the cold calculation of bloodlines and inheritance, but the choice to stand together, to claim each other despite everything.

Albinia was openly crying now, blood and tears running down her face, soaking her ruined dress. Her brothers surrounded her in a protective huddle, offering comfort and handkerchiefs and awkward but genuine affection.

Seraphim had been standing to one side with Gabriel, giving the Blakley family their moment. Now he cleared his throat gently. "I hate to interrupt," he said, "but Michael really does need to rest. He's been through quite the ordeal."

Michael started to protest, but Gabriel held up a hand. "Your brother is right. You're exhausted and likely injured. But—" he looked around at the gathered group, "—I think we all need a moment to work through what's happened. Perhaps we should reconvene in a more comfortable setting?"

One of the Blakley servants, a middle-aged woman, braver than the rest, had crept back into the hall. "Begging your pardon, sirs, but the drawing room is prepared. And I can have tea brought, if that would be helpful?"

"Tea would be excellent," Tristram said, sounding relieved to have something practical to focus on. "Thank you, Mrs. Lawrence."

The group moved slowly toward the drawing room, the brothers still clustered protectively around Albinia. Michael fell into step beside her, ignoring Seraphim's pointed look. He was tired, yes, and he probably should rest. But he wasn't leaving. Not yet. Not until he was sure she was well.

Gabriel walked beside Seraphim, and Michael caught fragments of their quiet conversation. Something about Fairyland, about the political situation, about allies and enemies. Seraphim made a sound of impatience. The word "alliance" emerged from his mouth scathingly.

But Gabriel made no move to leave, which Michael found both reassuring and slightly concerning. His brother didn't usually linger unless there was something important still to be done.

The drawing room looked exactly as Albinia had described it in their conversations on the path—oppressively decorated with heavy dark curtains and severe furniture that appeared to have been chosen to intimidate rather than comfort. The group settled themselves awkwardly, the brothers arranging themselves around Albinia as though forming a protective wall.

Tea arrived, brought by a succession of nervous servants who kept glancing at Gabriel as though expecting him to do something alarming. He ignored them with the ease of long practice, accepting a cup of tea and sitting with perfect propriety despite the power that radiated from him. He sipped the tea as though it were ambrosia

Michael found himself on a settee near Albinia, who looked like she might fall asleep at any moment sitting upright, in her tattered, soaked dress. Her brothers were discussing where everyone would work, now that they were adults and had their own passions—the house was large enough for all of them, apparently, though it would be crowded—and what they should do about the servants, and whether they should send word to anyone about what had happened.

Through it all, Albinia sat silent, her hands wrapped around a teacup she wasn't drinking from. Michael could see her mind working, could see the exhaustion warring with something else. Some decision she was trying to make.

Gabriel watched her, too, Michael noticed. Gabriel watched her with complete fascination. His brother had that look he sometimes got, the one that suggested he could see futures branching out before him, possibilities and probabilities all laid out like a map. But he said nothing, simply sipped his tea and waited.

Tristram had disappeared briefly and returned with a notebook, already sketching what looked like modifications to one of his inventions. The man really couldn't help himself, Michael thought with amusement. Give him ten minutes and he'd be deep in his work, the rest of the world forgotten.

The brothers' conversation had turned to more practical matters—who would manage the estate now that Augusta was gone, whether they should hire a proper steward, what to do about the oppressive décor.

"We could let Al fix it," Geoffrey suggested. "She's always had better taste than Mrs. Blakley, anyway."

"I'm not sure I'm qualified to redecorate an entire manor," Albinia said quietly. It was the first thing she'd said since they'd entered the drawing room.

"You're more qualified than any of us," Samuel said. "Left to our own devices, we'd probably just move all our projects into the drawing room and forget furniture exists."

That got a small smile from Albinia, but Michael could see the sadness beneath it. She was thinking about her lineage, he realized. About what she was and what she wasn't. About being the daughter of the deposed king and not belonging anywhere. Not belonging here.

Seraphim caught Michael's eye and tilted his head toward the door, a clear signal that it was time to leave. Michael shook his head slightly. Not yet. There was something unresolved here, something that needed to happen before he could go. He couldn't leave Blakley Manor like this. He couldn't leave Albinia.

Gabriel set down his teacup with a quiet click that somehow drew everyone's attention. "Miss Blakley," he said, his voice gentle but carrying clearly through the room. "You've been very quiet. I suspect you have questions."

Albinia looked up at him, and Michael saw something complex in her expression. Fear, yes, but also curiosity. And beneath it all, the kind of desperate hope that came from being offered something you'd always wanted but never dared ask for.

"I do have one," she said slowly. "But I'm not sure I should ask it."

"You may ask anything you wish," Gabriel said. "Though I cannot promise to answer everything."

The room fell silent, everyone watching as Albinia gathered her courage for whatever she was about to say.

The Great Trade

ALBINIA LOOKED AT THE king of Fairyland—at Gabriel Penn, who was also Michael's half-brother, who was also somehow her cousin by virtue of shared royal blood of Fairyland she'd never wanted—and tried to find the words for what she needed to ask.

Around her, the drawing room had gone silent. Her brothers—she still thought of them that way, even knowing they weren't truly hers by blood—were watching. Tristram Blakley had set down his notebook. Even Seraphim, who'd been trying to shepherd Michael toward the door, had paused to listen.

"You said," Albinia began, then stopped. Her voice sounded small and uncertain even to her own ears. She cleared her throat and tried again. "You said Fairyland owed debts to someone. Was it... Were you speaking of me?"

"Yes," Gabriel confirmed. He was watching her with those too-knowing eyes, and she had the uncomfortable feeling that he already knew what she was going to ask. But he said nothing, waiting for her to find the courage to speak.

Albinia set down her untouched teacup. "May I ask for...for a boon?"

Gabriel's expression softened slightly. "You helped unmake my uncle. You prevented him from using your power to attack Fairyland and reclaim his throne. You protected the infant king of the gryphons, thereby preventing a civil war among the bird folk. You saved my younger brother. And you did all of this at great personal cost, while exhausted and injured and having just learned truths about yourself that would have broken a lesser person." He paused. "Yes, Miss Blakley. I would consider that you've earned a boon."

Albinia's heart beat so hard that she was sure everyone in the room could hear it. This was it. The moment where she could ask for what she wanted, or she could stay silent and remain what she was. The daughter of a monster. No, two monsters. Half-elf. Half-calculating dark-magic user. Forever marked by a heritage she'd never chosen.

"I want to be mortal," she said. The words came out in a rush, tumbling over each other. "Fully human. I want to be—" She looked at Tristram, at his seven sons who'd claimed her as their sister despite everything. "I want to be really Tristram Blakley's daughter. Not his stepdaughter. Not the child his second wife forced on him through deception. I want to be his daughter by his first wife whom he loved and I want to be fully his sons' sister. Truly. In blood and bone and magic. I want my mother to have been his wife, his real wife, not Augusta. I want—"

She stopped, aware she was babbling, aware that what she was asking was enormous. Impossible, probably. You couldn't just rewrite someone's entire existence, their very being, and make her the daughter of a woman who'd died before she was born. Could you?

Gabriel went very still. The room had gone so silent that Albinia could hear the clock ticking on the mantelpiece, could hear the whisper of fabric as someone shifted position.

"You understand what you're asking," Gabriel said. It wasn't a question, but Albinia nodded, anyway. "This isn't a simple transformation. I wouldn't just be changing you. I would be rewriting history itself. Reality would reshape around the change. Documents would alter. Memories would shift—for everyone except those in this room, whom I can shield. But even those will have dual memories, and little by little, the one that they know now will become faded and unimportant, like a dream they had. Like a dream we all had. The portraits in the manor's gallery would show different people. Your mother, your new mother, will have to have lived longer. Everyone will remember her living longer. Everyone will know you as her daughter."

"I know," Albinia said. Her throat felt tight. "I know it's asking too much. I know it's—"

"It's not too much," Gabriel interrupted gently. "It won't be complete. Even I can't sever you wholly from Fairyland, but you'll retain only a bare touch of it. Of kinship to me." He looked very intently at her. "I don't mind if you don't. I don't know if you'll retain immortality."

"I don't want immortality," she said. Then, with a sudden flash of amusement, "I, too, don't resent calling cousins with you. But the rest..."

"The rest is well within my power to grant," he said, then made a gesture, which somehow encased the crystal armored guards of fairyland and the Princess Royal's own regiment in a shimmering blue wall of magic. "We'll proceed with family only," he said. "Now we're as though in a separate room. I need to make it clear and for you to understand the cost. Not to me—the magical expenditure is substantial but manageable. The cost to you."

Albinia blinked. "Cost to me?"

"You'll lose most of your Fairyland heritage," Gabriel said. "The power that comes from being the deposed king's daughter. The potential for enormous magical ability. The connection to Fairyland that's in your blood. All of it will be gone, replaced with human magic. Substantial human magic, certainly—you'll be a talented witch. Both Tristram Blakley and his wife were powerful in magic. But nothing like what you could have been as a halfling. Just a faint spark as someone with a long forgotten magical ancestor. Royal, but distant."

"I don't want to be what I could have been," Albinia said. "I want to be who I choose to be."

Something flickered in Gabriel's expression. Pain, perhaps. Or longing. "Not everyone has that choice," he said quietly. "Some of us give up our humanity to save those we love, and can never get it back."

Albinia realized with a start that he was talking about himself. That he'd chosen to embrace his elf nature, to become fully the king of Fairyland, and in doing so had surrendered the human half of himself. Had become something other, something powerful and strange and no longer quite the brother Michael and Seraphim remembered.

And he envied her. Envied her ability to choose humanity when he'd had to give his up. Not spiteful envy, strong nonetheless.

"I'm so sorry," she said softly. "I didn't mean—"

"Don't apologize." Gabriel's voice was firm. "You're making the choice that's right for you. That's all anyone can do." He stood, and the movement drew every eye in the room. "But I need to be certain. Once this is done, it cannot be undone. You will be almost fully human, fully Tristram Blakley's daughter. You will have two memories. One of growing up here, with Tristram and the boys, the other what you remember now. And no one but those in this room will know that the latter is true. You'll never be able to speak to anyone else about your true past. Are you sure this is what you want?"

Albinia looked around the room. At Tristram, who had offered to be her father by choice, even knowing she wasn't his by blood. At Samuel and Geoffrey and Edmund and the rest, who had claimed her as their sister when they had every reason not to. At Michael, who was watching her with his intent green eyes, and she saw in them no judgment, only support for whatever she chose.

"I'm sure," she said. "If...if the Blakleys don't mind."

Smiles, nods, acquiescence erupted from her chosen family.

Gabriel nodded. He walked to the center of the room, and Albinia felt compelled to join him there. She stood before the king of Fairyland, and was suddenly very aware of how small she was, how insignificant compared to the power that radiated from him.

"Kneel," Gabriel said, not unkindly.

Albinia knelt. The floor was hard beneath her knees, but she barely felt it. Her heart was racing, her hands clenched together to stop their shaking.

Gabriel placed one hand on the top of her head. His touch was light, but she felt power surge through the contact, making every nerve in her body light up. "Albinia Blakley," he said, and his voice resonated with authority that went beyond mere sound. "You have served Fairyland and its king faithfully. You have earned a boon, and you have named your wish. By the power of Fairyland, by the ancient laws that govern wish and want, by the threads that bind reality together, I grant your request."

The power that had been gathering around him suddenly focused, pouring into Albinia like a river of light. She gasped as it hit her, as she felt it reaching into every cell of her body, every strand of her being.

It hurt.

She hadn't expected it to hurt, but it did. It felt like being unmade and remade at the same time, like every piece of herself was being taken apart and reassembled in a slightly different configuration. Her elf blood—the power she'd inherited from the deposed king—was being pulled out of her strand by strand, and something else was being woven in to replace it.

Human blood. Human magic. A different heritage entirely.

She felt her features shifting subtly. Felt her bones restructuring themselves at the most minute level. Felt her magic—the deep well of power she'd always had—changing its very nature from faery-touched to fully human. From what it had always been to something different.

And beyond her own transformation, she felt reality itself reshaping.

History was rewriting itself, spreading outward from her like ripples in a pond.

Albinia felt tears streaming down her face, whether from pain or relief or something else entirely, she couldn't say.

The portraits in the gallery changed. She could sense it even from here. Where they had once shown only Tristram, his first wife, and seven sons, they now showed eight children. A daughter with red hair and freckles, held in the arms of a woman who looked like an older version of Albinia herself as she was becoming. Of how Albinia looked now. Tristram's first wife Emma, who had been a redhead and who in this new reality had lived longer. Long enough to bear one more child. Long enough to raise her daughter through early childhood before illness finally claimed her.

Documents shifted. Birth records, baptismal certificates, letters and notes scattered across fifteen years of life. All of them now showed Albinia as Tristram's legitimate daughter. Always had. Always would, except in the memories of those in this room, excluding the guards. In which, she noted, no servant remained.

And in Albinia herself, the deepest change was taking place. Her very genetics were being rewritten, faery blood replaced with human. She was becoming what she would have been if Tristram's wife had conceived one more time before her death. She was becoming their daughter in truth.

The pain crescendoed, and Albinia heard herself cry out. But she didn't pull away from Gabriel's hand. Didn't try to stop what was happening. This was what she wanted. This was her choice.

And then, as suddenly as it had begun, it was over.

Gabriel removed his hand from her head, and Albinia swayed, fell, catching herself on her hands. She was breathing hard, her entire body shaking from the effort of the transformation. But she felt...different. Lighter, somehow. As though a weight she hadn't known she was carrying had been lifted.

"It is done," Gabriel said. His voice sounded strained, and when Albinia looked up at him, she saw that the transformation had cost him as well. He looked paler, and the power that normally radiated from him had dimmed slightly. "You are now and have always been Albinia Blakley, daughter of Tristram Blakley and his wife, Emma. Sister to Samuel, Geoffrey, Edmund, Aaron, Jeremy, Joshua, and William. Fully human. Fully theirs."

Albinia tried to stand and found her legs wouldn't support her. But before she could fall, strong arms caught her. She looked up to see Tristram—*Papa,* some part of her whispered, *he's Papa now, really Papa. Papa who raised me*—holding her steady. She remembered Papa reading to her, Papa consoling her when Mama died. Papa solemnly enduring pretend tea with Albinia and her dolls. She'd had a governess a brief time, after Mama died. Even then, Papa and the boys had been the heaviest influences in her life.

"Welcome home, daughter," he said softly, and there were tears in his eyes. "Your mother would have adored you."

Her brothers surrounded them then, all seven of them, pulling her into an embrace that threatened to crush her ribs but that felt more like coming home than anything she'd ever experienced.

"Still a brat," Samuel said, but his voice was thick with emotion.

"Still our sister," Geoffrey added. "Always were, just...more official now."

Edmund said nothing, but he cried openly, and that was enough.

Albinia clung to them, to her father, to her brothers—her real brothers now, in every way that mattered—and let herself cry. For what she'd lost, yes. The potential power, the faery heritage, the connection to a world of magic beyond anything most humans would ever know. The familiar face in the mirror now subtlely but permanently altered forever.

But more, she cried in gratitude for what she'd gained. A family. A real family. Not built on deception or convenience or desperation, but on love and care and the fierce determination to belong to each other.

When she finally pulled back, wiping at her eyes, she saw that everyone in the room looked shaken. Michael stared at her with an expression of wonder. She'd worried briefly if her new features would shock him, but it didn't look as though they had. Seraphim looked like he was trying to process what he'd just witnessed. And Gabriel—

Gabriel smiled. A real smile, sad and genuine and full of something that looked almost like joy.

"I envy you," he said quietly. "I gave up my humanity to save my family, and I can never reclaim it. But you—you chose humanity, chose family, chose love over power. That's a rare thing, Albinia Blakley. Cherish it."

"I will," Albinia promised. And she meant it.

Gabriel turned to leave, then paused. He looked at Albinia—still tear-stained and bedraggled, her torn and bloodied dress hanging in tatters, her hair a wild tangle around her face—and something shifted in his expression. Almost amusement, but gentler than that.

He waved his hand, a casual gesture that belied the power behind it.

Albinia gasped as she felt magic wash over her like warm water. The cuts and bruises from the kelpie ride healed instantly. The blood on her face vanished. Her suddenly clean and shining hair lifted and arranged itself into an elegant style that would have taken a lady's maid an hour to achieve. And her ruined dress transformed into something beautiful—deep green silk that complemented her red hair, with delicate lace at the collar and cuffs, the kind of dress a young lady of quality might wear to a very special occasion.

She looked down at herself in shock, then up at Gabriel.

He smiled slightly. "My brother deserves to see you once more at your best," he said, too quietly for anyone but her to hear. "And you deserve to feel beautiful when he does what he's about to do."

Before Albinia could ask what he meant, Gabriel turned to Michael. "Take care of her," he said, his voice carrying to the whole room now. "She's worth it."

"I know," Michael said, and there was something in his voice that made Albinia's heart skip.

Gabriel nodded, satisfied. Then he simply stepped out of reality, disappearing as though walking through a door that only he could see. And his warriors followed him through the same door, marching, crystal armored rank on crystal armored rank. The human guards behind the Duke shifted on their feet, as though worried they'd magically vanish.

The drawing room seemed dimmer without the king of Fairyland's presence, more ordinary. Albinia touched her hair wonderingly, felt the silk of her dress, marveled at the absence of pain from injuries she'd carried for hours.

And then she became aware that everyone was looking at her. At how Gabriel had prepared her, as though for something important.

Michael cleared his throat. He looked nervous, Albinia realized. More nervous than he'd looked facing the deposed king.

"Not yet," he said, and there was something in his voice that made everyone pause. "There's something I need to do first. Before Seraphim drags me away to rest, before everyone scatters to their rooms. There's something I need to say."

Seraphim opened his mouth as if to protest, then closed it, as a knowing look crossing his face.

Tristram set down his notebook with a soft smile. "Let the boy speak," he said.

Michael crossed the room to where Albinia stood among her brothers. "May I?" he asked, holding out his hand.

She didn't understand what was happening, but she placed her hand in his and let him lead her to the center of the room. They stood there together, and she was acutely aware of everyone watching them. Of her beautiful new dress and her arranged hair, and the way Michael was looking at her like she was something precious.

"Albinia," he said, and his voice was steady despite the nervousness in his eyes. "There's something I need to ask you."

The Future

MICHAEL HAD FACED DOWN a deposed king. He'd been trapped in magical bindings designed to break his will. He'd watched Albinia unmake a creature of immense power through sheer precision and determination. He'd survived adventures that would have killed most people.

And none of it had required as much courage as what he was about to do.

He stood in the center of the Blakley drawing room, holding Albinia's hand, very aware that both their families were watching. Seraphim looked curious and slightly amused. Tristram had that distant expression that suggested he was already thinking about his next invention but was trying to pay attention. And Albinia's seven brothers were arrayed around the room like a protective wall, watching Michael with expressions that ranged from suspicious to openly hostile.

Albinia was looking up at him with those eyes that were somehow both wary and trusting at once, and Michael found himself momentarily forgetting every carefully rehearsed word he'd planned.

"Albinia," he said again, then stopped. This wasn't coming out right. He was supposed to be eloquent, supposed to have this all planned out. Instead, he sounded like an idiot.

Start over. Approach it like a problem to be solved. State your premise, show your work, arrive at your conclusion.

"I know we haven't known each other very long," Michael said. "A few days, really. Most of which were spent in mortal peril, which some might argue isn't the best foundation for—" He stopped, realizing he was babbling. "What I'm trying to say is that I've never met anyone like you. The way you think, the way you approach problems, the precision of your magic, the courage it took to ride a kelpie through the sky just because I called for you—"

"Michael," Albinia said gently, "what are you asking?"

Right. Get to the point. Michael took a breath and turned to Tristram. "Sir, I would like to formally request permission to address your daughter with a proposal of marriage."

The room exploded.

"Absolutely not," Samuel said immediately. "She's fifteen years old!"

"And you're what, seventeen?" Geoffrey added. "You're both children!"

"I'll be eighteen in less than a year. A little less than a year," Michael said, which he realized immediately was not a strong argument.

"Oh, well, that changes everything," Edmund said with heavy sarcasm. "Less than a year. Practically ancient."

Seraphim had his hand over his face, though Michael suspected his brother was trying not to laugh rather than expressing actual dismay. "Michael, while I appreciate the impulse toward propriety in asking permission first, perhaps you might have waited for a more...appropriate time? After you've both rested, recovered from your ordeal, had time to think clearly?"

"I am thinking clearly," Michael protested. "I know exactly what I want."

"You're exhausted, possibly concussed, and running on the kind of mad bravery that comes from having just survived the impossible," Seraphim said. "That's not the same as thinking clearly."

Tristram had set down his notebook and was looking at Michael with interest. "Let the boy finish," he said mildly. "I'd like to hear what he has to say."

Michael shot Tristram a grateful look and turned back to Albinia. "I know we're young. I know this seems sudden. But I also know that I've never met anyone who understood me the way you do. Who could work with me the way we worked together to defeat your— To defeat him. Who would risk everything to answer a call for help."

"That's very romantic," Aaron said, "but it's still not a reason to marry someone you've known for less than a week."

"I'm not asking to marry her tomorrow," Michael said, his patience beginning to fray. "I'm asking permission to court her properly. With the understanding that when we're both older, when we've both finished our educations, when it's appropriate—I'd like to marry her. If she'll have me."

That brought another round of protests.

"Court her properly means what, exactly?" Jeremy demanded. "Letters? Visits? Chaperoned walks in the garden?"

"All of the above," Michael said. "Whatever is considered appropriate. I'll follow every rule of propriety, attend every tedious social function, endure every suspicious glare from her brothers—"

"You're already enduring those," Joshua pointed out.

"Then I'll continue to endure them," Michael said. "I think I liked you better as geese."

"We were never geese!" Samuel said. "We were swans."

Michael sighed. "The point is, I'm not trying to rush anything. I just want—" He looked at Albinia, at her wide eyes and slightly parted lips, at the way she was watching him like he'd surprised her. "I want the chance. That's all."

"Your Grace of Darkwater," Samuel said, turning to Michael's brother, "surely you see how inappropriate this is?"

"Oh, I do," Seraphim agreed. "But I also know my brother. Once he's set his mind on something, there's very little point in arguing. The question is whether Miss Blakley—"

"Albinia," she said softly.

Everyone turned to look at her.

She was blushing, the color high in her cheeks, and Michael thought she'd never looked more beautiful than she did in that moment. Oh, her features had changed, but they were still hers. Gabriel's magic had cleaned and dressed her, yes, but it was the expression on her face that took Michael's breath away. Wonder and hope and something that might have been joy.

"I'm sorry?" Tristram said.

"My name is Albinia," she said, louder this time. "And I believe the question is whether I'm willing to accept Michael's proposal. And I am."

The brothers erupted again, all talking over each other. Something about her age and propriety and had she lost her mind and absolutely not.

But Tristram held up a hand, and remarkably, they all fell silent. "Let me see if I understand," he said. "Lord Michael Ainsling is not asking to marry my daughter immediately. He's asking permission to court her, with the eventual goal of marriage when they're both of age and have completed their educations. Is that correct?"

"Yes, sir," Michael said.

"And you, Albinia, are agreeable to this arrangement?"

"Yes, Papa," Albinia said, and Michael saw her smile at the word. At being able to say it and mean it fully.

Tristram nodded slowly. "Well, then. I suppose we should discuss the particulars."

"The particulars?" Samuel sputtered. "You can't possibly be agreeing to this!"

"Why not?" Tristram asked. "The boy seems sincere. He's clearly intelligent—took him less than an hour to help unmake an elf king, after all. And unless I'm much mistaken, he's the younger son of the Duke of Darkwater, which means he comes from good family."

"Brother to the Duke," Seraphim corrected. "I have inherited. But yes, the connection is legitimate."

"And his other brother is the king of Fairyland," Tristram continued, warming to his subject. "That's quite a pedigree. I'd be hard-pressed to find a better match for my daughter."

"She's fifteen!" Geoffrey protested again.

"And by the time they're married, she'll be what? Eighteen? Nineteen? Twenty?" Tristram shrugged. "That's perfectly reasonable. Your mother was nineteen when we married."

"But what about contracts?" William asked. "Settlements? Negotiations? These things take time to arrange properly."

"Then we'd better start now," Tristram said. He looked at Seraphim with a wry smile. "I assume the Darkwater family would expect appropriate provisions for any bride entering the family?"

"Standard marriage settlements, yes," Seraphim said. He'd given up trying to hide his amusement and was openly smiling now. "A dowry, if you can muster it."

"Her dowry," Tristram said, and seemed to calculate in his head. "Well, it was established at fifty thousand when she was born, but it has grown through judicious investments, of course."

"Fifty thousand!" Albinia said. "Fifty thousand! Mam— I mean Augusta always said we were poor. And there was never money for anything."

Tristram made that deep-thinking expression again, and sighed. "Oh. In that timeline... Well, even if she had me legally declared dead, she was not in my will. Everything would be held until Samuel inherited when he came of age. All she would have was what came from the manor, but that's not my income. My income is from shares in my inventions. The patents on the carpetships alone have made us wealthier than the dreams of avarice." He looked from Albinia to Seraphim. "Yes, my daughter has a dowry worthy of a ducal family, both in money and property. And she's been educated at an excellent establishment for young ladies these last four years and is properly versed in music, drawing, art, and the magical gifts young ladies should know. She had excellent marks."

Michael saw Albinia shake her head, as if trying to get something clear, but suddenly, in the new timeline, he remembered meeting her at a lecture, which she'd attended with the young ladies of Mrs. Eversley's establishment. The others were a gaggle of smiling fools, but Albinia was really interested in the effects of magic on electricity, and they'd talked and—

"And I would expect provisions ensuring my daughter's welfare and independence," Tristram countered. "A household allowance under her sole control, the right to continue her magical studies, guarantee that any children would—"

"Of course," Seraphim said. "Property, pin money, widows' rights, should the worst happen. All perfectly normal and proper."

"Perhaps," Michael interrupted, "we could discuss the actual marriage contracts later? After we've all had some rest and time to think?"

"Excellent suggestion," Seraphim said. "These negotiations can take months, after all. No need to settle everything tonight."

But the brothers weren't finished. They surrounded Michael, a wall of protective suspicion.

"You'll treat her with respect," Samuel said.

"Of course," Michael agreed.

"You'll write to her regularly when you're not in residence," Geoffrey added.

"Absolutely."

"You won't rush her into anything," Edmund said, his voice hard. "Just because you're older—"

"I'm only two years older," Michael protested. "And I would never—"

"You'll keep your hands to yourself," Aaron said. "None of this modern nonsense about unchaperoned meetings."

"I'll be a perfect gentleman," Michael promised.

"See that you are," Jeremy said.

"Because we'll be watching," Joshua added.

"And if you hurt her," William finished quietly, "there are seven of us and only one of you. And we know how to create pocket universes. We know how to hide bodies."

"William!" Tristram said, sounding shocked. "That's completely inappropriate."

"But not inaccurate," Samuel muttered.

Seraphim was definitely laughing now, though he was trying to hide it with a cough. "I assure you all that Michael has been raised with proper respect for propriety and honor. He knows how courtship is conducted."

"Do I?" Michael said, suddenly uncertain. "I mean, I've read about it, but I've never actually—" He stopped short of saying he'd never thought he'd marry, because women were such tedious widgeons. It wasn't true. In this new timeline, he'd been mulling it for months, and when he'd attended Albinia's graduation ball to celebrate her graduation from Mrs. Eversley's establishment, he'd already known he wanted to marry her. And in the real timeline, the one they'd lived through, he had realized he couldn't live without her...probably from the beginning. But he'd admitted it while they unmade the elf king.

"You write letters," Seraphim said. "You visit when invited and when there's proper supervision. You attend social functions together. You do not compromise her reputation in any way. It's all very straightforward."

"It sounds tedious," Michael said.

"It is tedious," Seraphim agreed, and grinned. "But that's rather the point. Courtship is meant to be respectable and boring and absolutely above reproach."

Through all of this, Albinia had been standing silently beside Michael, her hand still in his. Now she made a soft sound that might have been a laugh.

Everyone turned to look at her.

"I'm sorry," she said. "It's just— We defeated the deposed king of Fairyland. We unmade a creature of pure malevolence. We rewrote reality itself.

And now we're arguing about chaperoned visits and letter-writing schedules?"

"Well," Tristram said reasonably, "one must have priorities."

That broke the tension, and even her brothers smiled a little.

The chaos began to wind down. Seraphim and Tristram moved to one side and discussed settlement negotiations in low voices, both of them looking entirely too pleased with themselves. The brothers argued among themselves about who would serve as chaperone when Michael visited and whether they needed to draw up a rotation schedule.

And Michael and Albinia stood in the center of it all, largely forgotten for the moment.

"This is mad," Michael said quietly, for her ears only. "I should have waited. Should have given you time to rest, time to process everything that's happened. Instead, I just blurted it out in front of everyone—"

"I'm glad you did," Albinia interrupted. "If you'd waited, I might have convinced myself I'd imagined the way you looked at me and what I felt. Or that it was just the aftermath of the adventure, the way people feel close after surviving something terrible together."

"It's not just that," Michael said. "Al, when I was trapped there, when he was trying to break me, the only thing that kept me going was the thought of you. Knowing you'd come if I called. Trusting you, even when I had no logical reason to. That's not just proximity or shared danger. That's—"

He stopped, not quite ready to name what it was. Not here, not now, with both their families arguing about contracts and propriety and everything except the only thing that actually mattered.

"I know," Albinia said softly. "I feel it, too."

The room had grown quieter. Michael looked up to find everyone watching them again, the earlier chaos settling into something more solemn. This was important, he realized. This moment, these promises they were making to each other and their families. It deserved to be treated with proper gravity.

He took both of Albinia's hands in his, very aware of the watchful eyes around them. "I know I'm asking a lot," he said, speaking to her but loud enough for everyone to hear. "I'm asking you to wait while I finish my studies. I'm asking you to endure what will probably be tedious courtship rituals and my brother's lectures about propriety and your brothers' suspicious glares. I'm asking you to take a chance on someone you barely know."

"You're asking me to take a chance on someone who called for me across worlds and trusted me when I came, despite my parentage as it was," Albinia said. "Someone who saw my magic and thought it was brilliant instead of frightening. Someone who worked with me like we were two parts of the same mechanism, perfectly calibrated to work together."

She was quoting his own words back to him, Michael realized. From when they'd been fighting the deposed king, when he'd marveled at how well they complemented each other.

"Yes," he said simply. "That's exactly what I'm asking."

"Then I say yes," Albinia said. "Yes to the courtship, yes to the tedious propriety, yes to waiting. Yes to a likely marriage. Yes to all of it."

Michael felt something in his chest loosen, some tension he hadn't known he was carrying. "You're sure? Because if you need time to think about it—"

"I'm sure," Albinia said. "I've never been more sure of anything."

Seraphim cleared his throat. "Well, then. I believe the next step is to formalize the arrangement. A formal betrothal contract will be signed in a few months by both parties and their guardians, outlining the terms of the courtship and the conditions under which a marriage might proceed."

"How very romantic," Edmund said dryly.

"Romance and legal protections are not mutually exclusive," Seraphim said. "In fact, I'd argue that protecting Albinia's interests is the most romantic thing we can do."

"I'll need to consult with my solicitor," Tristram said. "Make sure all the proper provisions are in place."

"As will I," Seraphim agreed. "These things must be done correctly."

The brothers were already discussing what should be included in the contract. Provisions about how often Michael could visit. Requirements for supervision. Rules about correspondence. It was all becoming official and complicated very quickly.

But Michael barely heard it. He looked at Albinia, at the way she was smiling up at him, despite her obvious exhaustion. At the freckles standing out against her pale skin and the red hair that Gabriel's magic had arranged so carefully and the green dress that made her look like something out of a fairy tale.

"I'll see you this summer," he said quietly, just for her. "At the Darkwater estate. We're having a house party, and you're all invited. Your father and brothers, too, of course."

"Of course," Albinia echoed, her eyes sparkling with amusement. "It wouldn't be proper otherwise."

"Nothing but proper from now on," Michael agreed. "Exceedingly tedious and absolutely correct in every way."

"I can hardly wait," Albinia said, and they both knew she was talking about something other than propriety.

The room had settled into a more comfortable chaos now, with Tristram and Seraphim discussing dates and the brothers arguing about who would accompany Albinia to Darkwater and whether they all needed to come to ensure proper supervision.

Michael knew he should let go of Albinia's hands. Should step back to a proper distance, should demonstrate the respect and propriety he'd just promised. But for just a moment longer, he wanted to stay exactly where he was. Holding her hands in his.

"Thank you," he said softly. "For coming when I called. For trusting me. For saying yes."

"Thank you for calling," Albinia said. "For trusting me, despite the truth about what I was. For not caring that I was the daughter of a monster."

"You were never that," Michael said firmly. "You were always exactly what you are now—brilliant and brave and far too good for me."

"Now you're just being silly," Albinia said, but she was blushing again and smiling a little.

Seraphim had moved closer, and Michael knew his time was up. "Michael, we really do need to leave. It's past midnight, and you're falling asleep on your feet."

He was right, Michael realized. The exhaustion was catching up with him, making his limbs heavy and his thoughts slow. He'd been running on pure determination, but that couldn't last forever.

But there was one more thing he needed to do. One more moment before the families swept them apart and turned this into contracts and negotiations and sensible waiting periods.

He raised Albinia's hand to his lips, very aware of the sudden silence that fell over the room. This was allowed, he was fairly certain. A gentleman could kiss a lady's hand in greeting or farewell without impropriety.

Her skin was soft and warm, and he let his lips linger just a moment longer than was strictly necessary. "Until summer," he said.

"Until summer," Albinia agreed.

Their eyes met, and despite all the chaos around them, despite the families watching and the brothers glaring and Seraphim trying to hurry him along, there was a moment that belonged only to them. A moment of understanding and promise and something that felt like the beginning of a wonderful new life.

Then Seraphim pulled him away, and the brothers were closing ranks around Albinia, and Tristram was already sketching something in his notebook, having apparently lost interest in the proceedings now that the important points were settled.

"That was..." Seraphim began as they made their way toward the door.

"I know," Michael said.

"Our sister Caroline is going to have opinions," Seraphim continued. "Very strong opinions about you getting betrothed to someone you've known for less than a week."

"I know," Michael said again. Like Caroline could talk. She was betrothed to a centaur prince.

"And the contracts alone will take months to negotiate properly. Possibly longer, given that Tristram Blakley is famously distractible and might forget to attend meetings with the solicitors."

"I don't care," Michael said. "It's worth it."

Seraphim smiled. "Yes," he agreed. "I rather think it is."

"I'm finishing my education, Seraphim. I will not be a prisoner at Darkwater. I will go to Cambridge at the next term. Don't think of denying me."

"I wouldn't dare," Seraphim said, somewhere between impressed and amused.

They paused at the door, and Michael looked back. Albinia stood surrounded by her brothers, all of them talking at once. But she looked up and caught his eye, and she smiled. Just for him.

Michael smiled back.

"Come on," Seraphim said, not unkindly. "Let's get you home before you collapse. You can compose your first proper courtship letter tomorrow."

"I'll need paper," Michael said, his mind already working through the problem. "And ink. Good ink, not the cheap stuff. And I should probably read some books on letter-writing. There must be guides. Protocols."

"I'm sure there are," Seraphim said, amused. "Though I suspect Albinia will appreciate your letters regardless of whether they follow proper form."

"Still," Michael said. "If I'm going to do this, I'm going to do it properly."

They stepped out into the night, and Michael took one last look at Blakley Manor. Somewhere in there, Albinia was probably being lectured by her brothers about propriety and caution and not rushing into things. And he was about to endure similar lectures from his own family.

But none of that mattered. What mattered was the promise they'd made to each other. The beginning of something that felt right in a way Michael couldn't quite explain but trusted completely.

He'd called, and she'd answered.

And now they had all the time in the world to figure out what came next.

Home

THREE WEEKS AFTER THE transformation, Albinia stood in the drawing room of Blakley Manor and tried to decide what to do about the curtains.

Turned out they hadn't changed, because they weren't of Augusta's choosing. Being a peasant, with no knowledge of the ways of the gentry, she'd bowed to the taste displayed in the manor. Which was not Emma Blakley's—Albinia's mama, now—but that of Tristram's mother, Albinia's grandmama. Albinia's mama, between eight children and helping Tristram with his inventions, had not had the time to redecorate.

Which left the manor decorated in the ponderous taste of another generation. And these horrible curtains which were oppressive things, heavy burgundy velvet that blocked out most of the light, even at midday. They matched the severe dark furniture and the somber paintings on the walls—none of which were portraits, she noted, because those had all changed and were now in the gallery upstairs. These were just gloomy landscapes and still-lifes of dead game birds that made the whole room feel like a tomb.

It all had to go.

The thought was liberating and slightly terrifying in equal measure. This was her house now. Hers to manage, hers to change, hers to make into a home instead of the cold, controlled space it had been. Papa had made it clear that domestic matters were entirely her domain—he'd disappeared into his laboratory that first morning back and had barely emerged since, except for meals and the occasional announcement that he had, in fact, invented something revolutionary and would she like to see?

She always said yes. Papa's inventions were genuinely brilliant, even if she only understood half of what he was trying to explain. And she loved the way his face lit up when he talked about his work, the way he got so absorbed he forgot to eat or sleep or notice that he'd been wearing the same ink-stained shirt for three days.

The boys were no help with household management. Samuel was already planning an expedition to map some remote region. Geoffrey spent all his time with his birds. Edmund had gone back to the gryphon kingdom to visit Bug and sent regular reports on the young king's progress. Aaron and William were absorbed in their own magical studies. The twins had disappeared into the library and seemed to be attempting to read every book it contained.

Which left Albinia to figure out things like menus and servants' schedules and whether the curtains in the drawing room were salvageable or should just be burned.

"Al!"

Aaron's voice echoed through the house, followed by the sound of running feet. He burst into the drawing room looking harried and slightly wild-eyed, his hair standing up in all directions.

"I've lost my pen," he announced. "The good one. The one with the gryphon feather. I had it this morning, and now it's gone, and I need it because I'm cataloging the new plant specimens from the marshlands and—"

"Stop," Albinia said, holding up a hand. "Just stop and breathe for a moment."

Aaron stopped midsentence and took an exaggerated breath.

"Good. Now, where did you last see it?"

"If I knew that, I wouldn't have lost it," Aaron pointed out.

Albinia sighed. This was familiar territory. She'd been helping her brothers find lost things since she was old enough to cast her first locating spell. The only difference now was that she was doing it as their actual sister, not the half-faery daughter of their father's deceiving wife.

That still felt strange to think about. The transformation had been complete—her memories hadn't changed, but everyone else's had. The servants remembered her as Papa's youngest child, the daughter who'd always helped keep the household running. The neighbors who'd occasionally visited remembered her as the poor motherless girl being raised by her father and brothers. Even the portraits showed her as she'd always been meant to be—red-haired and freckled, the image of Papa's first wife Emma. And the neighbors knew she'd been away at a very proper school, and came back full of airs, graces and a whole very modish wardrobe, even though she wasn't yet technically out.

Only those who'd been in the drawing room that night remembered the truth. That she'd been someone else once. Someone darker, marked by faery blood and a monstrous heritage. And that felt like a distant dream.

Sometimes, late at night, Albinia wondered if she'd made the right choice. If giving up that power, that potential, had been foolish. But then she'd remember the deposed king's empty eyes, the way he'd seen people as nothing but tools. The way Augusta had manipulated and controlled and destroyed lives in pursuit of her own security.

No. She'd made the right choice. Power without love was just cruelty wearing a crown.

"Al?" Geoffrey was watching her with concern. "Are you all right?"

"Fine," she said, shaking off the dark thoughts. "Just thinking. Come here."

She pulled a small measure of power—human power now, warm and familiar and utterly hers—and wove a simple finding spell. It was one of the first things Augusta had taught her, back when her mother had still been pretending to care about anything other than control.

No. Not her mother. That Augusta didn't exist anymore. Had never existed in this timeline. Her real mother had been Emma Blakley, who'd loved her children and died too soon, who lived on only in portraits and Papa's occasional wistful comments and the new shape of Albinia's own face.

The spell settled and pulled. "Your study," she said. "Under the chair by the window. You probably knocked it off the desk and it rolled."

Aaron's face lit up. "You're brilliant. Thank you!" He was already halfway out the door. "I'll name a fern after you!"

"You've already named three plants after me," Albinia called after him.

"Then I'll name another one!" His voice echoed back from somewhere down the hall.

Albinia smiled and turned back to the curtain problem. Definitely needed to be replaced. Something lighter. Cream, perhaps, or a soft gold that would let the light in. The furniture, too—most of it could be donated or sold. She wanted comfortable things, inviting things. Chairs you could actually sit in without feeling like you were perching on a throne.

She'd need help, though. Managing a house this size was a full-time occupation, and while she was willing to learn, she couldn't do it alone. Either one of her brothers would need to marry soon and bring a wife who could help—unlikely, given their general obliviousness to anything outside their immediate interests—or she'd need to hire a truly excellent housekeeper and train her properly.

Of course, in a few years it wouldn't be her problem anymore. She'd marry Michael and move to...wherever it was that younger sons of dukes lived. A house in London, perhaps? Or an estate of his own that Seraphim would settle on him?

The thought made her stomach flutter with a mix of excitement and nervousness. Marriage. To Michael Ainsling, who built magical machines and solved problems with mathematics and had looked at her like she was something wonderful, even when she'd been bedraggled and bloodstained.

They'd been corresponding regularly. His letters arrived every week, written in his precise hand, full of details about his studies and his latest inventions and careful, proper inquiries about her health and happiness. They were exactly what courtship letters were supposed to be—respectful, proper, revealing nothing that might scandalize anyone who read them.

But between the lines, if you knew how to look, there was warmth. Affection. The sense of two people getting to know each other and liking what they found.

She'd written back with equal propriety, describing her days and her brothers' antics and carefully edited versions of her thoughts on magic and household management. And between her lines, she hoped, he could read the same warmth she felt when reading his letters.

Summer couldn't come fast enough. The Darkwater house party was still months away, and she was already planning what she'd wear, what she'd say, how it would feel to see him again in person instead of just in carefully worded correspondence.

They'd have adventures together, she thought. His workshop and her magic, arguments over the best approach to solve a problem, collaboration that felt like two parts of a perfectly calibrated machine. They'd probably drive each other mad sometimes—he was stubborn and she was headstrong, and neither of them were particularly good at backing down when they thought they were right.

But it would be wonderful.

A soft sound from the doorway made her turn. Mrs. Lawrence, the head housekeeper, was hovering uncertainly.

"Yes, Mrs. Lawrence?"

"Begging your pardon, Miss, but the draper has arrived with the fabric samples you requested. Shall I show him to the morning room?"

"Please," Albinia said. "I'll be there shortly."

She'd sent for samples weeks ago, as soon as she'd decided the house needed redecorating. It was time to start actually implementing the changes instead of just planning them.

As Mrs. Lawrence bustled off, Albinia took one more look around the oppressive drawing room. By summer, it would be transformed. Light and welcoming instead of dark and forbidding. A place where people could gather and talk and actually enjoy themselves instead of feeling like they were under constant surveillance.

Like the rest of her life, she thought. Transformed from something dark and controlled into something bright and free.

She was still smiling when she went to meet the draper.

The village was the same as it had always been—small and practical, with shops clustered around the central square and houses spreading out in neat rows beyond. Albinia had come with Mrs. Lawrence to order some specialty items that could be found locally.

She was examining a display of lace in a tiny shop when she felt the distinctive tingle of magic nearby. Not powerful magic, but skilled. The kind of subtle, practical work that a good hedgewitch might do.

Curious, she followed the sensation to its source. A woman stood near the counter, discussing some herbal preparation with the shopkeeper. She was perhaps forty, comfortably dressed in practical woolens, with dark hair pulled back in a simple bun and laugh lines around her eyes.

Albinia's breath caught.

The face was wrong. Softer, rounder, marked by years of genuine smiles instead of cold calculation. The posture was different—relaxed instead of rigidly controlled. Even the magic felt different—warm and earthy instead of dark and manipulative.

But the bones of the face were the same. The shape of the hands. The way she tilted her head when listening.

Augusta.

No. Not the Augusta who had trapped Papa and enchanted the boys and lived her life in pursuit of control and power. This was who Augusta would have been if she'd never called on the king of Fairyland. If she'd stayed who she was and married a simple man and lived a simple, decent life.

The woman finished her transaction and turned, nearly bumping into Albinia.

"Oh! Pardon me, dear," she said with a warm smile. "Wasn't watching where I was going. My daughter's always saying I'm too scattered for my own good." She paused, looking at Albinia more closely. "You're from the manor, aren't you? Old Blakley's girl? I've seen you in church. You came back from school quite the lady."

"Yes," Albinia managed. "I'm Albinia Blakley."

"Gussy Fletcher," the woman said, offering her hand. "Hedgewitch. Born three villages over. Moved to Wullfen Downs when I married my Martin."

Albinia shook her hand, feeling the warm, uncomplicated magic in the woman's touch. There was no recognition in Gussy Fletcher's eyes. No memory of being someone else, someone darker. As far as this woman knew, she'd always been Gussy, had always had her husband and her children and her modest practice helping the local farmers with their ailments and charms.

"It's nice to meet you," Albinia said.

"And you, dear. Though I should warn you—" Gussy's eyes twinkled, "—my eldest is a year short of your age, and when she heard the young lady was back up at the manor, she got all sorts of ideas about making friends. You might be receiving a very enthusiastic visit soon."

"I'd like that," Albinia said, surprised to find she meant it.

They chatted for a few more minutes about inconsequential things—the weather, the upcoming harvest festival, the quality of the lace in the shop. And all the while, Albinia studied the woman who had been and hadn't been her mother.

This Augusta—Gussy—was happy. There was genuine warmth in her voice when she mentioned her family. Pride when she talked about her five children. Contentment in the life she'd built, modest though it was.

She'd lost nothing because she'd never had anything to lose. She'd never borne a half-faery child or trapped an inventor and made him a werewolf, or enchanted innocent boys into swans. She'd simply lived her life, made her choices, found her happiness.

And she didn't remember any of it. Didn't remember the daughter she'd borne in shame and desperation. Didn't remember the years of cold control and manipulation. Didn't remember being banished to the spaces between worlds by the king of Fairyland.

Gabriel's magic had been thorough. It hadn't just rewritten Albinia's history—it had given Augusta a second chance. A different life, a better life. One she'd never know she'd been given, a reprieve nonetheless.

It was merciful, Albinia realized. More merciful than Augusta had deserved, perhaps. But mercy didn't need to be deserved to be real and she'd made good use of it, it seemed like.

"I should be going," Gussy said. "My husband will be wondering where I've gotten to. But it was lovely to meet you, Miss Blakley. I hope we'll see each other again."

"I'm sure we will," Albinia said.

She watched the woman leave, cheerful and unhurried, completely unaware of the life she'd never lived. The daughter she'd never borne. The darkness she'd never embraced.

Mrs. Lawrence appeared at her elbow. "Are you quite all right, Miss? You look pale."

"I'm well," Albinia said. "Just... thinking."

She finished her errands in a daze, her mind occupied with thoughts of timelines and choices and second chances. And second lives. By the time they returned to the manor, she'd come to a kind of peace with it.

The Augusta who had been her mother was gone. Had never existed in this reality. And Gussy Fletcher would live out her days in happy ignorance, never knowing what she'd been saved from or who she'd lost.

It was sad, in a way. But it was also lovely. And right.

That evening, Albinia sat at the writing desk in her room and pulled out Michael's most recent letter. She'd read it three times already, but she read it again now, savoring the careful words and the warmth beneath them.

Then she took out fresh paper and began her reply.

Dear Michael,

Thank you for your letter of the 15th. I'm delighted to hear your latest invention of a self-rowing boat is progressing well, though I confess I understood perhaps half of your explanation of the regulating mechanism. You'll have to show me in person and explain it more slowly.

I'm glad you are enjoying the learning opportunities at Cambridge and making friends with such similar minds.

Secretly, she wished she, too, could go to Cambridge. Michael had shared that his sister-in-law, the Princess Royal, felt the same, so maybe things would change in her time. For now, Albinia had what tutors she wanted, and, as always, learned from her brothers. She didn't miss the elf magic much. She hadn't known she had it for most of her life.

Life at the manor continues much as before. Aaron lost his favorite pen again (I found it). Papa emerged from his laboratory long enough to eat dinner before disappearing again with a new idea. Samuel has decided his expedition to the North of Patagonia needs to be postponed until summer, which means he's underfoot and driving everyone mad with his restlessness.

I've begun redecorating the drawing room. The old curtains are gone, and I've ordered new ones in cream with gold embroidery. The furniture is being replaced piece by piece with things that are actually comfortable rather than imposing. Papa says the room looks "much more cheerful," which from him is high praise.

Edmund writes that Bug is thriving and has learned to fly properly, though he nearly gave his tutors heart failure by attempting to fly off the edge of the suspended isle. Apparently he'd heard of my escape and wanted to see if gryphons could fly as well as kelpies. Edmund has since instituted a strict "no unsupervised flying" rule. Bug also now turns to human form, now and then, and is an adorable curly-haired blond imp.

She paused, considering whether to tell him about seeing Augusta. About the strange, bittersweet encounter with the woman who had been and wasn't her mother. But how to put it in a letter? How to explain the complexity of that moment to someone who hadn't lived through the transformation?

In the end, she left it out. Some things were better said in person, when she could see his face and know he understood.

I'm looking forward to the summer more than I can properly express, she wrote instead. *The house party at Darkwater seems impossibly far away, though I know it's only a few months. I find myself counting the days like a child waiting for her birthday.*

Is that terribly improper of me to admit? I suppose it is. But then, propriety is often overrated.

Give my regards to your family and your friends at Cambridge. Tell the Duke of Darkwater that Papa has agreed to all the contract terms he proposed, and the solicitors should have everything finalized by the end of the month.

I miss the way we work together, most of all, and hope we can have some adventure when I visit.

Yours, Albinia

She sealed the letter carefully and set it aside to be posted in the morning. Then she walked to her window and looked out over the grounds.

The gardens were visible from here, and beyond them, the road that led to the village. Beyond that, miles of countryside stretching toward the coast and the sea. And somewhere following that coast South, Darkwater. Michael. Her future.

A future she'd chosen. Not one dictated by blood or heritage or the machinations of others, but one she'd selected for herself when Gabriel had given her the chance.

She was Albinia Blakley, fully human, daughter of Tristram and Emma, sister to seven brothers who drove her mad and whom she loved beyond measure. She had a home to manage, magic to study, a life to build. And in a few years, she'd have a husband who understood her, who challenged her, who looked at her like she was something wonderful.

It wasn't the life she'd been born to. It was better. It was the life she'd found.

Albinia turned from the window and began preparing for bed. Tomorrow, she'd meet with the carpenter about new furniture for the drawing room. She'd help Geoffrey with whatever project he was working on that required seventeen separate binding spells. She'd remind Papa to eat lunch. She'd write another letter to Edmund asking about Bug and the gryphon court.

She'd live her life, the one she'd chosen, the one she'd fought for.

And in the summer, she'd see Michael again. They'd walk in the gardens at Darkwater under the watchful eyes of both their families, terribly proper and absolutely circumspect. And they'd talk about magic and mathematics and all the adventures they'd have together. And their minds and hearts would work like two halves of a perfect whole.

She could hardly wait.

As she drifted off to sleep, Albinia was smiling. The future stretched out before her, bright and full of possibility.

It was the future she'd stumbled into while trying to help Papa and the boys. But it was better than she could have designed it. Better than all her dreams.

And she intended to live it fully.

About the Author

SARAH WAS BORN (AND raised)in Porto, Portugal, where—at the age of eight—she decided she wanted to live in Denver and be a writer.

No, she still has no idea whatsoever why Denver.

Her understanding of the world, at the time, might be judged by the fact that she thought Denver was by the sea.

At any rate, having married a mathematician from Connecticut, she made her way to Denver in her late twenties.

She's raised two sons and a countless number of cats in the Rocky Mountains, and overall feels no need to repine for the choice she made at eight.

In a writing career spanning close to thirty years she's become a bestseller and received two prestigious awards (Prometheus: for Darkship Thieves, and the Dragon: for Uncharted, with Kevin J. Anderson.)

She's published over 30 novels and over 150 short stories, in genres ranging from science fiction to mystery, to fantasy, to historical. At the moment, she's not written children's books, men's adventure or romance. But she makes no promises. As the mathematician has instructed her to warn "No genre is safe from her."

www.ingramcontent.com/pod-product-compliance
Lightning Source LLC
LaVergne TN
LVHW091031080826
845145LV00002B/449

* 9 7 8 1 6 3 0 1 1 1 0 2 1 *